DONE
FOR A
DIME

DONE FOR A DIME

David Corbett

Ballantine Books • New York

This is a work of fiction. Names, places, and incidents either are a product of the author's imagination or are used fictitiously.

The city of Rio Mirada does not exist, but the region in which it has been placed—the hills and wetlands surrounding the conflux of the Napa River and San Pablo Bay, northeast of San Francisco—is real. So much has been altered, however, for the sake of dramatic effect and narrative clarity, that it, too, should be considered a fictional construct of the author's imagination.

A Ballantine Book
Published by The Random House Publishing Group

Copyright © 2003 by David Corbett

All rights reserved under International and Pan-American Copyright Conventions. Published in the United States by The Random House Publishing Group, a division of Random House, Inc., New York, and simultaneously in Canada by Random House of Canada Limited, Toronto.

Ballantine and colophon are registered trademarks of Random House, Inc.

www.ballantinebooks.com

Library of Congress Cataloging-in-Publication Data is available from the publisher upon request.

ISBN: 0-345-44753-0

Book design by Joseph Rutt

Manufactured in the United States of America

First Edition: August 2003

10 9 8 7 6 5 4 3 2 1

For Cesidia:

*I'll be looking at the moon
But I'll be seeing you.*

Poverty, not skin color, is the sin, and the key to the city of God is composed of property.

—WALTER MOSELY,
Workin' on the Chain Gang

Acknowledgments

The author was aided in many ways by many people, without whose assistance this book would simply fail to exist.

First and foremost, the author wishes to thank his agent, Laurie Fox, and editor, Mark Tavani, whose guidance and advice repeatedly steered him back from woeful errors, fruitless digressions, and shoddy work. Also, Marie Coolman, Michelle Aielli, Mary Seimsen, Kim Hovey, Joe Blades, and everyone else at Ballantine have provided encouragement and assistance on so many levels, in so many ways, and on so many occasions that it would be impossible to overstate.

A number of individuals provided guidance on factual matters, and if errors remain in the text, it is entirely the fault of the author and not these generous and informed sources. Mark Chubb, Assistant Fire Region Commander of the Transalpine Fire Region, New Zealand Fire Service, and John D. DeHaan, Ph.D.—whose *Kirk's Fire Investigation* is arguably the most useful, scientifically sound, and comprehensive text on the investigation of incendiary fires yet to be written—were invaluable in matters concerning arson, the physics of fire, and the specifics of firefighting. Detective Sid DeJesus of the Vallejo Police Department and Reserve Officer Rick Ruffatto of the East Palo Alto Police Department saved the author from many misconceptions regarding police procedure and investigative strategy and techniques. Patrick V. Garland and "Sarge" Hardeman helped regarding life and work as an MP in the 1970s, and Lyle Ferguson shared his Coast Guard experiences so the author could understand better how that agency patrols the Central American coast.

James Kern, executive director of the Vallejo Naval and Historical Museum, showered the author with more information than he could absorb concerning the history of the Mare Island shipyards and the community, housing, and culture that arose in the neighboring region. Kathy Blume proved invaluable on matters concerning local flora and fauna. Antonio Rangel's assistance concerning big rigs and tank trucks is especially appreciated. Brad Hughes, Diana Lang, and Marcus Shelby filled in some of the gaping holes in the author's musical knowledge.

Once again, the author was aided in his Spanish usage by Elly Sturm and Ana Ramirez, the latter of whom is also to be thanked profoundly for her guided tour of El Salvador.

Some of the author's helpers simply shared events from their lives.

Jerry Karr provided anecdotal tales concerning growing up at the northern end of San Pablo Bay and hunting and fishing amid the hills, sloughs, and salt flats bordering the Napa River. Linda Bixby shared her experiences concerning traumatic shock that gave the author a personal, visceral insight into how one survives terrifying helplessness. Jacqueline Morgan and her family, simply by being such marvelous friends to the author and his late wife, provided insights the author would never have grasped without their generosity, goodwill, humor, and kindness.

Tom Rickman, Ann Close, and Mark Childress all read portions of the manuscript prior to publication, and their encouragement and advice helped the author make this a much better book than he could have managed alone.

Although the textual research for this book covered a lot of ground, a few books proved particularly helpful. As already noted, *Kirk's Fire Investigation* by John D. DeHaan (Brady/Prentice Hall) was indispensable. *Understanding Police Culture* by John P. Crank (Anderson Publishing Co.); *Cop Shock: Surviving Posttraumatic Stress Disorder (PTSD)* by Allen R. Kates (Holbrook Street Press); *What Cops Know* by Connie Fletcher (Pocket Books); and *Practical Aspects of Interview and Interrogation* by David E. Zulaski and Douglas E. Wicklander (CRC Press) provided crucial insights into police work and life as an American law officer. *Slang Dictionary* (2001), compiled by the Communication Arts and Sciences Program, Berkeley (CA) High School, provided the author an invaluable source for reasonably current street vernacular.

Finally, portions of this book were written prior to the death of my wife, Terri. She believed in the book, felt a bond with its characters, and encouraged me to tell their tale. I wish she were here to see the fruits of that support, because I owe her more than I can say, and always will.

Downstroke

lancing up through the haze, he saw near his front door a shimmering radiance and wondered if it might not be a spirit, come to
welcome him. Blinking the rain from his eyes, he saw it was just
the glow from the porch light, filmed with cobwebs shredded by the
wind. He lay sprawled in the mud and gravel beneath the bare winter
branches of the sycamore—heels splayed, head bare, one arm cocked
beneath him like a chicken wing, the other pointed straight up the
path toward the house. His hat, knocked free, lay upside down, inches
from his outstretched fingers. His clothes, filthy and soaked through,
clung to his stone-cold skin. The draining heat, he knew, meant shock.
And the pain—it grew so total it stopped being pain at all, more a kind
of panic. He had strength to move his head, his hand, nothing more.
Bubbles of red saliva formed on his lips. A sensation like drowning
took hold.

One bullet had nicked his spine down low; another up high had
cut through his lung. A third had carved and twisted through the meat
of his shoulder. The exit wounds felt white-hot, and he guessed each
one to be about the size of a child's hand. The blood drained out past
his twisted arm into the rain-wet earth and rock.

He wondered if Toby's girl, the white girl, Nadya, had seen it all
from inside the house. So sudden. No warning. Maybe an ambulance
was on the way. He strained to hear a siren, at the same time thinking,
No matter. Mentally he counted and recounted the money in his
pocket—bills, coins—wondering if he had enough . . . *for what, old
man?*

His mind lost its grip on the present, his thoughts breaking apart. The night's events got mixed up with scenes from years ago, like snapshots tumbling out of a box. Scraps of remembered sound, too—music, years of it, a river of mindless ditties and intro hooks, ostinato runs and choruses, the refrains surging in crosscurrents like counterpoint, then trailing away.

In time, it came, like a whisper in his mind. Not a sound—more the sound within the sound. That haunting *yes*—the thing he'd hunted session to session, gig to gig, year after year—the truth of it, the tricky fluid soul of it, driving him slightly mad. Driven mad by music.

He'd sensed it almost every night—real, yes, any fool could tell you that. But so elusive. Too often, after the final set, he'd sat there alone onstage—the big brass ax in his hands, still warm from his breath—puzzling over how, despite every intent and effort, he'd somehow failed to get his talent around it. And so it chased him down a thousand nameless streets to the latest hotel room, horn case in hand, collar high against the wind. He'd left behind the other players at the bar, left behind the woman who'd made a point of hip-sliding up, smiling, saying he was the one she'd watched the whole night—and whose name he forgot almost instantly, long before he forgot that smile, or the spicy-flower smell of her skin all perfumed. And lying awake with a smoke, arm behind his head, he justified his loneliness, this strange madness, by saying it's an honest business, the pursuit of this sound that isn't a sound. This beckoning silence. It's the reason he played, the reason he'd never given up, never just said yes to the woman in the first place, telling himself, "I can live with this." Never put down the horn and said, "Okay. You win. Enough."

Like other players he knew, he'd gone so far as to give it a name: The Deep Sweet. And he learned then what a curse it is, to name a thing. For at one and the same time, as it finally feels solid, it somehow also slips away. And so a new word is needed, then another—till one day you're chasing it down those same nameless streets like a madman jabbering after his own delusions.

And now that elusive, crazy-making thing had come to find him here, on the ground, his life spilling away. It had come to tell him: Rise up. Remember who you are—Raymond "Strong" Carlisle, baritone sax. Veteran of The Basie Brotherhood, The Johnny Otis Revue, Grady

Gaines and the Upsetters. Road rocker for the likes of Ray Charles, Lloyd Price, Bobby Blue Bland. Listed on a hundred session sheets beside names like Wild Bill Davis and Thin Man Watts, Eddie Lockjaw Davis, Buddy Tate. Sideman for Gator Tail Jackson and Ruth Brown before their divorce, King Curtis before his murder. Held bottom on the reed sections of who knows how many house bands, pickup outfits, nightclub acts, roaming like a freebooter in cars of every make, buses in every condition—the chitlin' circuit to the Apollo, Central Avenue in L.A. to the Harlem Club in Atlantic City.

Then finally your own show: The Mighty Firefly Rhythm & Blues Orchestra. Not a juke joint, union hall, Baptist church, or Shriner Temple north of Monterey failed at one time or another to call upon MF R&B—sixteen strong, best sidemen and session guns on the north California coast. Packed dance floor every night. Smell of cigarettes and frying grease in the cramped heat, mingling with payday sweat and thick perfume. All fights called off with the band onstage. Cocktail waitresses rocking their hips while they call out orders at the bar. Bare-backed women in tight skirts and pumps, legs packed into shiny stockings, climbing on top of their tables, lifting their arms to the ceiling rafters to hoot and holler and sing God's praise for the Devil.

Years of music. And now Toby, accepting the torch. Father and son tied together, a lifeline of music. A lifeline. Toby. Good God, Son, know I loved you. Please know—

The front door to the house burst open. He arched his neck, craning to see. Through the milky haze of the porch light the white girl, Nadya, stumbled toward him.

Part I

———◆———

Moanin'

1

————•◦•————

Every black-and-white to be spared had come, seven of the ten on graveyard, drawn in once the watch commander broke the Code 33. Dennis Murchison studied the crowd while his partner, Jerry Stluka, parked their unmarked Crown Victoria as close as he could.

Onlookers gathered in the battering strobes of colored light. Even though the rain had stopped, umbrellas sprouted here and there. On the perimeter, one older couple, decked in bathrobes and slippers, clutched their pajamas to their throats and craned on tiptoe to see.

Murchison and Stluka pulled out their IDs, put the tabs into their jacket pockets so the badges showed, then drew latex gloves from the dispenser on the dash. Stluka, eyeing the crowd, said, "Am I free to assume this officially kicks off Black History Month?"

He was sable-haired, muscular, compact. A build referred to as *pyknic*, Murchison had learned once doing a crossword puzzle.

"Got any pills you can take, stem the flow for a little while?"

Stluka inhaled through his teeth, a hard, thin whistling sound. "Yeah. Keep 'em with the antiwhining tablets. Want one?" He stretched his glove tight. "Who's I-C?"

"Holmes."

Stluka cackled. "Sherlock!"

Murchison took stock of the faces swinging their way. Young men mostly, some with eyes like stones, full of what-the-fuck and who-are-you. "Once we get inside the tape, do me a favor. Lay off the Sherlock bit. Think you can do that?"

Stluka groaned. The pain of it. "Seems to me we could stand to lighten up a little. Get a sense of humor. You want, I could call him Maid Marion like they used to down around Dumpers substation."

"Oh yeah. That'll work."

"Hey—you want to be treated like one among equals, you take the damn chip off your shoulder."

"Whose shoulder? I'm the one asking."

Stluka made a little wave to suggest further discussion was beneath him. "I'm ready. You?"

They got out of the car and eased their way through the crowd from the back, checking faces. Murchison noted a player or two, known thugs, but that was hardly strange. They lived up here. One guy gripped an open Mickeys, talking smack into a cell phone. Others had their dogs in tow, pits and rotts. The animals strained against their chain leashes, sniffing the air. They'd caught the scent of the victim's blood.

Hennessey, who had the hill for patrol that night, stood in the middle of the street, ducking under one neighbor's umbrella as he jotted down her words. The woman wore pink sweats beneath a yellow slicker, bare feet in flip flops, her hair coiled meticulously into French braids.

Murchison came up, placed a hand on the officer's arm, and said quietly, "Hennessey Tennessee, toodle your flute."

The man was big, Irish—priestly eyes, wastrel grin. "Murch, hey." He nodded toward the woman under the umbrella. "Detective Murchison? Marcellyne Pathon."

She had high cheekbones in a round, childlike face. Behind thick horn-rims her brown eyes ballooned. She shook Murchison's hand. Her skin felt warm, her palm damp, not from rain. Nearby, a few young toughs in the crowd drifted back, far enough not to get dragged in, not so far as to leave earshot.

"She lives across the way." Hennessey pointed with his pen. Two little girls stood holding hands in the window, silhouettes, peering out at their mother. "Says she heard the shots, they woke her up, but—"

"Didn't see nobody." It came out quick. She adjusted her glasses. "I went to the window, you know, looked out, but—" A shrug. "All dark out here, you know?"

"Your children hear anything?" Murchison nodded toward her house.

Like that, she stiffened. "No, sir. All of us, the girls, too, we gone to bed already. Got church tomorrow."

"How about a car? Hear one? See one?"

She took in a long, slow breath, thinking it through. "No, sir. Don't remember no car." Her eyes held steady behind the Coke bottle lenses.

"Any voices, shouts, an argument?"

"No, sir. It was the shots, like sudden. Just them. Rest was real quiet. Especially for a Saturday. The storm, I figure."

"Mr. Carlisle hard to get along with?"

She recoiled just a little, as though accused. "How you mean?"

"Just trying to get an idea of who the man was, Marcellyne."

Her face relaxed a little, and she gave the question long consideration. She seemed conflicted. "What Mr. Carlisle was, was *big*— know what I'm saying? Spoke his mind. Stand back when he did, okay? But he was no trouble. I can't say nothing about him hurtin' nobody."

"The other neighbors. Any tension?"

Nearby, one guy with a dog craned to listen in. Hennessey edged over, herded him and his animal back.

"Not with me. Not with folks I know." Her eyes skittered around. Her voice quavered. "Have to ask them, I suppose."

Murchison nodded, glanced around at the nearest faces. Eyes fled his gaze. "Okay, Marcellyne. Great. Thank you. I'll get back in touch if I think we need some follow-up, okay?"

He didn't wait for her reply, but drew away, at the same time pulling Hennessey with him, turning him so their backs faced the crowd.

"This is your usual area up here, am I right?"

Hennessey shrugged. The polyester shoulders of his uniform beaded with rain. "Normally, yeah. Sure. Trade off from time to time— Brickyards, Dumpers—but I know the lay of the land pretty good up here."

"Look around. See any strange faces?"

Hennessey didn't have to look. "Here and there. But you know how it is. You're not a fuckup or his family, I don't know you."

From far back in the crowd, a voice shouted, "Pig white po-po motherfuckers!"

Murchison didn't bother to look. "You've got your Polaroid in the trunk?"

"Checked it out beginning of shift," Hennessey said. "Sure."

Murchison made a pressing gesture with his finger, the shutter button. "Don't wait, okay?"

Murchison joined up with Stluka just beyond the yellow crime scene tape, strung in a semicircle to keep the crowd back. An ancient sycamore loomed over a tall fence of rain-streaked dogtooth redwood that rimmed the property. A second ribbon of tape festooned the fence like bunting. A uniformed officer named Truax manned the gate, clipboard in hand, keeping the entry/exit log.

Murchison took a moment to survey the neighborhood. St. Martin's Hill shared the same high bluff overlooking the river as Baymont, the two neighborhoods divided by a shabby panhandle known for trade. St. Martin's was generally considered the better locale, working-class and stable, but the spate of foreclosures since the shipyard's closing had changed that.

Quicksilver mines once threaded the hill, part of a rim of upcroppings known extravagantly as the Sierra de Napa according to some old survey maps. Below, the Napa River flowed out from the salt marshes into San Pablo Bay. Only the western slope of the hill had been developed; the backside gave way to a broad, weed-choked ravine, former site of several sleeper mines. The ground remained too toxic from mercury for home building.

From this side of the range, though, on a clear night, glancing south from the bluff headlands, you could see San Francisco glimmering in the distance, like a wicked dream. Northward, beyond the salt flats, lay vintner paradise, the Napa Valley, with its thousands of acres of fretwork vines and the hundreds of tons of silt load they sent downriver. You could hardly head a boat upstream anymore except at high tide. An ecological disaster, those vineyards, but the yuppie-come-latelies couldn't love them enough.

In daylight, you looked west across the river to the Mayacamas Mountains, the interim distance greened with tidal wetlands riven by waterways—China Slough, Devil's Creek, Dutchman Slough. As a boy, Murchison had water-skied those sloughs with his older brother, Willy, breaking an arm once, his brother losing teeth, prelegal teens anesthetized with beer. Once, they'd traded chugs from a fifth of Four Roses bourbon—paint thinner with food coloring, basically—filched from a passed-out fisherman snoring in his boat.

The brothers had hunted together, too, looking for ruddies and stiff tails flying in to feed in the tidal pools, jackrabbits darting in and out of the fennel and coyote bush on the salt marsh levees, pheasant flushed out of the artichoke thistle around Five Brooks. Up near Dutton's Landing they'd helped buck oat hay for pocket money. After dusk they snuck into The Dream Bowl storeroom and helped themselves to a beer or two, then traded belches while the spinning tower light at the Napa Airport mesmerized them and they talked about girls they knew.

A lifetime ago, all that. As of 1972, Willy survived only in memory; you'd find his name etched in black granite among fifty-eight thousand others on the Mall in D.C. What hunting Murchison got to now concerned men. From time to time, he still felt the need for anesthesia.

He turned his eyes back to the immediate surroundings.

St. Martin's laid claim to being one of the few genuinely integrated neighborhoods in town, though halfheartedness more than highmindedness deserved the credit for that. Haywire zoning had let in the low-rent apartments, and they were nests of trouble. Absentee rentals were a blight. This had driven out a lot of the whites, and almost all the ones left behind worked in the building trades, cast adrift by the shipyard closing, traveling hours up and down the valley now for any work they could find.

In truth, the racial tensions in town were a good deal less edgy than you'd find in dozens of other places, though that didn't mean they didn't exist. Just because people intermingled didn't mean they mixed. The same held true for the force. Murchison got along with Black cops all right, or he had before being partnered with Stluka. Now he was an enigma, but he couldn't do much about that without undermining his partner, a cardinal sin the way Murchison saw it. Loyalty was a duty, not a bond. Besides, he knew only too well that getting along isn't friendship. And you didn't have to wonder much what secret feelings remained at work beneath the surface of things—on the force, among ordinary people.

As for the folks who lived up here, they did well to know their neighbors beyond hello, regardless of race, and the ones they did know owed that familiarity to trouble—a men's rehab center trying to get zoning for ten additional beds; or the duplex owners who'd phonied up a permit request, then painted the house in clown colors when the Planning Department turned them down. Here and there, you did still find a family who'd lived in the same house for decades, but now their children were taking over the property, hoping for a little of that inflation windfall so key to the California dream anymore.

Being close to the panhandle, this particular street was mostly Black, though scattered here and there in the crowd Murchison caught a white face. He'd be interested in Hennessey's Polaroids. Be interested in which faces Marcellyne Pathon could identify, which ones she couldn't. Which ones she wouldn't.

Across the panhandle in Baymont, things got worse. Up top there was a reasonably decent neighborhood called Home in the Sky, built by a man named Jameson Carswell, a local legend—only Black developer the town had ever seen. In the fifties and sixties he'd built almost all the new homes owned by African Americans up here, then formed his own finance company to loan out mortgage money when the local banks refused, hoping to ruin him. A fierce loyalty remained among the older home owners over there. Old folks, they remembered.

Almost everything below that one neighborhood, though, despite the stellar views, qualified for Section 8. More than shacks, less than houses, they were old federal housing units left behind by World War II, now with add-ons and renovations grandfathered in decade after decade. Shabby apartment buildings and four-room prefabs set onto concrete slab pretty much finished the picture.

Patrol units seldom ventured over into Baymont for so much as a barking dog except in teams of three. Narrow winding streets snaked downhill among eucalyptus trees and Monterey pines so ratty and thick with duff they almost qualified as tinder. At the bottom, where the panhandle ended, the streets on that side converged with those from over here on St. Martin's—it was the only way in or out of either neighborhood, another relic of the federal housing plan. Traffic bottle-necked down there every morning and every night. A renovation plan was in the works, but that had been true for thirty years.

Beyond the low stone wall demarcating the Baymont and St. Martin's Hill communities, twenty-five acres of vacant navy row houses sat empty. They'd been targeted for condo conversion—a contractor had the plans approved for 250 town houses, model units were due for completion early next year—but then cost overruns for heating and electrical upgrades halted work, or so they said. Meanwhile the project just sat there, inviting the worst.

To the south along the river, the warehouse district began. Boxcars tagged with graffiti turned to rust in the rail yards. Piles of pumice and concrete powder, heaped along the loading docks, sent gritty dust clouds sailing through town, ruining paint jobs and prompting asthma attacks.

The night trade down there, among the warehouses, made the action up here on the hill look like church. That's where you found the lion's share of meth labs and crack houses and shooting galleries—*if* you found them. They roamed spot to spot, week by week, to avoid crackdowns, and even with federal HIDTA money, the force had yet to build up the manpower to do much. Bangers ran roughshod, and where they didn't the bikers did, the two sides negotiating truces only money could explain.

Beyond that lay Dumpers and the rest of southtown, absentee rentals again, a lot of Section 8. Live there, you inhaled mold through your walls and looked out at the street through metal bars. What you saw, more than likely, day or night, was hookers working twists along the side streets off the truck route. Come morning, if you ventured very far outside, you had to watch your step to avoid the spent rubbers.

The whole town had started to backslide when the first big wave of parolees came back to town, trying to reclaim what parts of the street trade they'd surrendered when they'd gone inside. Crime rates were ticking upward again. Six murders already this year, first week of February. Six murders and fifteen fires, in an overgrown town. A community in transition, some bow-tied consultant hired by the mayor's office had called it.

Turning back to the murder scene, Murchison had to peer over the tall wood fence just to see a rim of roofline. The upper tip of an addition appeared near the back. Raggedy plum trees flanked the yard.

To either side, beyond the fence and the trees, two Queen Anne Victorians stood dark. The Victorians counted among about two dozen in this part of town, one of the reasons it bore the nickname Heritage Hill. In contrast to Homicide Hill, which it also got called from time to time. The Victorians were impressive despite long neglect— steep-hipped roofs, cross gables, spindlework. One had a veranda in front and a Palladian window on the top floor. The other had a tower and a widow's walk. More to the point, they both stood empty. There'd be no neighbors on either side coming forward with eyewitness accounts.

Murchison approached the gate. Stluka, already there, leaned against the fence, trading wisecracks with Truax.

"Just slammed it down," Truax said. "This green gunk. Said it had bee droppings in it, I kid you not. Bee droppings, not honey."

"There a difference?" Stluka shook his head, leaned down, and spat. "Health food. It's God's way of being passive-aggressive."

"The two Victorians." Murchison pointed at one house, then the other. "Anybody check them inside?"

Truax shook his head. "Inside, no. But they're secure. Doors all locked. Holmes sent me and Hennessey over to check both out first thing. No windows broke, except those must've got broke before. They're all boarded up tight."

"I still want both taped off. They're part of the scene till I let them go."

"Yeah, sure." Truax flipped to a blank page and wrote it down.

"And back people farther away, across the street and beyond the Victorians, both directions. Neighbor said she didn't hear a car, but just in case there's rubber out here, I want to be able to find it."

Truax puffed his cheeks. "Gonna need bodies."

"Call it in. Blame me. There's OT in it if anybody whines." He pointed again at the Victorians. "You said boarded-up windows. Remind me—we get calls on work site thefts up here? Lumber, tools, paint?"

Truax shrugged. "Don't look like much work got started yet."

Murchison took out his notepad. "I'll check. And fires. Unless I'm wrong, there were fires up here."

"Been fires everywhere," Truax said.

"I realize that." Murchison kept writing. "Jerry, we're gonna want to check property rolls, find out who the owners are, bring them in for a talk. See if they had words with the vic."

"Yeah," Stluka said, cracking his back. "Don't forget to remind me to remember that." He showed his badge to Truax, so he could log the number. "Let's bop on in, see what Sherlock's got."

2

———•◆•———

The halogen lights, erected just inside the gate, lit things up like a stripper's wedding. Five yards in, the body lay sprawled along the gravel path, covered with a plastic drape. The hands and feet stuck out from underneath, already bagged by the evidence tech. The bags made it look like the dead man had washed up in his own front yard, with jellyfish attached.

Holmes crouched close to the body, as though to defend it. Beyond him, spaced evenly across the yard, three patrolmen in rain slickers walked shoulder to shoulder, one small step at a time. Near the house, two others, one with a metal detector, checked the bushes.

The house was painted blue, a low squat cinder block structure like the kind used for rest rooms at the beach, except this one had windows and a front door. Flat roof, dry-rotted eaves, cheap metal windows pocked with rust. Behind it, the addition, made of wood plank and with a pitched roof covered in tar paper shingles, stood slightly higher and wider than the front. The effect was that of two completely different structures, trying to mate.

Seeing Murchison and Stluka, Holmes rose, rubbing his legs to get the blood flow back. At full height, he had three inches on Murchison, towered over Stluka. His slicker barely covered his knees.

Holmes had played basketball locally, starring in high school, then got lost in the rotation at Fresno State. Murchison, who'd been something of a local star himself fifteen years earlier—football, strong safety—had followed Holmes's career. He was ugly in the way that paid off for an athlete and a cop. He scared people: bony head, itty-bitty ears, nose like an ax blade. He had thick-lidded eyes that seemed both sleepy and pitiless. Especially when he looked at Stluka.

"I was going to hoist the tent. Keep all this dry. But the rain?" Holmes glanced up at the low clouds sailing inland. "Soon as I got here, pretty much stopped. Got to work."

"Got storms lined up halfway to Hawaii, Sherlock."

Murchison flinched at the nickname. Holmes, eyes steady, just nodded.

"Not the way I heard it," he said. "All clear."

Stluka uttered a throaty laugh. "Got yourself a real future with the weather bureau."

Murchison cut in. "Rain starts again, the tent goes up. Till then, we're here, let's get it done. Holmesy, take us through it."

Rio Mirada had eighty-five police officers. Only fifteen were Black, none were detectives, and only one was on track to change that. Sgt. Marion Holmes. Stluka, a refugee from Newton Precinct in South Central—the infamous Shootin' Newton—found nothing at all amiss in the numbers. But the current chief was a job hopper, more politician than cop, and he saw elevating Holmes to detective as a way to make his mark here before moving on. Holmes got more latitude at crime scenes than others assigned In-Charge. It rankled some on the force. Stluka, for starters.

Holmes pointed at the body with his pen. "Victim's known as Strong Carlisle. Raymond's his given name. It's his house here. Musician, headlined an outfit called The Mighty Firefly. Big band R&B, they do dances, Juneteenth, the festival and Shriner circuit. Once upon a time, man played with Ray Charles, King Curtis, Bobby Blue Bland—"

"Bobby Boo who?" Stluka rocked on his heels, sport jacket open, hands deep in his pockets. "I mean, am I supposed to know who that is?"

Murchison said, "We'll finalize the music appreciation aspect of this later. That all right?"

"Just a question," Stluka said.

"Understood. Holmesy?"

Holmes drew a line in the air between the gate and the body. "Gunshots from the rear, looks like three hit. Techs'll test the jacket for powder, but from the entry wounds alone I'd say close-range, probably ten feet or less. Exit wounds are big, real big, maybe hollow-points. Could be we're talking a .357, a .44—"

"You don't guess caliber from exit wounds," Stluka groaned. "Jesus."

Holmes locked eyes again. "I'll pass that along to the ME, Detective." Turning back to the body, he went on, "There's no casings, so revolver most likely. Got the guys here checking for spents."

Murchison's mind began to drift as Holmes crouched down beside the body again and got deeper into the detail, the science of it, the stuff that so impressed outsiders but didn't change the fact the situation basically reduced to: *Old guy got shot in the back by somebody who ran away.*

"What time we looking at?" he asked finally, snapping back to it.

"Dispatcher got the nine-one-one 'round midnight. Caller was a neighbor, said shots woke her up."

"Marcellyne Pathon."

"That sounds right. By the time she got to the window, nothing."

"Told me the same thing just now." Murchison glanced toward the gate, wondering whether the crowd outside had grown larger or thinned out, whether anyone had come up to Marcellyne and threatened her, told her everything she didn't see.

"EMTs got here inside of twelve but too late regardless. Did a hat dance all over the scene, messed up any chance you had at shoe prints. All that just to confirm Mr. Carlisle's no Lazarus. He means to stay dead. Lost too much blood and lost it too fast. Probably got a lung clipped, maybe both. Want a look?"

Murchison nodded, then crouched beside the body and tightened the fit of his gloves while Holmes removed the drape with one quick pull. As the victim appeared to him, revealed in an unintentional flourish like the culmination of a magic act, Murchison suffered an instantaneous series of fleeting regrets, intimations so momentary they could hardly be said to exist in time at all.

First, he pictured his wife and daughters, and feared for their safety. He'd felt this a lot lately, blamed middle age, the suspicion he'd somehow turned helpless: poor husband, bad father, weak man. Second, he indulged an inkling that life and death shared more in common than anyone knew, more like left and right than before and after. Third and last, he felt a disquieting sort of envy, wondering what it would feel like, to lay down that sword and shield.

The victim lay faceup, turned at the hip, like someone had tried to roll him over then stopped with the job half done. One arm reached forward, the other lay flung to the side. The feet were splayed a way you never saw in life, no matter how heavy the sleep. The face was long, narrow, with dark freckling across each cheek. A salt-and-pepper goatee. Deep eye sockets. Teeth, lips, and tongue all moiled with blood.

Murchison pulled up the pant cuff to check lividity. It was strong already, given the blood loss, leaving the skin an ashen purple-gray. The pant leg was mud-spattered, everything was. He drew the cuff back in place, smoothed it down. A little respect.

The man's chest was a pulpy mangled knit of fabric and skin. Despite the damage the shots had caused, you could tell from his clothes that this had been a proud man: tailored sport coat, natty red shirt with a black silk vest, gray pleated slacks. A black beret had been knocked off his head; it lay a few inches from his hand, upside down. His hair still wore the crease where the hatband had pressed into it.

The blood pooled beneath him had begun to dry. Hard to know how much he'd lost. There'd be a lot in his lungs, too, Murchison figured. He checked the gravel to see if a slug lay loose there. "After they take him away," he told Holmes, "let's check underneath." He had to hope the coroner's people would have the sense to undress the man carefully, check to make sure a spent bullet wasn't knocking around inside his shirt somewhere.

"Interesting position," Murchison said, gesturing to the body. "Paramedics roll him?"

"No. Found him like that."

Murchison glanced up, puzzled.

"There was a girl here when the patrols first arrived. She was shook up bad, could hardly get her words out. Got the idea she's the one turned him over, tried mouth-to-mouth. Knees were muddy. Had blood all over, her hands, clothes. Even the eyelashes and hair. Like the vic coughed it up in her face."

Murchison winced. "This girl, how old?"

"Late teens. Twenty tops." Looking up at Stluka, Holmes added, "Pretty little white girl."

The taunt ricocheted around the yard. Cops looked up, Black and white both. Stluka grinned, but his eyes were cold. "Love the one you're with."

Murchison said, "This girl, she's where now?"

"ER. Like I said, she was nonresponsive when we arrived. Just sitting up there on the porch, staring at the vic. Like a trance. Clawing at her arm, fingernails bloody. Inside of her arm, skin was tore up in shreds. Paramedics had their hands full just getting her to stand up. Took her off to get treated and tranqued."

"She see it go down?"

"Don't know. Like I said, I barely got a word—"

"Barely," Stluka said. "Come on, what's 'barely' mean? She say something or not?"

Holmes did a little shoulder roll. The sleepy, pitiless eyes came on. "Yeah. Matter of fact, she did. She said, 'I'm sorry.' Said that a lot."

Stluka let his jaw sag. "Sorry? Fucking Christ, Holmes, how you know she's not involved?"

Murchison said, "You got a man at the hospital with her?"

Holmes let his stare linger on Stluka. "Not yet. Needed the bodies here."

Stluka shook his head. "Ah, Christ."

"Get one. Call it in as soon as we wrap up." *For your sake as much as hers,* Murchison thought, turning back to the victim. The pant pockets were turned inside out, the contents placed into evidence bags. "What's missing?"

"Nothing, looks like," Holmes said. "This stage, don't see robbery. Somebody just came, pushed the gate open, pow. Then booked."

Stluka dislodged a snarl of phlegm from his throat. "You checked inside, right? Secured the house."

"Yeah. First thing. Yeah."

"Relax, Sherlock, it's a fucking question."

Murchison snapped his fingers. "Hey, boys and girls?" He gestured for Holmes to cover up the victim. "Back to the pockets."

Holmes drew the drape back across the body. "Wallet still in his jacket, fifty-two bucks and change inside. ID, credit cards. Untouched."

"Okay."

"Paper sack there? Got a pint inside. Sent another patrol unit, Gilroy, to canvas the liquor stores downtown, see what the counter help might remember."

"Good. Too bad it's Gilroy, but good. Anything else?"

"There's a son," Holmes said. "Showed up while I was securing the scene."

Stluka shot a glance at Murchison.

"He didn't get in here," Murchison said.

"No. No. I heard the commotion at the gate, went out. Got a little wild, you know? Son went kinda crazy. But I settled the young man down. Told him he had to stay outside."

"Okay, Holmes. Okay. That sounds good."

"He's a musician, too. The son. Coming home from a gig."

"He went crazy. How?"

"Upset, scared. Talked tough a little bit, said we couldn't keep him out. But I explained it to him. He sorta just caved in on himself then. Went all still, then boom, took a dive."

"Look real?"

"Yeah. Damn good if not. Eyes rolled back, legs went. Had to use smelling salts, bring him around. Came to, shot up, and spewed his supper out front in the gutter."

"Anybody else with him?"

Holmes shook his head. "Walked up alone."

"Walked—from where?"

"Never got that far with him. He was still fending off the little blue tweeties when I planted him in a car. He's down at the station now. All yours."

Murchison looked around the yard one last time, collected his thoughts. Older man, dressed sharp, a musician of some note, ho ho. Shot in the back, his own front yard, left to drown in his own blood. And a white girl, trying to save him, failing, perching herself on the doorstep while she clawed at her arm till the skin was gone. A real human-interest story, if anyone bothered to tell it.

"I'm ready to go inside, check the house."

Holmes said, "One last thing? The son, he IDed the girl." Holmes checked his notes. "Nah-dee-ya . . . Lah-za-rank-o. Think that's it. She's his girlfriend."

Murchison took out his pad and pen. "Spell it."

Holmes obliged. A little mischief flickered in his eye. "Could be one of your people, Stookles."

"Don't call me that."

"What is it—Po-lock? Slo-vock?"

"You hear what I just said?"

"You want, I can call you Cap'n Cracker, like they do around Dumpers in southtown."

Murchison couldn't help himself, he laughed. "Okay, that's it, enough. We got one body here. My guess is that's our quota."

"Tell you what, Sherlock—"

"Let it go, Jerry. Holmesy—the son, he say anything else about this girl?"

"Yeah. Yeah. Said she was with the vic earlier tonight, drove him home."

"From?"

"Club in Emeryville. Place called the Zoom Room. Where the son was playing."

"But the son," Stluka said, getting into it again, "he didn't need a drive. He walked." He looked back and forth, Murchison to Holmes. "It ain't just me. That doesn't make sense."

Holmes slapped his notepad against his leg. "Like I said, he's down at the station."

Murchison checked the time. "Okay. Holmesy. I got Truax calling in for more bodies. Connect with him. Get somebody to help Hennessey out there with the neighbors. Not just the crowd. Door-to-door, I don't care what time it is. Anybody has a story, get the particulars, then call me. Get a guy who's done some major accident work—Crawford's good, wake him up, blame me—have him check for rubber out on the street. Get a man over to the hospital, right outside the girl's door. She doesn't leave. Nobody in the room but hospital staff. I want first crack. We good?"

Holmes put his notepad in his slicker pocket and headed out. Murchison watched him go, loping like a giant through the gate.

"Talk about the high priest of half-assed." Stluka picked up the dead man's hat, checked inside. "Shoulda put a man with the girl down at the hospital first thing."

• • •

The house felt less gloomy inside than out. It was cluttered, dust motes sailing in the lamplight, but somebody'd put out the effort to make a home. To the right of the entry sat a cramped dining room, with an old oak table and chairs. To the left was the living room. A lumpy sofa sat against the far wall. Above it, family photographs covered almost every inch of plaster. Murchison went close, checked the faces.

"Anybody we know?" Stluka asked, meaning perps and players.

Murchison shrugged. "Come look."

The pictures seemed to be of family and friends. Three generations from the look of things: a matriarch, then the victim and his siblings, and after that nephews and nieces and others further removed. Murchison assumed the son was there—should have asked Holmes for a description, he thought—then shortly found the photograph he'd been hoping for.

Raymond Carlisle and a younger man stood side by side, each carrying a horn case. The victim was taller, a fact accentuated by his reedy build. He was darker, too, his skin a deep coffee color, with the spatters of dark freckling across each cheek Murchison had noticed outside, just as he noticed again the salt-and-pepper goatee, the deep-set eyes. In life, they'd perfected the man's intensity.

In contrast, the son, if that was who this was, looked studious. He had short-napped hair, and it set off his angular features, which resembled the victim's. His skin was lighter, a reddish cinnamon color, and he wore a pair of rimless spectacles. Behind the glasses, his eyes conveyed warmth, not heat. But there was wariness in them, too. This young man, early twenties from the look of him, was no hothouse flower. He had a strength about him, and his bearing suggested an easy grace tinged with formality.

"Think I found the son," Murchison told Stluka finally, easing aside so they both could look.

Murchison took note of Stluka struggling with his disbelief. The word *musician* conjured a distinctly different image in this town, given names like Pimp-T Junior, A. K. Hype, Treacherous Bo. The Violence Suppression Task Force had recently pulled in two rappers from

Baymont tied to a statewide bank robbery gang who had laid out their entire MO on a locally pressed CD. The mastermind producer of the local rap scene was himself a major player in the crack trade who was currently sitting in jail, awaiting trial for placing a bomb outside the south county courthouse, hoping to destroy evidence in a third-strike prosecution that would put him away for life. The FBI had just helped out in the arrest of a group of failed rappers who called themselves Pitch Black Night, tied not only to drugs but six murders in the area. The granddaddy of them all, though, was a rapper named Master De-Paul. He was the man who kicked off the turf war between Baymont and Dumpers that reached its peak body count in 1994. The city's reputation still hadn't recovered. Given all that and more, the general feeling on the force remained: if you were local, Black, and musical, you merited a watchful eye.

"Care to comment?" Murchison asked, standing back to take in the whole wall.

Stluka gnawed his lower lip, thinking. "Squeaky type, looks like. The son I mean."

"Yeah, but I was thinking more generally. These look like working people, church people."

"Spare me, Murch. Pictures lie." Stluka turned away, took in the rest of the room. "Every fuckwad in the world's got a snapshot somewhere makes him look harmless. And that'll be the one the family fawns off on the media when it's crying time."

There was a piano in the room, piled high with sheet music. Stluka drifted toward it as Murchison pulled back the curtain at the window. Unless this Lazarenko girl had been waiting, she most likely went to look only once she heard shots. Like Marcellyne Pathon. And saw nothing. The glass was filthy. Given the clouds, the rain, the sparse streetlights on the block, it would have been dark in the yard, nothing but an amber porch light strewn with cobwebs.

"Well now, looky here," Stluka said behind him.

He was standing beside the piano, holding a purse in one hand, an ID in the other. Shaking the purse, he caught sight of something inside. "Get that."

Murchison glanced in, spotted the wallet, took it out.

"There a driver's license inside?"

Murchison checked. "Yeah." He read the name. "This doesn't match what Holmes told us outside."

"Nadya Lazarenko." Stluka showed Murchison the loose ID he'd found first. "She's all of nineteen."

Murchison checked the other ID. "This one says she's Stephanie Waugh, twenty-one."

"Ta-da."

Murchison checked the photos. The faces were similar, not identical. Probably a friend's license. He dropped the wallet back into the purse. "She'd need phony ID to get into a club where her boyfriend's playing."

"The Zoom Room." Stluka grinned. "It's still deception, Murch."

"So's just about everything else at that age. She's our only shot at an eyewitness so far. I'm not going to bag that up and log it till I know it means something. Let the defense blow its own smoke."

Stluka sighed. "Fair enough. For now." He dropped the other ID in and set the purse back down beside the piano. "Join me for a stroll?"

He turned and headed down the hallway. Murchison followed, watching as Stluka checked in every opening he passed—linen closet, laundry hamper, bathroom shelves—sniffing at things like a disgruntled critic lost in the bowels of some minor museum. He lifted pictures, checking behind for wall safes. Kicked the baseboards, listening for hidey-holes.

They came to two bedrooms at the end of the hall, and Murchison supposed the son had been using the smaller one. There was one bed, a twin, covered with an old Hudson blanket. The desktop was neat. Stluka pulled open a desk drawer, peeked inside, then shut it again.

"Can we agree this room looks undisturbed?"

Murchison inspected the closet. The clothes hung straight, shirts stacked tidily on the shelf above, shoes lined up like little soldiers on the floor below. Not many. Not enough. Inside a plastic bag he found a turtleneck and denim overalls, hightops, and socks. All stuffed in together, like laundry, and small. A woman's. The girl had changed here, but no sign of staying.

"He doesn't live here. The son, I mean. His being here, it's short-term. And the girlfriend." Murchison set the bag back down, nodded toward the narrow bed. "She doesn't sleep over."

Stluka considered it. "Maybe she's a Thoroughbred, sleeps standing up." He pointed across the hall. "Or she spends the night with Daddy."

"You think?"

"I try not to make up my mind about people till they've had a chance to disappoint me."

The furniture in the larger bedroom across the hall was Sears-quality, decades old. No conspicuous sign of disturbance, just day-to-day carelessness. Worn slippers lay askew beneath the unmade bed. Drawers sat open, revealing nothing valuable or shameful, just old clothes, folded and clean. An old dusty TV sat atop the highboy.

Stluka opened the closet. "Here's where the guy's money went." He fingered the sleeve to a silk suit jacket. "Snazz 'n' pizzazz. Show Man." He dropped the sleeve, turned around. "Whereas this." He gestured toward the room. "Dressed with flash, lived in trash."

It was something routinely said of junkies. "You think?"

"No, we'd have seen more signs by now. Expression just leapt to mind." Stluka looked around again, shivered with disgust. "This guy got laid, he did it somewhere else. Unless he was paying for it."

Murchison checked the closet after Stluka, noted he was right: the quality of the wardrobe outpaced everything else in the house by far. Not surprising, Murchison thought, remembering the clothes on the body and what Marcellyne Pathon had said. He was *big*. Somebody with the guts to call his band The Mighty Firefly had to have style—thus the nickname, one supposed. Strong.

"ARF," Stluka said behind him.

Murchison turned, saw Stluka holding a prescription bottle, studying the label. "What the hell is 'ARF'?"

Murchison took the bottle from him. "Acute Renal Failure." He checked the other bottles on top of the bed stand. They were the usual garden-variety post-op brew: antibiotics, painkillers, some Halcion for sleep. They rested atop a checklist titled *"Nephrectomy: Expectations after Surgery. Convalescence."*

"Our victim only had one kidney."

"I think that's the least of his worries right about now."

"Dates on these scrips, I'd say it came out about two months ago."

"You going somewhere with this?"

"Holmes found a bottle in a bag beside the guy. He's putting it away, with one kidney."

"Unless his doctor killed him for being a crappy patient, why do I care?"

Murchison shrugged. "Thinking out loud." He crouched down, opened the bed stand drawer. "Well, well, what have we here, Mr. Carlisle?" Among reading glasses and ear plugs and Kleenex packs sat a snub-nosed .38, black metal with a brown wood grip. Loose shells rattled around in the bottom of the drawer. Careless old fool, he thought. He lifted the weapon, showed it to Stluka, then put it to his nose, shook his head. "Thing hasn't been fired in forever."

"Ah, piss." Stluka pulled back the bedcovers, checked beneath the pillows, found a Walkman but no second gun. "Bag the damn thing anyway. Give it to ballistics, let them confirm the obvious. Remind us what geniuses they are."

Murchison pulled an evidence bag from his pocket, shook it open, dropped the gun inside and then the cartridges. "Victim felt a need to keep a gun by his bed."

"In this neighborhood, come on. Wouldn't you?"

Checking the drawer again, Murchison found a photograph inside. An old one. He took it out. The face didn't register with the others he'd seen in the living room. A woman, in her mid-twenties or so. She had long hair drawn back with combs, setting off her eyes and smile. On the back he found an inscription: *Dear Raymond—With the warmest of hearts—Felicia.* The script, it was perfectly feminine. You could almost smell her perfume.

"Think we found the secret sweetheart."

Stluka took the picture from him, checked it front and back. "This thing's twenty years old, minimum."

Just then, the heater came on, erupting from the cellar with a sound like thunder. Warm air that stank of mildew began pouring through the wall vents.

Stluka shrank away from it. "I am really beginning to hate this case."

Murchison took the picture back, studied it one more time, then slipped it into his pocket. "Ideas?"

Stluka cracked his knuckles. "Maybe it's me, but I sense friction between the father and son."

"Style, you mean?"

"Everything in Its Proper Place versus I Do What I Want—Try and Stop Me."

"The vic looks like a character," Murchison agreed. "Headstrong. Daddy likes his drama. Son seems the dutiful type. And the girl?"

"I'm not sold on her being uninvolved. Not yet."

"Interesting." Murchison granted Stluka his instincts, which as a cop were often solid. His faults as a human being, those you had to deal with as they came. "And it's not just that the son's a neat freak, or that he's only here short-term. It's strange. He's made an effort to clear a space for himself, but there's no real stake in it."

"I'm here. Don't push it."

"Yeah."

"And I'm still hung up on this thing about him walking. There's a piece missing. He didn't walk thirty miles home."

Murchison headed for the door, glancing around one last time. "Check out the rest of the house?"

In the kitchen, a coffee mug lay in the sink, two cold tea bags shriveled inside it.

"Smell that?"

Stluka was already square with the next doorway. "I smell a lot of things. Pick one."

Murchison lifted the cup, sniffed, made sure. "Brandy, I think. Alcohol for sure."

Stluka closed his eyes, palms pressing his temples. "Murch, I got it. Okay? The guy was a lush."

"Bear with me." Murchison opened cabinets, peered in. He found the brandy bottle. The cap was sticky but loose, like it had just been reopened after sitting awhile. "The father had a bad enough drinking problem it cost him a kidney. The son's here to play caretaker. How long? Depends on how good a patient the old man is. Eight weeks of convalescence, he's already at it again."

"You think they fought about it."

"From the picture we saw, the son's no loser. He looks smart. And he's got himself a girlfriend, his own career. But he hauls himself up here anyway, to live in this dreary old hole." He nodded toward the cup in the sink. "Now this. Old man's mixing it in his tea, which is either some kind of homebrew cocktail or he was trying to hide it. And that means, yeah, maybe they fought about it."

Stluka stared back from the doorway, giving it thought. He blinked like a cat.

"You're the one brought up friction," Murchison said.

Stluka waved his hands in mock surrender. "I confess."

"I mean, given the neighborhood, the way he died, I wouldn't say this was a family deal. But in here—"

"Tells a different story, yes it does." Stluka tapped his hands against the door frame. "Wrap this up?"

The next doorway opened onto the addition. Mismatched chairs and music stands rested in haphazard clusters. Bookshelves, crammed with sheet music, lined one wall. The other three were covered with egg crate foam. The craftsmanship was shoddy—below, the rug buckled and curled at the edges, never tacked down; above, the ceiling lacked several acoustic tiles.

Stluka clasped his hands atop his head. "This guy had a real knack for unfinished business."

At the back of the room, a gold banner with black lettering hung from the ceiling, draped wall to wall:

STRONG CARLISLE & THE MIGHTY FIREFLY
MF R&B

It dawned on Murchison, finally, what the curious name was code for: Mother Fucker. He felt the spirit of the dead man in that house a little more profoundly. Strong, they called him. Big, Marcellyne Pathon said. Cagey and sloppy and stylish and wild. With an ambivalent son and a twenty-year soft spot for a sweet-faced woman whose picture he hid away.

3

———•◦•———

Toby Marchand sat alone in one of the police station's two cinder block interview rooms. He was still dressed in the clothes he'd worn onstage that night: gray serge suit, white Oxford shirt, Nino Mori necktie. He smelled of sweat, some of it rank from fear. His mouth tasted sour from vomit.

The memory came unbidden. Turning the corner, seeing too many people out and squad cars parked helter skelter in the street, strobe lights spinning. Feeling the bottom drop out of his stomach. Running up, pushing through the crowd—he got recognized, got ignored—reaching the gate, only to be hammerlocked by the cop standing there, told he couldn't go in. Shortly after, told why.

The images froze in his mind. Then the next moment he half expected his father to storm through the interview room doorway: Howling abuse. Ready to raise hell. The delusion brought to mind amputees complaining of pain in phantom limbs.

He'd been in the practice room, straddling a wood chair, reaming his trombone slide with a cleaning rod coiled in cheesecloth. Five o'clock, already twilight. His father charged in barefoot. His trouser legs flapped against his calves, shirttails sailing behind as he strode forward. He carried a large mug in one hand. The other hand rose up from his side, and a long bony finger sliced the air.

"Hey, boy wonder—yeah, you—eyes front."

Toby ignored him. Established habit.

"You gonna tell me what the fuck's goin' on? Or you want, I can guess. I'd love to guess."

Toby puffed his cheeks and sighed. "May I infer from your bellowing that your health is sound?"

"I'll bellow all I *goddamn* please. Got a fourteen-year-old white girl out there has the nerve to think she's some kind of fucking nurse."

From beyond the doorway leading back to the kitchen, a tiny female voice: "I'm sorry."

"I want somebody's face in my business, I'll call my sister."

Removing the cloth-wrapped rod from his slide, Toby inspected it for bits of flaking brass. The cheesecloth smelled of Slide-O-Mix.

"Not fourteen. Nineteen. Nadya is nineteen."

"Like hell she is. That girl's a virgin. I can hear the skinny-skin snapping like a snare head when she walks across the room."

Toby glanced up, his eyes a warning. "I seriously doubt that."

"You speaking from personal experience?"

Toby uttered a soft begrudging moan. "Unh-uh. You'll have to try harder than that. Meanwhile, back to the point, she's nineteen."

"You better pray to God she is, junior."

Toby opened the carrying case for his horn, placed the slide and the main assembly down into their velvet bed, and snapped the clasps shut. "Remind me, O ancient one—this the Jack Johnson speech, or the Chuck Berry speech?"

"Given I still say she's fourteen, it's the Chuck Berry speech. And good for you, child prodigy, to know there's a goddamn difference."

Toby rose from his chair. "Yes, well—"

"Jack Johnson went down because his woman was white. Not because she was young. Chuck Berry, that girl was young. And white. So yes, dear boy of mine, this is the Chuck Berry speech."

"Marie is only six years old," Toby sang quietly.

"Not that young."

"Ta-da."

"But white."

Toby lifted the necktie from the back of his chair and slid it under his collar. Fastening his top shirt button, he glanced to the ceiling and intoned, "The color white. 'The intensifying agent in things most appalling to mankind.' "

His father squinted. "Damn straight." A finger softly tapped the side of his cup. "Who said that?"

"Melville," Toby replied. "White guy."

"You're developing a serious case of snide, know that?"

As he passed his father, Toby caught the sharp sour taint coming from the old man's tea. He stopped, leaned forward, sniffed. "Tell me that's not what I think it is."

His father tipped the cup away and nodded toward the door beyond which Nadya still lingered, out of sight. "Seems to me you got your own business to mind."

"You are my business. I wouldn't be here if you weren't."

A car horn sounded from the street. "Good God." Toby checked his watch. "Nadya," he called out. "Go out, please, tell Francis I'll be there in five?"

The girl edged out from the shadow of the doorway. She was petite, finely boned, with jet-black hair, dressed in a turtleneck, overalls, hightop Keds. Fierce eyes dominated a bone-white face. Nadya Katarinya Lazarenko. Toby liked saying the name out loud, quietly to himself. Ukrainian, it conjured images of tormented exiles, seraphic ballerinas.

"Five minutes," he said again, gentler this time.

She nodded, held out her hand, every finger extended—as though to respond, "Gotcha, five, over." Toby half expected a cartoonish *fffuuttt* as she withdrew the hand, spun around, and fled. It was part of her charm, this comic, almost goofy eccentricity. A defense she'd concocted against her family.

Speaking of which, he thought, turning back to his father. He nodded at the cup. "You're light one kidney, remember? You got a death wish we need to talk about?"

The car horn blasted again. At the front of the house the door slammed open and closed as Nadya ran out to tell Francis, Toby's tenor man, to wait.

"Next time, you'll need a kidney donor. Don't come to me. Not if you're gonna play the fool like this."

He pushed past, squared himself before the bathroom mirror. His father ambled behind, sprawling himself in the doorway. "You wouldn'ta lasted twenty minutes in my day, know that?"

Toby shook his head, murmuring, "Here it comes," as he looped his tie into its knot.

"Woulda done you good. Play the juke joints down Grove Street. Only way to keep your job, win a cutting contest. Outplay the new guy or lose your chair."

"Spare me. Music as martial art. Funk Fu."

The bathroom wall was dotted with aging black-and-white portraits of his father in years gone by—standing with Frank Foster and Freddie Green of Basie fame, Ann Peebles, Etta James, Bill Doggett. The images hovered about Toby's reflection in the mirror like Sistine sibyls and *ignudi*.

"Know what you remind me of?" his father said. "One of them little old Filipino ladies here in town, think what we need is a *cultural center*. Museum for dust. Place for fat girls to fuck up ballet."

"Yeah, well, let me stop you before this gets too fascinating."

Toby smoothed his collar, made one last self-inspection, then eased past his father in the bathroom doorway. Gathering his jacket from its chair back, he shoved his arms into the sleeves, then grabbed his horn case and the beaten-up leather valise in which he carried his charts and lead sheets. He started for the door, but his father's hand sailed out, caught his arm.

"You're not really gonna leave me with that girl of yours, are you? All she does is sit there, screwed down tight, sadder than a map."

"You'll survive."

"Try to talk with her, she shrinks up like a sponge. 'I'm sorry,' she says. 'I'm sorry.' Like everything's her goddamn fault. When in doubt, blame her."

"It's commonly referred to as being shy."

"No, what it's commonly referred to as? Is white guilt. Or she got some new kind of ass-backward, fucked-up vanity they don't have a name for yet?"

Toby felt the heat swim up into his face, but he checked himself. This was an old game. Only his father kept score.

"Look. Talk to me how you want. Like I could stop you. But when it comes to her—"

"*You* a virgin?"

Toby flinched. "Excuse me?"

"Reason I ask—if you are, then that means it's your mother got you pussy-whipped like this. And that's just too sad for a man like me to contemplate."

Toby's jaw went slack. The breath got caught in his throat. Unsure whether laughter or fury was called for, knowing neither would make a difference. "I'll be sure to pass that assessment along," he said finally, and turned to go.

"Whoa!" his father called to his back. "Stop the presses. Mr. Shoes-Too-Tight-and-Oh-So-Sensitive runs to Momma. *And tells all . . .*"

Toby went to the front door and waited as Nadya, returning from the street, slipped back through the gate beneath the bare branches of the old sycamore. Overhead, twilight gathered in a threatening sky. As she darted up the gravel path toward the house, he thought how odd it was that not even hightops and overalls could hide how lovely she was. And she was, he knew, hiding. He wondered sometimes if he was the only person in the world who actually saw her.

They'd met at the music store where she marshaled the sheet music and taught piano. They'd flirted clumsily, sitting side by side at a Bechstein concert grand as Toby showed her the tonal colorings of Billy Strayhorn's "Chelsea Bridge." She in turn played two short pieces by Scriabin, one called *"Désir,"* the other *"Caresse Dansée,"* to show him how much, for her, the dense, chromatic harmonies and sadly playful melodies echoed Strayhorn's. Toby wondered if it hadn't been decided in those first few minutes. The curiosity they'd felt for each other, it seemed a kind of gravity, as though the next thing worth knowing lay secreted inside the other person. Not music, but the thing they couldn't get at except through music.

At twenty-two, Toby'd had his share of girlfriends—it was one of the perks of musicianship—but until Nadya, he doubted he'd ever been truly, honestly interesting to someone. And he doubted if he'd ever been as intrigued by someone as he was by her. It brought to mind one of his favorite sayings, by Coltrane: *"If there is something you do not understand, you must go humbly to it."* That's it, he thought. We go humbly to each other. And that humility, it formed a kind of tenderness, a depth of caring, he'd not known existed before. If that wasn't love, it was at least a kind of longing unlike any other he'd heard tell of.

She took the porch steps at a run. He opened the door and she ducked past him, clutching herself for warmth. He followed her into the living room, where she plopped herself down on the red leather ottoman. Crouching before her, he took her hands in his, kissed her fingers. They were ice-cold.

"The old man, that little fit he just threw—unless I'm guessing wrong, you caught him spiking his tea."

She flinched, shrank back a little. "I just came into the kitchen, he was at the sink. I didn't say anything, I just—"

Please don't say you're sorry, he thought, recalling his father's line about white guilt. "He's in a mood. Might be a good sign, all things considered. Means he's stronger. But it's not your job to do anything but drive him to the club and back tonight."

"I know."

"I'd do it myself—"

"I *know*."

She rolled her eyes, humphed, then smiled, revealing her slight overbite, like Gene Tierney's. Toby'd had a similar problem as a boy. From age eleven on, though, daily scales on the trombone, hour after hour, had gradually nudged his upper teeth into place. A minor medical miracle, his father had cracked at the time. Better orthodontics through practice, practice, practice.

Toby clutched her fingers tighter. "He's going to drink," he said. "My father. Stupid as that sounds, given his operation and all, he's going to do it and there's nothing you can do to stop him and I don't want you to try."

He got no further. The shock on Nadya's face told him, *Turn around.* He did so, in time to see his father, baritone sax poised before him like a battering ram, heading for the front door.

"Gonna go out and say hey to my man Francis," he said.

Toby stared out through the front door at the gate through which his father disappeared. As Nadya sidled up beside him, he said, "Scratch

the plan. I can't leave you with him. Not in this mood. It's like somebody lit a bottle rocket up his ass, pardon my French."

"*Baguette de fusée.*"

"Excuse me?"

"Nothing."

He checked his watch and groaned. "I wish I didn't have this feeling."

"It'll be fine."

"No, trust me, it won't."

"I can handle it, Toby."

She reached for his hand, clutched his pinkie, and shook it. It
broke his mood and he turned toward her, melting a little as their eyes
met. He'd seen pictures of her grandmother who'd fled the Ukraine
during the famine and pogroms of the thirties, and it was startling how
much Nadya resembled her. Down to the pitiless sorrow in those eyes.

"If I had more time, I'd never in the world do this to you."

She reached up and stroked his cheek. "You're not *doing* anything
to me, Toby."

"If he gets out of hand, dump him. I'm dead serious. Walk away.
Come back alone. Leave him to me or we'll just let him cab it home.
Won't be the first time."

Nadya searched his face. "Just leave him?"

"Absolutely."

She lowered her hand from his face to his chest, smoothing his
lapels, his necktie. "I don't think I could do that. I mean, just desert
him."

Toby shook his head and laughed. "You'll get tested. Trust me."

Walking out to the street, he heard the cry of his father's horn beyond
the fence. Once through the gate he saw him—still barefoot, standing
atop the hood of Francis's '72 Impala wagon. Eyes shut tight, the old
man bent over the windshield like he meant to melt it away.

He ended his onslaught with a fusillade of arpeggios swirling
down to a spine-rattling B-flat repeated in three fierce honks, the last
extended, then sweetened—a crooning whisper that faded away into
breath and silence. Eyes still closed, he smiled, satisfied. Turning, he

jumped down off the station wagon's hood and took a bow for the neighbors peeking out at the street from the edges of their lamplit curtains. The old man waved grandly, beaming a triumphant smile, then sauntered up to the driver's side window of the Impala as Francis rolled it down.

"Francis, who plays for dances." They pounded fists, then Toby's father stepped back to inspect the car. "What sorry-ass Injun begged you to take this pile of junk off his hands?"

Francis shrugged. "Runs good."

"So's your little sister, I hear."

Opening the curbside back door, Toby slid his trombone case in, resting it atop the other two horn cases already there—one for Francis's tenor, the other a Walt Harris baritone case connected to a ceremonial surprise for his father that, given events of the past half hour, Toby was beginning to regret.

His father turned his attention from the car to Francis's attire, which was nearly identical to his son's—crisp gray suit, silk tie, spanking white shirt. "Nice to see the two of you done up right for once. I mean, what was it, year ago, you two troop on outta here looking like a couple Rastafarians. Thought you were heading over to Valley View, chant the bitch outta my sister."

Toby put his valise on the floor between his feet and pulled the door closed. "One must be many things to many people."

His father cackled. "Yeah, I've heard hookers say that." He nodded toward the backseat. "You clowns must think I'm the village idiot. That or blind as Brother Ray. Think I don't know a baritone case when I see one?"

Francis and Toby exchanged glances. Neither spoke.

"Which one of you fools thinks he's gonna play that thing tonight?"

Toby gestured to Francis, *Let's go.*

"Takes a man to play the baritone."

"Then bring one with you," Toby said.

His father leaned in through the driver's side window, reaching across Francis. "I can still smack your head sideways, junior."

"Mister Junior, to you."

"Come here. Closer."

Francis fought his way through the tangled limbs, turned the key, cranked the ignition, and put the car in gear. He revved the engine, inched the car forward, and Toby's father backed out of the window finally, stepping away. Toby leaned across the front seat and shouted.

"Hey, Cranky McGeezer—you want to find out who's playing that baritone tonight, go back inside, lay off the juice, behave like a human being, and maybe your white fourteen-year-old nurse will be nice enough to haul that spiteful, mean-mouthed, old'n'tired ass of yours down to the club."

As they drove to Emeryville, Toby studied his lead sheets for the evening's set. Holding two side by side, he spotted at a glance an omitted flat, an undotted rest. Taking out his pen, he removed the cap with his teeth and made the required changes, the various parts trilling in his mind. Beside him, Francis tugged from his pocket the mouthpiece for the baritone, inserted it between his lips, and worked it with his lip and tongue, plying the reed with saliva.

For that night's set, as a surprise tribute to his father, Toby'd charted a septet version of Charles Mingus's "Moanin'." The number had been his father's signature piece in virtually every band he'd been in, even the blues acts, whose players never shrank from a little jazz if the chance arose and the crowd seemed willing. The piece began with one of the most celebrated hooks in the repertoire, announced solo by the baritone: brash, sinister, and yet with this raunchy mad laugh to it. Once the rest of the band kicked in, the tune just held on for dear life and ran.

The original had been scored for six horns. Toby was working with four, and a Hammond B-3 instead of a piano. He turned the organ into a plus, exploiting its throatier stops. To recover the texture lost by fewer horns, he stuck quick little crossing harmonies in obbligato behind the theme. All four horns and the B-3 got a solo. Everybody wailed.

Toby's mother, Felicia, attending one of their rehearsals, had sat there speechless and far-eyed when they finished their run-through, as though the music had conjured memories both too fond and too harsh to recall without feeling. Snapping back to the present when Toby stepped forward to get her reaction, she remarked, "You will make that nasty old creature very proud."

This from the woman who thought her son should study law.

The Zoom Room filled an old warehouse space in the Emeryville mud flats, not far from a portion of the freeway called the Maze near the bayfront border of Oakland and Berkeley. Inside, it had high walls fashioned of glass brick and cinder block, with cement floors and metalwork still intact overhead. The high, hard surfaces gave the room all the acoustical warmth of an empty swimming pool. Worse, the bar stood a good ways off from the dance floor, in an area built out from former office space. You couldn't sit with your drink and watch the stage. You had to mill along the edges of the dance floor, drink in hand, like some homely mope too sad to join in, too proud to go home. It meant the crowd often split into two distinct factions—one that danced, one that drank.

Near the stage, a poster propped on an easel announced the evening's acts:

RETRO RENAISSANCE & BEYOND

There were four acts on tap, with Toby's outfit up second. They'd get one set, forty minutes, following a group called Trane Stop and preceding an outfit named Miles To Go. The other bands were mixed but mostly white, the kind of California concept crew that relied more on theme and good intentions than talent—heavy beat with a funk accent, muddy chords, solos that slid around like a rainy night car wreck. Toby knew his men could blow the other players into dust, but this crowd might not notice, which kept him from getting too cocky. The evening's headliner, for whom most people there would be waiting, was named Yesterday's Memo, one of the few Neo-Swing bands that had survived the fad. It was a vamp act, Kid Coconut meets film noir, featuring a singer who called herself Carmen DiCarlo—a thin, small, throaty Kaye Starr impersonator who wore a turban and fishnets and smiled like a blind girl onstage.

Trane Stop wrapped up its set after a mere thirty minutes, leaving the crowd restless. Toby collected his band backstage after they'd set up their gear, running through his finalized lead sheets for "Moanin'" one last time before motioning them out into the lights.

Each man wore a prim gray suit, looking older than old school, almost Basie-esque. The crowd didn't seem to know what to make of them as they took their places. Toby snapped his fingers to sound the count, on the downbeat a two-stick crack hit the snare, and the band launched hard into Booker Ervin's "East Dallas Special." The freight train came alive with the horns: Roderick Coover on trumpet, Ikem Ononuju on alto, Francis on tenor, Toby on trombone. Rounding out the band, the rhythm section—Chubby Jefferson on six-string bass, Penny Tyler on drums, Jimmy Seagraves on Hammond B-3—they drove the horns from underneath, the organ humming, bass and drums kicking hard, testament to their background as a blues trio in the Groove Holmes mold.

Toby sensed a curious distraction in the room, but with the lights in his eyes he could make out nothing. He sent the band into its second tune without a pause—"Sack o' Woe," a Cannonball Adderley number. They were hardly through the second chorus before Toby knew he had to change tack or lose the crowd for good.

Instead of the Afro-Cuban treatment of Benny Carter's "Malibu" he'd planned, he shouted out Stanley Turrentine's "Sugar." They didn't have it in their charts; it was an upbeat head they used for warm-up at practice. Nobody balked. Toby counted it off and the Hammond B-3 howled the intro, driven from behind by a constant *tang-tang-tang* on the crash cymbal. The hook was in the bass line, a two-phrase minor second cadence tripping down from the top, then digging up from the bottom. As the horns chimed in, Toby sensed the bodies welling up from shadow toward the stage, not all of them but more than before—he could feel it, something turning. And yet that same unsettling discord remained in the background. He couldn't put his finger on it, but the rest of the room fell into their hands, to win or lose. He signaled one more solo from Jimmy on organ and Francis on tenor, then one last shout chorus and a fanfare to end.

Toby wasted no time. He called out Monk's "I Mean You," and from that point on it was one peak after another: Lee Morgan's "Speedball,"

Horace Silver's "Filthy McNasty," and for the Neo-Swing freaks a medley comprised of Basie's "Topsy," Ellington's "Cottontail," and Charlie Barnet's "Mother Fuzzy." They had the crowd firmly in hand when it came time for the set's finale. Ikem switched to tenor. Francis manned the baritone, took a few short toots to test the reed, then stepped forward to announce that deadly theme.

A hush fell. Toby pictured his father, out in the dark crowd, stunned despite himself. And, on some level, proud. Francis cut the silence with angular minor arpeggios that ended amid a cymbal fanfare, then reannouncement of the theme, a slow horn buildup underneath in minor harmonies with the rhythm building, driven on the backbeat. By the third announcement of the theme, it was time for the horns to do battle, rise and wail, finishing in a raucous, hair-raising dissonance from which Francis emerged alone on baritone to solo.

He hadn't finished his first full chorus before he had the room in his control. Keeping his lines short and clear, he made up in raw conviction what he lacked in technique. No showboating. It worked. He sold it, building it up, tearing it down to build it right back up again. As Roderick stepped up from the rear to claim the next solo on trumpet, the crowd erupted.

A police officer entered the interview room, bearing several plastic bags with blank labels on them and a kit of some kind. He was Black, rangy but strong, with a stooped gait, a few years older than Toby. His nameplate read: CARMICHAEL.

From his kit, Officer Carmichael produced a small vial and several cotton swabs. He set them on the metal table, then turned to Toby with a phony smile.

"One of the things we do," he said, "in a case like this, is try to make sure we've done everything we can to prove family members aren't involved." He nodded toward the paraphernalia laid out on the table. "The vial, it contains a nitric acid solution. Tests for gunshot residue. The way it works, I swab your hands, tops and palms, thumbs and forefingers, each with a different swab. We send them to the lab. Come back clean, whoever really did the shooting can't come up and say we didn't do everything we were supposed to."

This is a cop, Toby reminded himself, not a pal. "Nitric acid," he said.

"Doesn't burn," Carmichael assured him. "It's like point-five percent."

Toby stuck out his hands. "Do it."

"One at a time." Carmichael gestured for Toby to pull the left hand back. Wiping down the whole of Toby's right palm, he placed the swab into a plastic bag, marked the white label with Toby's name, the date and time, and the words "Right palm," then moved on to the top of the hand, the thumb, the forefinger, just as he'd said. He repeated with the left, then told Toby as he was labeling the final bag, "You want to wash your hands, I've got a towelette for you. Just a minute."

"This isn't just to rule me out. It's to see if I'm my father's killer."

Carmichael glanced up—not bothering with the smile this time. He studied Toby's face, his shoulders, his hands, as though searching out some tic, some flinch, an unconscious flutter of the eye that would signify guilt. Toby felt scared to so much as draw too deep a breath.

"When do I—"

"The detectives are still wrapping things up at the scene." Carmichael capped and pocketed his pen. "When they're done, they'll come down and fill you in."

He handed Toby the towelette he'd promised. "Just pitch it in the trash can when you're done."

The band regrouped in the former storage room where the musicians kicked back between sets. People straggled in and out, smiling, offering congratulations—members from the other bands, hangers-on, the young girls who showed up every Saturday night backstage somewhere. Jimmy, the organist, took out a flask of gin to pass around; they didn't know the place well enough to fire up a blunt. Toby declined a taste. He was waiting for Nadya and his father to come on back. Players from the other bands made a point now to introduce themselves. Toby smiled and nodded and shook hands and decided not to ask about the unsettling resistance he'd felt coming from the rear of the room.

A commotion came from the doorway. Toby hoped it was his father and Nadya and was halfway to the door before seeing it wasn't. Jimmy's twenty-year-old cousin, Javelle, stood there dripping wet, cursing, fresh from the parking lot. He wore a suit to match the band's, a ploy to attract girls, but now it sagged on him, soaked through from the rain.

Seeing the disappointment on Toby's face, Javelle barked, "Get that look off me, Tobo!" He pushed his hat back from his face. Droplets fell onto his shoulders. "Damn."

Toby made way for Javelle to pass, then peered out into the hallway. He checked the lines queued outside the Gents and Ladies, checked the crowd at the pay phone, made a quick reconnoiter out toward the stage. Wandering the dance floor, he accepted handshakes and compliments here and there, searching the faces. Near the back, he began to sense that same odd resistance he'd felt on stage. Inside the bar it got worse. A palpable tension charged the air. People stared at him a little too long, or they made a point of ignoring him. You're imagining, he told himself. Maybe.

At one end of the bar, an indie promoter who worked for Carmen DiCarlo dabbed at his face with a bloodstained towel. When he glanced up, his eyes met Toby's with unmistakable hate. Beyond him four guys in a cluster sat grinning. There'd been a fight, Toby realized. He came back to the musicians' room worried. Francis drifted up, bearing Jimmy's flask.

"You seen Pops?" Toby passed on the gin again.

Francis shook his head and handed the flask to an approaching Javelle, who, before taking his taste, said, "Fifty dollars for a goddamn jump. You believe that?"

Javelle drove the van that Jimmy used to transport his B-3 and Leslie cabinet.

"Leave your lights on?"

Javelle reached up, snagged the hat off his head, and spanked it against his pant leg. "Walked all the way to the Exxon off the freeway. Got back, you nizzels were done." He frowned, shaped his hat, and put it back on. "Fifty goddamn dollars."

The door opened again. Toby turned toward the sound with the last of his hope, but it was the club's owner, Vanessa. The kind of woman who made every musician who played her room uneasy, she carried herself with a jaded affectation that made her seem doubly cold. Despite the layers of makeup, you could spot at a glance she was well past fifty—dyed red hair, straight as a drapery to her waist, a man's white T-shirt beneath a suede cowgirl jacket, black leggings, red pumps. She held a cigarette stiffly between two straight fingers. Toby pictured her thirty years younger, saw a woman who made no secret about it: *I Fuck Money.*

Careful, he thought. You're sounding like the old man.

The whole band watched as she approached Toby. She placed the hand holding the cigarette on his shoulder, a certain dead look in her eyes. "Could I speak to you alone for a moment?"

Toby joined her near the door.

"Edgar said we had a little trouble in the bar tonight."

Toby felt his insides sour. It got worse as she ran down her version of events: Older Black man coming out of nowhere, completely unprovoked, wailing on Grady Bradshaw, Carmen DiCarlo's indie promo flack. A couple of guys who showed up at the bar from time to time waded in.

"Funny thing about it, these guys, the ones who jumped in, they were booing. But this old guy, he didn't stomp on them. He headed straight for Grady. And Grady was trying to play the diplomat, get these fools to shut up. I think Grady knows who it was, the old guy who clobbered him, but he's not saying. Being nice. Anyway, Edgar, my bartender, broke it up. Threw the old guy out. He had a young white woman with him. Tiny, pretty, pale. Ring any bells?"

Toby felt his face grow hot. Don't blame the messenger, he told himself, but there was something about her eyes that galled him. "This happen during our set?"

Studying him, Vanessa took a long draw from her cigarette and exhaled through the side of her mouth. "In the bar."

"I thought I heard something going on. But, you know, with the lights in our eyes, and the bar around the corner and all, couldn't see anything from the stage. But there was something off. I felt it."

"Have you heard anything? Since you've come offstage, I mean."

"Nope."

"Any ideas?"

"About?"

"Who it was."

Toby feigned reflection, shrugged. "Can't say."

She nodded and took another drag from her cigarette. "Just so you understand, bar fights are no joke. They cost money. Some loser gets himself kicked out, comes back at me with a lawsuit, doesn't matter if it's crap or not, my insurance goes out the window. I have to scratch up surplus lines coverage, and that costs a fucking fortune."

"Understood," Toby said, thinking: Loser.

"I like you. I like your band. Be nice to have you back. But I can't afford trouble."

Toby realized that was it. They were blackballed. And why not? His old man had clocked the lead act's promoter. The artery in his neck started throbbing.

Vanessa studied him for a moment. "My son," she said finally.

"Excuse me?"

"Edgar says the old guy referred to somebody in the band as 'my son.' Or 'my boy.' Mean anything?"

Toby felt his sour insides grow cold. "Not to me."

"He's not related?"

"Who?"

"Stop it," she said. "The guy we had to eighty-six. He related?"

"Not to me. My old man lives in Denver."

Vanessa nodded, pretending to believe. She peeked around him, wanting to inquire of the others. Javelle took the bait. He'd been listening in anyway.

"Phrase 'my boy,' " he said. "Kinda general, don't you think? He's Black. We're Black." He gestured as though, somehow, this might have escaped her. "His boys?"

"Don't," Vanessa cautioned.

"Javelle—"

"It's a Black thing. One of those famous Black things. Had something about it on the Nature Channel just the other night."

Vanessa dropped her cigarette on the floor and ground it out with the toe of her red pump. "Don't start that shit with me. It's really irritating."

Toby got Francis to leave with him, drive him back home. The rain had stopped, but a winter wind howled off the bay. The asphalt remained wet, oil slicks shimmering in the headlights on the freeway.

"You mentioned something," Toby said, "about a friend of yours, New York. Said he might have a lead on some session work, you and me. I know I said I wasn't interested before, but I've got a different take on that now." His mouth and throat were dry from rage. He licked his lips to get the saliva working. "First, though, I got some serious business with my old man."

Once beyond the Carquinez Strait, Francis turned west on Columbus Parkway, heading through the hills toward the river, then north into town. Toby looked out at the passing street. Lone figures huddled in shadowed doorways, cigarette ash flaring at their lips. Drab one-story bungalows with barred windows and scant yards receded into darkness off the main drag, the streetlights busted by the corner crews, the better to make trade. Dogs barked somewhere, everywhere.

"I'll have to talk to Nadya. Rather not just up and run."

"Sure," Francis said softly.

Toby could only guess at the humiliation of it, being the one standing there as the old coot went off, drunk most likely, the whole bar watching. And despite Toby's telling her to just leave him there, turn right around and walk off if he did anything stupid, Nadya hadn't done that. Just like she'd said, she'd seen it through, got his sorry old ass out of that club and brought him home. Uncanny, he thought, the mettle she had, for being so shy. He wanted to sit with her, apologize, thank her, tell her the plan, ask her to come with him. New York. Please. Do. Come.

Francis studied him a moment. "Kinda wondered just what, you know, it was gonna take."

Toby sighed guiltily and shrugged. "What doesn't kill you makes you stronger."

"Hell with that." Francis turned into the gateway to the hill and headed toward the top of St. Martin's. "What doesn't kill you just leaves you lyin' there."

"Francis—"

"Look, Tobo, it's not my place to come down on you for what you want to do, what your old man means to you, anything like that. He's your daddy, you're devoted, okay. Lot to be admired in that. It's just I don't want to see you end up like him. Be as good as he is, or was, only to gig maybe four times a year, if he's lucky, with a bunch of other sorry old men the business forgot long ago. Or never knew about to begin with."

"That's not fair," Toby said. The men in The Mighty Firefly were like uncles to him.

"Fair? Come on, Tobo. Your daddy, I like him, you know that, but his life ain't nothing nobody would say, 'Oh, please, one more time.' Looks back, he's bitter. Looks ahead, he's scared. That what you want for yourself? Be honest."

Like heading for New York will change that for us, Toby thought. Francis turned the corner onto his street, then braked so hard they both lunged forward toward the dash.

"Jesus motherfucking God."

Four police cruisers sat down the block, lights swirling in the darkness, splaying across the housefronts and through the branch-work of the trees. Two cops were holding back the crowd while another two stood in the open gateway to Toby's father's house, looking in at something on the ground.

"Oh Lord." Toby reached for his horn case and valise, swiped clumsily at the door handle.

Francis snagged his arm. "You can't say my name, Tobo, understand?" Panic hiked the pitch of his voice, his eyes crazy. He stared at the cruisers down the block, still clinging to Toby's sleeve.

Toby fought to free himself. He opened the door. "Francis, let go."

Francis clung harder. "This ain't no joke. I ain't here. I ain't the one drove you home. Tell me you got that."

4

The seven-year-old—barefoot, in pink pajamas, her hair twined into bow-tipped pigtails—bumped her hip gently against the doorjamb, staring out at the living room where Murchison sat. The girl's mother, Marcellyne Pathon, sat on the sofa, reviewing the faces in Hennessey's Polaroids as, in the background, a song titled "Ain't Got Time to Die" played softly on the radio, turned to KDYA: "Gospel by the Bay."

"Like I told you, these here are Mr. and Mrs. Toomey. They all lived up here for years." She pointed to the older couple in their robes and slippers standing on the edge of the crowd in the street outside the murder scene. "Same as for the Carvilles and the— Where are they? There. Mrs. Ripperton and her sons. Went to school with Jamal Ripperton. All these folks been living up here the longest. Nothing strange about it."

"Okay, Marcellyne. Good. But these guys." He pointed to the trio of young men unable to duck away from Hennessey's flash quick enough, their faces caught in quarter angles. One of them wore a skully, his hand raised to hide behind. His accessorizing gave him away—three gold rings on the fingers of the upraised hand, at least four gold chains around his neck. "Diamonds and gold and just paroled" was how Hennessey put it.

Marcellyne licked her lips as she took a shallow breath, adjusted her glasses. "Hard to see their faces here."

"I realize that."

She spun around. "Don't make me get up, Daijha."

The seven-year-old stared back at her, moody, fearful. Marcellyne made a move to stand up and the girl slid back into her room, rejoining her four-year-old sister.

"The name Arlie Thigpen ring a bell?"

Hennessey had pointed out his own hit parade from the crowd. There were several ballers, including the guy in the skully, from Long Walk Mooney's crew. Long Walk, a San Quentin grad, dealt in town, had for years, but now he hid behind the guise of party promoter. His parties tended to be wild, sometimes violent, so he moved them around, like the crews he had on hand to sell product—most recently brown tar heroin dissolved in water and sold in popper vials, and gooey balls, hash-laced Rice Krispie treats, favorites with the rave crowds. So went word on the street, at least. The police had no hard evidence, and they'd yet to come close to catching Mooney doing anything they could arrest him for. There'd been reports of an event that night down around the warehouse district, but the Carlisle murder had taken place before anyone could bother with breaking up a dance.

These young men here, in the photograph, probably worked bank. No one but juvies handled drugs on a Long Walk crew. Though he'd recognized faces and had tales to tell about several, Hennessey'd only been able to bring one full name to bear: Arlington Thigpen, age nineteen. He appeared in one of the Polaroids with the hood of his sweatshirt puckered tight around his face, but a webwork of whitish scars around one eye gave him away.

"I know Sarina, his mother. She works over the convalescent hospital. Has a retarded daughter. Her oldest, Robert, he lives in Richmond, I think, works construction."

"This is Arlie."

"Yes, sir. Don't know him. Not really."

"Any idea how his eye got like that?"

"No, sir. Couldn't say."

Hands trembling, Marcellyne shuffled the pictures together and handed them back to Murchison. One of the first things he'd learned about interrogation was when to pretend you believed, when to pretend you didn't. If someone's lying to you, act like every word is golden. String him along. If you think he's holding something back, accuse him of lying. Or her.

"You're not being up front with me, Marcellyne. You know, or Mr. Carlisle knew, Arlie or some of these other young men. That's the truth, isn't it?"

A flinch shot up her shoulder and neck. She couldn't look at him. "Everybody knows everybody up here, okay? But all I know is what I've told you. Did Mr. Carlisle know anybody in particular? I couldn't say. Anybody in those pictures?" She pointed. "I do not know."

"But *you* know them." He held up the picture again, took out his pen, and prepared to write on the back. "You just said it. Everybody knows everybody."

As he walked down from Marcellyne's door to the street he checked to see who took notice. In particular, he looked for J. J. Glenn, Waddell Bettencort, Michael Brinkman, Eshmont Carnes—the young men whose names Marcellyne had just delivered. Only three scattered groups of onlookers remained, and none of those were promising. It was, after all, Saturday night. Sunday morning now, to be exact. Money to be made.

Truax, looking almost lonesome, remained on guard with his clipboard at the gate to the scene. The coroner's unit had come and gone, taking the body with them. Two patrol units had left; the others had turned off their lights. The street seemed almost normal—dark, windblown, wet.

Glancing back at Marcellyne's home, Murchison spotted a sprawling bougainvillea, once high as the roof gutters, now sagging from its trellis, weighed down with rain. It littered warm-winter blossoms onto the patchy lawn. Here and there, daffodils, bearded iris, daylillies already bloomed in scattered flowerbeds down the block. Oxalis—yellow bell-shaped flower, clover-shaped leaves, a weed—cropped up everywhere. First week of February, Murchison thought. Might as well be Easter.

From across the street, Stluka bounded up to greet him, all smiles. "Oh man, are you gonna fucking love this."

Something feral lit Stluka's eyes. "Let me guess. One of the Victorians?"

"You kidding? Both of 'em, locked up tight as a nun's butt. Listen to me." Stluka pulled a notepad from inside his sport coat. "I figured, this close to last call, we couldn't wait any longer to contact the club, this Zoom Room in Emeryville where the so-called son played tonight."

"What do you mean, 'so-called'?"

"Spoke to the owner, woman named Vanessa. You should get a load of this broad. Oh, oh, oh, what a girl."

For what seemed the thousandth time, Toby looked around the bare interrogation room, seeing it finally not as a place but a state of mind. The state of mind was: *guilty.* He recalled his thoughts on the ride home with Francis: Leave the old man behind. Let him drink himself sick in that house alone. Let him die alone. He welcomed the sound of the door opening, someone joining him, anyone, even police. Glancing up, he saw there were two of them, both white, in plain clothes. They looked at him as though trying to figure him out. He felt a slight disorienting charge, like static electricity, as he picked up his glasses from the table and put them on, fitting the earpieces in place.

"Toby, is that right?" the nearer one said, sitting down. He was the older of the two, rangy and tall, with rust-colored hair and worry bags beneath the eyes. He had freckles, wore a modest wedding band, and carried himself with an air of rumpled loneliness.

"I'm Detective Murchison," the man said, then with a nod to the other added, "This is Detective Stluka." This guy was stocky and flat-faced, with black hair and cop eyes.

"Toby Carlisle?" Murchison, the sad one, asked.

"No," Toby said softly, clearing his throat. "Marchand. Toby Marchand."

The stocky one said, "You told Sergeant Holmes at the scene the victim was your father."

Toby flinched at his tone. "He is my father. Marchand is my stepfather's name."

"Stepfather?"

"He lives in Denver. He and my mother are divorced."

The two detectives looked at each other. Toby, feeling his skin grow warm, went to loosen his tie, only to discover his collar already undone, the knot lying at his breastbone. He remembered the officers hunched around him, the smelling salts.

Murchison said, "I wish we could give you time to get your mind around what's happened, Toby. Prepare yourself. But we can't. First seventy-two hours after a homicide are crucial."

The man's eyes, his voice, they were strangely gentle, inviting, like sleep.

"I understand."

"You told someone else tonight it's your father who lives in Denver."

Toby stiffened. "That's not true."

"What's not true?"

"My dad lives here. I mean, he did."

"But you said otherwise. Earlier tonight."

"I don't—"

"After your father was thrown out of the club in Emeryville. The owner, she came up to you, asked if you knew him. Asked if he was your father. You said no."

Toby sat back. A sickness bubbled in his stomach. The detectives waited. His mind cleared suddenly; he realized what the man had just said.

"Thrown out—you know about the fight at the club."

"We know a lot of things, Toby. The investigation's almost complete."

"But if you know about the fight, then Nadya—"

"She's at the hospital. She's fine."

One guilt fed the other. His father's death, Nadya's being left alone to deal with—what? "The officer at the scene, he—"

"She's being treated. She's safe."

"That reminds me." It was the black-haired one, Stluka. He reached into his pocket, took out a driver's license, showed it to Toby. "Stephanie Waugh?"

Toby took the license from him, studied it, puzzled.

"It was in your girlfriend's purse. Along with her real ID."

Toby tried to hand it back. Murchison said, "Been a lot of little white lies told tonight, Toby. Too many."

"Listen, I—"

"Let me stop you. This is important. I absolutely need to know you understand, Toby, we can't help anybody—not you, not your girlfriend, not your family—with false information. Won't help. Can't help."

Stluka got up at that point, whispered to Murchison, "I'm gonna get to that thing we talked about," then left the room. Toby watched him go as Murchison edged his chair an inch or so closer.

"The truth, Toby. No more stories. No more telling one person one thing, another person another. It's already caught up with you."

Toby turned back toward that voice, and as he did an odd sense of weightlessness came over him, the kind of sensation he associated with dreams in which he suddenly took flight. The thrill of terror. At the same time, he detected an echo of something else. An invitation to surrender. The two things fit together somehow. Don't be scared, he thought. Tell the man it was you. Say you want to confess—what part does truth really play in this? Your father was murdered while you yourself wished him dead. Even if somehow, someday, they find out who really fired the gun, it will never bring the old man back to life or wash away this taint. You'll feel filthy, soiled by your own shame, forever.

"I was thinking," he whispered, "just before you came in. . . ." His voice trailed off, his words suddenly unwieldy. He couldn't make sense of how to continue. Glancing up, he saw a momentary hardening in the detective's eyes, a shadow so fleeting he wondered if it had really been there. Regardless, something hungry, almost pitiless, revealed itself. It shocked him out of his phony guilt. He sat up straight.

"Thinking what, Toby?"

"Nothing. I'm sorry. You asked about my father."

"Toby, don't do this to yourself."

"I lived with my mother and stepfather till I was ten."

"Toby—"

"They separated, and Mom needed help. I've got two stepsisters; three kids is a lot. Pops took me in a few years. Went back to my mother's for high school so I could study in the jazz program at Berkeley. I've been staying here again the past two months. My father had surgery."

Murchison sat back a little, his eyes blank. Two seconds passed, five. Ten. "A kidney removed," he said finally.

"Yes." Toby felt caught in the man's stare. "He'd just been up and half his old self." His voice quavered.

Murchison leaned forward again. Their heads almost touched. "I can't help you, Toby, without the truth."

"I'm telling you the truth."

"The victim kept a gun in his bed stand, Toby. He was scared."

Toby laughed, looked away, thinking, *The victim.* "Scared? That'd be something."

"He had reason, or thought he had reason, to think he was in danger. Any enemies you know of? Scores to settle, old or new? Debts? Women he'd broken off with who took it hard?"

Toby felt relieved at this turning away of the detective's scrutiny. And yet, in response to the question, he found himself addressing a void. There was either too much to tell, or too little.

"Not recent, not that I know of."

"What about Felicia?"

That stopped Toby cold. "What about her?"

"She's—?"

"My mother. Have you spoken to her? Does she know what happened?"

Murchison sat motionless, as though he didn't hear. His brow knit almost imperceptibly, then smoothed again. Another long silence. "Your mother get along with the victim?"

"Get along?" Toby let loose a harsh chuckle, shook his head, thinking, There it is again. The victim. Could be just some cop way of talking. "My father wanted nothing so much as to get back with my mother. My mother wanted peace."

"Peace?"

"Shortest path to my father's heart was through his ego. Not my mother's style, pampering a man's vanity. And he had a temper. He never backed down, never, not from anyone."

"Not even you."

Toby laughed, nervous. "Especially not me."

"And when he got in your face, your mother's face, you stood your ground. Defended your mother."

"I don't recall saying my father got in anybody's face."

"Sure you did. Plain as day."

Toby bristled at the accusation. At the same time, he feared what the man said was true.

"It's hard, Toby, when you're caught in the middle. I understand that, I do. The victim, your mother, all those years, him wanting to be with her, your mother keeping her distance. And with his temper, I'm sure it got rough. I'm sure you got punished for things you had no part of."

"Detective—"

"And then you try to do the decent thing. He's sick, alone in that house, you come up here to lend a hand. It's a generous offer. A sacrifice."

Murchison edged in closer.

"You know, Toby, my father, he's old, he's sick. Needs me more than ever. Still treats me like dirt. He's proud, he's depressed, and sometimes he's just a little crazy. And it's hard, it's damn hard, to do what you've got to do, do what you know is right, when all it earns you is abuse."

"I didn't say—"

"So, you see, Toby, I understand. In particular, I understand how hard it must have been tonight. The brandy in his tea. Didn't think I knew that. Yeah, I knew that. And a few weeks after he's lost a kidney. Tells you a lot, Toby. Tells you it will never stop. Never. Whatever price he wants you to pay, or wants your mother to pay, he intends to collect, over and over, till the day he dies. And now he's got you right where he wants you, stuck in a small room in his house, a prisoner, giving up your life for his."

"I didn't give up—"

"You tried to be gracious, invited him along tonight, but that just rubbed it in. He had to punish you. Had to punish you for having a life with promise ahead, not just memories behind. Had to punish you for the fact he's never earned your mother's love. So he picked a fight. Got kicked out of the club. But he won't be the one to suffer. You will. It's your reputation now, not his. He knew that. You told yourself, 'I'm willing to do the decent thing, the right thing, but I won't let him destroy my life the way he destroyed his.' Burning every bridge he crosses, till he's left in that house all alone—that's how the neighbors saw it, we've talked to them—killing himself just to get someone to be there with him. None of that's fair. Anybody can see that, Toby. And so you came home from the club. Straight home. Enough's enough. Time the two of you had it out. Time you said what needed to be said."

To a point, Toby thought, it was eerily true. He felt the same disgust with himself.

"Where were you right before you came up to the gate outside the house, Toby? That's what I need to know. Sergeant Holmes stopped you, wouldn't let you come in the yard. Right before that, you were in a car coming back from the club."

"Yes."

"The driver of that car was . . ."

An icy pall came over him. "One of the guys in the band."

The look—it was like he'd kicked the detective's chair.

"He has a name, Toby. The guys in your band, you know them. They're your friends. A couple of them are still down at the club. They're helping us out. We're grateful for that. The one who drove you home, though. His name."

Toby tried to think, but all he could hear was Francis's voice. *This ain't no joke. I ain't here. I ain't the one drove you home.*

"Stop this, Toby. Don't. Stop it now."

"Stop what?"

"This is my job, Toby, I like to think I'm good at it."

"A guy in my band—"

"He's got a name, Toby."

"Jimmy Seagraves."

Murchison sat back, shook his head. "I'm gonna give you a chance to think about what you're doing. Don't think this is any fun for me, Toby."

"Jimmy Seagraves, he's the organist in the band."

"Drives a van."

Toby went stiff. "Actually, his cousin Javelle—"

"They're still down there, Toby. At the club. Never left. Can't get the van to start."

Toby felt light-headed. Tell him the truth, he thought. Now.

"Francis Templeton. That's his name."

Murchison tapped his hands together slowly, his eyes never straying from Toby's. "Francis Tyrone Templeton. He's an abscond, out of

Bellflower, in South Central L.A. Felony possession, two and a half years in Corcoran. Probation officer's sworn out a bench warrant for him, hasn't seen him in eighteen months. But you know all that. You just thought you could lie to me about it."

"Francis asked me to lie," Toby said. Funny, he thought, how the truth doesn't really help.

"What else did Francis ask you to do?"

"Nothing. He was scared. He asked me not to say he was there, that he wasn't the one who drove me home."

"So you lied for him."

Toby's head sagged. "What's going to happen to him?"

"Him? You're worried about *him*?"

"Why—"

"He staying somewhere here in town?"

"With his great-aunt."

Toby felt the way he had when he'd cut himself badly once, strangely calm, staring at the blood, thinking, Stupid. Then: Now what?

"The aunt," Murchison said, removing from his pocket a pen and tiny spiral notepad. "A name and address, Toby."

Toby gave him the information, imagining what would happen. A car would rush over, more than one, cops at the door, pounding, waking up that poor old woman and the neighborhood, too, taking Francis away. Toby pictured him, tottering in handcuffs down the porch stair at his great-aunt's house with a cop clutching his arm. A third of the guys Toby had known growing up were filing in or out of prison. Queasy, he put his head in his hands, thinking, So this is what it feels like. To betray a friend. What sort of prayer do you offer up, he wondered, to get right again?

Murchison clicked his pen. "Okay, Toby. Good. But this is just the first step. Right? You need to ask yourself: What will Francis say once he's in that chair instead of you? I can only help you for so long. If Francis decides to help, you have to understand, I'm going to listen."

Toby snapped to. "Listen to what?"

"This is your chance, Toby. Offer won't be on the table forever. Francis is your friend, okay. I can understand that. But that's not going to be the situation in a very short while. Down here, in these rooms, a guy learns quick. It's every man for himself down here. Francis, he's been through all this before. He's going to be afraid, Toby, afraid this deal down South he's running from will be a second strike. That ups the ante, huge. It's Corcoran they'll send him back to. You heard about the gladiator fights? Jury acquitted the guards, but you really think that doesn't happen?"

Toby's mouth and throat had turned to sand. He worked his tongue, trying to create saliva. Murchison watched.

"My point, Toby, is this. Francis, he's going to be willing—hell, eager—to do what he can to help himself. But that'll be later. Now, it's you and me. Here. I want to help. I do. I can see you're a decent young man. It's not the world we'd like it to be sometimes. Things go haywire. The feelings, they just come. Then we look at what's happened and wish to God we could go back, undo it."

Toby glanced down at his hands. Only then did he realize how tightly they were clasped. It took him a second to untangle his fingers. They were numb. He shook them out and, as he did, one of those feelings Murchison had just talked about, it came.

"I get it now," he murmured. "I understand."

Murchison offered a sad smile, but the eyes held steady. "That's good, Toby."

"I understand why Francis was so afraid. In the car. When he dropped me off."

"What was Francis scared of?"

"You." He made sure to connect—Murchison's eyes, his own. "This."

"Everybody's scared in here, Toby. But there's a way out."

"Why would I want a way out? I've just figured out the secret."

Murchison sat back wearily in his chair, his head cocked. "You playing games now, Toby?"

"No. Just lying. Again." Toby pushed his glasses up, rubbed his eyes, then shook the dull tired ache from his head. "Well, that's what you think, right? Not a word I say can be trusted, right? It's all one big lie. Unless, of course, I say I killed my father. That's the truth."

Stluka, hearing that as he came back into the room, jumped on it. "You ready?"

"I'm lying," Toby said again, louder. Sweat poured freely down his back now, his face wet with it, too. "Right? I came up, pointed the gun, shot my own father like some crackhead. Like my evil, worthless friend. I did it. Except I'm lying. I shot the man took me to music lessons, ten years old, my hand in his, walked me down the hill to Henderson's Music Store twice a week. Paid for those lessons when my mother refused. I shot him dead. But I'm lying. I'm glad, I'm glad, I'm just so goddamn glad he's dead. But I'm lying."

He shook with rage and, sneakily, the grief slipped in behind. A desperation tinged with longing—it choked him. He'd heard stories of family members throwing themselves into graves, wailing as they landed on the coffin, and others climbing down in their funeral clothes to drag them out. It had always seemed bizarre, false, comical.

"Damn you," he whispered, wiping his face.

Murchison said, "Damn me why?"

"He was my father. I loved him. Not perfect—"

"What wasn't perfect about it?"

Toby uttered a miserable laugh. "It was mine."

"Tell me the rest, Toby," Murchison said, leaning forward, not unkind. "Tell me now."

Toby glared at him. "I did not. Kill my father."

"Did you kill Strong Carlisle?"

"I just told you."

"He's not your father," Stluka said, impatient, like some deadline had just passed. "Everybody knows it. The neighbors. Guys in your own damn band. He pretended to be your father, hoping he could get a second shot at your mother. And she played him like a fucking drum."

Toby dropped his hands from his face. He was light-headed, short of breath, again. Stluka stood there, glaring. Murchison waited. So that was it. Not my father. The victim.

"Ah, no. No." Toby rose from the chair. His legs melted beneath him. The room swam with shadows and whirling dots. "This is nuts, just—"

"Tell me now," Murchison said. "There won't be a better time. It's Francis's turn next."

"Tell you what?" Toby turned this way, that, trying to figure out where to move.

"You know what," Murchison said. "Sit back down, Toby. Please. There's something you want to get off your chest. Tell me."

Toby caught himself before raising his voice again. It's just what they want, he realized. Emotion. Careless, wild, Negro emotion. He leaned forward, hands outstretched, and announced quietly, soberly, eyes locked on Murchison's, "I killed no one." He turned to Stluka. "Absolutely, utterly, no one. And neither did Francis." He straightened, realizing finally how right he'd been, how small a part truth would play in this. "As for *the rest,* as you call it, do what you're gonna do. I've run out of ways to tell you. I'm through talking to you. I want to speak to a lawyer."

5

Murchison worked his first murder in 1974—571st MP Company, Seventh Infantry, stationed at Fort Ord near Monterey. Because he'd had a year of college before enlisting, his superiors waived the four-year MP and rank-of-sergeant requirements—he was being groomed for Criminal Investigations Division. His workload consisted of on-base wife and child beatings mostly, off-base rapes and brawls and D & Ds, the occasional dope case. Once, a load of weapons gone missing.

The night manager of an hour-rate SRO on the breakwater end of Ocean View Avenue called in the case. He said he had a soldier on a bender in one of the rooms. "Make it quick. Girl he's with, she sounds unlucky."

Murchison and three MPs jumped in the Jeep and got there in fifteen. The night manager—almost thirty years later, Murchison still remembered his rippling fat, his yellow teeth, his sleek gray pompadour—met them in the lobby and they charged upstairs. Murchison knocked hard, got no response, used the manager's passkey, and, pushing open the door, discovered John T. Boyle, Specialist 4—Combat Infantryman's Badge, Purple Heart, Bronze Star for valor at Dak To—tottering on his feet with a broken bottle in his fist. He'd dressed out a woman he'd met in some drinking hole, slathering himself and the shabby room in her blood.

The manager, who came in behind, upchucked the instant he hit the door. By the time they had Boyle under control—whiskey-eyed, half-naked, and handcuffed to the headboard, mumbling,

"The whore had a blade, I swear"—the manager was popping a vein, spouting stuff like "I don't need John Law around here. That's why I called you guys, not the locals. Collect your own garbage. Get it outta here."

"Yeah?" Murchison stood in the bathroom doorway. "And whose garbage is she?"

The woman—maybe twenty-five, shag haircut, racoon eyeliner—had fled to the shower stall, like it was some sort of home base. Her body still lay in there, naked except for high-heel sandals, more a tangle of body parts than a human being, arms and face scored into shreds.

Murchison had enlisted two years earlier, April 1972—a matter of days after the family got word his brother was dead, killed during the NVA's Easter Offensive. Willy's truck took a freak direct hit from rocket fire while it convoyed relief supplies toward the siege of An Loc. The way Murchison saw it, there was no choice. Sign up and serve. Eighteen, he thought one sacrifice could redeem another. His father never forgave him. After Willy's death, seeing his lone remaining son star in football—he was rounding out freshman year on scholarship, the full deal, Oregon State—it was the only dream left. The prospect of losing both sons in the same sinkhole, especially at that futile and chickenshit stage of the war, it was too much. They fought about it, just once; then the old man went inward.

Once, during a week home for R & R, Murchison happened upon his father sharing a beer with a shipyard pal. They were discussing the pictures on the mantel, Willy's trimmed in black. "Yeah, hell, take a look. My sons. The Casualty and the Martyr."

One tour proved enough. Murchison's younger brother illusions were gone and the war was done. Once released, he walked on at San Diego State, earned Honorable Mention All-WAC at strong safety senior year. A free agent tryout with the Chargers thrilled his dad for a bit, but he was camp fodder: white, mid-twenties, too slow, too old. Jobs were scarce, the recession. Deciding to put the MP/CID experience to work, he joined his hometown force. In time he married, had two girls, rose to detective. A lot to prize. So little to make of it.

With every success he felt it, the nagging absence, wanting to confirm his hunches with his brother, hear his voice say, "Right, Denny. Absolutely. Good job." All these years later, it haunted him. He felt half a man with his brother gone.

Strangely, that truth hit home all the more with every murder he worked. John T. Boyle was just the first of many reckonings. Because, year after year, it was Willy's death he needed to get right. And couldn't. No matter what he figured out, no matter how many cases he broke, nothing came whole. In the end, there was always *just this*. He had to content himself with defending that, the unnerving, unsatisfying incompleteness to everything. Not merely letting it slip away, like it was nothing at all.

Just this is not nothing. That, he supposed, would be his last illusion.

Three black-and-whites were parked outside the home of Carvela Grimes, Francis Templeton's great-aunt, by the time Murchison and Stluka pulled up. Murchison glanced up and down the listing street as he stepped out of the car. The houses, once the best on the hill, looked unkempt, forgotten. Porches tottered with broken slats. Junk cluttered walkways. Pits and rotts charged fences that shook from the force of their bodies and their barking filled the night. At every window along the block, one or more backlit forms peered out.

An officer named Manzello stepped forward to report. Grinning up at the nightbirds, he said, "One minute they're staring out at us, the next they're watching *Cops*, see if they've gone live."

A second uniform, named Stritch, came up behind, sniggering through his gum. He was a north county boy, tall, farmhand thin, and knobby, with dingy blond hair he combed straight back along the sides. It made his face something of a shock. The smile didn't help; his teeth were a disaster.

"You guys seen these?" Stritch held up a handbill torn from a nearby telephone pole. Herbal Viagra, it advertised. Reading from it, he said, " 'Shoot ejaculate thirteen feet!' "

He laughed. Murchison tried not to look at his teeth.

Stluka said, "Goes to show you, Stritch. Ain't size that matters. It's distance."

"Yo, babycakes. *Go deep!*"

"What's the story so far?" Murchison asked, glancing up at the Grimes house.

Manzello answered. "The guy you're looking for, Francis Templeton, looks like we got a skip. We told the old lady lives here—"

"You didn't just bust in, right? You knocked."

"Detective, please. Think like a man, work like a dog, act like a lady—that's our motto."

"Talk old folks into anything," Stritch chimed in, "you say it nice enough."

Everybody looked at him. Manzello said, "Been moonlighting in sales, Stritch?"

"Gents?"

"Let's see." Manzello again. "The old lady, we told her we know this Francis character is staying here. Reliable source, blah blah. We explained our purpose, Detective, and requested admittance. She lets us in. We searched, found his clothes, that's it. Tried to get the old girl to give him up. She said she'd talk to her lawyer tomorrow at church and come down Monday to the station. Till then, she's not talking."

"A lawyer at church." Stluka took a stick of gum from Stritch. "The appointed time is nigh."

"The woman," Murchison said, "she still up?"

"Be a surprise if she wasn't. We just wrapped up inside the house about, what?" Manzello turned to Stritch, thumped his arm. "Five?"

"Five, sure." Stritch rubbed the spot Manzello had thwacked. "Ten tops."

"Thanks." Murchison turned around and took the steps two at a time, up the sloping front yard to the porch. Stluka trailed behind. Above the door, someone had nailed a hand-painted sign, its lettering carved into the wood:

JUST ANOTHER DOPELESS HOPE FIEND

Murchison knocked twice, tried the knob. Locked. He thumbed the bell, knocked again, harder. The door cracked open finally, revealing a bolt chain, beyond which a small, aged Black woman in a plaid robe peered out through eyeglasses with one cracked lens.

"Mrs. Grimes?"

"Miss," she corrected. Her voice was cool and proper. But a thread of fear ran through it, too. "I told the officer—"

"Miss Grimes, my name is Dennis Murchison. I'm lead detective on the matter we're working on. It's a murder, a man named Raymond Carlisle—"

"I knew the gentleman. I told the officer I would meet with my lawyer."

"Miss Grimes, you're not a suspect."

It wasn't entirely true. She wasn't a suspect in the Carlisle killing, obviously, but she could be charged for harboring a fugitive. It'd require specific intent, and even if they had it, given these circumstances—an abscond on a two-year-old warrant, an elderly woman—only a brass-assed head case would want to prosecute. Not that there weren't candidates available in the DA's office. Especially with a killing in the picture.

"Of course, ma'am, speak to an attorney. Please, do. But I'm wondering, did anyone actually explain for you what this is about, our being here?"

A small, finely boned hand appeared, gently clutching the side of the door as though for balance. The paint had been rubbed away on the door at the very spot her hand rested. He pictured her standing at that same spot, the same way, off and on for years.

"What I have been told," she said, "I do not believe."

"I'd like to explain things, if you'd let me."

Behind him, he could hear Stluka clearing his throat. The woman frowned and blinked.

"By all means. Do. Tell me."

"May I come inside?"

The woman's eyes flashed toward Stluka. "Just me," Murchison promised. The old woman stared silently for a second longer, then eased the door closed, slipped off the bolt chain, and opened up again, stepping back for Murchison to pass.

The house was a two-story saltbox, built turn of the century, long before the wartime federal housing took over the hill, Jameson

Carswell after that. The rooms were small, the walls thin, as though it had been a summer home for some old San Francisco family. Those days were long gone. Settlement cracks splintered out from every window and fanned across the ceiling; the paint on the walls had yellowed with age. Area rugs dotted a scuffed wood floor.

She led him into a living room furnished with a sofa, a recliner, scattered chairs. A TV, an old RCA console stereo, and a sewing machine lined the back wall. Needlepoint pillows dotted the couch.

The place had been dusted recently, and the job had been done right—none of that myopic, haphazard swiping you'd expect from an old woman. Maybe she had help, Murchison thought. Francis Templeton, felony abscond, dusting.

Murchison sat down on the sofa as Miss Grimes settled herself into the recliner, modestly covering her legs with the folds of her robe, beneath which she wore flannel pajamas, with white socks and bedroom slippers on her feet. Murchison waited for her eyes to turn toward his.

"The reason we want to meet with Francis, he's the only alibi Toby Marchand has at this time. You say you knew Mr. Carlisle. You know that he and Toby—" He gestured with his hands as though to suggest vaguely a relationship. He was hoping, out of impulse, Miss Grimes would fill in the blank. She merely sat there, hands folded in her lap, watching him. "If Francis Templeton can confirm Toby's story, it would help us eliminate Toby, Mr. Marchand, as a suspect. Now, I realize Francis has reason to fear cooperating with us. He's an abscond. There's an outstanding warrant, he's probably looking at incarceration."

"I know nothing of that."

"I understand." There goes specific intent, Murchison thought, unless we can prove she's lying. "What I mean is, whatever trouble your nephew faces, it doesn't have to be a major hurdle. He might be able to six-oh-two the whole thing, work it through his counselor, if he comes forward right away. The longer he puts it off, the less likely he'll catch a break. The judges down South can be harsh, I realize that. But I'll personally go to bat for him, if he comes in tonight. This morning, whatever. But it has to be soon."

He let another silence fall between them, hoping again it might encourage her to offer up some small detail they might be able to use. She regarded him as though he were drifting inside a fish tank.

"If you have truly and honestly stated your reason for being here, then you are even more misguided than I suspected." She lowered her chin and scowled over the rim of her damaged glasses. "Any suspicion you might have that Toby Marchand did anything whatsoever to his father except take care of him—devotedly, I might add—is nonsense."

Murchison felt grateful that Stulka wasn't in the room. For a small, frail old woman, there was a hardiness to Miss Carvela Grimes, a clarity, that Stluka would interpret as insolence. At the same time, Murchison thought, Father. She identified the victim as Toby's father. No hem or haw. He spread his hands, as though to say he would, or could, concede her feelings, but before he could interject a single word she resumed speaking.

"I never married, Detective. The man to whom I was engaged died in the Second World War. He enlisted so that I and he could live in a better world than the one we'd known growing up. I moved here from Birmingham, Alabama, with my brother and sister in 1942. I was fourteen, the youngest. My brother was drawn by the work at the shipyard the war offered. I met my fiancé—his name was Reginald— I met him at a USO function here at the naval base. He was one of the laborers loading ammunition at Port Chicago farther down the strait.

"Reginald trained with the navy in Michigan, he was looking forward to fighting. He was young and proud and he wanted to prove himself. He was not alone. When President Roosevelt offered combat training to Negro recruits, every man in the community wanted to enlist. Across the South, in the cities, out here. They wanted to make a statement, that they were Americans, second to none. They prized liberty more than anyone, and would defend it with honor. But the training was nothing but public relations. They were not assigned to combat, because white soldiers and sailors wanted Negroes nowhere near them. They would not even so much as donate blood if it would go to Negro casualties.

"My fiancé and the other men became cheap labor, getting sub-union pay for backbreaking work. Dangerous work. I assume you know about the explosion at the ammunition loading dock. I remember that day well, even today. I heard the explosion, felt the shudder in the air, and looked east and saw the smoke in the sky. I knew something terrible had happened. I knew where."

She reached out to rearrange the folds of her robe across her legs. A slight twitch in her cheek betrayed an effort to control an old emotion.

"Reginald was not one of the mutineers who refused to go back to work afterward—demanding to be assigned to combat instead, for which they were humiliated and court-martialed. And Reginald wasn't one of the ones who returned to loading ammunition. He was one of the ones they never found. He was on the dock at the time, doing his duty. Like everyone and everything around him, he was annihilated." She twisted her small, thin hands in her lap. "This happened, Detective, for the sake of your freedom and mine. Our freedom to sit here and ask and answer disgraceful questions. The freedom of your men to run roughshod through my home without notice, laughing like thugs. Enlighten me, please, Detective, enlighten an old woman, how exactly do you presume to honor my fiancé's sacrifice?"

If Murchison felt grateful before that Stluka wasn't in the room, it was nothing compared to how he felt now. He himself felt torn, resentful of the lecture—there's a body bag in my background, too, he thought. You want to traipse out the dead, use them as some sort of moral collateral, I'm wise to you. And yet he felt stung by her words, too.

"Miss Grimes—"

"No, sir, I am not through, not yet." There was a halt in her voice. The sound of fury almost spent. "You have asked about my great-nephew, and so I am obliged to respond. Francis has already paid handsomely any debt to society honestly owed for mistakes he made. And they were mistakes, Detective, not crimes. He has put that all behind him, moved on, and done well. For others as well as himself. For me. He has been my friend, my companion, my helper. Any further attempt to punish him is nothing short of sadistic. That is not to say, however, that it is surprising." She adjusted her glasses on the bridge of her nose, her hand trembling. "There is nothing worthy of us as a people, as a society," the word drawn out, *so-sigh-a-tee*, "to be gained from incarcerating a young man like Francis. Suspecting a young man like Toby Marchand. It is an outrage, the fact you are wasting your time on these two young men, instead of spending it wisely in pursuit of a killer."

Leaning toward him, for emphasis, she repeated, "*A killer.*"

Murchison waited a moment, to be sure she was finished. His stomach felt sour and knotted, all the bad coffee through the night, now this. "I can't remark on what may have happened to Francis before. The law at times, I agree, can seem perverse."

"Perverse? If it were only perverse, I could understand. Do you know, Detective, of a journalist named George Washington Cable?"

Not another history lesson. "I don't, Miss Grimes, but—"

"He investigated prisons in the Reconstruction South. Freed slaves, denied work, got snared in police sweeps and charged with vagrancy, petty theft, drunkenness. Black prisoners outnumbered white by eleven-to-one in Georgia, sixteen-to-one in South Carolina. A larceny conviction could earn you twenty, sometimes forty years in prison, during which you'd be rented out for work by the warden— slavery in everything but the name, it was said even then—building turnpikes and levees and railroads, or sent back into the cotton fields, down into coal shafts, shackled, dressed in burlap. Which is more malicious, Detective? For a starving man to steal a hog, or for twelve jurors to send him to the coal mines for twenty years for doing it?"

Murchison knew better than to say things had changed. "Too little," she'd reply, and he'd have no answer for that.

"Francis told me a little about prison, Detective. He had a cellmate who severed an artery in his wrist with a sharpened comb, did you know that? The blood just exploded from his arm. He went into seizures. Francis shouted and screamed for twenty minutes before anyone responded. The young man was dead by then, of course. Suicide, they called it. Negligent homicide—murder—is what it was."

"You're telling me that Francis will do anything rather than go back to prison." His tone was a little harder than he wanted. He was tired.

"Why should he go back? He's done nothing wrong."

"That's not entirely true, Miss Grimes. There are rules, to make probation meaningful."

"Meaningful?" She seemed startled by her own outrage.

"They may seem artificial. Or overly severe. But they're rules nonetheless."

Miss Grimes leaned forward. "There is a sadness about you, Detective. Are you aware of that?" Her hands were trembling more noticeably now. "A sadness—in your eyes, in your voice—a weariness that seems almost a kind of, if you'll forgive me, a kind of desperation." She took a deep breath, her chin lifting. "You might benefit from reflection on the cause of that."

She struggled from the recliner, took a second to secure her balance and adjust her glasses, then headed with short careful steps toward the front door. At the living room archway she stopped, turned back to Murchison, who remained planted on the couch. "I'm an old woman. I have seen many things in my time. I do not fool easily."

Three sudden loud hand slaps hammered the wall of the house. From the porch, Stluka shouted, "Murch, up and at 'em. Like now."

Outside, Murchison found Stluka folding up his cell phone. "Bag this. Let's head downtown. Hennessey's got something."

Fielding's Liquors sat on the same side of the block as an African braid-and-bead parlor, the Odd Fellows lodge, Downtown Tattoo & Piercing, and an adult video arcade with a banner in the window reading YOUR VALENTINE'S DAY HEADQUARTERS. Across the street, you had the jewelry and loan outfits, one of three SROs in the area, plus discount furniture and mattress stores and one of the town's two gay bars. Two buildings were boarded up, renovations on hold; the owners were waiting for things to change down here.

Somebody'd shattered the window of Fielding's Liquors. A maw of jagged glass gave way to the magazine racks, beyond which the beer coolers glowed. Another light glimmered behind the cash register where the liquor and cigarettes were kept.

Hennessey waited on the corner as they walked up. His eyes,

bloodshot, darted a little in their sockets. "Alarm went off about an hour after you guys left the Carlisle scene. Get this—they threw a boat anchor, I kid you not, a boat anchor, through the window."

"Pirates!" Stluka said.

"Better yet, could be we got us a tie-in to the shooting."

Murchison and Stluka glanced at each other.

"Tie-in how?"

"Holmes sent Gilroy down to canvas the liquor stores, see if any of the clerks remembered the vic. This guy, one who owns this store, he did. This is where the old guy bought his bottle, maybe half an hour, max, before he takes it in the back up the hill."

Stluka shrugged. "That a tie-in?"

"I'm not done." It came out hard. Hennessey looked edgy, beat. "Owner says there were slingers working this corner earlier in the night. One of them got into it with the vic."

Stluka rolled his eyes. "There anybody that old man *didn't* get into it with last night?"

"Gilroy was taking all the info down when, finally some luck, same kid waltzes in. Guess who?"

Murchison reached into his pocket, pulled out the Polaroid gone over with Marcellyne Pathon, now with the handwritten names on the back. "One of these guys?"

Hennessey waved him off. "You already got the name. I gave it to you. He was up there prowling the street outside the Carlisle house."

"Arlie Thigpen."

"One and only."

Murchison felt a pressure that had been building inside him give now, just a little. He'd not confided it to Stluka, but even before the harangue he'd endured at the hands of Miss Carvela Grimes he'd come out of the room with Toby Marchand thinking, Where's the fit? He'd lied, sure; he had at least one bad companion. And yeah, there was heat between him and the vic. But from everything he'd heard, a guy like Strong Carlisle, he made it his daily business to stir up heat.

On top of that, Toby's eyes weren't blank; you could see through them to who he was. A little too smart for his own good but also the kind who, if he'd done it, would have caved with less pressure than he'd taken. He hadn't messed with his face or hair, hadn't sat there guarding his breadbasket. His anger built during the interview, instead of going off first thing—all of which pointed more toward innocence than guilt. God only knew what the father-and-son story was or how long it would take to winnow it out. Regardless, it seemed irrelevant now.

"Gilroy have the sense to detain this Thigpen kid?"

"Oh well, now here's where it gets vivid." Hennessey shook his head, a story coming. "Kid strolls in. Owner nods to Gilroy, like, *It's him*. Gilroy goes hands-on, says, 'A word outside,' and the kid streaks. Being J. P. Stupid—I mean, they worked this same fucking corner tonight, you'd think he'd know—he tries to scoot down the alley just beyond Price Town, the sofa joint? It don't go nowhere. Even a box of rocks like Gilroy can handle him trapped like that."

"This Thigpen kid, he's in custody?"

"And Gilroy's at ER. Goofed up his wrist or something."

"Hot pursuit." Stluka's contribution.

"The owner, he around?"

Hennessey pointed inside. A small, miserable-looking man sat in the dimness behind the cash register. Murchison gestured for Stluka to follow him inside, but before he reached the door a faint sound caught his ear. Glancing up at the corner lamppost, he spotted the source—a small speaker, from which emanated a tinny rendering of what he believed was Mozart, *Eine Kleine Nachtmusik*. The broadcast came to them courtesy of the city council. It was a recent brainchild, offering a nightly assortment of classical favorites at key downtown gathering spots. The purpose was not aesthetic; the music was meant to discourage loitering, stave off drug deals, irritate the hookers.

The liquor store owner, like most in town, was known to the police. This one's name was Abdul Hussein, but he went by "Tony." He was a Fijian Muslim, bony and small, with a graying shock of matted hair. He wore horn-rimmed glasses, tube socks, and sandals, with a trench coat draped over flannel pajamas. A stocking cap rested so high and loose on his head it looked like someone else had perched it there without his knowing.

As soon as Murchison and Stluka were inside the door, Tony Hussein snarled, "Try to be good citizen. Tell what I see. Tell what I know. Look!" He shook his head, wincing in disgust at the rusty twenty-five-pound anchor on the floor, bedded in shattered glass. "Little shitfucks. You guys really scare 'em, huh?"

At the West County Med Center ER, Murchison heard Gilroy's voice from behind the last blue curtain.

"I've chased him into this blind alley, okay? He's figured it out finally, the cluck. No place to go. I start shouting into my radio—this thing here, on my shoulder—pretending the cavalry's on the way. Truth is, there's nobody but me. This kid, he don't know that. He jumps on top of a Dumpster, tries to snag a fire escape ladder. I grab for his ankle, he stomps on my arm, little prick, which is how the wrist got like this."

"Yeah," a second voice said. Breathy, young. Female. "Swole up bad."

"It's nothing. Line of duty. Any event, this kid hits the fire escape, he's gone. So I lean down, grab the backup piece from my ankle rig, lay it on the ground. I call up, 'Break yourself, skinnybone—see this? It's called a toss down. That's the weapon you pulled on me, you worthless piece of shit. Now climb your scrawny black ass down off that Dumpster or I'll defend myself, hear me?' "

The young woman chuckled and mewed, awestruck.

"The rest was routine. Used what we call the kneel down, pat down, and cuff technique. Here, I'll show you."

Murchison went to pull back the screen, but Stluka stopped him—finger to his lips, that wicked glee in the eye. Fifteen, twenty seconds, Stluka nodded okay. Murchison cleared his throat.

"Officer?"

Stluka drew back the curtain. A nurse's aide—maybe twenty years old, blond hair and baby fat, dressed in blue scrubs—knelt on the floor, hands cuffed behind her. She had bloodred nails, big teeth, hair pulled back tight with ringlets at the temples. Gilroy, left wrist bandaged, was patting her down with his good hand. He was big—square, muscular—with a chestnut-colored flattop and huge ears. The ears, they'd earned him the nickname Dumbo; due to other qualities, the nickname had stuck.

He was leaning close behind the girl. Her cheeks were flushed.

Stluka said, "Confirm all wants prior to arrest."

They froze, the girl and Gilroy, looking like some randy statuette at a novelty store.

"That thing on your belt. You know that's a baton, right? Not a marital aid."

They gave Gilroy time to undo the girl's cuffs, help her up. She fled. He couldn't wipe away the bad boy grin.

"You took a suspect into custody," Murchison said. Given recent activity, he felt the need to add, "Downtown."

"Thigpen kid. Yeah. In the raghead's store. I hear somebody bitched up his window after, too."

"This Thigpen kid, he's where?"

"Holding, waiting for transport to County. That's where I left him, anyway."

"You written anything up?"

"Not yet." He lifted his bandaged wrist, waved it a little side to side. Queen of the Rose Parade.

"What was your reasonable suspicion?"

Gilroy looked stunned at being asked such a thing. "Hennessey didn't—"

"Let's hear it from you."

"Store owner IDed him as a potential suspect, the Carlisle thing. Him and the vic got into it, rough stuff, less than half an hour before the shooting. Outside the liquor store, which is just down the hill from the old man's house."

"But you decided to detain him. This Thigpen kid. Not just give him a Beheler and invite him down to the station for a chat."

"He got itchy feet. I went in pursuit. In the course of pursuit, we got in a toss. Plus this." He held his breast pocket open with the bad hand, reached in with the good, and pulled out a popper vial of brownish liquid, holding it top and bottom, index finger and thumb. Murchison took it from him, careful not to touch the sides, shook it, watched the fluid darken.

Stluka said, "Imagine that. Best drugs in town. And they're free."

Murchison followed up: "You open this?"

"No."

"No secret sniffs?"

"No." Pissed now.

"You found it where?"

"Dropsie. Right there at his feet, in the alley where I made the arrest."

Stluka groaned. "If only life were as simple as you, Dumbo."

Gilroy crossed his arms, get that bulge thing going. "Excuse me?"

"First, don't feed us dropsie stories." Murchison shook the bottle again, watched the fluid cloud, a little lava lamp. "Second, the Thigpen kid, he's not young enough. This is Long Walk Mooney's crew. He's got kids to handle product. You tell me you found a wad of cash, I'd believe you."

"Cash," Stluka said. "You know, it's fungible."

"You accusing me of taking this kid off?"

Neither Murchison nor Stluka answered.

"Look, I'll run this down again, though I guess you heard it the first time."

"Sure," Stluka said, "practice makes perfect. Except it didn't happen that way. You had the kid cuffed, your wrist is goofed up, God knows how—and don't tell me he stomped you, I don't wanna hear it—regardless, you're pissed. You plant him in the car, see some juvies sending the fuck-you eye from up the street. You charge, they book, and either you find their stash spot or they get sloppy, leave that bottle behind. Either way, you can't tie it to your collar without being a hell of a lot more clever than you've been so far."

"What is this?" Gilroy did the shoulder thing, the one lifters do. "You guys think you're IA now?"

"If we were IA, Dumbo, one of us would be teamed up with that pudge you just cuffed."

Murchison dug an evidence bag from his pocket and dropped the popper vial inside.

"Hey." Gilroy puffed up, red in the face. "What the hell is with you two?"

"Some advice." Murchison pocketed the bagged vial. "You write something up, make sure it can pass the smell test. And back to the subject of cash, you'll be logging into evidence every single cent you found on that kid when you apprehended him. So how much was there?"

Gilroy's eyes flitted from one face to the other.

Stluka said, "Tick tock."

"Two hundred."

Murchison looked at the floor. Stluka said, "You wanna lie about how much you stole off a suspect, don't pick a round number."

"I was guessing."

"Yeah?"

Murchison looked up and held out his hand. "Empty your pockets."

The blood left Gilroy's face. "I don't have to do that."

"You're absolutely right," Murchison said.

"Five." Gilroy licked his lips. Glancing at Stluka, he added, "Five-twenty."

"He didn't say pick a number, Dumbo. He said empty your pockets."

Gilroy froze, nothing moving but his eyelids as he blinked. He stuck his hand in his pocket, withdrew a money roll with a hundred showing on the outside, bound tight with a rubber band. Murchison took it from him as Stluka said, "Unless that's a sucker roll, I'd say it's a grand easy."

Murchison counted it, rolled it back into a wad, and fastened it tight with the rubber band, then took out his notepad and jotted down the amount, saying it aloud as he wrote. "One thousand three hundred and forty dollars."

Stluka let go with a soft whistle. "Viva Las Vegas."

Murchison handed the roll back to Gilroy. Gilroy took it, put it away, then nodded toward Murchison's pocket. "The bottle?"

Murchison thought it through. Can't save the world, choose your fights. "Sure." He grabbed it from his pocket and handed it back to Gilroy. "I'll be following up. Remember."

Stluka turned back toward the intake desk. "I'll go track down where they've stuck our witness." He started to walk away, singing under his breath:

"You got the eggs, I got the bacon.
But it ain't breakfast that we're makin'."

Gilroy's eyes followed Stluka's exit, his face still pale. Turning back to Murchison, he said, "Nothing I can do or say to keep all this ten-twelve with you guys, is there?"

Murchison felt like choking him. "You want to rethink what you just said to me?"

Gilroy coughed up a bitter little laugh and dropped his head. "I'm gonna get ass-fucked on this."

"I'm willing to overlook this other nonsense you were trying to pull. Even the money. But you go find that girl you were trying to impress. Tell her that routine about the toss-down was a load of crap. And then write it up just like it happened. Because if the kid you took into custody is our perp on the Carlisle killing, his defense team is gonna retrace every step he took from the time he crawled out of bed this morning to right now, this minute. And they're gonna find everything with a pulse that saw you take the kid down, not to mention that young lady you were just here with. She gets bit by the truth bug, you know they'll call her to the stand. Then the last thing you'll have to worry about is what I wanna do to you."

"Yeah. Sure. I'll talk to her."

"Damn right you will." Murchison snapped his fingers to get Gilroy to look at him. "By the way—Arlie Thigpen. You swabbed the kid's hands, right?"

Gilroy's head swung up, his eyes met Murchison's, but whatever they saw belonged to a whole different world.

"For gunshot residue."

"I know what for."

"Then answer me."

"No."

"No what?"

"No." Gilroy looked away again. "I didn't swab his hands."

The choking impulse, it spoke a little louder this time. "Any particular reason, Officer, why you didn't?"

Gilroy wasn't talking anymore. He'd set his jaw, tilted his chin up, like a kid daring you to do your worst.

"Call in," Murchison told him. "Tell the watch commander you're still here. And tell him to send a tech or somebody, anybody, down to the holding cell—don't wait one minute—send him down and swab that kid's hands."

6

As Nadya blinked the grit from her eyes, the murk of half-sleep gave way to a soupy dance of broken planes suspended in a cold light. Little by little, things tapped into gravity, arranging themselves like actors searching out their marks. She lay flat on her back in a strange bed. Against her skin, the starchy sheet felt crisp as butcher paper. The too-clean smell told her: *hospital.* I don't remember getting here, she thought, at the same time feeling little surprise.

The door was closed. Beyond it, echoes formed a dull clamor—soft-soled footfalls down a long corridor, a screeching metal cart, bottles rattling—above which two Latinas bantered as they passed the room.

"Donde hubo fuego, quedaron cenizas."

"Amor de lejos, es de pendejos."

The two women broke into little shrieks of laughter that faded as they moved on.

Nadya rose, struggling through haze. Drugs, she guessed, wondering which. Her throat clenched, a sandpaper tongue, she could barely swallow. Setting her feet upon the floor, she had to guess her legs would bear weight. The floor itself seemed oddly immaterial, like the surface of a pool.

Testing her balance, she clung to the bed rail, then worked herself hand by hand to the end, where she lunged toward the sink, caught it, collected her balance, and stood upright. Opening the chrome spigot, she ran the cold water at full force, and it formed a backwash as she fussed a plastic cup from its cellophane. She threw back a half dozen mouthfuls, pausing between each, the cup against her breastbone as she breathed in, breathed out. The edge of the cup thudded against her lips as she drank, like a clumsy kiss. Within the water's mineral after-taste she detected a hint of blood.

Only after the final swallow did she take full note of the bandage covering the inside of her left arm. Running her hand across the dressing, she wondered at its being there. The tape was rough to the touch and thick, the bandaging deep with gauze. It disturbed her—again a dull, faraway fear, but edging closer.

How much time had passed? The last thing, she was sitting at the piano in Toby's father's house. The image caused her heart to pound— *last thing*—her breath grew short and something coiled tight in her stomach. Other memories flashed and vanished, trailing dread, the way the water down her throat left its bloody aftertaste. Her emotions were gaining momentum, but still she couldn't quite bring anything to bear.

She looked up into the mirror and beheld the reflection of what seemed a sickly twin. Same black hair, same deep-set eyes, but all washed out, ghostly, lost. She wondered if this odd, misremembered self now possessed the memories she could feel were missing.

She'd left the water running. Closing the faucet, she almost lost her balance, and as she steadied herself it occurred to her that if she let go with both hands, her body would drop like a stone. Her head would strike the edge of the sink with a sound like a kettle-drum. She might lie there on the floor for hours. And would that be so terrible—wasn't being left for dead precisely what was called for?

Toby and Francis had driven off; Toby's father returned inside the house, carrying his baritone. Nadya hadn't budged from her chosen spot—perched on the old red ottoman, hugging her knees. He closed the door gently behind him, a wistful look in his eye as he set the big brass horn down.

"You got a sweet face, know that? Your heart half as sweet as your face?"

She sat motionless, eyes wide. "I—"

"God knows that'll change if it's true, but for now it's a gift and I won't begrudge the boy that." He smiled, staring at her as though she reminded him of someone. "Your eyes, Jesus. Kind to break an old man's heart."

His mood, it seemed so different from before, the storminess gone, replaced by a kind of longing, almost sorrow. "Thank you," she said. A whisper.

"A princess." He turned toward the kitchen. "Mr. Sensitive's gone and found himself a little Russian princess."

"Mr. Carlisle?"

He disappeared, and Nadya listened as he made himself fresh tea. She rose, tiptoed to the doorway, and watched from behind while he spiked the mug with brandy, just as he had before—not much, barely a shot. *Medicinal,* she imagined him telling himself. He has to know this is madness. And yet she suspected the impulse had a life all its own. He lifted the cup to his lips, shivered with the jolt, and then his entire body sagged as though with sad, fond recognition. He closed his eyes. A moment later he was chuckling.

"Fourteen-year-old nurse," he muttered. "Pretty little white thing."

Nadya drew back from the doorway, returned to the ottoman, and sat down again to wait.

She felt out of place in Toby's father's home, but that was nothing new. Most of her life, she'd felt out of place.

She'd graduated from high school at sixteen, and left home within the week. She'd not spoken to her family since and the story of that was a big fat boring book. As for college, she wanted no part of it, considered the prospect dreary, conventional, creepy. Given her grades and test scores and letters of reference, though, the choice was hers. Anytime. Anywhere.

She lived in a tiny studio apartment above the Berkeley music store where she worked, where she'd met Toby. She'd furnished it so far with one table, one chair, a futon, a space heater, and a hot plate. There was one window—she'd put up curtains and lined up potted succulents along the sunny ledge. She had five changes of clothes, hanging from the shower curtain rod above the claw-foot tub. Rather than move her clothes every time a shower was called for, she took baths. Bubble baths, if time permitted. She'd never had one before living alone.

The studio served as her hideaway with Toby the nights he could get away, and she still at times could barely endure the agony of her good fortune, having him as her lover. The great vulgar myth about shy women—there's always a swaggering male in the picture, all hormones and sweat. *This is how it's done.* Toby ached with a shyness almost as excruciating as her own. Almost, that was the key. Patience—that, too. A gentle suitor just slightly less clumsy than her, guiding her through the grand messy business of lips and tongues—banging their teeth like ten-year-olds sometimes, tasting each other's saliva, feeling his breath on her face like steam from a teapot. Then his skin against hers, the contrast stunning and lovely when she lay naked in his arms. Feeling complete only in his nearness. Knowing her body had been meant for no one but him, knowing that the way she knew her name.

It was not her nature to trust happiness. Life's gifts got stolen back, that had been her experience. But she was trying to learn otherwise, in some way knew that living itself depended on it.

Toby's father sailed back into the living room, gripping his mug of tea. "Up off your lily pad, Froggy." His voice struck like thunder. "Sit your skinny ass down at the piano. Got something I wanna address with you."

He took a spot on the bass end of the piano bench and patted the spot to his right for her to sit. Nadya blinked, stunned. He cleared his throat. "Now, princess."

She got up, sat beside him, and put her hands in her lap.

"No no no." He placed his tea on the floor. "Get your hands up where they belong. This morning, I heard you playing something. I'd like you to try it for me again right now."

Nadya looked at him, puzzled to the point of anguish.

"Monk," he said. "You were playing Thelonious Monk. Put your hands on up to the keys, let me take a listen."

Nadya flushed bright red. "Oh well, I was just—"

"Anh-anh-anh. None of that. The tune was 'Well You Needn't.' The instruction is: Yes, you must. Go on."

Nadya could not move.

"Don't you be sitting at my mother's piano and not do as I say. Hands up. Eyes forward. Play, girl."

His voice was a barely contained roar. Nadya's hands shot to the keyboard. She hesitated but, sensing his wrath, began. The melody was simple enough and one of Monk's catchiest, with nothing but a flattened sixth to make it different from any number of Tinpan Alley standards. It was the tonal clusters in the left hand, with their minor second grinds and clustered fourths, that led her astray. Nadya knew her problem. Years of classical study had her thinking, Popular music, tonal chords. The song came off as slight. Overpretty. He stopped her.

"The reason," he said, "a great many perfectly capable players never trouble with Monk is that if you employ too much technique, you come across as missing the point. And if you just bang at it, you come across pretty much the same."

Her hands remained arched over the keys.

"You studied," he remarked, nodding at the curve of her fingers. "Long time?"

"Since I was four."

She returned her hands to her lap. He reached down and gently took her wrists, placed her hands back up on the keys.

"Competition?"

The question embarrassed her. "Tchaikovsky," she murmured.

He laughed. "You studied for the Tchaikovsky Competition and you sit here acting like it's a disgrace?"

"I felt like a trained monkey."

"Well, yes, there's that side."

"It's the only side."

"You've got technique. You gonna sit here and tell me that's not important?"

Her defiance softened. She felt lost.

"Play me something," he said. "Not Monk. Not something you *want* to know. Play me something you *do* know."

"No. I mean, thank you, this is kind, but—"

"I'm an old man. And old men do get tired of being contradicted."

"I haven't—it's just that—"

His hand slammed down. "Don't sit at my mother's piano and tell me no. This is my home. Where's your manners? Play, damn it. *Now.*"

Nadya could only sit there, looking up at him as though waiting to be swallowed.

He got up with a sigh of disgust. "Fine. I thought so."

He was five steps toward the kitchen—to freshen his tea with more brandy, she guessed—when the impulse came. Whether to protect him from that next drink, draw him back, or to defy him, prove him wrong, whatever, her hands came down in a windstorm of sound.

Later that night, on the way to the club, he would tell her that had he sat and tried to imagine what it might be like for days ahead of time, he would never have conjured what he heard. Brahms, *Hungarian Dance no. 5 in F-sharp minor.* He knew the piece from Warner Brothers cartoons and comedy bits—it was one of those pieces so inherently rife with self-parody, so torturously overplayed and played badly, that few people knew what it was supposed to sound like. "But you do," he told her. Her fingers didn't linger on notes. The attack was bright, her arpeggios crisp, her releases and pedal work balanced. She didn't turn it all into a drone of sappy, pseudo-gypsy mush. You could hear the wildness in the tune. The heartbreak.

The truly spooky thing, though, he told her, was when he turned around to see her bent over the keys, he'd noticed her eyes were closed. "How many thousands of times have you played that thing?" he asked.

While she'd been in the throes of it, she realized, too, how much she'd wanted to mock him. *Play what you know.* Well, Toby's little Russian princess, what does she know? Bugs Bunny music—isn't that what you think? That's all I'm capable of, right? No fire, no blood, no passion. The little princess wants passion, she has to steal it from you, from your son. Just like Brahms ripped off the gypsies with these phony little dances.

But back in the moment, the fury of sound—as suddenly as she'd started, she stopped. Biting her lip, she sat there rocking a little, forward and back.

In time, he said to her, "Whatever it is that's going on, I don't care what it is, how bad it feels, don't you ever, for the love of life and music, don't you ever forget it. Do you understand?"

She cackled, couldn't help herself, opening her eyes to look right at him.

"Cartoons," she said.

He winced. "I'm sorry?"

"Cartoons. 'You want to learn how to feel, Nadya, watch cartoons. Why do you think you like them so much? When cartoons are happy, they are real, real happy. Right?' " She wiped her eyes, her nose. " 'No ambiguity. No double bind. And when they're angry—' "

The words came out like rote; she was quoting a therapist she'd seen the first year after leaving home. Her voice caught at the end.

"And when they're angry," he said gently, "they what? Tell me."

She responded with a forced and clumsy little laugh, then put her hand to her face. Eyes clenched shut, she shook and gasped for air.

"This is going to sound terrible," he said softly, putting his hands on her shoulders, "but I would really like you to stop, okay? As a young man, I learned some of my hardest lessons from women who got prettier when they cried."

That made her laugh. Waving her hand, she said, "I'm fine, really," but she wasn't, and instantly she plunged right back into it.

"If you're up to talking about it, I'm up to listening."

She wiped her face. "No. No, it's—"

"Seems to me, we already danced to this tune. Don't make me bully you, all right? You got something to get off your chest. You keep it inside, it just finds some other way to sneak out. You think you're getting a handle on it, but it's smarter than you. So tell it."

It went like that for the next half hour, giving in to him, letting him hold her, wanting him to, rocking back and forth. Toby'd never mentioned this side of his father, perhaps had never seen it. She felt privileged. And guilty. Gradually, he got her to tell him why the tears.

Jeremy Vanderheiden, MFA, Ph.D. Plump, blond, dapper, eccentric: he'd been her mentor, hired to prepare her for the Tchaikovsky Competition. And though he lectured her about discipline and possessed the required obsession with all things *élevé*, he was also at times a devilishly silly man, a kind man. A perceptive man. It became clear to him early on that though she might very well possess the talent to compete, she lacked the monomania, the fire. She was gifted, yes. But not great.

He saw something else, though, too. She needed her lessons for reasons far removed from music. She ran there to get away from the sadistic little psychodrama at home: feckless dad, icy mom, vindictive sister. Only her grandmother provided anything like warmth, and even that came tinged with need and bitterness—then, when Nadya turned eleven, the old woman got shipped off to a home. Six months later, she suffered the massive stroke that transformed an aging Ukrainian émigré into a bedridden ghost.

And so Jeremy Vanderheiden, piano guru to Berkeley prodigies, became the one human being in her life Nadya could not wait to see. He indulged her, serving petit fours and maple creams, tittering as he gossiped about divas, letting her begin each lesson with the music she loved, lifted from cartoons—as long as she played *con fuoco*. With fire.

Then, five years after she'd begun her course of study with him, he shriveled up before her eyes. Scalded with sores, badgered by delusion. One day she came to the door and a man she didn't recognize answered. He asked her name and then retrieved an envelope from a small stack lying on the entryway desk. He handed it to her, then closed the door.

She ran to a nearby park, tore the envelope open, and read:

My dearest Nadya:

I am writing this note long before it will be necessary for you to read it, because I fear, if I wait much longer, I will not have enough of a mind left to say what I must say to you.

How I wish we did not have to say good-bye. You charmed me, Nadya, with your passion, your silliness, your shyness. How brave you are. I wish I could live forever to enjoy you, to protect you. I will miss the sound of your laugh. I like to think, sometimes, that there will be something like it where I am going.

Now I must be honest—your family, "music," "your future"—these are lies. They are a prison. Continue to be brave, Nadya. Be happy. From where I sit now, I believe to

*be brave and to be happy might well be one and the same
thing.*

I will be your loyal friend forever, wherever

Jeremy

Toby's father sat there with her, handing her tissues, gently rubbing her back as she finished the story. Finally, he said, "Now I understand why you're always saying you're sorry. I think I know what it is you feel so sorry about." He tapped his fingertip gently against the bridge of her nose. "You're alive."

Behind her, the door to the hospital room opened. The sound of a man's voice filtered in.

"No lie, I heard it from one of the nurses. Guy howled in here with his girlfriend, maybe two o'clock. They'd had sex, he rolls off, she says, 'I can't feel anything in my legs.' He thinks she's complaining. Then boom, lights out. Aneurism. Died in here this morning." A snort, a murmur of disbelief. "Understand? The guy fucked his girlfriend *to death*. Twenty-three years old. Try getting a hard-on after that."

She turned away from the mirror toward the sound and came face-to-face with a tall, mournful man with rust-colored hair, dressed in a wrinkled suit. Behind him, a beefy black-haired man with a squinched face was ending his exchange with a police officer sitting just outside the door.

"Nadya," the first man said, "my name is Detective Murchison." He seemed surprised to see her up and out of bed. Gesturing to the black-haired man, he added, "This is Detective Stluka. We'd like to speak with you a moment."

She looked up into his eyes and felt a knifing sadness. The opening bars of "Flee as a Bird to the Mountain" filtered through her mind. A spiritual, Toby had taught it to her, then showed her how Jelly Roll Morton had turned it into "Dead Man Blues."

"Would you please tell them to stop giving me whatever it is they've got me on." She lifted her hand toward her head. "I feel like I'm going a little crazy."

Murchison offered his hand. "You need help getting back into bed?"

Nadya lurched beside him while the other one glanced around the room. Stluka, she thought, a Slavic name, maybe Polish. Her grandmother always hated the Poles, a Ruthenian Catholic versus Roman Catholic contempt Nadya had never comprehended. Religion seemed the last of this detective's concerns; he looked a merry thug. She worked herself back into the bed and covered herself.

Murchison pulled up the room's only chair and sat. At close range, his eyes were a large, warm, watery brown. Stluka rested his back against the wall, cracking his neck.

"We're working on the incident involving Mr. Carlisle." Murchison folded his hands. They were freckled, with graying red hair. "I understand you were there, when the first officers arrived."

It's not a question, she realized, and yet it felt like one. *The incident.* His words evoked an image, she believed it to be true, but it all seemed tagged with "could be." If it happened, she thought, it happened to someone else. My sickly twin.

"You were sitting on the porch." He nodded toward her bandaged arm. "Clawing at your skin."

The panic came like a thunderclap, lancing through her body, more like a seizure than any kind of fear she recognized. A shudder knifed up her back. Her throat clapped shut. The air in her nostrils smelled thick, warm and coppery like blood, then greasy and sweet.

Murchison shot up from his chair. "You all right?"

Behind him, Stluka opened the door, telling the officer outside, "A nurse. Like now."

Nadya lurched upright, her lungs clenching as she tried to draw breath. Murchison hovered near her face, his eyes chasing hers. Her throat opened up to expel a racking sob. She clutched at his jacket, the wool smelling of rain and sweat and musty cologne a thousand years old. He put his hands on her arms.

"Deep breaths."

A nurse appeared—middle-aged, African American, her hair bobbed, gray at the temples and parted on the side. She wore an open white hospital smock with a navy turtleneck underneath. A pair of reading glasses, hanging from a chain around her neck, bobbed on her plump chest. She moved Murchison aside, rested her haunch on the bed, and pulled Nadya toward her.

"About time." She stroked Nadya's hair. "What you've been through, what you did, about time."

Nadya clung to her, embarrassed at the need, the two detectives watching. It seemed an eternity. *What I did*, she thought, confused. Her throat went raw, sandpaper again. The nurse reached for a Kleenex dispenser and pushed tissues into Nadya's hand, one after the other, as she wiped her face and blew her nose and said, "I'm sorry," over and over, to which the nurse murmured, "No sorries required, dear, none whatsoever."

In time the nurse looked over her shoulder at Murchison and Stluka. "She's crying." Said to a pair of dopes. "You call in a nurse, like she's popped an artery. She's crying." She shook her head and turned back to Nadya. "Ain't that the way."

"She couldn't breathe," Murchison said, a little testily. "She said the meds are driving her nuts."

Stluka said nothing.

"Breathing all right now, aren't you, dear?" The nurse's voice was warm, like the sound from a sleeping cat. Holding Nadya at arm's length, she inspected her eyes, felt for the pulse in her carotid artery, then her wrist. She ran her hand along Nadya's bandaged arm, checking to see that the adhesive was secure. "I do believe, little one, that you are going to live." She took Nadya's hands. "These two rough-tough crime-fighting-type fellas need to ask some questions. Could get sloppy. You up for that, or you still need a little time?"

"These meds—"

"You're on Xanax and Valium, dear, nothing more. You just got it intravenously, so it feels a bit more personal. We can slide back a little now, if you want. Nothing else in your system, really, except some antibiotics, for your arm. Pretty tore up, it was. Took a bit of needlework."

Nadya stared at the bandage, feeling another wave of dread, but gentler now, with the nurse there. "I don't remember."

"No surprise there, dear. You're gonna find your memory shooting around on skates for a while."

Murchison made a face. The nurse ignored him and got up, mov-

ing with a droll sashay toward the door. "If she needs anything else—
a coif, pedicure, some chilled white wine—you gents just holler.
Holler good. We'll come a-runnin', oh my yes, God a'mighty." She
opened the door and said to the officer stationed outside, "You gonna
move sometime today, or shall I get the girls from Housekeeping to
drop by and water you?"

Once the door closed, Murchison returned to his chair. He nodded
toward Nadya's arm. "That seems to bother you."

She followed his gaze. It was as though they were both standing a
little off, regarding her arm. It made her feel ashamed.

"I don't remember anything about it."

"Does it hurt?"

"Not yet."

"Why don't you tell me what you do remember."

Nadya looked up from her arm and saw Stluka against the wall,
his eyes fixed on her.

"It's all in pieces." She tucked a strand of hair behind her ear. "I
have these emotions—they're, they're very raw, very intense—but
there's no picture. Or, if I do see something, it just flickers by. Never
connects to anything."

"What's the last thing that doesn't feel like that? That feels whole."

She gave it thought. "I was at the piano."

"The one in the living room?"

"Yes." She closed her eyes, trying for a mental picture—stomach
tight, heart thumping, but she tried—unsure if she was remembering
or imagining. Music echoed faintly in her mind, one of the Hungarian
dances again, but not the fifth this time, the eleventh. No cartoon
associations with the eleventh: elegiac, in A minor. Poco andante.

"I was playing, waiting for Mr. Carlisle to come home. I got this
sense that he was outside. I don't know, just a feeling. Then I heard the
gate. I got up to see—"

"See what?" It was Stluka.

Her head felt light and she found words failing her. Again, an eternity passing. "I heard the gate."

"You told us that."

"I mean a second time." She looked at Stluka, then Murchison. "I
heard the gate a second time. That's when the shots—" Her pores

opened up and sweat beaded on her skin, but she was cold. She felt so cold.

"You want us to call the nurse back?" Murchison said.

"I was confused, I just sat there." Drawing breath, it felt like sucking air through a long, thin tube. "I've never heard a gun go off before. And for a moment, I didn't know, or couldn't believe, what it was. The shots, they were so close, just outside. So loud. I remember thinking that I should get down, on the floor. One bullet, I think, hit the house. But I couldn't move."

"That's not so strange."

"But you did get up finally." It was the other one, Stluka. "Go to the window."

Her head began pounding again. "I should have gotten up right away, I know. Done something."

She shut her eyes and it felt good, the blankness, but then Murchison, the kind one, was struggling with her, holding her by the wrist. "Stop. Stop it."

Nadya blinked open her eyes. Her face was damp, her whole body was wet. She glanced at the wrist Murchison was gripping. The hand was balled into a fist and throbbing.

"Don't hurt yourself." Murchison loosened his hold. "There's no need to hurt yourself. It's not your fault."

Nadya unclenched her fingers. They felt like wax.

"Tell us what you saw, Nadya. Please. All right?"

Stluka said, "Where was he lying?"

She glanced up. "Excuse me?"

"In the yard, Mr. Carlisle, where was he?"

Like a fish dying at the bottom of a boat, she thought. Eyes bulging, mouth gaping, formed around a silent *No*. But a human face, an arm reaching out for her.

"Just inside the gate." She had to swallow, breathe. "Beneath the sycamore."

"Anyone else there with him?" Murchison asked.

She tried to picture herself back at the window, looking out, but when her imagined gaze tracked up his body the yard telescoped, the fence receding fast, growing small, the gate vanishing into the distance. It made her dizzy.

"It still feels like I'm on something." She held her head. "And my memory, it's like it's gone crazy, or stuck."

Stluka shuffled his weight from one foot to the other, then leaned back against the wall again, hands in his pockets. The look on his face said: *This is worthless. This*, meaning me, she thought.

"There are times," Murchison said, "especially when danger's involved, or violence, or something particularly horrible has happened, when we—I mean police here—we just react. And trying after the fact to put into words or even figure out what we did can be almost impossible. It's the way the mind works. The part that explains isn't the part that reacts. So I think I understand how hard it is for you, trying to tell us what happened. And why."

"Thank you," Nadya whispered.

"Are you aware you called nine-one-one?" Murchison asked.

"I did?"

He smiled. "You didn't say much. I listened to the call-ins before we came over. Yours was first. Pretty frantic. You dropped the phone."

Nadya shook her head, blinking. "I'm not helping, am I."

"What the paramedics think, you ran out to the yard, tried to give the victim mouth-to-mouth, got a face full of blood, and probably watched as Mr. Carlisle died right in front of you." He reached out and gently tapped her bandaged arm with his finger. "Then you went back to the front porch and did this to yourself, until help arrived."

Her throat gave up on her again. The coppery scent became a taste and she felt her eyes swimming in their sockets. Neither of the detectives moved toward the door. They wouldn't be calling for the nurse this time.

"Your memory a blank about all that?"

She steadied her eyes, glanced up into Murchison's face, wanting to say, *Help me.*

Behind him, in a voice like a face slap, Stluka asked, "You know a guy named Francis Templeton?"

Murchison's eyes went strangely blank, as though a switch had gone off.

"Yes." So hard to get the word out.

"Know where he might be?"

Murchison, gentler, added, "If he were in trouble, where would Francis go?"

"Is he in trouble?"

"Where would he go?" Stluka asked.

Nadya glanced from one man to the other. Something was going on between them, a competition of some sort. Or maybe she was making it up. Like everything else.

"There was a fight at the club. In Emeryville. Three men followed us to our car. Has anyone told you that?"

The minute they'd entered the bar, Nadya felt a pair of eyes on them. Dapper old black man, young white girl, you had to expect that. No worse lie on earth than the one you heard on right-wing radio: *post-racist America*. But these eyes went beyond even that. They shot out from beneath blond bangs, the boy ham-faced but hard—twenty-something with a pseudo-Celt tattoo on his neck, tiny ears, and a preciously crude haircut. He had friends with him, a foursome. One had dyed black hair and a vampire pallor, drumming his fingers on the bar as he ogled the chest on a woman three stools down. The other two faced away, each of them broad and thick-necked, with close-cropped hair.

They were strangely out of place, given the rest of the crowd—by and large a college mix, the guys animated and smart with their first ventures into facial hair, the girls even smarter and vaguely depressed and clustered in chatty groups. Nadya's eyes held the blond's for several seconds, till his glance moved on. Following it, she saw that now it was Toby's father staring back at him. In response, a smile played on the young tough's lips. The smile did not say, *Hello.* It said, *Any time.*

A voice broke through the crowd noise: "Strong Carlisle. Am I right?"

The man sailed in from out of nowhere. He was tall and good-looking, with pale blue eyes and thick brown hair combed straight back. Even his stubble looked well considered. He offered his hand. "Grady Bradshaw."

Wary, Toby's father practically sniffed the air. "Do I know—"

"I saw The Mighty Firefly play a Juneteenth gig on Lake Merritt last year. Or no, two years ago. Two years. That's right."

Toby's father finally accepted the outstretched hand and shook it politely.

"That was a hell of a show." The man's voice was full of good graces, but his eyes remained strangely cool. "Nobody blows like that anymore."

"You're very kind."

"I still remember you counting off those tunes."

He recited songs he remembered from the Mighty Firefly playlist—Joe Morris's "Weasel Walk," Arnett Cobb's "Mr. Pogo," King Curtis's "Honeydripper"—rattling them off so fast it was like listening to Willie Dixon's "Song Title Jive." When he got to "Okie Dokie Stomp," Toby's father cut in.

"You know your tunes. Either you're a freak for fifties big band blues or you're in the business."

"Promotion. I'm an indie. Carmen DiCarlo, she's one of my acts."

The look in Toby's father's eye said, *Aha. The enemy.* "This that new brand of payola you hear so much about?"

The promoter's smile faltered just a bit. "It's nothing like that, really."

"That's good to hear. Really. Back to the tunes you were running down, 'Okie Dokie Stomp,' yeah, that was our flag-waver. Cornell Dupree number. Original had Seldon Powell on the baritone. That's my horn."

"Oh, I know."

"We did a Mingus number, too. 'Moanin'.' Everybody got to stretch out on that one, even me. Crowd went crazy. Maybe you recall."

The younger man's eyes jittered with face-saving calculation. Despite herself, Nadya made a nervous little chirp at mention of the Mingus tune.

"And who is this?" The man seemed thankful for something else to talk about. His face recovered its blank good humor.

"This is Nadya, my son's young lady."

Offering his hand, Grady Bradshaw eyed her up and down. She'd changed into a cowl neck sweater, a short pleated skirt, black hose. He seemed taken by the outfit. Nadya half expected his fingers to slither up her arm.

"Your son," Grady said, his eyes returning to Toby's father. "I'd have thought he'd be playing with you in The Mighty Firefly."

Nadya couldn't tell whether this was a compliment or a dare. Toby's father answered back with a wicked smile, "Toby needs about five more years of practice, and forty more years of being screwed by the music business, to earn a chair in The Mighty Firefly."

The man laughed too quickly. Too loud. As though quoting his favorite bumper sticker, he said, "Gotta pay your dues, you wanna play the blues."

Inwardly Nadya cringed. What would you know about it, she thought. To save them all, she said, "I think the band's starting."

At the bar, the four hoods continued their haul at the tap. The same meaty blond sat watching them.

Toby's father extended his hand. "I thank you for flattering a vain old man."

"Not at all."

Grady Bradshaw melted back into the crowd. Once he was gone, Toby's father said, "You didn't like that fella."

It was embarrassing sometimes how little slipped by him. "Yes, well, you didn't, either."

"If there was a game show for guys who bragged about getting laid anytime they wanted, he'd be the host." He gestured for her to lead the way back to the dance floor. "Don't think I didn't see the way he looked at you. I mean, girl, you gotta admit, that skirt you're in— barely covers your home life. Any shorter, it'd be a hat."

They came out from the bar to find Toby's band assembled onstage at the far end of the echoing room, beneath the lights. The music started—Booker Ervin's "East Dallas Special." The song cried out for dancers, but only a handful moved forward in the dark. Mostly the crowd, larger now, preferred to wander the vast dance floor, chatting, drinking.

Peering through bodies in the dim light, Nadya thought she spotted friends of the band in front. She wanted to move up, join them. Toby's father resisted, gesturing that he wanted to hang back. He motioned for her to go on ahead.

"No." To disguise her worry, she took a sip of her drink. "I'd rather stay with you."

He began searching the crowd, too. Nadya suspected he was looking for Toby's mother, Felicia—he'd been warned she wasn't coming, some church function, but apparently he'd held out hope regardless. By the time his eyes returned to the bandstand they had an ugliness in them. His jaw set hard, he downed his drink in one swallow.

Onstage, Francis stepped forward on tenor to announce the theme and claim the chorus, building his solo from climbing triplets that ended in a scream. Snapping to, Toby's father shouted, "Yeah! Get *on* it!" Kids standing near him shrank away. "What is wrong with you people?" Sweat broke out on his face. He tugged at his collar, licked his lips.

Nadya touched his sleeve. "Do you need some air?"

He waved her off as "East Dallas Special" ended to scattered cheers. A round of boos erupted as well, deep within the bar. Toby's father spun toward the sound. Before Nadya knew what was happening he was moving. She grabbed at his sleeve, but he shook her off, making her follow as the septet launched into the next tune, Cannonball Adderley's "Sack o' Woe."

He charged through the crowd into the packed bar, dodging the clustered groups that provided cover for his approach. Grady Bradshaw stood with his back to the room, addressing the four roughnecks, some kind of argument. As Nadya rushed up behind she heard them shouting over each other.

"—any your business?"

"I'm just saying—"

"Hey, chilluns. Look who's back. Spook Ellington."

Toby's father came up on Grady Bradshaw fast and yanked him around. "Two-faced son of a bitch." He caught him quick with a straight flat shot to the bridge of his nose. It landed like a hammer. Grady's head jerked back, his knees buckled. Threads of blood spumed everywhere.

Toby's father got jumped from behind by someone in the crowd and locked into a bear hug. The man was young, large, and soft, with darkish skin but whitish features. Grady howled through bloody hands, "What the fuck is *wrong* with you?" Nadya tried to step in, get the man with his arms locked around Toby's father to let go as the four hoods shot up off their stools, grateful for the excuse.

Still wrapped tight in the big stranger's arms, Toby's father managed to duck two punches and caught one on the shoulder that was meant for his head, the whole time kicking wild. Nadya screamed, the sound barely audible above the crowd noise and music. Onlookers in the bar shrank back. The bartender barged in from the perimeter, gripping a golf club like a baton and shoving everybody apart. "That's it! Over! It's over!"

The hold around him loosened, Toby's father circled fast and delivered a quick jab to the eye of the soft, bearish stranger who'd held him. The young man crumpled. Toby's father got a good kick in before the bartender grabbed him by the scruff, dragging him off.

"The fuck I say?" the bartender said.

Toby's father tore free, shook off the punches he'd taken. His skin glistened with sweat. "You're goddamn lucky you got something in your hand."

Grady Bradshaw, his back against the bar, pulled a handkerchief from his pocket and applied it to his face. Toby's father pointed. "Get religion, motherfucker. Insult my son—"

Grady Bradshaw just shook his head, perplexed, disgusted.

"You're outta here," the bartender said.

"Yeah, yeah." Toby's father snatched his beret from the floor and reached out for Nadya's hand. "Let's catch the rest of the set." He started toward the dance floor, but the bartender grabbed him by the scruff again, dragged him through the crowd to a side exit beyond the bar, saying, "No, no, no, old man. Not a chance."

The door banged hard against the iron rail of the landing. Toby's father shook himself free. "I'll walk." He squared himself, framed by the doorway. "One man against five, you kick the one out first."

"You started it."

"Kick the nigger out first."

"Yeah, yeah. Here it comes."

"This is about your motherfucking tip, ain't it?" Toby's father jammed a hand into his pocket, withdrew a few bills, and tossed them at the bartender's feet. "There. Now I'm going back inside to hear my boy."

"Like hell. You're gonna pick up your fucking litter is what you're gonna do. And I see your ass inside this bar again, you'll sleep it off in Santa Rita."

Nadya squeezed through the doorway past the bartender to join Toby's father. She took his hand. "Let's get out of here."

Toby's father stood his ground. "Send out your boys. We'll finish this up right." For the sake of finality, he spat at the bartender's feet, but the man had already turned away.

Nadya, tugging his arm, led Toby's father down the metal steps as the door slammed shut. Their steps rang loud on the metal, then softened to a flagging thud on the asphalt. They were halfway through the parking lot as, back inside, "Sack o' Woe" ended to polite applause.

"No use in bein' scared." He lurched beside her toward the car. "You want to be with my son, about time you learned what it's like."

She looked back over her shoulder, quickening her pace. He stumbled as they turned down the alley where the car was parked.

"Please," she said. "Try."

He shook free of her hold. "Don't you start with the weepy, boo-hoo bullshit again. Damn, girl. Cried enough already tonight." He adjusted his coat collar, shook his head to clear it. Not far away the freeway roared with traffic. "Besides, you ain't the one gonna take the ass kickin' regardless."

They were maybe fifty yards from the car. The shout Nadya had been fearing came from behind, at the far end of the alley. One word: "Hey!"

Three silhouettes, lined up beneath the streetlights.

Nadya pulled at Toby's father's sleeve. "Hurry."

He pulled back his arm. "Not my style."

Nadya shot another glance back, saw the three shapes closing. Why just three, she wondered. Which one had stayed behind? Or was he circling around behind them somewhere? She turned and ran, leaving Toby's father where he stood, gaping at her, dumbfounded. She reached the car, got in, and fired up the engine. Toby's father spun one direction, then the next, looking back at the three punks closing in from behind, then around again at Nadya.

"Little Russian princess," he hooted. "Well, ain't that just it. Go on, run off. Good riddance."

She backed the car out fast, flipped the headlights on. Toby's father turned back around toward the three hoods, ready to do whatever. He put a hand in his pocket to suggest a weapon. "Not goin' down without one of you going with me!"

Nadya slammed to a stop as the car pulled abreast of him, leaned across the passenger seat, flinging the door open. His body responded before he had time to change the look on his face. He barely got the door closed before Nadya jammed the transmission into reverse and, head turned back over her shoulder, gunned the motor. The car sped backward away from their pursuers, who, in frustration, hurled stones.

"You're good at this," Toby's father mused.

At the alley's end she stopped, lodged the transmission into drive, turned hard, and sped off between parked semitrailers down the side street and away.

"Well now. Where did you learn—"

"I drove a cab."

"Backwards?"

Nadya headed for the freeway. "One of the older guys. He took me to Sears Point, the high-performance course they teach there."

Toby's father went slack-jawed. "You are just one bottomless sack of surprises, young lady, know that?"

"Why did you hit him? Grady Bradshaw. Why him?"

"You hear what he said?"

"It wasn't him. It was one of the others."

"Naw, I heard different." He wiped the sweat from his face. "And don't you go righteous on me here. You hated him every bit as much as I did."

"That's no excuse."

"Naw, naw, I mean it now. Don't you start in shaming me, girl. It's not like I planned to have a bunch of loudmouth rednecks pop up tonight. Grady, no Grady, pretty much all the same, you know? Put some thought under that, why don't you."

"I just—" Her voice faltered. She swallowed and tried again. "I hate that sort of thing."

"Yeah, well." He folded his hands in his lap. They were shaking. "You hate that kinda thing too much, all you'll ever do is run from it. And all that means is you'll spend the better part of your life running."

• • •

"You're saying the fourth man, or one of these other three—somebody followed you back home," Murchison said.

"I didn't see anyone. I was busy, driving, arguing with Mr. Carlisle."

"Arguing?"

The way Stluka said it made her turn. He was chewing gum now. Maybe he had been all along.

"I was angry at him. I knew how much the night meant to Toby. He had a tribute planned for his father, but—"

"Toby good and irked about that?" Stluka again.

Nadya blinked. "Is Toby in trouble?"

"Toby and Mr. Carlisle, they mixed it up serious earlier tonight, *before* the show, correct?"

"You don't think Toby—" She looked from one man to the other. "Can I see him? Is he all right?"

"He's fine," Murchison said. "He's at the station."

"Be a whole lot better," Stluka said, "once the truth comes out."

"You want me to tell you Toby had something— That's insane, you can't—"

Murchison stopped her. "Go back to what you saw when you looked out the window, saw Mr. Carlisle on the ground. Take your time. Picture it. Clear as you can."

It was confusing, the two moods, clinical and snide. Feeling less threatened by Murchison, the clinician, she did as he asked, closed her eyes and tried to focus. Shortly she saw the same unchanging thing— Toby's father at the edge of the dim porch light, facedown in the mud like he'd been dropped from fifty feet up, convulsing in shock, fish-eyed, the hiss of air through his bloody teeth while one hand reached out, *Help me.* Not a memory. Happening all over again, inside her head.

"Try to picture the gate," Murchison said.

"Toby, don't forget. He was where?" Stluka added.

Her eyes shot open. "Toby? I don't know."

"But home already." Stluka, pushing.

"No."

"Francis there, too."

"No, I told you." Nadya pulled the covers off her legs and dropped her feet to the floor. "The nurse—"

"Nurse says you're fine," Stluka said. "Gave us crap for calling her in the first time, remember?"

"You're not calling her this time. I am." She tried to stand. "I have to see the nurse."

She put weight on her legs, but they gave way. Murchison reached out quick, caught her, saying, "Whoa, whoa."

"Help me," she whispered to him. "Please."

He shrank from her glance, then turned his head, nodded to Stluka.

Stluka didn't move. "Arlie Thigpen," he said.

"Who?"

"Arlie Thigpen. Tell us about him. Francis introduced him to Toby. Or was it the other way round?"

She had no idea what he meant. Murchison, still holding her, whispered, "If you know, it could help explain a great deal. I know it's difficult. Please—"

She tried to squirm free of his hold, couldn't. Looking up into his face, she saw a gentle and fatherly insistence. But it was a mask. Behind the mask was something unspeakable.

She tore free then, screaming, "I want the nurse!" So loud, she thought, a howl. Not me. But who? She fought through his hands, toppled in a heap to the floor, fending him off with kicks as she ripped at the swath of bandages girding her arm. I do know, she thought, I know, I know—clawing at the tape, wanting her skin, wanting to strip it away next, layer by layer, strip it away to see the blood. See beneath the mask.

Murchison and Stluka hovered over her, dumbstruck. The nurse threw back the door and hurtled in, pushed them aside, kneeling in a rush to grab her wrists and tell her, "Stop. Now—listen to me, *listen to me*—stop this!"

Nadya, blinking, saw the room bathed in a pall of grainy light. As she glanced down, her hand and arm took form before her as a faint growling whimper rose in her throat. Things melted into a welcoming misery, through which, in the background, as though from a different place, a different time, she heard the nurse say, "That's all for now. Leave. Both of you."

7

urchison got out at the door for Custody Transfer as Stluka triggered the rattling chain-link gate to the parking lot. A stench fouled the air, the usual Sunday morning whiff of aqueous ammonia discharged from the refineries across the strait. Murchison punched in the security code at the dial pad and, once the lock clicked free, walked through to the holding area just beyond the door. It didn't smell much better inside, but the stench was human, not chemical.

Glancing through the smeary Plexiglas window of each of the cells, he finally spotted Arlie Thigpen alone inside the last lockup. He was skinny and short, all the more boyish because of that, something he no doubt played to good effect in presentencing interviews. He'd pulled the hood of his sweatshirt tight around his face—same as in Hennessey's Polaroid—his legs tucked up on the bench and his shoulder leaning into the corner as he tried to catch some sleep. How many times, Murchison wondered, have I seen a kid brought in on a killing think a nap would make it all disappear?

He slapped three times hard on the cell's metal door. Arlie jerked upright, hands swinging fast to his cover his head. Good for you, Murchison thought—at least some part of you knows you're scared. Peeking through his fingers as he spun his head around, Arlie squinted blearily at the overhead light first, then found the door, meeting Murchison's eyes through the square of Plexiglas. The boy's face, with its nettle of white scars around one eye, went blank. Just like that, nobody home. He stayed like that, coiled, watchful, as Murchison drew away.

The overnight custody log bore eight names, but the only one Murchison recognized was Arlie's. The other seven bodies awaited up-county transfer, the usual Sunday morning assortment from what Murchison could tell given the code citations listed beside their names: three drunks, two hookers, a wife basher, and a doper. On the blotter where the log rested someone had scrawled in a faint hand: *Johnson's Law: The Lower the Altitude, the Greater the Reptile Density.*

Heading upstairs, he checked his watch to make sure he still had time to catch the end of the change-of-shift walk-through for the Sunday morning crew. The briefing room sat at the top of the stairs, low-ceilinged, small in size and made smaller with the dozen officers crammed inside. They sat wedged shoulder-to-shoulder at three tables surrounding the duty sergeant who stood at a lectern, reading out beat and car assignments. Murchison waited in the doorway till the roll was finished, then whistled softly. Catching his signal, the duty sergeant knocked three times on the side of his lectern and called out in a Central Valley drawl, "Listen, people. Detective wants a word before you head out to your cars."

A distinct switch in mood settled in. Murchison, feeling like the school principal everyone respected but nobody liked, waited it out. He assumed they'd been briefed on what had happened the preceding night, but decided to run it down again just in case, then added, "From what we know now, it's possible, maybe likely, the Carlisle murder and the Fielding's Liquors vandalism are linked. We're tracking down leads right now, but what I'm going to need from you are want-and-warrant checks on the following names."

He took out the Polaroid he'd shared with Marcellyne Pathon, its edges already worn, the image thumb-stained. He read the names handwritten on the back—Eshmont Carnes, Michael Brinkman, Waddell Bettencort, J. J. Glenn. He added the names Arlie Thigpen and James "Long Walk" Mooney, noting that one was in custody, the other wasn't.

"Don't waste time. As soon as you're in your cars, crank up the Panasonics. Apply some percussive maintenance if they screw up like usual, but do your checks. Stay in touch with each other so you can lend support if somebody pulls a runner. I want everybody in that crew, all known associates, talked to. And after them, if need be, their mothers, their sisters, their cousins, their friends and neighbors. You bring up eight-fourteens on anybody—they got so much as a fix-it ticket that's overdue—I want them down here. Lock 'em up, make 'em sit. Separate cells if you can—if you can't, put somebody who's not in the crew in there with them. They don't get to work up their stories while they sit down here, not without somebody else in the cell who can tell us about it. And they don't get transferred up-county, understand? I find out somebody got processed out and he's walking around again with nothing but a court date to worry about, I'm gonna have something to say about it."

He glanced around the room, hoping for a little fervor. Heads nodded, eyes stared, not so much keyed in as just polite. Once upon a time he could have expected more, but with Stluka as a partner his words got taken in ways he could never predict. It had gotten to the point where he had to either explain everything he said five different ways or just say nothing. And the only thing cops distrusted more than a guy who talked too much was someone who said nothing at all.

"If somebody in the crew doesn't come back active with a want or warrant, go to whatever address you've got anyway, drag him out of bed, give him a Beheler, and bring him down. He doesn't want to come, keep at him. Double up, second uniform talks to the parent, the girlfriend, the roomie, whatever. Apply pressure. Let him know: Silence equals suspicion. We'll be on him, day and night, till he talks to us. And if we find out he's lying, we'll be back."

Murchison scanned the room, thinking, And by us, I mean me.

"Last, there's a young man who's identified himself as the murder victim's son."

Finally, a reaction. Eyes danced a little jig, here and there a grin.

"Young man's name is Toby Marchand. He's upstairs, and he's lawyered down." He let that sink in. "His alibi, for lack of a better word, is an abscond out of South Central, name of Francis Tyrone Templeton. Mr. Templeton is a fugitive at this point. We want him picked up. And we want to know of any connection between him or Toby Marchand and Long Walk Mooney. Or anybody in his crew."

He pushed off the doorjamb, turned halfway into the hall, then added over his shoulder, "Sorry if that all sounds complicated. But that's where we're at."

Just outside the detective bureau, he pulled up at the last door in the hallway. Easing the door open, he peeked inside. Tony Hussein, the liquor store owner, sat hunched beneath a crane lamp at a broad wood desk, squinting through his eyeglasses at the photo book he'd been given. He'd changed his pajama bottoms for corduroys but for some reason hadn't bothered to trade the top for a shirt as well. One hand rummaged through his wild hair; the other flipped through the pages of mug shots. He hardly seemed to be looking, just turning pages, like it was punishment.

Murchison knocked gently on the door and ventured in, noticing, as he approached, that the storekeeper hadn't marked a single head shot. The Post-its he'd been given remained wrapped in their cellophane. Frustrated, Murchison felt tempted to show him Hennessey's Polaroids, get to the point, but he knew better. They'd have to work up an eight-pack for that.

Taking up position behind the storekeeper's chair, he prodded, "No luck?"

Tony Hussein squirmed in his seat, nudged his glasses up his nose, and shook his head. "Fucking stupid. Waste my time." He waved his hands above the books in disgust. "Like I see some guy, okay? Think, I know him, he been inside the store." He frowned, reached inside his pajama top, and scratched. "Second look? Hey. Not so sure."

Murchison leaned down, picked up the Post-its, and unwrapped the cellophane. "Even so, keep track of the ones who hit you like that, okay?" With one hand he crumpled the cellophane; the other deposited the Post-its on the desktop beside the photo book. For emphasis, he tapped them twice with his index finger. "Every little bit helps."

"Yeah, sure, yeah." A coffee cup rested by the storekeeper's hand. Peering into it, he grimaced. "This stuff's worse than the piss I sell at my store, know that?"

"Yes, sir. I do." Murchison turned and headed back for the door. "But we can't be undersold."

• • •

Murchison walked slowly down the narrow corridor separating the station's two interview rooms. Though the rooms themselves opened onto the hallway leading to both the squad room and the detective bureau, you could only enter this corridor between them by going all the way around through a rear passageway. Suspects brought into the rooms through the main area didn't know this corridor existed.

Inside the secret hallway were two monitors connected to the video cameras positioned in the ceiling corners of the two interview rooms. It apparently had been beyond the foresight of the mastermind who'd thought of putting them there to think as well that it might be wise to conceal them. As it was, some suspects mugged for the cameras, some ignored them, a rare few actually remained oblivious to their existence.

Murchison leaned down toward the video monitors. One of the two rooms was empty. Inside the other sat Toby Marchand, as he had for hours now. Framed within the small screen, he rested forward, arms on the table and chin on his balled fists. His eyes bleary and open wide, he just sat, waiting. And nine out of ten things he's waiting for, Murchison guessed, will never happen.

Holmes sat alone at his desk in the squad room, finishing up his paperwork from the last shift. He didn't glance up as Murchison crossed the room but instead remained hunched over his report forms, gripping his pen like a dart.

"Holmesy." Murchison pulled up and rested against the next desk over. "Mr. Marchand. Anything to tell?"

Holmes looked up at last. His eyes swam, like he was breaking off a trance.

"He asked if he was free to go. I asked if anybody'd told him he was. That confused him enough, or annoyed him enough, he just went back in and sat down. About the third round of this, I told him even if he wanted to go anywhere he'd need a hotel room because you hadn't cleared the scene yet. That was maybe, what, an hour ago."

"He tell you anything else?"

"Usual." Holmes yawned and stretched, his long arms extending in each direction beyond the edges of his desk. "Can't believe he's a suspect in this, loved his father. They had problems, but—" He completed the thought with a shrug.

"Okay. You fired up to get out of here, or can I fill you in?"

Holmes grinned, the look in his eye half calculation, half surrender. "Sure. I'm square for the OT. Go ahead."

Murchison took out his notepad, flipped through the pages. "First thing, there's some confusion as to what the real relation is between Toby in there and the vic."

Holmes sat back, puzzled. "Serious?"

"What? Tell me."

"I'm just going on what I saw."

"When he showed up at the gate."

"Exactly. His dive. That kinda thing, hard to fake."

"Yeah, but why?" He thought not just of Toby but of his girlfriend, her traumatized memory. Her guilt. "I mean, I'm not contradicting you, I just want to be sure. It looked real, why? Because it caught him by surprise? Or he didn't think it would look *that bad*."

Holmes tapped his pen against the papers stacked on the desktop. "You honestly think he's in on this."

"I don't want to find out two weeks from now that he's disappeared like his friend the Bellflower abscond and everything else we've been looking at has fallen apart."

Holmes nodded, thinking. "Makes sense."

"Let me run down the time line, at least as we know it now." Murchison chafed his face, get some blood going, then ran through the chronology. The victim's kidney surgery, his drinking regardless, him and Toby arguing about it. Then the bar fight in Emeryville, being followed into the parking lot, the drive home, maybe followed. As Murchison described the tussle with Arlie Thigpen outside the liquor store—third altercation of the night—Holmes had to laugh.

"Guy's like a machine. Crankin' out the reasonable doubt."

Murchison stared across the room, his mind hazed. "We don't get a confession? We're never gonna wrap this thing."

Holmes took out his own notepad then, shuffled pages. "You mentioned Long Walk Mooney, the crew outside Fielding's Liquors. They were out there last night, for sure. There was a rave down at the warehouses. Long Walk was running it, and he had jobbers working the dance floor, giving directions to where you could cop."

Murchison sat up straight. "You found this out how?"

"A source." Holmes closed his notepad.

"He'll come forward?"

"I didn't say it was a he."

"Your source will come forward?"

"Not likely."

They sat like that for a moment, staring at each other.

"I understand, Holmesy, wanting to protect your guy. Girl. Source. Could be good down the road, who knows how many times. But this is now."

"Murch—"

"This is murder."

"And what I've got is information, Murch. Not evidence. Okay? It gets where we need this link, I can get the name of the tout. Maybe. We can pressure him or get visual IDs from other kids who were at the dance. But my guy?"

"Guy. Thank you."

"You're welcome. He will never, I mean never, hang numbers on Long Walk Mooney. He'd rather fuck us on the stand than wear a snitch jacket. And I don't have to tell you why."

Murchison waited, hoping for some sign of Holmes weakening, but none came. When the silence became uncomfortable finally, he said, "By the way, Stluka and me, we went to see the girl you found on the stoop outside the house."

"I guess I'd know by now if she saw anything."

Murchison let out a sick little laugh. "Like talking to a bat." He winced, remembering the nurse screaming at them to get out. "That may change in time. Let the meds wear off, get her head on straight." His glance drifted up to the ceiling. "Any event, just in case we're seeing this wrong right now, I'd like to keep her away from her boyfriend, if I can. For as long as I can."

"Any idea how?"

"Keep him here. Meanwhile, not to take advantage, but this source of yours. Run the names Francis Templeton and Toby Marchand by him. I'd like to know sooner rather than later if they tie in with the Mooney crew."

Inside the detective bureau, Murchison turned on his desk lamp and opened the black binder he'd use for a murder book in the Carlisle shooting, searching his drawer for three-hole paper. He was thinking through things done, things yet to do, when Stluka sauntered forward, carrying a file folder that he dropped onto Murchison's desk so he could read the label: *Arlington Nehemiah Thigpen.* A date of birth and a CII number were listed beside the name.

"Ran the kid through the computer," Stluka said, "saw he had a court date coming up."

Cracking the folder open, Murchison started with the rap sheet. The boy had a handle, "Blink"—a touch of the needlessly cruel, given how his eye looked, but that was the street. First arrest at age twelve, six arrests thereafter, mostly drug and theft charges—seven bookings in as many years, but only one taken through to conviction. That case, for possession, included a battery allegation; he'd created a cop toss in the course of his arrest. Maybe Gilroy was telling the truth, Murchison thought. Reading further through the code, though, he saw that the count got dropped in a plea.

"Ah, crud."

"The invisible battery?"

"Yeah."

"Don't despair. Read on."

Arlie'd done a stint with the CYA at Mount Bullion for the possession rap. Fourteen months after his parole lapsed he'd been arrested again, possession with intent this time. He was free on bail, with trial set for six months out.

"If Gilroy can make something real out of whatever happened between him and this kid, could turn out to be the boy's third strike."

"I did the math. Yeah."

"That's good, I think."

"Could cut both ways, yeah. He could cave, he could fight."

The sentencing report took particular note of the mother, Sarina Thigpen, a churchgoer who worked six ten-hour days a week at Overlook, the local convalescent hospital. She had a daughter at home with Down's syndrome and an older son, another parolee but with a clean slate the past five years, working construction in Richmond. Murchison remembered hearing pretty much the same report from Marcellyne Pathon.

"Boy's got a stand-up mother," he said.

"Like many of her kind." Stluka turned away, heading back toward his own desk. "Fat lot of good it's done him."

After the sentencing report came an internal memo that ran down Arlie's known associates. They were all there: Eshmont, Michael, Waddell, J.J. Plus, yes, Long Walk Mooney. But not Toby Marchand. Not Francis Tyrone Templeton.

Arlie Thigpen got brought up from his holding cell and put in the second interview room. Murchison stood in the secret corridor, watching on the monitor as the young man paced around the room alone before taking a chair. He was wearing an orange jumpsuit now. They'd made him hand up his clothes so they could check for traces of blood and gunshot residue. The jumpsuit's bright crayon color made Arlie look younger still. Fourteen, fifteen tops.

The more Murchison studied him, the more the kid appeared to be the type to have taken an ample share of blows to the face. The older brother, maybe. The hoods on the street who called him Blink. It wasn't just the mottling of scars around his eye. His stare seemed to emanate from a place inches inside his skull.

Murchison had arranged the room so the table rested against the wall. That way it couldn't be used as a barrier between them once he went inside and joined the kid. They'd sit face-to-face, as close as Murchison could get.

On the table he'd placed two sets of blank forms. The first was to process Arlie in on a 148 violation—willful resistance of a peace officer. Depending on how things went once Gilroy got a credible story down, that could get upped to combined 241 and 834 charges—battery against a peace officer, use of force in resisting arrest. For starters. The other form was a material witness questionnaire. Between them lay a yellow legal pad. For Arlie to write on, when he was ready.

It's your choice, Murchison thought, watching Arlie as he sat there, a study in attitude. He'd barely glanced at the blank forms, preferring instead to feign a little more shut-eye. He sat slouched, legs stuck out in front with the ankles crossed—*fend off trouble, protect the genitals*. His arms lay folded across his chest—*constrain emotion, shield the heart*. The final touch: his lips were pursed, teeth clenched, his jaw set hard—*say nothing*. And they wonder why we don't believe them when they say they're innocent, Murchison thought. Their own bodies don't back them up.

This is the one, Murchison thought. Don't second-guess yourself. Doubt your instincts going in, you'll get nothing.

Stluka sauntered in, silent as he took up position beside Murchison. Both men stared at the video image of their chief suspect. Glancing sidelong for a moment, Murchison caught something amiss.

"Hey, skipper," he said. "You might want to think about hoisting the mainsail."

Stluka looked down at his crotch. "Whoa." He reached down, zipped up his fly. "Froggie went a-courtin'."

They returned to their study of Arlie Thigpen. Stluka broke the silence this time.

"Got a call on my voice mail. Owner of the club down in Emeryville. Vanessa." He sighed. "I think the romance is off. She's got a lawyer."

"Before dawn? On a Sunday?"

"I'm guessing retainer." Stluka held out his hands, embracing an invisible basket of money. "Nice big fat one."

"They've already nailed down their story."

Stluka smiled. "You're a smart guy. Ever think of being a detective?"

Murchison locked his fingers behind his head and turned at the waist, slow, till his back cracked. "Go on. Tell me the rest."

"The club denies any liability for any act or failure to act that may or may not have occurred tonight or any other night on or off its premises. Something like that."

"There's still this three versus four thing—"

"Not now." Stluka ran his hand across his chin, as though trying to gauge from the stubble how soon he'd have to shave. "She cleared that up."

"How?"

"Ran through the whole thing again. My guess? She and her lawyer, they rehearsed. And I bet she taped the phone message on her end, too. This is going to be the story, period. Said her bartender remembered one guy stayed behind, never left. Watching everybody's drinks, the cheap little shits. Black hair, pale skin, tall—guy who stayed behind, I mean. The other three went to make sure the old man, this Carlisle character, didn't come back with a gun. Basically, she says it's all his fault. Anyway, after him and the girl drove off, the three amigos came back and all four together tried to pick up chicks, without luck, and drank Watney's till closing." He chuckled. "Watney's. 'It's a pale ale.' She wanted us to know that."

"And this promoter, the guy the vic clocked?"

"Grady Bradshaw. His act was on last. That's a definite. He never left."

"So it's her and her bartender. They're the alibi for the bar crowd."

Stluka didn't answer. He leaned down a little closer toward Arlie Thigpen's image. "Your grandmother ever tell you she was going to sell you to the ragman?"

Murchison wasn't sure he'd heard right. "The who?"

"My grandmother, she was first-generation. She used to tell us—if we were roughing it up inside the house or whatever—that if we didn't behave, she was going to give us to the ragman. You know, like we were just another hunk of garbage." He chuckled, but it wasn't laughter in his eyes. "I even remember seeing this ratty old man riding a horse-drawn junk cart down on the street, which I know isn't real, I must've made it up, but there it is. In my head."

He looked at Murchison, inquiring.

"My grandparents didn't do the discipline bit," Murchison told him, sensing, finally, where this was going. "My folks took care of that all by themselves. And their line was usually 'Don't come home complaining they hit you at school, or we'll just hit you again.' "

Stluka laughed, kinship in his eye. "That's why we're who we are, Murch. Instead of the sorry little sack of shit in there." He tapped his finger against the video screen. With his other hand he scratched beneath his arm, where his shoulder holster bit into his skin. "Know who he reminds me of? Couple of my neighbors, they're Unitarians. They hired this kid to help rake leaves, weed the garden, do odd jobs around the house, you know? Thinking, Let's help the kid out. The poor, unfortunate, misunderstood Black male. One day, they come home, find a side window jimmied. In the bedroom, a set of rings, been in the family for generations, they're gone. Plus about two hundred cash hidden in a sock drawer."

He waited, and Murchison could almost feel, like some small gravitational force, the tug of his craving for eye contact. Murchison refused to give in, keeping his gaze straight ahead.

Stluka said, "Just about everybody you know has a story like that. Ever wonder why that is?"

"I don't have a story like that," Murchison said.

"That's a lie. This job, it's nothing but stories like that."

"Jerry—"

"Know what I read the other day? A kid had a better chance surviving combat in World War Two than he does surviving childhood and adolescence in Washington, D.C., today. That's after Black mayors since way back. And as much or more spent on social services as anywhere in the country."

"The seventies, Jerry. We've had this talk."

"No, Murch."

"Factories closed down, jobs got shipped offshore. Black community got slammed. Crack came right after."

"Murch, stop it. Capitalism ain't the problem. Japan is the greediest country on the planet, money is king, and nobody cares how you make it, especially now that the so-called Asian Miracle's tanked. Porno is huge there, and I'm talking seriously sick shit—S & M, child porno, even. And yet they've got the lowest violent and property crime rate in the world. Scandinavian countries have incredibly low crime rates. What do they have in common?"

"Just a guess—cannibalism?"

"Racial homogeneity."

Murchison felt trapped and yet he blamed himself for that. Stluka was hardwired; any leeway to be had wouldn't come on his end. Murchison resented that, resented all the things he knew he couldn't do about it, and resented the stranger to himself and everyone else it had turned him into. But none of that, in the end, was Stluka's fault.

He turned—toward the door, not his partner. "The world is a ghetto, Jerry. I dunno. You tell me." He started to walk away.

From behind, Stluka said, "No, that's my point, Murch. It's not the world. It's here. It's us."

"Okay, Jerry. You win." He got as far as the door. Feeling a curious kind of guilt, like he'd failed to remember something that once had been second nature, he turned back for one last attempt at connection.

Stluka stood there, eyes shining, lips creased into the coldest of grins. "Come on, Murch, don't sulk. Admit it, you're gonna miss me when I'm gone."

8

───────•◆•───────

Murchison made his way back through the narrow winding hallways to the lunchroom and slipped in coins to the vending machines for two packets of cheese crackers and a carton of chocolate milk. He put the crackers in his shirt pocket and shook the milk carton as he walked back through the hallways to the interview room in which Arlie Thigpen sat. Murchison punched in his code at the dial pad, unlocking the door.

"Hey, how we doin' in here?" There was no recent mention of a father in Arlie's file, so Murchison assumed the position was open. A common tactic. Uncle Dad, they called it. "I'm still scrambling around, putting this and that together, but I figured you might be hungry, so I got you these." He laid out the crackers, the milk. "Not much, but it's the best the vending company gives us."

"I want a lawyer."

"I'll be back, we'll talk then."

Murchison turned to go. Behind him he heard the cellophane snap on one of the cracker packages. Over his shoulder, he saw the kid going at it with his teeth. Glancing up, Arlie froze, then spat out a sliver of wrapper.

Murchison punched in his code and slipped back out the door. He crossed through the squad room toward the detective bureau, stopping one door short. He knocked.

"Mr. Hussein?"

He opened the door and the storekeeper cringed. Murchison checked the photo books. Three Post-its stuck out above the pages, flagging head shots.

"These the only ones that look familiar?"

Tony Hussein frowned, scratching his neck. "You know, those things, they don't—" He shrugged. "It's not like, you know, how they look. When you see them."

Murchison checked the pictures. Not one matched a name they'd already come up with, not even Arlie Thigpen. The guy got scared, Murchison thought. All this time alone.

"Would you mind coming with me for a second?"

Murchison lifted him out of his chair and led him—straggling, hand clutched to the waist of his trousers to keep them from sagging around his hips—back through the maze of hallways to the corridor between the interview rooms. Murchison talked as they went.

"There is nothing about what you're going to see, Mr. Hussein, that should be interpreted as an indication of guilt in any way. We're talking to people, a lot of people, about the fight outside your store. The murder. The anchor heave-hoed through your window. And we're going to talk to a lot more people. Witnesses, not just suspects.

"For the moment, there are two young men in particular we've had the chance to speak with, and before they move on I'd just, for the sake of being thorough, like to know whether either young man looks familiar to you. And if so, why. I'm not saying either one will. It's entirely possible both young men are strangers to you, and if that's the case, fine. There's no pressure. Don't say you recognize somebody you don't. But if either young man is familiar, I want you to tell me precisely why and how, tell me the last time you recall seeing him, what makes that occasion memorable. Okay?"

The routine was called a show-up. Murchison gestured Tony Hussein through the final door. Once inside, the store owner took barely a glance at either monitor before he spun around.

"What happens next, huh? Smash my window this time, but next time. Tell me."

What is this, Murchison thought, a dare? "Mr. Hussein, I understand your concern. I do. We'll catch the men who came after your store tonight. We'll catch the ones who try anything else. We'll put them away." Murchison didn't try to sound convincing and the storekeeper didn't pretend to believe. Murchison gestured toward the monitor. "Just one look, okay?"

Tony Hussein turned, adjusted the glasses on his face, and

squinted at the screen. "Him. The one, outside my store, yelling, fighting. With the old man." It came out more like a complaint than an ID.

"You didn't pick his picture out of the book." And how could you miss him, Murchison thought, with those scars around his eye?

"Him." The storekeeper said it again, but quieter now. "Him. The face I remember. Okay?" He turned back around with a look of almost defiant neediness. "And that's that, right? I go back, you go back, everything normal, everybody happy. Everybody safe. Tuck tuck, night night."

Murchison pointed to the second monitor. "Before we head back, could you look at the other young man for a moment?"

Hussein adjusted his glasses again, then stared at Toby Marchand. "Who the fuck is that?"

Murchison said nothing. Tony Hussein leaned a little closer, squinted, then straightened back up again. He shrugged, pitching his head left and right. "Him I don't know." The fear came back. "Should I?"

"Do me a favor. Look again. Imagine him in different clothes, if you can. Whatever the young men were wearing outside your store. Be sure."

Hussein turned toward Murchison, blinked. Stared.

"Not me, Mr. Hussein. The young man in the room there."

Arlie didn't bother to look up as the door opened. He had crumbs on his chest. Cracker wrappers and the now empty milk carton lay scattered on the floor beneath the table. Murchison closed the door, crossed the room to the one empty chair, and sat, pulling it close till he and Arlie sat barely a yard apart. The kid made no move to increase the distance, but he kept his arms folded tight, legs stuck out in front of him, ankles crossed. His feet quivered like a current ran through them.

They taught you to first determine the suspect's dominant need. Respect. Safety. Flattery. Sympathy. Then you were supposed to stimulate and exaggerate that need, and finally offer to gratify it in exchange for a confession. Tell him you understand how it could've happened, reduce the moral weight of the crime, suggest a less repelling motive for it than the evidence reveals. But never back down from your conviction the guy did it. And never offer a scenario for him to buy into that would remove intent.

There, simple. The less intuitive guys loved it. They could recite it back to you in a heartbeat. Only trouble was: What about the perp who thought respect was safety? By the time you figured out *his* confusion, he'd sealed up on you. Game over. And what about the guys who invited flattery but then turned on you, figuring if you kissed their butts you didn't respect them? Same with sympathy—if you really understand me, you hate me. And I hate you. The dominant need turned out to be a smokescreen, behind which hid an enigma. The psyche. A human being.

"Feeling better now that you've eaten a little?" Murchison set his file on top of the table and pulled toward him the nearest stack of papers. "You get a chance to look at these?"

Arlie just glared. "I want to see my lawyer."

The kid wasn't mealymouthed about it. No: *Maybe I need.* Or: *Would it be possible if.*

"This questionnaire here, it's for witnesses." Murchison held the blank material witness form up so Arlie could see it. "Thirty-six questions."

Arlie responded by tugging at the front of his orange jumpsuit, then glancing at the door. "I'm a witness? Well, damn. When do I get my clothes?"

With the *Dickerson* ruling, cops could be held personally liable for any violation of a suspect's rights. The California Department of Justice had issued a memo about it, warning there'd be no more coaching about interviewing outside *Miranda.* You could lose your home, your life savings, for doing now what they'd been training you to do for years. It was a miracle they could get cops to work through to retirement anymore, the number of times the rules got changed— especially now that it was you, not just the department, left holding the bag.

Still, as long as you didn't threaten, there was room to maneuver.

"What I mean, Arlie, is that if you're a witness, I can try to intervene on your behalf. Depends on what you're a witness to."

Arlie squirmed in his chair, face full of disgust. Murchison nudged his chair closer.

"Arlie, I'm not stupid. And I'm not one of those cops who think every Black kid who comes in here is stupid, either."

"Whoa. Mighty Whitey."

"I can't help unless you let me."

Arlie broke eye contact, shook his head. "My lawyer."

"You have a lawyer?"

"You gotta get me one."

"Aren't you a little ahead of yourself?"

"You can't hold me on one charge, pretend we just talkin' on another charge. Don't work like that. Not if I ask for the lawyer. I ask for the lawyer, *poof*, magic words." He did a little side-to-side in his chair, a challenge. "From here on out, every word *you* say will be used against *you*. That's the motherfucking law."

"Just to fill you in, Arlie. Only warning ignored more often than *Miranda* is the one on the outside of a cigarette pack."

"Ignored by who—you?"

"I got told once, by a judge right here in this county, I open a trunk and find a pound of weed, I lacked probable cause. I find a dead body, the opposite applies. That's not us, that's the court. Damn few lawyers are dumb enough, or dishonest enough, to file *Miranda* motions. They never work."

"Not the way I heard it."

"This isn't TV, Arlie. This is right here."

"Always a first time."

"You're not that lucky." He looked straight in the kid's eyes. "Are you?"

Arlie made a half-dozen faces at once, ended up staring at the wall.

Murchison said, "I was watching this program on the Discovery Channel the other night. The average person swallows six spiders a year during the night, did you know that? They crawl into your mouth while you're sleeping, I kid you not. Spiders, they like warm, wet places. I wonder—think that happens more often in prison?"

"I *want* to see my *lawyer*."

"Fine." Murchison reached for the booking sheet. "Officer who brought you in, he had to go to the hospital." He checked to see how that landed. Arlie recoiled a little further into himself. "Didn't get a chance to finish the paperwork that's required."

Actually, Murchison had torn up the intake form Gilroy had filled out when he placed the kid in holding. Murchison wanted to redo it himself, try to build some rapport.

Arlie said, "I ain't saying another word to you."

"This is just the paperwork that allows us to track you through the system, Arlie. It's not subject to *Miranda* warnings. So first thing we do is go through the basics, name and address and birth date. You know the drill." He took the pen from his shirt pocket, clicked. "Arlington Nehemiah Thigpen, am I right?"

He started to write it down. Arlie said nothing.

"Arlie, if you don't confirm that I have it right and I get it wrong, it's only gonna make it harder for you to get processed out. Understand?"

Arlie's eyes glimmered, moving slow behind half-shut lids. "Yeah." A murmur.

Murchison wrote it out in block letters. "Thigpen. There's a receiver, played for the Steelers, then the Titans. Yancie Thigpen." He opened Arlie's file, checked the address on his rap sheet, and left the file open so Arlie could see it. "You follow football?"

"Maybe."

"Still live with your mother?"

Arlie bristled. "You want an address, I give you one."

Interesting, Murchison thought. He tapped his pen against the rap sheet. "Just tell me if that one's right."

Arlie leaned close, read the address, then read a little more. All his arrests were listed in the dense, semicryptic code the computer spat out. "Yeah." He slouched back in his chair again.

Murchison wrote out the address, slow. "I'm not much of a poker player, Arlie, but I know enough not to show my hand. All right? You know why you're here, and it's not for the bottles—"

"There ain't no bottles. Damn cop set me *up*."

"And it's not for the dustup with the cop who brought you in here."

"What am I supposed to do, just let him swing the damn stick?"

So that's how Gilroy fouled up his wrist, Murchison thought. "You're not going to rustle up bail and get right back out there. Not this time. You've hit it big. Uniforms are out on the street right now, gathering up your friends."

Arlie fussed with his nose, then his lips. The Facial Touch Zone, textbooks called it. Lot of capillaries in that part of the face, and when the blood really starts to pump, the skin itches. Once or twice, his fingers strayed to the scarring around his eye.

"Maybe sooner, maybe later, we'll hand it off to the DA, and his sole focus will be to put you away for life. Or have you executed."

"Go ahead." It was almost convincing, the bravado. Except the face touching, the jittery legs, the eyes. "Talk talk talk." Arlie stuck out his hands, turned them over. "That deal they did with the Q-Tip thingies? Gonna show I ain't shot nobody."

The words came out with a clicking sound, the insides of his cheeks catching on his teeth. Whitish threads of dry saliva formed at the corners of his lips.

Murchison said, "Come on, Arlie, you're smarter than that. Results come back negative, doesn't mean squat, really. Not with the other stuff we've got."

Arlie crossed his legs. Another textbook move. "Get real. Ain't no other stuff."

"If there's a gun out there somewhere, tossed into the bushes or a sewer? Anywhere somebody, like a kid, could happen onto it? We've got a public safety problem. So I've got to ask you, where's the gun?"

"You can't *talk* to me. Said it already. Ask for a lawyer, boom, that's it."

Murchison shook his head. "Arlie, if I had a few hours, I'd give you my little lecture on the court rulings chipping away at *Miranda* the last thirty years. But to be brief, like I said, this is a public safety issue. I've not only got a right, I've got a duty. Time's a factor. You toss the gun? Where is it?"

"Fuck a gun," Arlie said, louder now. Eyes not sailing left or right, dead on. Defiant. "You think I'm stupid. Try to chump me up. Forget it. My lawyer, how many times I gotta say."

"If it ends up we find the gun ourselves, Arlie, somebody hands up a tip, this little exchange is part of the record. It'll come up at sentencing—you had the chance to take the public's safety into account and refused. You with me?"

Arlie laughed. "Listen to you. Already got me beat. On somethin' I didn't do."

"Arlie, I want you to listen to me." He edged his chair another inch closer. Arlie's legs reached out between his own. "If you didn't kill Mr. Carlisle, why would the girl inside the house identify you as the guy who did?"

They called it the enticement question. As worded, it wasn't exactly a lie. Get scared, Murchison thought. Come on, get scared. So I can protect you.

"There's a thousand reasons why it could have happened, Arlie, and I can understand every single one. Did you shoot him to save face? Or did somebody say, 'He pays, or you pay'?"

Arlie began shaking his head in violent little jags, whispering, "No, no, no. . . ."

"You've asked for a lawyer, Arlie, and that's your right. I mean, you've heard it before, but I'll say it now—you've got a right to remain silent if you don't remain silent anything you say can and will be used against you in a court of law and you have a right to a lawyer, duh, and if you can't pay for one, one'll be provided." He spun the waiver around on the tabletop so Arlie could sign. "Now—having those rights in mind, do you want to hear what I have to say?"

"That's all I'm *doin'*. Shit."

"You want to tell me your side of the story?"

Arlie shook his head. "This ain't happenin'."

"Arlie, you get a lawyer, I'm out of it. And that's not a good thing. You get a lawyer, he's gonna plead you not guilty as soon as you're arraigned, and the switch goes off at that point. The papers'll carry it, public opinion'll turn against you, and the DA—he's elected, remember. Meanwhile, if you get tired of the public defender constantly begging you to plead out, you'll need a private lawyer, and you know what that means. Your mother has to take out a loan on her house. One more debt. One she can't afford. All that because you told me to get lost." He sat back, folded his hands behind his head. The open position, nothing to hide. "Remember, Arlie, the cops—we're the guys out there with you, on the street. You may hate our guts, but we're the ones who know what really goes down out there. Deal with you day in, day out. Know the shit storms you deal with, the kinds of pressure that come into play." He paused, to make sure the next part had the proper effect. "We even know who's going to let you go down, just to take the heat off himself."

Arlie's eyes went stony and yet, at the same time, he yawned. Tension, Murchison guessed, not fatigue.

"Just the way of things. We know what stunts your friends will pull just for an angle. But you get a lawyer, from that point on, we do what we're told. And we'll get told, 'Nail it down.' DA's not gonna care if you really did it or not. Close it out, that's the plan. One of your buddies is desperate for a play, decides to point the finger at you, it'll be your job to prove he's lying. Not ours. By that time, things'll be stacked against you pretty good. And because you lawyered down, I'll be out of it. What help I can provide, I can provide now, not later. You want to clear the air, I'm gonna listen. But the chance won't be there for long. I can understand how it might have happened. I know a lot about this guy, the one who was shot. I know a lot about you, about your crew. Waddell, Michael, J.J., Eshmont. Long Walk."

The kid's breathing came faster. He started blinking a lot.

"You got something you think I should know, tell me now. You're not in this thing, fine. But you gotta tell me who is. You gotta give me a name."

Come on, Murchison thought, knowing enough not to prod. You've sold him the product. Don't buy it back. The wait drew out, the tension faded a little. Murchison sensed he was losing the kid.

"You're not going to be the only one dealing with this, you know. Your family, they're gonna go through it, too. Your mother."

Arlie winced, did a little put-upon dance in his chair, and a vein in his neck fluttered.

"I'm gonna need to talk to her, Arlie. Your mother. Explain why you're in here. There anything you'd like me to tell her?"

"Yeah! Tell her I ask for a lawyer, you don't listen. Tell her my rights been violated."

Murchison felt it slip away. The kid wouldn't bend. Not without more to leverage.

"Anybody you want me to call?"

"Didn't ask you to make *my* call."

"You don't want me to call your mother?"

"No!"

"What's the problem? Your mother gonna take the news you're in here—again—a little hard? Could be your third strike."

Arlie shook his head in disbelief, glancing away. He looked about ready to cry. Back in business, Murchison thought. Most welcome sight in the world, a suspect ready to cry.

"I'm here to listen, Arlie. It's all I'm here to do."

"You gonna do what you wanna do," the kid muttered.

Murchison leaned forward. "I didn't hear that, Arlie. I'm sorry."

Arlie snorted and grinned. "Go ahead, ask your damn questions. Fuck yourself up. I done asked for my lawyer." His voice rose. "Say what you want. You see nigger in front of you, you think, Fool. Brothers know all about this shit. Got guidelines from the motherfucking DA, tell you how to talk 'off the record' and shit, so you can twist me up, get me to say something stupid, make sure I don't take the stand. Well, I'm innocent. There. Off the record, on the record, on the stand, off the stand."

He tried to clear his throat, but there was nothing there—his lips, his tongue, everything bone-dry. He shook his head and made a spiteful little laugh, then glanced down at the floor, chest trembling as he breathed.

"Ain't gonna make no difference regardless. Only thing goes down is what you wanna go down. What you don't wanna go down, don't go down."

9

———•◦•———

arina Thigpen shuffled blearily through the worn, dimly lit lobby of Overlook Convalescent Hospital, heading toward the electronic glass doors opening onto the parking lot. She'd stayed late to help the understaffed relief crew as they launched the new day, lifting patients from their beds, guiding them to the closet-sized bathrooms that the old folks soiled in their blind, palsied, or delusional efforts to relieve themselves. With the patients occupied, Sarina changed the bed linens, thick with a toxic urine stench or the bitter chalky smell of sweat. If no voice called out from the bathroom, she knocked, entered, lifted the frail thin body off the toilet, wiped it clean, and guided it back to its fresh bed. Returning to the bathroom, she picked her rag out of the ammonia bucket and washed down the walls, the floors, the toilets inside and out. By the time she removed her uniform at shift's end, it peeled away bearing unspeakable stains.

That wasn't the worst, though. The worst was the slurs and insults shrieked or hissed in her face by white patients, their minds all but gone. An RN had explained the medical reasons once—strokes degrade the frontal regions of the brain, she'd said. The regions involved in social inhibition. "They don't mean the things they say, any more than they mean to soil themselves."

Sarina knew better. In fact, as she saw it, the exact opposite was true—they meant it all too well. They'd been harboring the bile in their hearts their whole lives, and only a quirk of fate—one stroke too many—kept them from being able to keep up the pretense all the way

to the grave. Every time she got called "nigger bitch," "gorilla," everything else imaginable—the women as bad as the men, worse sometimes—she reminded herself that this was the real them. This was the
racist inside every last one of them, screaming to get out. And she
would pride herself on not retaliating. No, she thought, the Lord will
not have it. Vengeance is His alone. And so every last one of those
nasty, ignorant, loudmouth bigots lay clean as a whistle in a spanking
white bed with an immaculate bathroom waiting.

Outside, the eastern sky was cold and blue with daybreak, with
night receding in the west. She searched her purse for her keys. Finding them, she looked up again to find two men in sport coats, waiting.
Detectives, she guessed. How could you not tell?

"Mrs. Thigpen?"

The one who spoke was tall and thin, homely, with reddish hair.
The other, she could see at a glance, was a devil. Sarina snapped her
purse shut, crossed her hands in front of her. "My name is Sarina Thigpen, yes." She cocked her head a little to one side, indulging them.

"My name is Dennis Murchison, I'm with the Rio Mirada police. We
have your son Arlie in custody, Mrs. Thigpen. He asked to see you."

It was the first time they'd come for her at work. "I suppose I got
a stop to make at the bondsman," she said, and began moving toward
her car.

"Bond's not an issue, Mrs. Thigpen. Your son's being held in connection with a murder."

A thread of bile slithered up into her throat. "That can't be."

The one who'd spoken, the one with the rust-colored hair, held out
his arm, as though to guide her. "I can explain in the car," he said.

Stluka got behind the wheel, providing Murchison the role of confi-
dant, bearer of bad news, and negotiator. He sat sideways in the seat,
the better to talk with her. She was a short, muscular woman with
small, strong hands. Atop her broad neck sat a square face, with high,
round cheeks and thin, almond-shaped eyes. As they pulled out of the
parking lot, the light from the street lamps played across her face, dappling it with angular shadows. She sat there with her purse in her lap,
gripping it to her midriff.

"As you probably know, Mrs. Thigpen, your son is up for trial in six months on possession with intent charges."

"You said murder. I got in this car 'cause you said murder. Not drugs."

Over his shoulder, Stluka said, "I thought you got in because your son asked to see you."

It was out before Murchison could stop him, and instantly Sarina snarled back, "You gonna try to blame me? This country stinking with drugs, no good jobs, more jails than schools, and you wanna blame me? My God, you are the devil. Stop the car. Stop it here. I'll walk to see my son."

She slapped at the door handle. Murchison glared at Stluka, then reached out his hand in a calming gesture. "Mrs. Thigpen, he chose his words poorly."

"It's the devil in me."

"You get your goddamn hand away from me." She glared at Murchison. "Don't you dare touch me."

Murchison withdrew his hand. "I meant no offense, Mrs. Thigpen."

"You don't mean nothing but offense. You drag me away from my job, what are people to think? You say my son's a killer."

"Mrs. Thigpen—"

"I am a woman of the church. I put my faith in God, not you. Certainly not you. I have prayed for my son, and I have worked hard, but I cannot be all places at all times. I cannot save him from a street you refuse—"

She was shouting. Murchison, nerves frayed, found himself shouting back, "Mrs. Thigpen, we have an eyewitness. Nod your head if you understand."

He regretted it, not telling her eyewitness-to-what, but he was unwilling to suffer any more sermons. Besides, deceit was permissible, that was the law. Blue lies, they were called. Sarina leaned back in the seat.

"Witness," she said. Her glance floated from Murchison's face to the back of Stluka's head—right, left, then right again. "What did this witness see?"

"The victim's name is Strong Carlisle, he's—"

"Raymond Carlisle?" Sarina sat up straight, incredulous. Her eyes brightened. "My son has no stock in killing Mr. Carlisle. My Lord, I took care of that man's mother up there at the hospital 'fore she passed. No, you're wrong. You're confused."

"Eyewitness," Stluka repeated. He didn't call them blue lies. He called them weasel prods.

Sarina's fingers kneaded the thin vinyl strap of her purse. "That can't be right."

Murchison took a moment to think through his next step. He saw no point in trying to convince her Arlie had done anything; it was enough she thought they were convinced. Her role in this was to bring the whole immeasurable weight of tortured motherhood to bear on her son, make him see who was going to suffer. But to make that work, Murchison had to give her hope.

"Mrs. Thigpen, I'm not going to lie to you. We know pretty much all we need to know about what happened, but that's not saying we know everything about why. I don't doubt there are some pressures in play that we'll only find out about as time goes on."

"He did not do it. My son did not kill Raymond Carlisle. That's just—it's crazy. Crazy."

Sarina looked out the window at the empty street rushing by, the hardscrabble housefronts, the blighted yards. "Poor man," she said quietly. Then, locking her hands in prayer, she whispered, "Dear Lord, Who knows the weakness of our natures, bend down Thine ear in pity." Eyes closed, she continued in a hush, lips barely moving.

When she reopened her eyes, Murchison said, "I'd like to explain a few things before we get to the station, Mrs. Thigpen. Would that be all right?"

There was a chance that Arlie, upon talking with his mom, might cut his losses and confess. Even if the kid didn't sign a waiver and talk, something might spill out as he tried to make his mother feel better—something Murchison could tie to something else, weave together, work up. This, in legal parlance, was the difference between an admission and a confession. The courts were far more willing to consider an admission reversible error. No big thing, no matter how bad you tooled with the suspect's rights. And even if Arlie's lawyer did end up getting it suppressed as evidence, it was still information. Prosecutors could bitch all they wanted, *Information isn't evidence,* but the truth remained: Information could be molded. It could be handed around, like money. It could be used for bait.

"I used the word *murder* before, and that can be misleading. What we have is a killing."

He explained to her the three main concepts involved—malice aforethought, depraved heart, heat of passion—and let the terms sink in. They were the juicy words, the ones juries loved. Then he ran down how impossible it would be for a jury to think Raymond Carlisle's killing deserved anything but the most severe charge, the harshest penalty. Shot in the back—malice. Followed into his yard—aforethought.

"Sometimes people think they can lower the charge to manslaughter. Heat of passion. It usually means the victim did something or said something so vile, so degrading, any reasonable person would be unable to control his rage. The law is surprisingly wise in this regard, Mrs. Thigpen." Remembering her near-silent prayer of just moments before, he added, "It recognizes the weakness in our natures."

Her eyes flared. Bingo.

"We lose it sometimes. Work ourselves up and can't work ourselves back down. All because some jerk pushed too far. A depraved heart is not an angry heart, it's an empty heart. That's why manslaughter, a crime of passion, is the lesser crime. In theory, anyway. But again, Mrs. Thigpen, nothing's as simple as it ought to be. The law demands there not be a cooling-off period if a defendant's going to claim heat of passion. If there's time to cool off, any time at all, then there's no real heat."

"Cool off," Sarina murmured, trying to fashion the phrase into some form of good news. Her eyes narrowed again. "Time—"

"You got time to cool off, Mrs. Thigpen, bye-bye manslaughter. You follow a man and shoot him in the back, that's bye-bye murder two. Which pretty much boxes the thing in. Murder one. In a death penalty state."

Sarina shook her head. "Follow? You said time—"

"Now, I admit, anything can happen. We've got a saying: Inside the courtroom, the rules of gravity no longer apply. And that's true twice over inside the jury room. Only takes one juror. Feel a little twinge of doubt. Feel a little pity. The number of hung juries is up, way up. Not just that, it's happening most in trials of young Black men, and it's Black women who are hanging those juries. So there's always a shot. Except, well, I feel obliged to tell you, every case where you've got a hold-out juror? Case gets retried and the second trial results in conviction. Hung juries just slow the process down, make it more expensive, they don't stop it. Besides which, capital cases here draw their jury pools mostly from north county. Which means white people. I'm not saying it's right, Mrs. Thigpen, I'm just saying that's the situation."

"Time," Sarina said again, this time loudly, as though the concept hovering just outside her grasp had finally come to bear. "Cooling-off period. You said you had an eyewitness. Then you talk about time. Time between what and what? This eyewitness, what did he see?"

They'd reached the police station. Stluka pulled the car into the public lot, so they could take Sarina in through the front.

"I'm not at liberty to divulge what the witness did or didn't see." Inwardly, Murchison cringed at how lame it sounded. "And since time is short, there's one more thing I need to explain to you before we go in. One more term. Not a legal term, a street term. I don't know, maybe you already know it. The term is *juice*."

Sarina had resumed the pose she'd struck upon first entering the car: handbag tight to her waist, small, strong hands clenching the strap. Back where we started, Murchison thought.

"You work the street, Mrs. Thigpen, like your son, you gotta have juice. Gotta know who else has it. In particular, you gotta know who among your so-called friends has it, who doesn't, who wants it, how bad they want it."

Sarina's defiance melted a little. The fear returned to her eyes.

"Think about all those other young men working that street corner with your son."

"Street corner?"

Stluka groaned and looked at his watch. Murchison said, "Your son was spotted downtown, working a corner with maybe half a dozen other young men."

"Downtown?"

Stluka said, "Peddling them powerful powders, ma'am. As he has been known to do."

"I don't believe that."

"Eyewitness," Stluka intoned, his hands thrumming a little tom-tom on the steering wheel. "Hate to keep bringing that up, inconvenient and all, but—"

"You still haven't told me—"

"The witnesses saw what they saw, Mrs. Thigpen." Murchison was irritated—with both her and his partner. "The point I want to make before we take you in to speak with your son is this: Which one of those other young men has got juice?"

Sarina stared.

"Put yourself in their shoes, Mrs. Thigpen. We're going to be bringing down here every single one of them. The guys working that corner with your son. Most are in trouble already, and they're going to be trying to buy their way out of it. There's eight times as many Black men in prison as there are in college, four times as many for drugs as whites. You think people are pissed off about that? John Q. Public, he's delighted. Crime's down. He thinks, Three strikes? Hell, let's make it two. Make it one. And your son's so-called friends, dragged in here— it's already happening, Mrs. Thigpen, right now, this minute—they'll know all that. If they don't know it coming in, they'll catch on quick. I guarantee it. And the writing on the wall, it's gonna say: Time to get a little juice. Time to say, 'You know that old man got popped on the hill? I may have something to say on that.' "

"On the hill. But you said Arlie was *downtown.*"

"One of your son's pals, he's looking at hard time, years of it. No way out. Except your son. He's got your son to hand up."

"No," Sarina said, shaking her head violently.

"He's got juice."

"This is wrong. This is evil."

Stluka blew out an annoyed gust of air, opened his door, and said over his shoulder, "You want evil, we'll take you to the freezer, let you talk it over with Mr. Carlisle."

"You can't do this."

"You willing to bet your son's life on that?"

"Your son's friends," Murchison pressed, "they get brought in— and like I said, that's already in play, Mrs. Thigpen—you really think they're gonna be looking out for your son?"

Tears welled in Sarina's eyes. She sat transfixed.

"No taint to snitching like there used to be, Mrs. Thigpen. Now it's just one more way to look out for number one. They don't even call it snitching anymore. They call it getting down first. Your son's friends—maybe one, maybe more—somebody's gonna have his ass in a jam and he won't think twice. He's gonna get down first. To hell with the snitch jacket. Man's gotta do what he's gotta do. Get himself some juice and walk on out into the light of day. And your son will be what's left behind."

Sarina reached for the door handle. "Let me see Arlie." She wiped her face with one hand, fumbled to get the door open with the other. "I want to see my son."

Murchison got out, hurried to open her door. "I'm sorry if all this upsets you, Mrs. Thigpen, but I'm just trying to lay it out for you. Murder two? Manslaughter? Forget about it. Not with this set of facts. Not unless your son wants to plead out."

"And if he's innocent? Do you even care?"

Stluka glanced around, to see if anyone was watching. The parking lot was empty. Beyond it, the station house glowed in the early morning haze.

"Your son wants to plead," Murchison said, "there's always room to maneuver."

Sarina took a trembling breath. Murchison waited. Just beyond him, Stluka stood there with arms crossed, wearing an expression that betrayed his thoughts, which were: Go ahead. Cry. Feel fucking sorry for yourself.

"I'd bet good money, Mrs. Thigpen, it wasn't even Arlie's idea."

It took a second, but Sarina glanced up. She'd caught on. A way out?

"There's somebody else," Murchison continued, edging closer to her. "Let's suppose. Somebody else on that corner, somebody who saw Arlie and Mr. Carlisle. They argued, Mrs. Thigpen. Nasty. Loud. Physical. Arlie got tired of Mr. Carlisle's abuse and shoved him off the corner, told him to go home. Then this somebody else, the one whose name we don't know, he stayed behind with Arlie and started to push. Mess with Arlie's manhood. 'You ain't gonna put up with that? Settle the score. Shut him up.' And this somebody else, he takes out the gun."

Murchison reached into his jacket, removed a ballpoint pen, took Sarina's wrist, and pressed it into her hand.

"And he says, 'Are you a man or not?' And all your son's so-called friends are there, waiting. Like they're banging him in. But we need Arlie to tell us that."

He let go of Sarina's wrist, but her arm remained fixed in mid-air, as though hung there by wire. She looked at the pen, then let it drop to the ground, lifting her eyes to Murchison. He stepped back, extending his arm as though to say, *It's time.*

"A name, Mrs. Thigpen. Tell your son what we need is a name."

Murchison delivered Sarina into the interview room with her son. He and Stluka then went around and listened in from the monitoring box in the corridor between interview rooms. What they heard was twelve minutes of motherly pleas on one end, on the other angry protestations of innocence. They watched as, on the video screen, mother and son clutched hands, they wept, the mother prayed out loud as her son begged her not to.

Murchison took heart that most of what he'd told Sarina Thigpen had sunk in. She begged Arlie to give them a name, pass the blame to someone who deserved it, spare himself, but Arlie's defiance was absolute. He had nothing to do with Strong Carlisle's death and knew no one who did. Watching him, Murchison wondered at the young man's seamless air of conviction, unable to tell if it came from the heart or just practice. Finally Arlie got up, faced the corner where the camera hung, and slapped his hands against the wall, shouting, "Take her home! Hey! Take her home!"

Once outside the interview room, Sarina turned on Murchison. "What on God's earth have we done," she said, "to make you hate us so?"

"Nobody hates your son, Mrs. Thigpen. I want to help him. But I can't do that as long—"

"As long as he won't confess to what—"

Stluka cut her off. "Your son, those scars around his eye, how'd he get those?"

Sarina recoiled from him. "What are you trying—"

"Face get pushed through a window? And where were you when that happened?"

The rest was garbled screaming, conducted while those in earshot prairie-dogged, heads bobbing out from doorways to watch. Holmes bolted out from the squad room, took one look, then stepped forward to steer Sarina away as Murchison tried to do the same with Stluka, pressing his hands to his shoulders to ease him toward the detective bureau doorway. Stluka was having none of it, not yet. Before Murchison could talk him down, though, an officer called out from the doorway leading out to the lobby.

"Detective Murchison? Someone up front. Said urgent."

Stluka used the distraction as an excuse, finally, to collect himself. "Go on," he muttered. "It's over here." He straightened his tie, shook his head in one last show of triumphant disgust, then headed into the detective bureau. Around the corner, Holmes pinned Sarina Thigpen against the wall, collecting her between his arms, his face in close as he soothed her with an onslaught of consoling words: "I understand . . . I know . . . I realize . . ."

Murchison turned away, headed out toward the lobby. His mind rattled with things he wished he'd said, other things he regretted saying, botched questions, bad guesses, assumptions gone wrong. That was a killing for you—one man lies dead and everyone else gets stupid or goes nuts. You really did have to wonder sometimes who had it worse.

Past the final door, he greeted two women, both middle-aged. One white, one Black. It took a moment, but he realized he knew who the Black woman was.

Murchison guessed she was forty-five, fifty tops, but she could pass for mid-thirties. Cinnamon skin, high cheekbones, almond eyes. No more than a hint of crow's-feet edging those eyes, same at the lips. Her long hair, coarse and straight, was a coppery brown, slightly darker than her skin, swept back and tied into a high ponytail that emphasized her brow. On a white woman, the ponytail would have looked too cute, phony young. On this woman, the effect was simple and prim, like her clothes: white blouse with a Peter Pan collar, navy cardigan, gray wool skirt, modest black flats.

Felicia Marchand. Toby's mother. Strong Carlisle's secret sweetheart.

It was the white woman, though, who stepped forward. She was a little zaftig, but voluptuous, not matronly. Murchison felt embarrassed by his arousal. No makeup, but her skin was flushed and her eyes didn't need it—they were a stark clear blue with thick lashes. She carried a briefcase but wore sweats and her black hair was finger-combed with renegade strands everywhere. She'd shot up from a deep sleep at the sound of the phone, he guessed, dragged herself out from under the covers, thrown on whatever lay tangled beside the bed (he pictured her hopping one-legged as she pulled on her socks). Strangely, the dishevelment made her more attractive; you could almost smell the sleep on her skin, and the next picture that came to mind was her crawling right back into bed. Luxuriant, happy, naked. The Queen of Naps.

She held out a business card.

"My name is Tina Navigato. I'm a lawyer. I've been hired by Toby Marchand's family to represent him. Could I see him?"

Murchison took the card and read it. Her office was local, but he'd never heard of her. The areas of specialty listed beneath her name were estate planning and probate litigation.

"Come on back."

He gestured for the desk officer to buzz them through, then led the two women down the long hall past dark offices into the squad room and, beyond it, the interview room in which Toby Marchand waited. Murchison opened the door and stepped back, letting the two women pass. He waited in the doorway, watching as the young man— rumpled, stiff, bleary—glanced up and spotted his mother. His eyes knotted, then his whole face caved in. She rushed toward him, wrapped his head in her arms, and pressed it tight to her midriff, stroking his hair, weeping herself now as she murmured, "Oh, child, my Lord, dear God . . ." Toby's hands clung to her back, squeezing the white wool of her cardigan. Tina Navigato glanced away, tucking a strand of hair behind her ear as she drew back toward the door and gestured that she wanted to speak with Murchison alone.

"If you're not going to charge him, I'd appreciate it if you'd let him go home with his mother."

"He can't leave town." Murchison pulled the door shut. Cops in the squad room were peering out at them.

"His mother lives in Oakland."

"I'll be clearing the scene in a bit. He can go back there."

"That's not his home."

"He lives with his mother?"

"No. No. She just thinks it would be best—"

"What about the white girl? Ms. Lazarenko."

Her eyelids narrowed. "I don't know who you mean."

"Your client's girlfriend? Discovered at the scene. She's at the hospital now, not doing so great."

She glanced away, puffed her cheeks, then let out little spurts of air. A pensive, self-effacing gesture, childlike, strangely charming.

"I need to speak with my client, obviously."

"Obviously."

Her eyes didn't seem quite as lovely now. The blue in them, the cold came out. "Are we getting off to a bad start here, Detective?"

"Came out wrong. Sorry."

"As for the house, his father's, I mean. After what happened, good God. Could *you* stay there?"

"We keep a list of local motels. Hotels."

"These people aren't made of money." Even her voice was frosty. "You do intend to release him."

"With the understanding he doesn't leave town. He skips, I'll swear out the warrant myself."

She looked away again, shaking her head. "You can't honestly believe he had anything to do with his father's murder."

Murchison smiled. Father, he thought. Came right out, like the honest-to-God truth. Probate lawyer. "The investigation," he said, "is continuing."

He opened the door for her again and, without comment, she slipped past him. Closing the door, he turned to find Stluka coming up from behind. He'd calmed down, and a familiar wickedness lit his eyes. His old self.

"That broad in the sweats—she a dyke, or just trying it on for size?"

Across the room, Holmes draped a willowy arm across the shoulders of Sarina Thigpen, soothing her as, with the gentlest pressure, he bent down to ease her along the corridor toward the lobby. Another officer brought Arlie out for his return to the isolation of the holding cells downstairs. Sarina, feet pointing one way, head spinning back, spotted her son and then her whole body pivoted. She reached out across the intervening space as Holmes collected her short, strong body in those arms of his, leaning down still farther to console her in whispers.

Murchison handed Tina Navigato's card to Stluka. "She's a lawyer."

Stluka took it, read, then his jaw dropped. *"Probate litigation?"*

Arlie Thigpen, hands cuffed behind his back, bristled at Stluka's voice and glared back over his shoulder, one last look of defiance before passing through the doorway to the stairs.

"I need to work on the murder book." Murchison turned toward the detective bureau. "Lot to sort through. Don't want to overlook anything."

Stluka was right behind him. "This kid's already angling for what he's gonna inherit?"

"I think his mother's the one who hired her."

"No," Stluka said. "No. This means something."

"I didn't say it didn't. I said—"

"Our instincts were solid the first time, Murch. Inside the house?" He tapped the business card against his knuckles. "Fuck me. We spent the last couple hours looking at the wrong son. So-called son. Whatever."

Part II

Rip, Rig, and Panic

10

———◆———

Richard Ferry had a sense of humor, but he seldom laughed. Too many times, he'd seen men use a laugh as a kind of bluster, a way to pretend they weren't scared. Even men who knew they were about to die. He sometimes wondered if that wasn't why jokes were invented in the first place—as a device, a probe, a way to expose a man's defenses. Make him laugh.

He sat in the rearward employee lounge of an empty suite of offices in an industrial park just off the Napa Highway, a mile north of Rio Mirada. The room was painted in earth tones and furnished with a table, two swivel chairs, a sink, a small fridge, and a microwave, plus a portable TV Ferry had bought himself. He'd lived there secretly for nearly two months, sleeping on the carpeted floor, sponge-bathing before dawn in the Men's down the hall. He'd been given access by the real estate outfit that leased the offices—in the present case, leased to the phony plumbing company Ferry would identify as his employer if anyone bothered to ask.

Presently, he sat with a young man named Manny, whom he'd found and recruited for this particular job, exerting no small effort doing so. Given recent events, the kid resembled nothing so much as the most regrettable mistake Ferry had ever made.

"Look on the bright side, I guess," Ferry said, shooting the boy one of his mirthless smiles. "Get sent back to stir, you won't be just the big tubby firebug everybody lines up to punk. You'll be a bona fide killa."

"That's not funny." Manny pressed an ice pack against his eye. "And no way I'm going back to stir."

He was a tall, soft, hulking boy—a man actually, but his mind had never quite made the passage—part white, part Black, the rest Filipino, a walking-talking totem of the U.S. Navy presence at Subic. It gave him one of those go-figure ethnic looks.

"I like that. Power of positive thinking."

"Stop with the jokes already. This is serious."

"Gee, you think?" Ferry checked the gun Manny wanted him to get rid of. The "weapon," as it would now be known. A Smithy .357, two live rounds, four spent. Casings still in the cylinder. Plus a box of hollow-points to dispose of. "Some poor old fool, doesn't haven't jack to do with why we're here, takes four in the back. Every cop in town looking for the guy responsible. What's so serious?"

"It wasn't my fault."

Ferry slammed the cylinder shut. "You need some original material."

"I'm asking for your help."

"No, you're making excuses."

"Motherfucker hit me."

Ferry shook his head in dismay. "See what I mean?"

Withdrawing the ice pack, Manny fingered the cold, wet skin left behind. "Yeah, well, I don't make the fries."

"What the hell does that mean?"

"You're Mr. Fix-it." He pressed the ice pack to his face again. "Fix it."

"Come again?"

"Nothing."

"You sure?"

Manny made a whimpering sigh and leaned over to check his reflection in the chrome of the sink. The eye had swollen shut. Bruising rimmed the socket.

Ferry said, "Think you've iced that thing enough?"

"Still all swollen."

"Yeah, well, you apply cold right off, might've had a shot at that. How many hours has it been?"

Manny shrugged and turned back to the portable TV. It was tuned to a Mexican channel, *Televisión Azteca*. This particular program was part of a genre known as *Los Mascarados*, which Manny loved. The heroes were masked wrestlers who served as vigilante avengers. The drama tended toward juvenile, the plots spectacularly stupid—almost as contrived as the wrestling scenes interspersed with the action. If one of the *mascarados* lost in the ring, he was obliged to remove his mask forever. It was considered a great disgrace, being unmasked.

The kid was born Manuel Turpin and by his eighteenth birthday had accomplished even less than your average blubbery, broken-home American teen. One night, that all changed. Using nothing more ambitious than gasoline in five-gallon cans and standard matchbook fuses, he set fire to seven houses under construction on the outskirts of Portland, in a suburban-sprawl subdivision near where his mother's latest excuse for a boyfriend lived.

Manny was hard pressed to explain even to himself why he'd torched the buildings—only the framing and roof and subfloor were in place, but that meant exposed wood and plenty of cross-draft. Basically, he just liked watching them burn. He felt happy for once, freed of his shame as he stood there in the night, listening as the wood shuddered and screamed like an animal, the flames rippling up the four-by-fours with a palpable hunger—the fury of it, the quivering rays of heat, the mysterious sense of life—all set against the vast dark backdrop of Mount Hood.

It took six weeks to trace it back to him, by which time half the local papers, abetted by the wise use crowd and nameless law enforcement sources, had all but convicted a local cabal of militants, radical anarchist ecotage types. Manny, luxuriating in the wrong headedness of the blame, nonetheless came to find the rhetoric alluring. Especially that one word, repeated like a drumbeat: *terror.* It appealed to him in a way he could explain no better than he could the erotic rush he'd felt, standing out there in the darkness, eye-to-eye with the fire.

I am an instrument of terror.

It gave substance to the emotions roiling inside, a sense of himself as one of a kind. That new sense of calling, it gave him something solid to hold on to when two special agents—tough-talking Mormons wearing flannel suits and clip-on ties—showed up at the house. His mother and her boyfriend had headed off for an impromptu weekend alone on the Columbia River. The FBI claimed an anonymous neighbor had called in the tip, but Manny would always suspect it was his mother's boyfriend who'd dropped the dime.

Virtually the first thing asked was, "Do you, Manuel—can we call you Manuel?—do you have or have you ever had any affiliations with the environmental underground?"

Manny couldn't say yes fast enough. So scared he couldn't stop crying, he secretly hoped, once his name went public, the movement would step forward and claim him as one of their own. They'd done it before; he'd read about it. But the movement disavowed him instantly. The U.S. Attorney, though, was three steps ahead on that one.

"The radical underground prides itself," the government's press release said, "on its clandestine communication channels. The suspect himself affirms his connection to environmental terror groups. Those groups have not offered one shred of evidence to disprove that fact."

The perfect ploy—can't prove a negative and can't disprove the possible. And so Manny got to be who he claimed to be and was promptly despised by all. Meanwhile, prosecution and prison inflicted their customary indignities. He did thirty months, reentering society punch-drunk, flinchy, shabbily tattooed.

Unmasked.

Ferry took a sip of orange juice from a carton he'd bought at a nearby minimart, wiping his lips with the back of his hand. "How many punked-out jailbird junkies does it take to screw up a perfectly good plan?"

"He *hit* me."

"He was old. If you'd bothered to look, probably could've seen the punch coming from, I dunno, Mars?"

"You weren't there."

Ferry rummaged in the paper sack at his feet, broke off a piece of an apple fritter he'd bought at the same minimart, tossed it in his mouth, and chased it with another swallow of OJ. "You're absolutely right. I wasn't there. Which brings us back to my favorite question— why were you?"

Ferry had identified the kid, researched him, tracked him down. He'd come across the Portland arson story in an Internet posting. First stop, the mother. She'd married the boyfriend by that time and was apparently unaware, unconvinced, or unconcerned that her new husband had likely been responsible for her son's imprisonment. Ferry pretended to be a private investigator working for an insurance company that had a claimant pretending his fire had been set by their son. From what Ferry could tell, the mother—source of Manny's Black and Filipino genes—had more vested in her latest marriage than her son. And to his new stepfather, a cracker from the Cascades, Manny meant less than nothing. Like everyone else in Manny's life, they couldn't disclaim him fast enough. But as Ferry thanked them for their time and got ready to go, the mother stood up with him and said, "I'll walk you out."

In the front yard, she confided that a few months earlier she'd received a one-page letter from Manny, postmarked from a town in Northern California called Susanville. "There's a prison there," she added. "Basically, he asked for money." As she turned to go back inside the house, she added, "I'd appreciate it if you wouldn't tell Manuel I gave you that information."

The trail in California proved complicated. Manny wasn't in custody at the Susanville Correctional Center and never had been. He'd taken half a course for big rig drivers at the local community college, then disappeared. Given the fact that he could be anywhere, Ferry decided to employ the help of law enforcement. It continued to amaze him how trusting some cops could be once they recognized you as a former member of the tribe.

He told them he was working for the family, trying to get the young man home for a little tough love. The cops he befriended confided that Manny's name was related to arson fires throughout timber country. In Susanville alone, pipe bombs took out a log loader at a chip mill and a hijacked truck had been set afire. But Manny's name came up across the state in Arcata, too, where a tree farm run by the Humboldt State agriculture department had gone up in flames. Then back to the foothills, a town called Quincy, where they wanted him for questioning in a torch job involving two more lumber trucks in a storage yard. Despite the legwork, the pattern gratified Ferry. Showed the kid still wanted to be known as the next great solo eco-warrior. And he had the good sense to keep moving.

In the end, it all turned on the fact that a Plumas County deputy Ferry'd befriended stuck his neck out. The kid got picked up with no ID on a drunk and disorderly out near Antelope Lake. The deputy suspected this sulky mound of crossbreed lard was Manny Turpin and for a slight fee was willing to let Ferry spring him, nothing more than a fine to pay and a promise to get the kid out of the county for good.

Once Ferry had Manny in hand, he drove him to a deserted trailer in the woods where he'd been crashing. Manny picked up his stuff, all of which fit in a knapsack; then it was south, fast, out of the sheriff's jurisdiction. In Downieville, Ferry sat the kid down for breakfast at a knotty pine diner. The kid ate like a pound mutt while Ferry let him know the extent of his good fortune. If he'd been made, which would have been assured once his prints got back-checked, he would have faced investigations, charges, and most likely convictions in at least three locales.

"Thank you," Manny mumbled, hunched over his plate.

"Not gratitude I'm after," Ferry told him. "I'm interested whether you want to get serious." He said he worked for a certain party paying well to stage a particularly dramatic event. "I'll tell you what the target is at the proper time. You can understand my reluctance at this point, I'm sure."

When Manny smelled setup, Ferry explained that if all he wanted was Manny in jail, he'd have left him where he was. And he wasn't using Manny to get to anyone else; they wouldn't be bringing anyone else on board. "Just the two of us." That, and the naming of sums, proved to be all it took to recruit the kid. What was the alternative? How far did he expect to get if he just walked out?

On the drive down to Rio Mirada, the kid opened up, told the sorry tale of his life up to that point. As though to impress Ferry with his competence, he confided that his whole time in prison, all he'd done, besides get hassled or get high, was bone up on arson. Getting paid to set fires? Tell him where to sign.

If anything, it was hard to hold him back. And that, combined with the timing problem, almost caused the whole thing to fall apart.

Ferry had hoped to find the kid, keep tabs on him, then bring him on board when the moment was right. Then Manny ended up a print check away from long-term custody. It forced his hand. But it was weeks too soon. Stuck in Rio Mirada, the kid had nothing but time on his hands. You couldn't keep him locked up, though Ferry'd been tempted. He'd suggested once they room together here, in the office, but the kid freaked, spewing the most wildly paranoid rant Ferry'd ever heard. The prison thing, he guessed, and backed off. Rather than lose him altogether, he'd bargained the kid down to just staying in daily touch in return for an allowance. Out on his own, though, the boy went wild.

Thank God arson's so hard to prove, Ferry thought, more than once. Manny, admittedly a first-rate sneak, had set nearly twenty fires around Rio Mirada in six weeks' time. Cars mostly, SUVs and high-end sedans, a whole carport of them once when the chance arose. A few Dumpster fires, too, downtown. It had stirred up something of a local panic, and Ferry had considered cutting the kid loose. At this particular moment, that seemed like an opportunity missed.

But Ferry had latched onto Manny because he recognized what a curious little gem he was—precious not despite but because of his many flaws. His self-pitying pride, his obsessiveness, his lack of friends. Ferry would never find a replacement half as perfect, not given his time frame for the job.

If only an obsession with fire had been his sole vice. The kid still had his prison jones—nothing worse than a maintenance habit, a morning nod at a shooting gallery, another about five at night, it kept him even keel most of the day. But to feed it, he needed to connect, and the people he'd connected with had steered him to an empty house up on St. Martin's Hill, telling him he could crash there for a sum. And so Manny ended up in a deserted Victorian, right next door to his future victim.

"You stalked her, the little white beauty you saw visiting up there."

"I *followed* her. To the club."

"We think we like her, do we, Manuel?"

"Shut up."

"Then you followed her back and waxed the old dog you thought was boning her."

"I didn't—Jesus. You're not listening."

"Sure I'm listening. Especially to the parts you leave out."

"It's like, the way you think, the fight at the club never happened."

"Kinda wish it hadn't, you want the truth."

Manny fingered his eye again. "Old man just sailed into the bar? Swung around this white guy he'd been all friendly with not ten minutes before. Nailed him. Boom! It was crazy. Thought I was doing the old fool a favor—"

"Doing the girl a favor, you mean." Impress her, Ferry thought. Who *was* that masked man?

"Lock him up, get him away, before, you know, the crowd got at him."

"The crowd, it got at him anyway, didn't it? With you holding him."

"Not my fault."

"God forbid you just butt out."

"I loosen my hold? Old dude spins around and clocks me in the eye. Kabam! Worse, I'm 'zontal, he slams his heel down hard. I mean, damn hard."

And disgraced you in front of your secret darling, Ferry thought.

Manny felt along his rib cage, winced. "You fight like that, you got what's coming."

"Now you really sound like a punk."

"If I was a punk I wouldn't be sitting here. I'd be giving you up as fast as they'd let me."

Ferry rose from his chair, crossed over to where Manny sat. He nodded at the boy's ice pack. "Can't be much more than water in there now." He gestured toward the fridge. "Got another tray of cubes in the freezer. Give it to me, I'll fill it up."

He held out his hand. Manny's good eye twitched as he thought about it.

"I thought you said it wouldn't do any good. Too late."

"Seems to make you feel better. Come on, give it."

Ferry wiggled his fingers. Finally, Manny let go of the ice pack. Ferry took it, raised it to his ear, shook. "Just like I thought. All water." He smiled. Then he reared back, slapped Manny's face with the ice pack as hard as he could, did it again, fast, grabbing the kid by the hair, pulling up so the kid couldn't hide, harder, flogging him. Manny broke free and lunged from his chair to the floor and tried to fight off the blows with his hands. The bag broke, water flew everywhere, and then the damp cloth was like a little whip, the sound a low, fierce whistle in the air.

Ferry threw the bag down finally. "Old man kicked you? Kick you here?" He aimed for the rib cage. "Kick you here?" The kidneys. Manny curled up into a ball, arms shielding his head, knees tucked up to protect the stomach, the groin. He lay there perfectly still, taking it like he had in prison, just the sound of his breath leaking through his teeth as he panted.

"How stupid could you be?" Ferry shouted. "Tell me, please, tell me you didn't have your car parked out front when you shot the old fuck."

"No." A small voice, the fat boy, the raped boy, deep inside himself.

"Everybody in the neighborhood, they hear the shots, they look out, there you are."

"No."

"You better hope to God not."

"I parked down the hill, block and a half away. I waited next door."

"Lying in wait? You simple shit."

"I got away."

"They saw you."

"I ran. I'm here."

Ferry collapsed into his chair. His chest heaved as he wiped his hands on his pant legs. "See what you make me do?" The oldest reproach.

They stayed like that—Manny on the floor, curled up, head buried deep within his arms. Ferry watched him from his chair, skin damp with sweat. An electric clock above the doorway hummed. Manny spoke first.

"I'm gonna need to leave town."

"Talk like that, I'll kill you right here."

"I can't just—"

"You think I'm not wise to you? Finally get a chance at some real money, not this firebug stuff you're used to, you can't fuck it up fast enough. Because you're scared. You know what a chickenshit loser you really are and you're scared. So you pull a weapons-grade fuckup, thinking it's your way out. Think again, you little piss pot. I've shelled out plenty to you already. Bought you that fucking car."

"I'll pay it back."

"No, no. Like *way* too late for that."

"I can get the money."

"Shut up!" Ferry picked up his chair by the arms, slammed it down again. "Hear me? Fucking shit weasel—you listen to me. Think I'm Mr. Fix-it? Well, here's how things get fixed: plan gets sped up."

"Like when?"

"Like tonight, if I can figure it out."

"That's crazy."

"Tell me about it."

Manny stared out between his elbows. The bruised eye wouldn't open. "Richard, please. The guy fucked up my eye. I can't see. I'm no help to you."

At that, Ferry laughed.

11

———◆———

Toby couldn't dispel a vague suspicion as Tina Navigato took control with the police. Not that he wasn't grateful, and there was no questioning her competence. But she hadn't brought up money yet and where she came from proved curious.

She'd been contacted by his mother. The bigger surprise, though, was that she'd also been his father's lawyer. When he asked if that didn't pose a conflict, her representing both of them, father and son—victim and suspect—she responded, "You're innocent. Besides, I'm no longer your father's lawyer. Agency terminates at death." The last part was one of about five things she'd said that stopped him cold.

She recited for him what she described as the same disclaimer she'd given his father. There were several first-rate African American estate planning and probate laywers in town—all smart, at least two smarter than her, one way smarter—not to mention criminal defense lawyers, and she would gladly provide referrals and harbor no ill will. Toby responded by asking what his father had said when she'd posed the same question.

"Your father," she said somewhat sheepishly, shooting a glance toward Toby's mother, "said that, frankly, he got a silly little thrill—his words, I remember them well—having a white lawyer. Especially a white woman lawyer."

With respect to the murder investigation, she added that she had, some five years back, worked for a small boutique criminal defense firm, specializing in prosecutorial abuse cases and death penalty writs. Though that no longer constituted her specialty—she'd moved on when her mentor, the firm's managing partner, died at age forty-six from a brain tumor—she still knew the lay of the land. It didn't take a genius to infer from the way she told this part of the story that her mentor had in fact been her lover.

For a number of reasons, some he only dimly understood, Toby liked her. He felt something less than a silly little thrill, but he liked her. He prayed to God that didn't mean keeping her on was crazy.

He sat on her right side, his mother her left. Across the table, Murchison and Stluka sagged a little in their chairs, arms crossed, ties tugged down from their collars. A vexed exhaustion hazed their eyes. Toby could sympathize. He chose not to.

"I've had the opportunity to confer with my client, and there appear to be several areas that could use some clarification. You realize I'm under no obligation to make him available for questioning, and I have associates who'd consider me a fool for even going this far. But Toby has insisted I tell you: He did not kill his father. And the victim was, yes, his father. Perhaps that's the first confusion we should deal with."

Like everything else about her, Toby thought, her voice was an enigma; a sexual huskiness softened the edges of her words. She pulled a burgundy three-part legal folder from her briefcase and withdrew from it a thin stack of documents clasped together.

"Mr. Carlisle came to me two weeks ago concerning a problem with his sister. He'd received a tax notice from the county concerning his property, and only then learned that title had been transferred without his knowledge or consent into joint tenancy with that sister, whose name is Veronique Edwards. I have a copy of the quitclaim here from the Recorder." She found the deed in the stack of papers and spun it around so the detectives could see. "First, observe the date. Mr. Carlisle was in the hospital, heavily sedated at that time."

"His kidney surgery," Murchison said, picking up the deed. "Day of?"

"Day after. The second thing to notice is the signature. It's a reasonably good forgery, but the first name gives it away. Mr. Carlisle's *y* had a distinctively large below-the-line flourish."

"Low impulse control," Stluka said, glancing over Murchison's shoulder.

"It's notarized." Murchison handed the document back.

"I've spoken to the notary. She works at the same title company where Ms. Edwards works. She says a Black male adult who showed her Mr. Carlisle's driver's license and seemed to bear a resemblance to the photograph came in with Ms. Edwards and executed the deed."

"Her husband," Toby's mother said. Her voice betrayed a bitterness long in the making. "His name is Exeter."

"We don't know it was Mr. Edwards for certain," Tina advised. "Not yet."

"It's not the first time they've pulled something like this," Felicia said.

"Not like *this*," Toby countered. "When Pops was on the road, pay the gas bill, deposit a check, sure."

"Maybe you see something I don't," Murchison said, directing his words to Tina, "but I don't get how this settles anything about your client being the victim's son."

"Mr. Carlisle intended to leave his house to Toby. It's why he added the practice room addition—not just for his own band, but Toby and his bands, too. And he knew it's not income, but assets, passed on through generations, that secure your place in the middle class. He wanted that for his son. He also knew the poor chances involved in trying to qualify for, let alone afford, a mortgage on a musician's income. Especially here in the Bay Area."

Toby had already heard this recitation and still felt stunned by it. To learn like this, under these circumstances, that his father had intended the house to be his, it seemed a kind of hex. And when he thought of his father's abuse right up until the very end, his relentless unforgiving disapproval—tempered now forever by this secret generosity. How like him, Toby thought. How like him to devise a way of sharing his love that would, at the same time, perfect my guilt.

"He told you this young man was his son," Murchison said, nodding at Toby but not looking at him.

"He made it explicit, in the estate planning documents he had me prepare." Tina produced next from the clipped stack of papers a will, an advance health care directive, and a durable power of attorney for property and personal affairs. "If you look at the will, Article One, 'Introductory Provisions,' you can see under the second paragraph he identified Toby Marchand as his only child, and that all references to 'his child' in the will are to Toby."

Stluka picked up the power of attorney, shook it, thumbed through the pages to the back. "This isn't signed."

"Neither is this," Murchison said, checking the second-to-last page of the will.

"No," Tina said, faltering a little. "He had an appointment to come in to execute them this coming week."

"But he was killed before he could do that," Felicia said.

"It does, perhaps, speak to motive," Tina said.

Toby cringed. He didn't want to save himself by letting this lawyer, a white woman, cast blame inside the family. And yet he hadn't tried to stop her.

"Mr. Carlisle confront his sister over the forged deed?" Murchison asked.

"I can't say," Tina replied. "Judging from what I know of his character—"

"Did he?" Murchison posed it to Toby.

Toby snapped to. "If he did, he didn't tell me."

"Which would not have been unusual," Tina snuck in.

"Raymond to a T," Felicia affirmed.

"I'm lost," Stluka said, tossing the power of attorney back onto the table.

"Perhaps," Tina said, "I haven't explained it as clearly as I might."

"Not the problem," Stluka said. "This old man gets cheated out of full title to his own house but doesn't tell his much-beloved son? His chosen heir? This from a guy who spared no words, the way I hear it. Got into three fights the same night."

"He'd been drinking," Toby said.

"Not every day, all day. Am I wrong?"

"Raymond, for all his windiness," Felicia said, "was a very private man about his personal affairs."

"He never—and I mean *never*—mentioned any of this stuff to me." Toby nodded toward the documents on the table. "I would've been dumbstruck if he had."

Murchison leaned in toward the table, reaching out his hand to suggest they all slow down. "Something we've heard," he began guardedly, "is that it was common knowledge that Mr. Carlisle accepted Toby as his son. Even though, in fact, he wasn't."

"Common knowledge?" Tina said it sarcastically. "And you *heard* that from—"

"Veronique." Toby's mother rolled her eyes. "That has to be Veronique."

"No," Murchison said, "it wasn't. We haven't spoken to Mr. Carlisle's sister yet. We got this information in follow-up interviews with a few of the neighbors. And we also heard the only reason Mr. Carlisle accepted Toby as his son was to win you back, Ms. Marchand."

All eyes turned to Felicia. She sat there frozen.

Tina tried to reassert control. "I only brought this up to clear away a confusion. If paternity is relevant to Mr. Carlisle's murder—"

"Wait," Felicia said. "No. It's time this got settled." She met Murchison's stare. "It is astonishing to me that rumors so old, so wrong, so mean-spirited, could spring back to life at a time like—" Her voice caught. Tina reached over to touch her arm, but she waved the gesture off. "All right then." She squared herself in her seat. "This is not easy for me. I do not enjoy recounting my failings. I've made my peace about what I did. But I understand. You need to know. Well, then—"

She lowered her eyes and folded her hands as though in a silent, preliminary prayer. Toby felt an immediate desire to go to her, offer consolation, and at the same time gave in to a curious refusal to move.

"I was married at the time I met Raymond. Separated from my husband, yes, but still married. The Oakland Church Council had a citywide benefit. Raymond was with Johnny Otis at the time, and they headlined the show. Raymond knew a woman in my choir. She introduced us. You already seem to know that Raymond had a strong personality. He could be persuasive. And charming. And generous. I was lonely."

She stopped. Tina said softly, "I think that's—"

"Of course, of course, of course, of course I got pregnant. But not in my wildest imaginings did I expect the response I got from Raymond. He asked me to divorce my husband, get it final, then marry him. He'd be proud to raise the child, my two daughters, too. I could not do that. There was fourteen years between us. And Raymond, well, Raymond was Raymond. Exactly and forever who he was. I couldn't change him and I couldn't live with him. So I called my husband. I cried on the phone, told him I missed him, begged him to see me. The tears were genuine. I was so scared. He came back to the house, thinking it was just to talk, feel things out. I took him to bed as quick as I could, so he'd never suspect."

It was the room, Toby thought. He knew this story, knew the broader strokes at any rate, but he'd never heard it with such an edge of self-contempt. The room was to blame. It brought it out of you.

"Raymond, unfortunately, could not take no for an answer. He called the house, snuck by. Sonny, my husband, figured it out soon enough. To his credit, he did not just turn back around right then and leave me and the girls for good. Or Toby, once he was born. Sonny was a decent man. Not perfect, Lord knows, but better than I deserved, I suppose. He stayed longer than he wanted, longer than I had a right to expect. But when he finally did leave, I was desperate. I called Raymond, asked him to take Toby for a while. A year, maybe, till I got better work and saved some. Three children on what I made part-time with the church council? Not possible."

"And Mr. Carlisle, he did take Toby in," Tina said. "There are school records to verify that, which I intend to obtain, giving the address here in town as Toby's residence, listing Mr. Carlisle as father."

"Call me dense," Murchison said. "But I still don't see how that *proves—*"

"It suffices," Tina said, "under the Probate Code. The first presumption is always that a child born into a marriage has the husband as father, regardless of biological paternity. Which, in this case, would mean Sonny Marchand is Toby's legal father. But there's a countervailing presumption. The biological father has a right to reassert legal paternity if three conditions hold: the mother affirms him as the biological parent, he takes the child into his home, and he holds the child out notoriously to the public as his own. All three apply here."

"Notoriously?"

"It's statutory language. The Family Code and Probate Code crossreference each other on this point. It's not clear whether preponderance of the evidence or clear and convincing evidence is the standard, but I think we can meet the higher burden."

"You mean it's for the court to decide."

"Absent an executed will, but—"

"The deed's joint tenancy. It'll pass outside probate."

"I'll be filing a quiet title action. We'll also petition for probate at the same time."

She'd explained the mechanics to Toby, and it had made sense, after a fashion. First, without the house, there wasn't enough property to probate, so you had to show Veronique didn't gain the house outright through the phony joint tenancy. *Fraudulent conveyance* was the term. But even if they won that round, they'd have to go on to show that Toby was the rightful next of kin. Left unsaid: Even if he got the house, he'd have to mortgage it or sell it to pay her. What was the point, then? What was he inheriting, really, except a fight?

Murchison said, "Sonny Marchand, he's where?"

"In Denver," Toby replied. "I told you earlier."

"He'll confirm what I said," Felicia told him. "I will provide you with his number."

"And though I have not spoken to him yet," Tina said, "Mr. Carlisle has a brother. He lives in Bremerton now, took the transfer when the shipyard closed. It's my understanding he'll confirm Toby's relationship with his father, too, though he won't much care for getting caught in the middle between his nephew and his sister." She began collecting her documents together. Glancing up at Murchison, she asked, "Would you be needing copies of these?"

Murchison seemed a thousand miles away. Gathering himself, he said, "On your way out. That'd be helpful."

"There's something else," she added, snapping her briefcase shut. "It's probably the most important thing, but this other matter needed clearing up, and what I've got to say next is speculative. Evidence Code Section nine-fifty-seven says there's no privilege still existing between me and Mr. Carlisle relevant to issues between parties with a tangible interest in his estate. So it's my understanding I'm free to say what I'm about to say. He discussed with me why he did not want money or real property, just certain family personal effects, left to his sister."

Toby squirmed in his chair, his uneasiness worse now. This part he'd learned just a little earlier as well.

"Mr. Carlisle didn't explain to me how he came by this information, and I neglected to ask him. It didn't seem relevant at the time. But he said he was aware that his sister, through her position as a title officer, had helped facilitate some questionable real estate transactions in town, up near his own property, involving a local convict."

"Long Walk Mooney," Murchison said.

Tina's eyes shot open. "You know this?"

"I know that man's name."

"No. That wasn't just a lucky guess."

"Like I said. His name, it's come up. Property?"

"He uses straw men, usually just other people in the community, family members of kids in his—" She flailed her hand, struggling for the word.

"Crew," Murchison prompted.

"Thank you. I was going to say organization—"

"Knights of Columbus is an organization," Stluka said. "Mooney runs a crew."

She smiled, unfazed. "Yes. In any event, he secretly buys these properties, and Ms. Edwards converts his cash into cashier's checks for deposit into escrow and makes sure the sales go through smoothly. If he rents out the properties, Ms. Edwards handles all that, too. In a few cases, he's paid for renovations for people who couldn't find credit, then taken out a second mortgage against the property, again using others as stand-ins. Sometimes he just loans out cash, with the same arrangement—repayment secured through the property."

"She's laundering for him," Murchison said.

"Mr. Carlisle seemed to have a grudging respect for it all, as though his sister wasn't so much wrong in what she did as too smart for her own good. He said capital's hard to come by for people up in Baymont and St. Martin's Hill and he hadn't heard anyone complain about terms."

"People don't complain about loan sharks." Stluka, arms crossed, eyed her like she was a fool. "It's unhealthy."

"I don't think Mr. Carlisle saw it that way. Perhaps he was just jaded about it all. He also mentioned a couple of businesses—a body shop, a liquor store, a Laundromat—all owned secretly by this Mr. Mooney as well. But my point here is, two of the properties he owns through third parties are the Victorians to either side of Mr. Carlisle's home. Mr. Carlisle suspected that the reason his sister wanted his house so badly was because she'd promised it to Mr. Mooney."

"Or sold it to him already," Felicia said.

Finally, Toby got the will to stand. Maybe what was being said about his aunt was all true, but he had no stomach for stirring up this kind of trouble inside the family.

"This is my cue to leave," he said.

Tina, startled, glanced up at him. "Toby—"

"My aunt is many things. Content with what she has is not one of them. But she did not kill my father."

"I'm not saying—"

"Or arrange it through anyone else. It's just—no. And this—what is going on here? Don't make me part of it."

"You don't know her like I know her." His mother sat with her hands folded in her lap now, an air of almost wily contentment about her. Justice at last. Veronique made to pay. "Way that woman cries after a nickel, God only knows what she'd do for a dime."

"I'll grant you, she's a hard woman," Toby said. "And greedy. God, yes. But—"

"Why do you think I never even made an attempt to try to make things work with your father—think it was just him? After Sonny left, I had a mind to, believe me. I did. Your father was a trial, God yes, but all men are. Even sons."

Here it comes, Toby thought.

"But your father was nothing compared to his sister." Felicia turned a little toward Murchison, to include him. "There are women who never let go of their brothers. Girlfriends, wives, they come and go, but a sister like this? Her hold is relentless. These outsiders, these other women—and their children, Toby—they can't be allowed to stake a claim on the family. That was Veronique. How do you think I knew to call Ms. Navigato? Your father told me about her—the usual, some offhand snip in a two-minute phone call—said to watch out for you, beware of Veronique if anything should happen to him. I wish all this"—she fluttered her hand to suggest the room but, beyond that, the police, the investigation, the murder—"surprised me. But it does not. She will ruin you, Toby. See you squander every dollar of your inheritance, one court battle after the next, before she ever allows you to claim one penny of it for your own."

"That doesn't mean she killed Pop or had anything to do—"

His mother shook her head. "You're blind."

I need to get out of here, Toby thought, before I say what's truly on my mind. He turned to Murchison. "My girlfriend is at the hospital, correct?"

He shot a final glance toward his mother and saw the disbelief, replaced quickly by a wounded resignation. They'd had this talk. A white girl. And musical, like his father. It was doubtful he could have done worse dating a goat.

"I've been advised by my lawyer I'm free to go. So if there are no objections." He pushed himself up from the table—light-headed, the stress, no sleep—and collected his jacket. He could feel the eyes boring into his back as he headed for the interview room door.

Murchison said from behind, "I still have to insist you stay in town."

Toby shot a weak smile over his shoulder. "I wouldn't dream of doing otherwise."

Reaching the door, he turned the knob and pushed but needed the force of his hip to get the thing open. The blinds on the window rattled. Outside, gazed upon by a half-dozen uniformed men and women assembled at desks beneath the fluorescent lights of the squad room, he searched the various doorways, trying to divine the quickest way out.

Pushing his arms into his jacket sleeves, he made his way down the hallway he hoped led to the lobby. It did. Once there, he found waiting for him a short, powerful, broad-faced woman clutching a small purse to her midriff. Seeing him, she rose from her chair, eyes fierce with sorrow.

"You're Mr. Carlisle's son."

Toby straightened his jacket collar. "Yes, ma'am."

Her lips flattened against her teeth, almost a grimace, as she blinked away tears. "I am so sorry for your loss. Your father."

Toby, again, said, "Yes, ma'am."

"I work at Overlook. I cared after your grandmother when she was there."

Toby nodded, glancing at the clock. He patted his pockets, checking for his folded-up necktie, his money.

The woman stepped closer. "The police are wrong. Understand? They think my son had something to do with killing your daddy, and that's wrong. He did not. Doesn't know who did. It's the truth, I swear to God in heaven. Please say you understand. Please." She reached out, took his hand, her grip strong, her eyes not just sad now. Scared, too. "I am so sorry for your loss, a terrible thing. But you can't let them do this to Arlie. You can't."

12

erry, at the wheel of the white long-bed van he'd been driving around for weeks, followed Manny as he headed north toward Napa to ditch his car. A winter sun flooded the stark blue sky with buttery light. The air smelled crisp, touched with wood smoke and pine, the sheltering hills to either side of the highway a lush green. It was one of those mornings, Ferry thought, that made you wonder if it hadn't been created to help you forget the night before.

Manny chose the parking lot for a mall of retail outlet stores not far from the wine train depot, hiding the car among a handful of others belonging to employees who'd already trudged in for the morning shift. When Manny climbed inside the van, Ferry told him they'd be back for his car before the lot was empty again late that night—patrol units would be trolling through, running plates on the cars left behind.

From Napa, they returned south, heading for Sky Valley Storage. Manny sat in his own private realm, curled up inside himself on the van's passenger side. He'd convened with his works and completed his morning nod before the drive to Napa, hitting that feel-good stride before getting in his car, so this mood couldn't be blamed on his habit. Must be my company, Ferry thought, fighting a smile. The brooding proved a mixed blessing. The silence was welcome, but without the kid's usual me-me monologue there was no way to tell how badly his thoughts were bouncing around inside his brain. He just touched his face a lot, especially the puffed-up eye, staring out at the Sunday morning hills like a kid being dragged to church.

Not everyone can kill a man, Ferry thought, let alone do it right—in the back, Christ, an old man. Over a girl the kid had never even talked to. Barely a step up from drowning cats.

Turning into the storage facility's driveway, Ferry punched in the code and the tall gate shuddered back. Steering the van past the empty aisles to the last row, he turned down and stopped midway to the end. Getting out, he glanced up, saw wisps of white cloud sailing east in a brisk wind. Gusty but clear, he thought. And warm for this early in the day. All things considered, good fire weather. As good as he could hope for this time of year.

The storage space was street-level, full-size, the kind rented by vintage car freaks, antique dealers, gun show vendors. The van blended well enough—Ferry'd bought it at a bankruptcy auction and it still had the plumbing company's logo on the side. Nobody ever puzzled much over a plumber's van roaming around, whenever, wherever.

Manny stayed put in the passenger seat as Ferry worked the combination on the padlock. The sliding door rolled up with a howl, slid home on its runners along the ceiling, then rocked a little. Ferry walked up to the driver's side window, knocked hard, saying through the glass, "Now's the time."

Once Manny was inside, Ferry rolled down the door again and switched on the timer for the overhead light. There were a dozen five-gallon plastic buckets in the locker, the kind used for powdered laundry detergent, and an equal number of five-gallon jerricans filled with diesel fuel. Bags of ammonium perchlorate, a box of road flares, and three sacks of aluminum cans collected from a recycling Dumpster comprised the rest of the materials.

That was the great thing about storage facilities, Ferry mused. Everybody has a secret locked up here. You could hold black masses, use naked virgins for altars, eat their flesh, and make marionettes out of their skeletons afterward—as long as you paid your rent and didn't bum too many cigarettes, no one said boo.

Sensing that he might need to be ready at a moment's notice, Ferry had bought all the bomb components once Manny had started his arson spree. It seemed eerily prescient now. I should have kept closer tabs on the kid, he thought. Should have played the pal, encouraged him to unburden his moldy little feelings. Maybe then I might have seen it coming.

The diesel fuel gave off a dense, greasy smell that hung heavy in the closed space. For some reason, it alerted Ferry to the fact that he'd just lost his last decent chance to back out. Manny knew where the locker was now, could describe exactly what was in it. Even if Ferry tried to be nice about it—pay him a little on-your-way money, drive him back to his car, tell him, "Too bad, didn't work out, maybe next time"—Manny wouldn't go quiet. He'd cause a scene, he was scared. And on his own, loose in the world, the kid posed a real threat. Tagged out there somewhere, as was sure to happen, maybe soon, he'd hand up Ferry in a heartbeat.

It rankled, the fact that a perfectly good plan, an excellent plan, could fall apart because a dog fart like Manny Turpin committed the world's most mindless screwup. It wasn't right. You're better than that, Ferry told himself. Smarter than that. No such thing as a plan that fails, just planners who can't think on their feet fast enough. You have to know how to improvise. You can do this. It's your peculiar gift, turning crap into gold.

For the next forty minutes, he showed Manny how to mix the powder oxidizer with the diesel fuel, stirring it slowly till the slurry stood thick enough to support one of the road flares straight up. Next, a half-inch floater of diesel fuel to serve as a timed fuse. Any more than that, the smoke would tip off neighbors or passersby. Any less, the thing might go up before you're far enough away.

"Cut the cans up with these," Ferry said, digging a pair of tin snips from a small toolbox he brought in from the van. "Put the shredded-up pieces in the mix. That'll speed up the burn rate." Finally, he showed Manny how deep to plant the flares for a five-minute fuse. "Okay, that's how it's done. Do the full dozen."

Manny looked torn. Resentful of being bossed, intrigued by the task. "This stuff isn't motion-sensitive, right?" With his foot he nudged the one completed bomb just slightly. "Needs flame."

Ferry wiped his hands on a rag. "Be a good idea not to smoke. And stay out of sight. I gotta figure out how much the locals know about you."

• • •

The truck stop was named Tullibee's, located along Route 37, the two-lane highway that scrolled west across the salt marshes and the wildlife refuge to the Sears Point Speedway and Sonoma County. The tables sported blue-and-white checked tablecloths, the windows clouded with steam. The waitress on duty had her hair pulled back in a sloppy bun and patrolled the room bearing two coffeepots. "Regular or irregular?" she asked before pouring.

Only four tables were occupied at that hour—a pair of long haulers sitting together, a deliveryman by himself, a woman with a wasted, naked face that spoke of drink. At the last table sat a cop. Ferry always made it a point to befriend someone in local law enforcement. This one's name was Gilroy.

Off-shift but still in his blues, he sat by himself at a four-top along the wall, attacking a breakfast known as the Sixteen Wheeler: four-egg omelet, four rashers of bacon, four link sausages, two biscuits with gravy, and a short stack. Ferry joined him and, when the waitress appeared, turned his cup over in its saucer and told her preemptively, "Regular." Once she was gone, he said to Gilroy, "Hear you guys had a shooting up on the hill last night."

That's all it took. Gilroy liked talking. He launched into a monologue of what had happened, gracing the narrative with homely truisms and folksy metaphors that often made no sense. Ferry imagined Gilroy regaling himself with much the same monologue as he drove around in his car. As the story wound on, Ferry examined Polaroids of a kid named Arlie Thigpen. Gilroy had shot the pictures through the grating of his squad car. Souvenirs.

"Kid's part of a crew linked to some guy named Long Walk Mooney. Name ring a bell?"

"Yeah," Ferry said. Manny had brought it up, said the guys he bought from knew him, worked for him, something along those lines. It was addled, cryptic, and vague, like much of what Manny said.

"Guy like him? Mooney, I mean. We had the money and the manpower, he wouldn't be out there, doing what he does, hiding behind this rave promoter bullshit. He'd be locked in a box, where he belongs."

Ferry half listened as Gilroy went on, bemoaning now the general state of local law enforcement, the gutless chief, the two-faced mayor, the tightfisted council, the ungrateful public. The diatribe wasn't hard to tune out. Ferry had more important worries—like what a load of bad news this was, the fact the main suspect at this point had ties to the same group of losers who knew Manny. Sooner rather than later, somebody'd let it be known that Manny had been crashing right next door to where the murder took place. And then all eyes would turn.

Ferry put the pictures down. "So this Thigpen kid, he's everybody's best idea at this point."

"So far? Sure. Yeah." Gilroy chewed quickly and hard. It made his huge ears move in an unsettling way. The flattop didn't help.

"That mean they're laying off the son?"

Gilroy downed an inch of juice, then wiped pulp off his chin. "So-called son."

"What's that supposed to mean?"

"I hear his claim to being family is a reach."

"From who?"

Gilroy whirled his fork in the air. "Seriously. You ever talk to jigs about their family?"

Ferry sighed. Gilroy launched on.

"So-and-so's the second cousin of the half sister who married Aunt Nibby's stepbrother's nephew's grandson's uncle on his mother's side." He shook his head, stabbed a sausage. "They say hillbillies are inbred. You're writing it down, somebody rattles off that kind of crap? Hard enough to take it seriously, let alone make sense out of it."

"Back to my question, though. This kid the chief suspect or not?"

"For now, yeah, maybe. Him or his pals in the Mooney crew." Gilroy poured syrup over his hotcakes, catching the last drip from the pitcher with his finger, licking it.

"Give me the story on the guys working the investigation," Ferry said, gesturing to the waitress for a refill.

"Murchison, he's primary. Dick Tracy without the squint and chin. Grew up here. Thinks he's a genius. Worse, thinks he's everybody's boss. Righteous fucking know-it-all."

"This the rust-haired guy you pointed out to me last time?"

"Right. Him."

The waitress appeared, refilled Ferry's cup, and shot him a bleary smile of jagged teeth before trudging off to another table.

"What about his partner?"

"Stluka. Head case asshole. Former LAPD."

"How'd he end up here?"

"Way I heard it, he only moved north after the Ramparts scandal. Wife's idea. Get out now, before it all turns to hell, or save your off days for visitation."

"He know what he's doing?"

Gilroy shrugged. "There's one good thing to say about him—he makes no bones about the Third Worlders. Told this bitch from the public defender's office once, I swear to God, 'Soon as they stop acting like animals, we'll stop putting them in cages.'" Gilroy shook his head, admiration in his smile. "That said, he's a prick with a problem. Gets along with just about nobody."

"Except Murchison."

"I don't know that either one of those guys 'gets along' with anybody. Even each other. I mean, a joke here and there, palsy-walsy, but nothing tight."

"And this detective-in-waiting, the one running the scene?"

An ugly light came on in Gilroy's eyes. "Marion Holmes. Stluka calls him Sherlock. Affirmative action promo fuck. Kind of guy makes you wanna turn in your tin."

"Okay, but—"

"Watching his back big-time, so damn scared he's gonna blow it. Sticks his neck out for nobody."

"Which means, relative to what we're talking about?"

"This case closes out, won't be because of him. He'll wait in line for a good idea."

Ferry thought all this through. Within tight parameters, he trusted Gilroy's judgment. He was reliably paranoid, hostile but not unstable, with a decent eye for things around him, an eye informed more by self-preservation than ambition. That lack of ambition, it was why he'd never make it out on his own. Needed the security of the big blue brotherhood, even though he despised or distrusted most of the guys in it.

"Realistically, how close do you think they are? To closing this thing out, I mean."

"Close?" Gilroy howled through a mouthful of food. "Little banger piece of shit lawyers down the minute Murch gets close enough to say boo. Gotta chase down the rest of his set at this point.

Got the whole Sunday morning squad out on a mutt hunt, known associates."

Ah, Christ, Ferry thought. "Any luck?"

"Beats me. I'm off-duty." Gilroy chafed a napkin across his lips. "But one other thing? After the Thigpen kid hunkers down, Murchison hauls the mother in. I swear, if ugly was a stick we could've booked her for assault."

"They brought the mother in? Whose idea was that?"

"Murchison's, I guess."

Ferry chuckled and looked off. *"People versus Mayfield."*

Gilroy blinked, puzzled. "Percy Mayfield?"

"People," Ferry corrected. *"People versus Mayfield.* It's case law. You bring a family member in, like the mom, let her talk to the suspect, then try to break her down afterward. Mom's not a suspect, no *Miranda* warning required. Constraints are a little more fluid."

Using his last wedge of toast, Gilroy sopped up the bleeding pools of egg yolk, syrup, and meat grease on his plate. "Whatever."

"You say Murchison thought of that?" Ferry was impressed. "That shows smarts."

"Yeah, yeah." Gilroy popped the last corner of toast in his mouth, chewed with abandon, then sat back, studying his immaculate plate. "If farts were smarts we'd all be Einstein."

"Where do you get these things?"

"Not like it led anywhere. Little banger denies all. Momma screams, 'Set my baby free!' Fucking joke. And that's another thing. Murchison may think he's Eliot Ness, but—and this ain't just me who says this—he goes into a room with a suspect? You'll see ducks big as trucks before he walks out with a confession."

Okay, Ferry thought. We've established you won't be having the guy's child. "What about the girl you mentioned? The one they found at the scene? What's her story?"

Gilroy shook his head. "From what I caught during the shift change? She's strictly a case of see-no, hear-no. And wiggy to boot."

Finally, Ferry thought. A little tiny bit of good news. He drained the last of his coffee, gesturing to the waitress for the check. "Before we wrap this up, tell me the rest about Murchison."

Gilroy stared at him like he'd asked for the radius of the moon. "The rest? Like what?"

"Like start with anything you can think of. And when you get to everything you know, stop."

They walked side by side down the hospital corridor, the nurse—her name was Marjorie, Nadya had learned—keeping a dutiful pace. Movement still came sluggishly, Nadya's legs working only in jerk-step. The slippers didn't help. Made of paper, they felt like envelopes on her skin, and if she didn't drag her feet they came off, tripping her up.

Sunday morning, the hallways were heavy with shadow and deserted. Patients slept or had their TVs turned down low, just the flickering screens and a humming undertone. The vast space, the long corridors, the quiet—it felt a little like the end of the world.

"They said I called nine-one-one. I don't remember that. I don't remember a lot."

Marjorie reached over, pulled a strand of hair off Nadya's forehead, smoothed it back against her skull. "I can't say about nine-one-one. And what I know I can only guess at from what one of the EMTs said when they brought you in. That and the way you looked." Her voice was calm, a throaty alto. "You were covered in blood, young lady. Your skirt, your sweater, your face. Your hair. I know, because I'm the one dealt with your clothes and scrubbed you off."

Nadya felt her heart start to pound, her breath grow short, but the panic didn't rise up and choke her like before.

"Some people remember these kinds of things crystal clear. Others, like you, go blank. At least at first. It'll come back, nighttime especially, in bits and pieces." Marjorie guided Nadya around a corner, said hello softly to a white-haired man and his gaunt wife with her IV pole, shuffling the opposite way. "We remember the things we can talk to ourselves about. This is how it started, then this, and so on. Things like you went through, when it just runs right over you, the mind hits overload. You'll be piecing it all together for the next few days, weeks. Months, maybe. Emotions coming at you left and right, you're gonna feel like you're dodging traffic. Buses, not bicycles."

"What if the memory's gone forever?"

It was a strangely hopeful thought. Marjorie's eyes, though, said no.

"What troubles me, little lady, is the stuff you're forgetting. You tried to save the man's life. You ran out, knelt down in his blood, turned him over, tried to breathe life into him, he coughed it all right back into your face. What you did, it was courageous, dear. But that you don't recall. I believe you should. Maybe you're stronger than you care to admit."

They came to an empty waiting room, its chairs arranged along the wall, a table with jigsaw puzzles and board games piled atop it. What caught Nadya's eye, though, was the piano.

"I'd like to sit here, just a little while, if I could."

Marjorie checked her watch. "I need to get back to the nurses' station."

"I'll be fine. Really."

Nadya guided herself along the chairs to the piano bench, pulled it out from the keyboard, and sat. A sad old upright, scarred from years of schoolroom use, its wood dull, its keys yellowed, three with the ivory chipped and the low C-sharp gone altogether. A simple test of octaves revealed, to her surprise, it didn't need tuning too badly.

She centered herself, raised her hands to the keys, and began. Once again: Brahms, the Eleventh Hungarian Dance. Originally written for four hands, she played the transcription for solo piano made famous by Julius Katchen, just as she had the night before, waiting for Toby's father to return home. No matter what comes up, she thought, no matter how fierce, how awful, keep playing. You may not have a story for what happened, not yet. But you have this.

She forced her fingers deep into the keys. The sound became the backdrop to a kind of movie—whimsical but sad, the old modal church harmonies mixing with Romany tremolos and displaced accents. In time, the images arose—the house, its lamplit interior, this same music. The gate outside opening, once, twice. Shots.

She stopped playing, as she had last night. Sat there stock-still. How long? Finally rushing to the window, the curtain pulled back. There, in the yard. Toby's father.

Play what you know.

Her skin beaded with sweat. It took her several moments before she could swallow. This is your life now, she thought. Pounding heart, cold wet skin, the gooey sweet copper smell of blood. Make peace. Make peace with it and try again. Remember. Toppling backward from the window, yes. Tripping over the ottoman, I suppose, yes. The phone, dialing the phone—was she really remembering it now or simply fabricating images to coincide with what they'd told her?

Did it matter? Of course it mattered.

"Why did you stop?"

Nadya jumped at the sound. Turning, she saw him in the doorway. "Toby." A whisper. His shirt collar open, jacket unbuttoned, he looked spent and rumpled and wonderful. Except—

"What's wrong?" she said.

She saw something in his eyes. A terrified revulsion.

"No." He shook it off. "Nothing's wrong. Are you—"

She put her hands to her face. "I must look—"

"No, no." He sat beside her. "Don't say that."

She leaned into him, pressed her face against his shirt. "Are you all right? Oh God, you're all right, you're all right, you're all right." She clung to him, gripping his jacket as though hoping to crawl inside.

He wrapped his arms around her, swaying gently. "Shush, shush, hey, I'm okay, I'm fine. What about you?"

What about me? she thought. My mind's a *danse macabre*. I'm sick with fear and I want to die from guilt and I missed you and thought I might never see you again, or if I did you'd hate me, like I thought you did when I first saw you in the doorway, that look in your eye.

"I was so scared." She jerked her head back. "You smell like you were scared, too. Oh God, what happened?" She reached up, grazed his cheek with her fingertips. "Where were you the last few hours?"

He took her hand. "I'm sorry, I didn't have time to shower."

"No, no, that's not what I meant. My God, it smells wonderful. You're here. You're here."

13

Murchison took what solace he could from the fact he'd had the good sense to extend the crime scene to the two Victorians on either side of the Carlisle property. He sat in a patrol unit, waiting for a callback from the watch commander, while officers manned the front and rear of each house, making sure no one made it in or out.

The watch commander was himself waiting—expecting word from down the chain of command, men who were tracking down the owners of record for both premises, so Murchison and his officers could gain permission to enter. They'd knocked, hoping someone was inside and would have the good sense to open up, but no such luck. Lacking anything concrete to claim exigent circumstances, they couldn't just plow on in with neither a warrant nor permission. And they lacked anything solid enough yet for a warrant.

What they had was dribs and drabs—scraps of information collected bit by bit from members of Long Walk Mooney's crew, their friends, hangers-on. They'd been brought in one by one by patrol units or questioned in the field. The bad news—every single one denied any involvement by Arlie Thigpen or Long Walk Mooney in the Carlisle killing. Alibis, such as they were, abounded, contradictory and otherwise. But what they did hand up got confirmed by Holmes's nameless source, who checked in when word of the mutt hunt made the rounds.

He'd told Holmes it was true, there was a mixed-race male—*skittle*, Holmes said, was the word used—heavyset, six feet tall, went by the name Manny. He'd hung around the fringes of the Mooney crew the past few weeks, then got tipped he could crash at one of the houses next to the Carlisle home. No one as yet knew which one, which was why Murchison had men stationed both places.

Tight as a nun's butt, Murchison thought. In Stluka's defense, not to mention Truax and Hennessey, who'd done the first check, both Victorians were indeed secure. The search would probably reveal how the kid had gotten in and out, but still, it felt embarrassing, to be so close and at the same time so clueless. Good thing Jerry went home for a few hours' sleep, he thought. Otherwise he'd be sitting here howling.

The radio call came through. Murchison picked up. "What've we got?"

"We tracked down your owners." The watch commander this shift was an old-timer named Durbin. "Gotta tell you, Murch. I mean, it was like pulling teeth, getting them to cop to the fact they were listed on title."

"They're straw men." Murchison had to hand one to Toby Marchand's lawyer. The Queen of Naps. "What about consent to enter?"

"You're good, go on in. But get this—neither one of these owners had keys."

"I'm not surprised."

"You're not?"

"Who does? Have keys, I mean."

"Woman named Veronique Edwards."

Murchison laughed. Victim's sister. "That's too perfect."

"Both owners said she handled the sales, these are investment properties, blah blah, she's in charge of the renovations."

That made Murchison look, just to be sure. "What renovations?"

"Guys I had making the calls, they said these people couldn't even tell for sure if the Edwards woman had keys, you want the truth."

Didn't want to tell you, Murchison thought.

"My guys told them we needed access, keys or no keys, now, not next week, what's it gonna be? After some real sandbagging they finally said yeah, sure, okay. My guess is they're calling this Edwards woman right now. Her or their lawyers."

Or both, Murchison thought. He ran it over in his mind, tried to imagine what he'd do in their shoes.

"Durbin, it's time to bring this Edwards woman down for a sit. Might be past time. Send a car over to get her. Her and her husband, no excuses. Whoever you send, make it clear, don't say anything about keys or anything else. Offer condolences, sweetie her up. If pushed, we want to hear anything and everything she has to say about her brother. Tell her it's all routine, but it can't wait. Homicide, first seventy-two hours, you hear where I'm going. Same with the other owners, they don't get a choice. Put 'em in different rooms, if you can find that many. Or out in the squad room where they can be watched. Regardless, they sit tight."

He signed off, got out of the car, and signaled to both crews to grab their tools. They were free to go in.

Toby and Nadya rode in the back of a Yellow Cab from the hospital, sitting close. Toby wrapped his arm around her as she nestled her head into his shoulder.

The clothes she'd worn last night had been claimed by the police. Toby'd not thought to bring anything for her, so it had been up to Marjorie, the nurse, to loan from her locker a cable-stitch sweater and jeans four sizes too large. Nadya'd rolled up the cuffs, and they'd found twine to cinch the waistband tight, the denim billowing at her hips and thighs. For shoes she wore the same paper slippers. They were ridiculously thin in the cold air, and she shivered beside him in the backseat of the cab.

As he held her, something his father once told him came to mind. It was one of the best lessons the old man had ever given him, actually, about something he called at one time or another The Deep Sweet. Music is a living thing, he'd said. Inside every piece you ever play there's a pulse, a real one—not made up in your head, in the music itself. It's your duty to find it, connect. Do that, commit yourself to it, you'll discover the reason you play. Discover yourself, reflected back in song. You don't, you're just blowing notes.

Toby had felt it maybe a half-dozen times, no more. But the point was to know you'd felt it. To know that was to understand that inside every true thing there's a welcoming beauty, even as simple a thing as a song. That kept you hungry. And that was the point—to keep on the hunt, to crave that echo, to know it's there, and to never stop wanting it.

Toby'd come to think of love that way, too. There were technicians in that realm just like in music—men and women who thought what happened between them was a matter of skill, a craft you refined. He'd fallen hard for a woman like that, almost proposed—a woman, sad to say, whom his mother still considered perfection—fashion model elegant but educated, too, Stanford Law, a worldly future ahead of her. But inside?

As Nadya curled up beside him, he felt a deepening suspicion that this sneaky, mercurial truth toward which his father had pointed the way resided closer than he'd guessed. No sooner did this feeling arise, though, than he shrank from it. Maybe, he thought, it's just need. Or guilt, trying to twist itself into something good. You're a walking wound, he thought. Be careful. Let all this sit till your father's death and all it means isn't so raw.

A long lore accompanied the Black male, white woman fascination—hiding from the harder truths, needing someone who embraces your self-delusions, saving each other. Hiding behind each other. You can drive yourself crazy, he realized, undermining your affections like that. Then again, returning to the feel of her body burrowing into his own, his former feelings—his admiration for her talent and mind, his attraction to her beauty, his affection, his curiosity—they all seemed shallow, equivocal. Inadequate. There was more going on here. For the first time, he felt a hint of that ineffable pulse echoing between them. And yet he realized, too, how suddenly, like his father's life, it could be destroyed. And that returned to him his guilt. She was the one who tried to save him, he thought, at the very same moment you were turning your back on the old man for good. It shamed him. He found himself despising her a little—what good did she accomplish really, what help did she deliver, what did she see, *she's weak*—even as he tightened his hold around her, despising himself more.

They took the last corner and, in an eerie replay of the night before, police cruisers sat waiting, lining the street. Like they'd never left, Toby thought. It caused an odd sort of vertigo—wanting to find out what was going on but wanting to flee. Feeling at the same time both lost and right back at the beginning.

The cabbie turned around in his seat and queried them with his eyes, as though to ask if they really wanted out. Toby slid his arm out from around Nadya's shoulder—she'd clutched that hand in her own so tightly he'd lost sensation in three fingers—took out the last of his cash, handed it across the seat, and motioned to Nadya.

"It's okay. Let's go."

An officer with a clipboard—not the same one as last night, Toby noticed, the one he'd wrestled with—stood guard at the gate, tipping one foot to the other in the wind. He was the youngest cop Toby'd seen so far, and he carried himself with an affected squaring of his shoulders, like a TV Texan. As the cab drove off, the baby-faced officer jotted down its license number on his clipboard.

A small display of flower garlands and paper-wrapped bouquets cluttered the sidewalk. The flowers were joined by condolence cards, candy boxes, stuffed animals—even a balloon in the shape of a heart, made of Mylar and filled with helium, bobbing at the end of a string. Left by well-wishers, Toby guessed, neighbors. Same neighbors who told the police I wasn't my father's son.

"My name is Toby Marchand," he told the officer, walking up. "I live here."

The officer held up the clipboard, gesturing for them to wait, then turned his body away, leaning his head to one side to speak into the walkie-talkie attached by Velcro to his epaulet. With the sound of the wind, Toby couldn't hear much of what the officer said, but he did catch his own name and that of Detective Murchison, plus the word *girl*. The officer ended his call and turned back. "Detective be out in about five, ten minutes. Wait here."

Toby led Nadya to the sidewalk, where she hunched down, her back against the trunk of the sycamore. With pained eyes she studied the mound of flowers and gifts, pulling the sweater hem down over her knees to the ground and tucking her feet inside, then stretching the neckline up above her nose. Once she stuffed each hand inside the opposite sleeve, only her eyes and the top of her head remained visible.

Why were the police still here, Toby wondered, or here again? He felt like asking, but the young cop might as well be wearing a sandwich board reading: DON'T BOTHER ME.

He returned his focus to Nadya, and she glanced up, meeting his gaze. *I am the ruin of everyone I love,* her eyes seemed to say. *And everyone who loves me.*

"You know how much I care about you, right?"

It didn't come out quite the way he'd wanted. She seemed shocked at first, but the agony in her eyes dissolved a little. As she worked to free her face from the collar of the sweater, the slightest smile appeared.

"Thank you."

He dropped next to her, wrapped his arm around her again, pulling up his jacket collar with the other hand. The wind seemed gentler near the ground. Nadya tensed up beneath his arm, her head swinging left, then right.

"Can you smell that?"

Toby sniffed the air. "What?"

Her head stopped turning. She gazed at him with terror in her eyes. "Nothing."

He took her chin in his hand, wouldn't let her look away. "Tell me."

She swallowed. "It's nothing."

"You're sure."

"Yes."

"It's in your head."

"I think so. Yes."

He stroked her cheek, the darker skin of his fingers accentuating her pallor. "Does it help, knowing it's not real?"

She looked away, trembling as she buried her fists deeper into the sleeves of the huge sweater. "Someday. I hope."

"When the flashbacks come, are they visual, too? Can you see him?"

It seemed too personal, too needy a question. She took a long time to answer.

"It's like what you see when you switch the lights on, then off, real quick. It's there, just an instant. Then it's gone." She shivered. "And it's awful. But the fear, it's there the whole time. I can't make it stop. My heart's going a mile a minute, I'm sick to my stomach. My whole insides, just—"

She closed her eyes and he held her again, tight, till Murchison appeared. He came wearing the same expression of buried rage smothered in despair that Toby had come to think of as the face of the law.

"Why didn't you tell me there was someone living in the house next door?"

Toby glanced at Nadya, who stared back. They struggled to their feet.

"I didn't know," Toby said.

"There was?" Nadya asked.

The young cop stepped forward, into Murchison's orbit. The detective ignored him.

"Big guy, bearish, on the chubby side, mixed-race."

In the corner of his eye Toby caught Nadya staggering a little on her feet. Turning, he saw her eyes swell. "What?" he whispered.

"Could you describe him again?" Nadya asked.

Murchison did. Nadya went white.

"There was someone like that. At the club. When Mr. Carlisle got into the fight."

"You didn't mention that before," Murchison said.

"He wasn't one of the four who caused the real trouble." Her voice barely rose above a whisper, but even so the words came out shrill, defensive. "He was just somebody in the crowd. He came up, put his arms around Mr. Carlisle, like he wanted to help break up the fight. When he loosened his hold, Mr. Carlisle turned right around and hit him. Hard." She winced at the memory. "And kicked him, after he fell." She looked up at Toby as though wanting to be forgiven for having to admit that.

Murchison asked, "He follow you out to the car?"

"I don't know. I don't think so, but I don't know."

"Okay." Murchison toed a spot of grass cropping out of a crack in the sidewalk, then looked off at the Victorian from which he'd come. "From what we found inside, looks like he lived on cold canned soup, vanilla cake frosting, and peppermint schnapps. Cellar dweller. Except he liked to sit up at the window on the top floor, too." He pointed up toward the widow's walk. "Bit of a smoker. You never saw an ash glowing red up at that window? Or any other lights at night?"

Both Toby and Nadya looked, following the direction of his finger with their eyes.

"He also liked making little flamethrowers with hair spray. You never saw that?"

"No," in unison. Nadya shook her head for emphasis, her eyes brimming with self-reproach. Toby said, "That house, it's been empty months, maybe a year. You stop paying attention."

"Too bad for your father."

Toby couldn't believe he'd heard right. "Are you saying that just because—"

"Your father, he mention seeing anybody in that house?"

"If he had, I'd have told you."

Murchison, to Nadya: "You?"

She shook her head. Toby said, "I want to get her out of the cold."

Murchison leaned away, murmured something to the young cop, who ducked his chin as he listened, then leaned back. "One, given what we know now, I'd have to say it's unwise for you to stay here. Could be your father's killer was holed up next door, and he may have an inkling you can identify him. Two, I haven't released the scene yet. Given what we just found, I'm not going to, not anytime in the next few hours. Three, I've been thinking about what your lawyer told me. I want to look at your father's financial records, his checkbook, tax work papers, anything he didn't give his lawyer. Your lawyer. But I still want you here in town. You want, go down, stay with Ms. Navigato for now."

Nadya edged forward, her paper slippers chafing the sidewalk. "Why are you being so hostile? What have we done?"

Murchison didn't answer, just stared back at her with a kind of wounded bafflement.

"You think we're guilty."

Toby touched her shoulder, whispering, "Choose your battles." He tried to turn her away. She refused to move.

"If you feel so much hate for us, who are you doing this for?"

"I don't hate anybody."

"Oh my God, you don't see it in yourself?"

Nadya shook her head and broke out of Toby's hold, spinning away. Toby clung to her hand, to keep her close. "We'll need to get some things from inside the house, Detective. Clothes, my shaving kit, things like that. I assume you'll want to come with us, or have one of your officers come along."

Murchison tore the edges of the crime scene tape away from the gate as the younger cop jotted down everyone's name on his entry/exit log. Once the tape was clear, Murchison turned to Nadya.

"You sure you're up for this?"

He seemed more cautious than concerned. She stood there, staring at the gate. Toby said, "I can bring your clothes out to you, if you want."

"No. I want to go in."

Murchison pushed open the gate, and she looked through the opening into the yard. Standing perfectly still, she swayed a little on her feet, her skin blanching a ghostly white.

"Let's get you inside," Toby said, taking one arm.

Murchison tried for the other, but she tore her hand away, clasping it across her mouth. Hissing through her fingers, "The bathroom."

Toby fumbled with his keys for what seemed an eternity, and as soon as he got the door open she fled past him, hurtling through the living room, then slamming the bathroom door.

"Still think it was a good idea to bring her back here?" Murchison eased past him in the doorway. "Where did your father keep his mail and financial records?"

Toby went to the china cabinet in the dining room, opened one of the lower panels, and withdrew the shoe box full of receipts and bill stubs, the checkbook. Placing them on the tabletop, he said, "My father was extremely private about all this. I won't be able to make any better sense of it than you will. So if you'll excuse me."

He left Murchison at the dining room table and ventured back toward the bathroom. He leaned toward the door, listened, caught the sound of Nadya gasping in and out, the sound strung together with whimpers. He pictured her on her knees, the cold tile, the bile on her lips. He lacked the heart to make her face him like that, so he drew away, went to his father's room.

It felt like a violation, being there. Raiding a tomb. He sat down on the unmade bed and stared at the open closet, the array of suits and sport jackets, lime-green polyester to worsted Italian wool. Weary, he put his hand out to brace himself on the mattress, and as he did, his hand brushed something hard beneath the pillow. He recoiled on impulse, even as his mind recognized what it was: his father's portable CD player and headphones. Toby removed the unit from beneath the pillow and out of curiosity popped open the play port, to see what the last thing was his father had listened to.

It was a disc by the baritone saxophonist Hamiet Bluiett and his sextet: *Old Warrior, Young Warrior.* Toby had given it to his father as a Christmas present; he'd meant it as an homage. His father, unwrapping it Christmas morning, sniffed the scent of free jazz and listened to no more than the first three tracks before turning it off. "Music to get lost by," he'd said, then gone off to make tea. The crack had sparked one more round of insults between them. And now here it is, Toby thought, the thing he listened to at night before drifting off. Cherished in secret.

He removed the small, shiny disc, holding it in his hand like a mirror as the bathroom door opened. Looking up, he saw Nadya appear in the doorway. She'd washed her face, gargled; he could smell the soap and mouthwash. He gestured for her to sit beside him.

"You okay?"

She buried her hands in the sleeves of the sweater. "Better. Some. What's that?"

"Present I gave Pops." He turned the disc this way and that in his hand. "Reminded me of something."

"Tell me."

He shrugged, but she placed her hand on his shoulder. "Please. I'd like to hear it."

Toby puffed his cheeks and thought about where to start. "I was nine. Pops took me to see Illinois Jacquet's big band. We went backstage before the first set. Pops knew Rudy Rutherford, he played clarinet and baritone in the band, and they did a little howdy-doo, you know, two old guns cracking wise. Then Pops asked if he could introduce me to Illinois."

He chuckled, remembering.

"It was like meeting the pope in a bar. He was sitting in this tall, wobbly wood chair, a barber's bib around his neck, while his manager fussed at his hair, straightening it with a heating iron. So damn proud of that wavy gray hair. Rudy introduced Pops and me, and Illinois played the gracious big shot. Asked me how I liked 'playing the bone.'"

Toby looked down at the CD player, reinserted the disc.

"The band, they did a lot of old stuff. 'White Heat,' 'Stompin' at the Savoy.' You'd have thought nobody could blow the dust off those tunes, but they did. I watched Pops as he listened—eyes almost glassy at times. Real quiet afterward." He glanced up, to be sure Nadya followed. "That was the first time I think I actually understood my father. The dream always just outside his reach. All it takes is one signature tune. Illinois had it with 'Flying Home.' Lee Morgan had 'The Sidewinder,' Ahmad Jamal, 'Poinciana.' One tune, so people have something to hang your name on.

"Pops almost had it with 'Moanin',' or so he always said. He'd packed off for New York, and somehow hooked up with Mingus, who took him under his wing." Toby chuckled. "The Angry Man of Jazz, he got called. Mingus had this reputation—he was a junkyard dog when his temper blew. Small wonder my old man admired him. But he could be gentle, too, and generous, even to guys like Pops, who was raw and young, but fearless. With Mingus on his side, Pops thought this was it. His shot. Mingus showed him lead sheets for 'Moanin'' and a few other tunes that got laid down in the *Blues and Roots* sessions. Pops said he memorized what he saw then holed himself up in a Harlem cellar for weeks practicing. But come time to cut the wax, the record label wanted a name, so they went with Pepper Adams."

Toby glanced up again, offered a wan smile, then winked.

"At least, that's the way Pops always told it. God only knows what the truth is. Could be Mingus was just blowing smoke. Young dude fresh off the bus, why crush his pride? Maybe Pops just decided the tune was his after hearing it so many times when he tagged along with the band. That would've been like him. I've never looked into it too hard, afraid the whole thing's a lie. But the moral's true, even if the story isn't. That's how close you can come. And still be nowhere near."

Nadya reached for his hand and gripped it hard. "You're not like that. You'll never be like that."

"We're all like that." He lifted her hand to his lips, kissed her fingers, then got up and headed to his room. "Just some more than others."

He gathered a change of clothes together. Nadya, following him in, sat on the bed, watching. Once he had his things packed, he pointed to her sweater and baggy jeans. "You want, I can leave you alone while you change out of those."

"I'd prefer you stayed, actually."

They traded places, Toby on the bed now, watching as she kicked off the paper slippers, untied the rope cincture at her waist, let the baggy jeans fall, then pulled the sweater over her head. She stood there naked a second, frail and small. The overalls and turtleneck she'd worn yesterday, before changing into her dancing outfit, lay in the closet, stuffed inside a plastic bag, along with her socks and hightops. She didn't put them on. Instead, she turned to face him.

"When you're with me like this, here, please don't think I'm awful, saying this, I feel this overwhelming need to—I want you so badly. It sounds sick, weird, I can't help it. I feel so ashamed. I've heard of things like this, how death does this, like instinct kicks in, but I always thought it was stupid and—"

"I feel the same way," he said, unable to get up from the bed, unable to look away from her. "I mean, wanting. I've felt it, too. Don't think I'd be able, though."

"No." She didn't move. "Would you like to have a baby?"

"Nadya—"

"Someday?"

He got up, took her in his arms, feeling the wiry smallness of her, rocking. "It's cold. Get dressed."

She put on her turtleneck and overalls. They hung wrinkled on her. "I look like a bag lady," she said, pulling on her socks. Once she'd knotted her hightop shoelaces, Toby reached out for her hand. "Let's get steppin'." One of his father's phrases. They walked back to where Murchison sat poring through canceled checks in the dusty prismed glow of the dining room chandelier.

"I want to bring my father's horn with me," Toby told him, setting down his bag. "I don't want to find out somehow it turned up missing."

He didn't wait for a response but marched back to the practice room. He spotted it in the far corner, the wood shell case propped open, about the size of a child's coffin. The big brass Selmer horn with its lacquer finish lay inside, bedded in dark red velvet.

Murchison returned to the Victorian where he reconnected with the officer-in-charge, a corporal named Coover—African American, short and moonfaced but hard in the body. Nose tackle material. He closed his eyes every time he laughed, and he laughed often.

Coover pointed vaguely toward the street. "Anything new?"

"Tell you in a minute. What about in here?"

Coover nodded at the door to the cellar. "Just what we found down there, the funky, nasty, smelly soup cans and such. Jesus. Nobody knows the rubble I've seen." He laughed, softer than usual, but even so his whole torso shook and the eyes narrowed to slits. He pointed to the ceiling. "And his little crow's nest up top. No weapon. No stash. This floor, second floor look clear. What's naked to the eye, any rate." He ran his fingertips along a window ledge, rubbed the gritty dust away. "Messed up, but clear."

"Anything to suggest the guy had a cell phone, a recharger, batteries, anything?"

"No such luck, and that'd be luck, Murch, admit it."

"Evidence tech on the way?"

"Yeah, and the stuff in plain view we got bagged."

Murchison liked working with Coover. He did things. "Okay." He took a pair of gloves out of his pocket, slipped them on. "Let's get busy on outside plain view."

Coover shot him a wary look. "Sure that's not a little gung-ho?"

"We've got permission from the owners to search the premises. And the kid staying here had no expectation of privacy, he was an intruder. Add to that what I learned outside. The girl who was with the vic last night? She remembers a guy matches the visual on our slob in here getting into it with the old man at the club where the son was playing. Besides, the guy looks like a firebug, and we've had too may fires around town not to act on that. I'll take the risk. Public safety. We're looking for a weapon and any further evidence of arson." And any safes, he thought, where Long Walk Mooney stashes his cash. He looked around the empty, filthy space. "Okay. You want, start downstairs. Do the wall sockets, check for loose floorboards, ceiling panels, everything. You find anything, leave it where it is, holler. Let me make the judgment call before we actually bag it up. If it looks like I should have gone for the warrant—"

"I can keep a secret," Coover said.

Murchison nodded, grateful and at the same time uneasy. "I appreciate that. I'm gonna take one last check upstairs."

On the second landing, a pull-down spring ladder led to the third floor. Murchison scurried up, entering an attic, half built out. Plywood sheets had been laid down for flooring, and where they hadn't been, knob-and-tube wiring ran exposed along fiberglass insulation decades old. He lifted the nearest edge of the dense stuff, once pink, now gray, checking for a stash spot—a gun, shells, a cleaning kit, anything—then made a mental note to make sure they ripped up every square inch of it before they were through.

The whole place smelled like an ashtray. Murchison, bowed at the waist to make the low clearance, headed for the window at the far wall.

They'd taken away the cigarette butts and logged them into evidence, but the burn marks remained, rough black smudges on the knotholed wood, marring the window ledge, too. They'd also found and bagged up a half-dozen spray cans and hundreds of spent matches. The kid was making flamethrowers up here, entertaining himself with practice—but nobody'd seen that. In a high, curtainless window on a dark street. Sometimes it seemed a miracle they ever solved anything.

Manny had come and gone through a basement door, a padlock protecting the place while he was away, a broom handle propped up against the door when he was inside. That would clear Stluka for any blame in not discovering he'd been getting in here. He slept and ate in the cellar, out of sight, but then, to pass the time, climbed up here.

Looking out the window, Murchison could see the whole front yard of the Carlisle property, much of the back. The angle was wrong for peering in beyond the curtains, but Murchison harbored little doubt why Manny, whoever he was, had sat up here. Same reason he'd turned up at the club.

He had a thing for the girl.

How that played into the victim's fight with Arlie Thigpen—or the fact that the victim's sister and Arlie and Manny all had ties to Long Walk Mooney—he couldn't say just yet. A cell phone and its record of calls would help, but Coover was right, that was a long shot. One thing remained obvious, though, from just the way they'd found this window. Manny obsessed. Murchison would bet anything the object of that obsession was Nadya Lazarenko.

He cringed, remembering what she'd said—*Why are you being so hostile?* It echoed with the contempt he'd felt from her at the hospital, with the disdain he'd felt everywhere the past few hours. *What have we done? . . . There is a sadness about you, Detective . . . a kind of desperation.* Marcellyne Pathon had wanted him out of her house, though she'd been too Christian, or scared, to tell him so. And the way the nurse at the hospital had screamed at him and Stluka to get out, you'd have thought they'd been going after the Lazarenko girl with razor blades.

Again, he felt puzzled by how much it bothered him. Only rookies expect gratitude; it was one of the first casualties of the job. And yet he wasn't like Stluka, dividing the world into cops, fools, and assholes. But there were times he found himself driven by little more than habit and a shameless need not to look ridiculous. He didn't have any ideals or convictions anymore. The job beat them out of you.

Who are you doing this for?

The problem, he knew, was him. Arlie and Toby, they'd been suspects; he had every right to go at them, even with the liberties he'd taken, the lies he'd told. Not everyone would back him up on that, but their resentment didn't trouble him, at least not as much as the others. The others had sensed something he'd been unable to hide. *You don't see it in yourself?* Unsettling, having his expression unpacked like that, the way he unpacked the faces of men he interrogated. And once he realized that the accusers who troubled him most were women, it came to him.

It had happened several months ago, in the dead of night. Joan thought he was asleep, lying on his side with his back to her. Sliding behind him, she loosened the drawstring of her pajamas, reached inside, and fingered herself to climax, trying to disguise her breathing so as not to wake him. He didn't stir—it felt cowardly at the time, more so in retrospect—just listening. He wondered if she'd needed him near her, needed his scent, the warmth of his body, to feel aroused. If so, it seemed a dismal kind of flattery.

Sex had seldom been easy between them. Catholicism? Too easy to blame. She never looked at him was one problem. On her back, or her on top, straddling him, she closed her eyes. Or, her preference, being taken from behind. Was it her or him? He knew what his face looked like; even back in his playing days, he'd hardly turned heads. He couldn't find the words to tell her how it made him feel—again, that manly, cowardly inability to talk.

Once she'd finished, she retied her pajamas and slid back to the far side of the bed. In time, her breathing settled and she drifted off. He remained awake, engulfed in a loneliness he supposed there was a word for.

14

---

erry returned to his lair in the office complex, plugged in his laptop, and logged on. He'd needed to get the lay of the land first before connecting with Marisela.

He typed in her E-mail address, and like most Central Americans, she had a Mexican ISP. True to their routine, he wrote in English, the better for her to practice. He wrote simply, mentally translating his words first into his own rudimentary Spanish, then back again, knowing her shaky understanding of his language matched his own feeble grasp of hers. Six years, you'd think one or the other would have improved in the foreign language department, but given the nature of the attraction, talk had never been their first priority. Besides, they spent a lot of time apart anymore.

> *Querida Marisela: My work is complete tonight. I drive to Baja tomorrow. Tell Ovidio that somebody, one of his friends or contacts, needs to meet me with a boat. Pick a place, Bajamar to El Rosario. Sorry I did not know sooner. Things just happened quick. I realize it's a lot to ask, but I'll pay. I miss you, and think of you every day.*

They'd met a few years after the UN-brokered peace accord removed the odious Salvadoran military from any law enforcement role. An exchange program developed between a few American and Salvadoran police departments. Ferry—at that time Bill Malvasio, his given name—had ten years behind him with Chicago PD. He'd spent the last three working undercover with the Area Six tac team—mocking up tracks on his skin with mortician's wax and mascara; waiting as robed women from Nigeria crapped out balloons filled with Karachi white; breaking down teary strung-out hookers in shooting galleries, manhandling their crotches searching for the little knotted Baggies. It was great fun. He and a few of his pals on the squad called themselves the Laugh Masters.

He got teamed up with a squad of Salvadoran officers scheduled for antinarcotics work and befriended a few. They were tough types, a little of the old macho swagger, but generous guys, a trait he learned was typical. They invited him down for a visit, meet the families, see their own mean streets, such as they were, and get a feel for what they did shift to shift.

He'd never seen such beaches—Costa del Sol, Playa El Tunco, Playa El Sunzal—all within a stone's throw of tin hut villages and beggars. Fifty-year-old school buses painted Halloween colors carried *campesinos* through the dense wet heat from La Libertad into the interior for starvation-wage work, trailing flatbeds stacked with sugarcane. Women carrying baskets atop their heads made their way along roadside culverts where derelict cattle grazed. Despite so many wretched poor, the bratty rich, the grimy heat and the hard life, he told himself, I could live here. Strange, how idle dreams sometimes harden into necessities.

He'd met Marisela in Santa Tecla. She was the sister-in-law, *la cuñada*, of one of the narcs he'd trained, Ovidio Morales, and she worked for her father's lumber business. A true *morena*, she had the kind of deep dark eyes Ferry could get lost in. Her body was slightly plump—she bemoaned the poundage on her hips, patting it sometimes like a pair of holstered guns, calling it *mis pistolas*—but the soft skin, the high cheeks, the full lips, they did the trick. Not to the point he'd marry her, bestow the much-wanted green card, but they were *amantes special..* Amazing, the degree of heat a gringo lover could excite in that country, especially once prices shot sky-high when the dollar muscled the *colón* aside as the official currency.

Soon, the whole issue of a green card became moot. Everything went haywire when he returned to Chicago. He had to flee—two unforeseen benefits of his undercover work: new friends south of the border and a master class in phony documents. He told Marisela he'd left the force to do private security work of a decidedly sub rosa type for rich men and that explained his need to slip back and forth across the border twice yearly for longer and longer periods. Since he brought back dollars, no one second-guessed him, not openly. Besides, it was the truth, more or less. And Marisela's family had secrets of its own.

It turned out Ovidio, Marisela's brother-in-law, had friends not only among the former thugs in the National Guard and Treasury Police but within *La Mara Dieciocho* as well, a bunch of gangbangers deported from East Los Angeles, specializing in the usual: stolen cars, weapons, shakedowns, drugs. So Ovidio had no problem turning a blind eye to the secretive comings and goings of Marisela's American *marinovio*. On the contrary, a mutually beneficial arrangement was forged. Thus the ability to ask for a boat at a moment's notice and trust one would appear. For a price.

Before leaving the office complex, Ferry collected Manny's .357. He reloaded the revolver, keeping the spent casings and putting them back in the box of extra shells, storing it all in the van's glove box, being careful to wipe away prints.

He drove into Rio Mirada, heading for Baymont, wanting to reconnoiter the scene once more before meeting with the big fella. Once he got to the hill and started up the incline through the winding, cluttered streets, he took heart from what he saw. Rainwater from the recent storm sat backed up in the sewers. They had infiltration problems up here, the storm drains and sewer lines decaying underground and their runoffs flowing into one another. That, plus the jerry-rigged add-ons, the bathrooms linked illegally to storm drains, not sewer lines; roof leaders linked backward the other way; cracked service laterals, leaking sewer lids, and rusted cleanouts. It meant every home up here was vulnerable to storm drain fumes rising up through their sewer lines.

It wasn't the hillside's lone vulnerability. The high foreclosure rate up here had created about a dozen vacant houses. Most lenders liked work-outs with defaulting borrowers, given the hassles of flipping the lots. Frontline Financial, the most aggressive subprime lender in the area, had a different plan. Targeting borrowers with nosediving credit, they jacked them into impossible loans, drove them into foreclosure, then either planted dummy bidders at the trustee sales to drive up the prices or slipped them off auction and back-channeled the sales to insiders or others willing to kick back for the privilege.

These were the houses Ferry had targeted. The past two weeks, he'd gone around, jimmying the locks, making sure he could get inside at his pleasure, testing to see if or when someone might come around, make repairs. There were eight houses that had stayed good, spaced pretty well evenly around the hill.

He checked each one again on his way up to the top. No change, easy in, easy out. No squatters or druggies to deal with. He tooled around inside each one for a few minutes, to make it look like he had real business, before heading back out to the van and continuing on.

Near the top, he came upon a testing crew running smoke into the storm drains. Three guys in hard hats and coveralls watched with dismal expressions as, sure enough, plumes rose up from the sewer lids. Ferry slowed the truck, hailed the nearest man in the crew.

"What's all this?"

The guy put his hands on his hips, eyeing the plumbing company logo on the side of Ferry's van, then offering a thin smile. "Tunnel system up here's just totally screwed." He made three separate gestures of resigned disgust. "You got cross-connections all along here botching up both lines, half-ass laterals from the old federal housing, inflow leaks, drain tap-ins way outta code—"

"Figured something must've gone seriously haywire, you guys out here on a Sunday."

"We've been out here Sundays—hell, Saturdays, holidays, goddamn Christmas Eve—since I can't remember."

"How long you think till the storm drains clear?"

The guy just laughed. "What they ought to do? Huff and puff and blow this whole damn hill down. Pay people off, start over. You know?"

Yes, I do, Ferry thought, easing his foot off the brake and waving good-bye.

The very top of the hill rose up beyond the last houses, forming a bluff that created a shallow box canyon. Beyond it, the hill gave way to a sloping meadow once home to quicksilver mines, now cluttered with old red rock tailings and thick with star thistle and field mustard.

Ferry looked back the way he'd come. You had houses built on piers into the hillside, which provided just the right ventilation. Cheap single-pane windows that would shatter with the temperature differential, creating even more ventilation and amping radiant heat. Wood shake roofs with dried-out, curling shingles—airborne embers could embed themselves there. Years of ladder fuel accumulation, shaggy brush and vines and overgrowth nudged tight against houses and trailing across the roofs. Pine duff inches thick in places, at the bottom of which embers could burn unnoticed for hours, days, weeks, even after the top layers got hosed down.

Add to all that the bottleneck at the bottom of the hill—one way in for the engine crews, same way out for the evacuees—and the fact that fire races uphill, the only thing you could ask for to better the situation was two months' more time, until the Santa Ana winds of April kicked in.

And of course, the coup de grâce—the hydrant couplings were World War II vintage. Two and a half inches. Nearly every fire company for miles around had upgraded to three-inch. Their hoses wouldn't fit. Rio Mirada would have to rely on its own four pumper crews to fight the blaze and whatever CDF could drop from the sky.

Before driving back down the hill, he made a pass through the uppermost neighborhood—Home in the Sky, they called it. His point of interest was the little mom-and-pop filling station and food market at the very top. A boon to the locals, walking distance for kids and old folks. And people up here were loyal. Despite higher prices, folks bought their gas here. Every two weeks the owner phoned in his order, and every other Saturday night the tanker wound its way up the hill.

Ferry drove past the pump island, like he meant to turn around, in reality checking to see if the owner'd put up the sign that they were out of gas. Sure enough, third pump, unleaded. OUT OF SERVICE. It wasn't just luck. Luck was for the unprepared. When you're ready, it's fate.

For good measure, he checked across the panhandle, to see what was up with the Victorian where Manny'd been crashing. Once he got there, all the good fortune he'd just tallied up in Baymont seemed stolen back again. Squad cars lined the street. He saw cops gathered around the Victorian's yard, they were searching it high and low. The rust-haired detective with the sad-bag eyes was there, too. Murchison. Ferry wondered how much they knew about Manny, whether an APB had been radioed out, full name and description and criminal record.

It all seemed to be happening at hyperspeed, good luck and bad. He wished he knew what that meant. Regardless, it was time to bring the big guy on board.

Ferry drove past the warehouse district and down to the riverbed to a place called the Slaughter House. The card room, named for a spit of land near where it sat, had opened during World War II, same time as the brothels and bars along the Little Liberty boardwalk, a wartime gambling haven for servicemen and the shipyard crews.

The current owner was trying to clean up the place—put in a restaurant, a conference room, a sports bar—but Ferry had hired himself out to a few card rooms in one of his first stints back in the States after fleeing Chicago. He knew the scams reasonably well, and his first time here, he'd gleaned from a railbird's bragging that he'd been placing sports bets through a phone spot and getting his payoffs out of a bogus player bank.

Ferry walked in and saw Asians and Filipinos already thronged around the Pan Gow and Pan Nine tables. Sucker games. Across the room, the rest of the local rubes played Texas Hold 'Em and Lowball, two-dollar ante, four-dollar raise; it was impossible, no matter how good your luck, to so much as break even given the pots involved. Table fees ate up your winnings, not to mention management's propensity to advance the clock. At one of the tables, Ferry spotted a guy he pegged for a prop player, a cardsharp employed by the house for rough play on fools and drunks.

Ferry moved through to the sports bar. It was a different world in here. In addition to the half-dozen TVs mounted around the room, there were also windows looking out at the sunlit river. A small marina lay right out back, another recent upgrade, and the local honchos liked mooring their boats there, to show what characters they were. It made the Slaughter House a sort of unofficial yacht club for candy-ass degenerates.

At the bar's far end stood the conference room. Acting as though he didn't know where he was going, Ferry opened the door and poked halfway in, did a double take when he heard voices, glanced up and around the room, then mumbled an apology, and closed the door again.

They were all in there.

Clint Bratcher, the big fella, Ferry's paymaster, held court. At his side sat his prime pick for city council in the upcoming special election, Ralston Polhemus—insurance broker, respected in his community, a big shot at Mission Baptist. Like everyone else in Bratcher's pen, Polhemus sold his allegiance up front. Bratcher arranged the money.

Polhemus was needed as the swing vote in an upcoming eminent domain push Bratcher had masterminded. Polhemus was expected to provide cover for city staff working the deal, and Bratcher needed his vote to approve the debt and forestall any challenges to tax diversions or bond terms. He was running against the school board president, Sheila Hampton-Dawes, also African American but tied to the affordable housing clique through her brother.

It was Bratcher's job to keep Hampton-Dawes off the council and, more important, deny her the seat on the board of the redevelopment agency that came with it. It was Bratcher's special notoriety, not so much his power to elect, but his power to defeat. His attack ads were legend. The ones focused on Hampton-Dawes detailed her attempts to get permits revoked on all the development projects around town—projects stalled by the dot-com bust and the subsequent lending squeeze—and to have those permits secretly reissued to her brother or his friends.

"Biggest racket in the world," Bratcher told anyone who'd listen. "Affordable housing. And the phony nonprofits pushing it."

Beside Polhemus sat Walter Glenn, a local architect and contractor best known for expediting building permits, for himself and select others. You hired Glenn as a consultant for your project or watched it get snarled in red tape and die.

Beside Glenn sat Bob Craugh, a developer and redevelopment honcho who, along with four other landowners in Rio Mirada, decided what got built, what didn't, in town. Not a mitigation plan or review process devised by man he couldn't humble. There were six strip malls in town with over 40 percent vacancy that Craugh had pushed through the redevelopment agency, every one funded by bonds secured by projected increases in tax revenue that never materialized—a sweet deal, since the city, not Craugh, held the debt. But now he had three work sites idle in town, faced permit cancellation, and was accused of land banking. Thus the sit-down with Bratcher. They'd teamed up before, together with Glenn, during the last election cycle.

The others around the table Ferry hadn't recognized. But that wasn't the point. He'd caught Bratcher's eye, and now it was time to wait.

He took a stool at the bar, ordered coffee, and watched the basketball game on an overhead TV. In time, the conference room door opened, a brief surge in noise, the voices within competing for an instant with the ball game commentary, then dying again as the door closed. Bratcher came forward—a large man, six-four, two forty, with squarish, clean-shaven features marred by pocky cheeks and a broken nose. He had meaty arms, thick hands, hard blue eyes. He dyed his hair and combed it neat as a colonel.

"Who's on top?" Bratcher directed the question at the bartender. He didn't so much as glance sidelong at Ferry.

The bartender, adding egg whites to a gallon jar of Collins mix, glanced up at first Bratcher, then at the screen. "No clue." He shrugged. "Haven't paid much attention."

"Game's over, all intents and purposes." Ferry slipped off his stool and tossed a couple singles onto the bar. "Might as well catch some fish."

"You got a favorite spot?" It was Bratcher. Like they were strangers. But the eyes were cold. He was ticked.

"I'm open to ideas."

"Try Dutton's Landing, across from Cuttings Wharf. End of Green Island Road. Some late-run salmon and steelhead can still be had, and there's always stripers. Even if you don't catch anything, nice just to be out there. Might spot some gadwalls or mallards starting north. Kinda early in the year, but warm as the weather's been, who knows?"

Listen to you, Ferry thought. A real hook and bullet guy.

15

---

oby parked at the curb outside a stately Mission-style home on the edge of downtown. A low stucco wall, rimmed with red clay tiles to match the roof on the house, surrounded the yard, which was filled with massive oaks and smaller chinaberry trees.

Getting out from behind the wheel, he collected from the back-seat his father's horn and his own. He felt oddly protective of the baritone, almost paranoid. Its weight in his hand seemed oddly personal. This was the one part of his father's life he understood—devotion, practice, ambition, disappointment. He wanted the horn near him. If it got damaged somehow or lost, it'd feel like he'd killed the old man all over again.

He joined Nadya on the sidewalk as she pushed open the iron-work gate. Side by side, they walked up a curving brick path beneath the trees, sunlight dappling the ground through the oak leaves, which rustled in a midday wind. Climbing the steps to an arcaded porch, they found a brass nameplate beside the front door: CHRISTINA NAVI-GATO, ATTORNEY-AT-LAW.

Toby prepared to ring the bell but then noticed the door stood slightly ajar. He glanced at Nadya, who shrugged. It was an office, after all, not just a home, Sunday notwithstanding. He nudged the door open.

"Hello?"

Two large rooms with coved ceilings flanked the entryway, one for waiting, the other a conference area lined with bookshelves. Both were empty, as were the small offices lining the hallway. At the rear, the hallway zagged. A rustic kitchen stood to one side. Toby heard voices, then saw, at the very back, a carpeted stairway leading to the second floor. He turned to Nadya, shrugged—she answered back with a shrug of her own—and led the way up.

Just beyond the landing stood an archway leading to a large, recessed, wood-paneled library with a low ceiling, lit by skylights above, antique sconces along the walls, and Tiffany table lamps elsewhere. A dense oak table dominated the center of the room, piled high with case files, pleadings, three-ring binders, and document boxes.

Four people sat around the table—Tina, two other women, and a man. Atop their heads they wore blue-and-white FedEx envelopes, pulled down to the eyes or pushed back to the crown—all of them laughing giddily, like kids at a birthday party.

"Hello?" Toby said again, Nadya behind him in the archway.

The laughter stopped in halting chirps; everyone turned. "Oops," someone whispered.

Tina rose, pulled the FedEx envelope off her head, and eased forward, smiling sheepishly. "It's Sunday," she explained. "We're here working, instead of at home. Needed a little boost." She held the envelope up, to demonstrate. "Rally hats."

Introductions ensued. The man was Tina's brother, Dan, who dominated the room the instant he stood up. One of the women, Shel, was his wife, a reedy woman with graying red hair. Something haunted her eyes, Toby thought, and in that regard they reminded him a little of Nadya's—inviting but uneasy, too. She did not stand; a cane was hooked to the back of her chair.

Tina introduced the last woman as her partner—bespectacled and prim, a thirtyish Filipina with dimples and a pageboy haircut. Joyanne was her name. Toby wondered, Partner in love or law? Taking her small hand, he remembered there'd been only one name on the door. But earlier, when Tina'd mentioned her male mentor, he'd inferred they'd been lovers. Now this. Maybe I got it wrong, he thought. Maybe I've got everything wrong.

He put the horn cases down. "Nadya can fill you in on what just happened at the house. You'll want to know. In the meantime, I need to make a phone call. Is there somewhere private?"

Tina led him to a small office just off the landing, with little in it but a single desk, a lamp, and a telephone console. As soon as she left, he closed the door, selected an outside line, and phoned the number he knew from memory. A frail voice answered.

"Miss Carvela? This is Toby Marchand."

On the other end of the line he heard a faint gasp, like she'd nicked herself with a pin. "My poor boy, I am so sorry, so terribly sorry."

At the sound of her voice, the feelings came. He bit his cheeks. "I have an apology to make."

"Whatever for?"

"The police."

"They were here. Earlier."

"Yes, I know, Miss Carvela. I was the one who told them where to come."

The line went still. Toby filled the silence with recriminations.

Finally, she said, "Oh, in the history of such things, it was hardly too bad." The cheerfulness seemed forced.

"I'm so sorry."

"Yes."

"Is Francis—"

"He's fine, dear. He's found a place with some friends. I suppose I can tell you that. He asked me not to tell you where. For your sake, not just his."

It sounded like a lie. Toby said, "I understand."

"You mustn't blame yourself. I can only imagine what you've been through."

"No. That's no excuse."

"Toby—"

"I didn't know, they had me alone, I thought—" He stopped himself. No excuse, but listen to me. "I don't know what I thought. I wish—"

"Yes."

Neither spoke for a moment. Toby coiled the phone cord around his finger.

She said, "Do you have a place to stay?"

Toby had to think. "I'm guessing Pop's house, I don't know. But there's some talk that the guy who shot him was hiding next door."

"Oh dear. Take care, you must—"

"I'm at my lawyer's now."

Another pause, then: "Would it be too much to ask . . . Oh, this may be, how shall I . . . It's a bit to ask. Would you mind terribly staying here with me?"

It seemed a clumsy touch of grace. Like being forgiven.

"Everything that's happened, it has me a little, I don't know, uneasy." She chuckled sadly. "All those years living alone, then just a few months with Francis here, in the house. See what a spoiled old woman I've become?"

When he returned to rejoin the others, he saw his father's horn case open on the large oak table. The baritone's pearl keys and nickel-plated body glimmered in the light. Everyone looked up—not a word from anyone, staring at him in the doorway. He wondered if they felt guilty for having stolen a peek without asking first. Silly, he thought. Then Nadya got up, holding a crumpled white envelope, which she held out for him to take.

"They wanted to see your father's horn. We found this in the compartment that holds the extra mouthpiece and reeds."

The envelope had "For Toby" written on it, his father's handwriting. It was sealed. He checked with Tina, who nodded. He worked the seal open. A letter lay inside, written on hospital stationery.

Dear Toby,

It's been a couple hours since Veronique drove me to the emergency room. The whole time, she's hounding me about, "Do you have a will? Have you made arrangements?" Like she can't wait. Drive me straight to the graveyard, not the hospital, if she could.

But it got me to thinking. Before they put me under the knife, I want to say a few things.

I wasn't the man, the musician, the father to you, or the friend to your mother I should have been. Time like this, that looms large. Wish I could change it, know I can't, may never get to say I'm sorry.

In particular, I rode you hard, too hard. God knows there's reasons for that I should be ashamed of, but I wanted you ready. Ready to take on the phonies and the users and the thieves who will hound you throughout your career. I know your mother wants something else for you, can't blame her. But I sense in you the gift. Sensed that a long time, actually.

I want you to have the house. It's paid in full, your grandmother took care of that. I built it out so I could practice with the Firefly, but not just that. For you, too. If you want, take over the band. They're good men, strong players. I think they'll follow, if you have the spine to lead. Don't be shy. As they retire or pass away, replace them with players you know, players you respect. Carry on.

Any money or other valuables I leave behind—there won't be much, I'm sure that's no shock—divvy them up among the family as you see fit. Don't let Veronique badger you into something you don't think's right. But don't listen to your mother, neither, just walk away. Please do as I ask. It will give me some comfort, knowing that.

The nurse is here. They're ready. Please know I loved you, Son. I always have. I have shown that badly. But I've paid.

> *Your loving father,*
> *Raymond Carlisle*

Toby read it again, twice, beginning to end, needing to sit finally. He found himself in a strange mental state, not wholly there, not wholly elsewhere, wishing for a time and place he could answer this letter.

Tina walked up, hand held out.

"May I?"

Always the lawyer. Toby passed the letter to her and glanced up at Nadya, who came close, resting her hand gently on the nape of his neck. Her skin felt cool against his own.

"Do you know what this is?" Tina asked.

It seemed a kind of trick question. Toby shrugged.

"We'll have to verify it's your father's signature."

"I can do that."

"Someone other than you."

"Why?"

Tina folded the letter closed and handed it back. "It's called a holographic will."

Following Bratcher's directions, Ferry drove past the rock yards and auto dismantlers and salt ponds lining Green Island Road. At the very end, he parked the van beyond the blacktop at a gravel turnaround rimmed with bulrushes and fennel that had died back with winter.

Rusting track led to the old rail bridge, a two-tower structure of low-carbon steel painted a puke green and tagged with graffiti. The county had taken out its center section, so boat traffic could sail up and down the Napa River at will. Trash littered the muddy weeds leading up to the rail bed. Nice just to be out there, Bratcher had said. Some joke. It was the kind of place teenagers came on Friday night to get ripped or blown, and only foreigners would bother to fish here.

He locked the van and headed toward an old rotting bench, looking across the river. Cattails lined the riverbed, their flower spikes shorn away, harvested by local florists for winter decorations. On the far side, a derelict pleasure boat, complete with paddle wheel, listed to one side in the mud flat. Beyond it, redwood piers tethered with speedboats led up to a line of houses atop the levee. The county loners lived over there, their homes accessible only by water or a two-lane road snaking down from Cuttings Wharf.

The slough-laced wetlands stretched to the south. Ferry spotted a great blue heron in the distance, making one last turn of the marshes before returning to its rookery. It was high tide; the heron scoured the levees, waiting for the mice and voles to clamber for high ground, exposed. It reminded him of Manny. Unmasked. Exposed.

He guessed the kid worked off two core principles: *I am disgusting, even to myself,* and *The world must burn.* With no inkling of how the one fed the other, let alone why. It might almost inspire a kind of pity, Ferry thought, if you weren't obliged to clean up after him.

Ferry had to make sure Manny's misadventure of the previous night never reached Bratcher's radar. Not till payment was in hand, at any rate. Given the big guy's history, you had to guess he'd find a way to make everybody suffer the cost but him.

Bratcher had begun as a fireman—there was an irony for you, Ferry thought—getting in just before the pay scales skyrocketed. Few people realize how well you can make out as a fireman in California. He moved on to business agent for the union, where he honed his lobbying chops. He liked that, the arm-twisting, the hustles, the brinkmanship. And again, there was money in it. Some of it came in cash.

Cash builds up, you gotta find a way to invest. Only so many new safes in the house you can justify. Looking for opportunities he could monitor firsthand, Bratcher turned to flooring—offering short-term loans to car salesmen who'd left dealerships to open lots of their own. Being salesmen, they wildly exaggerated their chances of breaking even, overspent, and ran to men like Bratcher for cover. He was smart, always demanding a secured debt, and took away a half-dozen homes through foreclosure, right when property values went wild.

Bratcher cashed out, then teamed up with his lawyer to invest in closely held real estate concerns bankrolling motels at South Lake Tahoe during the casino expansions, and high-rise apartment buildings around Sacramento as the state government mushroomed. He hit bliss every deal he made, a knack for timing. Then came his first bad move.

He saw a bargain in some high-rises in south Sac. Too cocky, he figured he could boot all the subsidy tenants. He didn't foresee the gang upsurge of the mid-eighties. Within three years, his sly investment transformed into two of the tallest crack houses in the West. He spent ten years trying to go through the police, the courts, community groups, only to see every meager victory stolen back within days, hours sometimes.

Bratcher wasn't the kind to live with that—getting jobbed by the underclass was for social workers—which led to his linkup with Ferry. Bratcher's lawyer was the one who heard about him—former narc, contacted through the Internet, already wielding a heavy, if slippery, reputation.

Ferry's strategy was twofold.

One, focus on women in the family. Make it plain—the trouble goes or they go. You get a fight, plant evidence if need be, drop the dime. Women hold the whole thing together. Send the women to jail or put them on the street, the men won't stand tall—they'll vanish.

Two, scope it out, see who travels with whom, then pick off a low-rung slinger or tout—better still, a family member—leave a telltale mark on the body if you can, kick off a war. Bodies buy action. The ones left behind kill each other off, get popped in a street sweep, or, with the jacked-up heat, scurry on down to the next relation in line. Home is where they have to take you in: Elk Grove, Rio Mirada, Vallejo, Pittsburg, Richmond, Oakland, Hunter's Point, East Palo Alto. Skip tracers, bail bondsmen, parole officers, the police—they all knew the circuit well. But for Ferry, all he needed to know was there was somewhere else for Bratcher's problems to head. As long as they went, problem solved.

That was four years ago. In the interim, Bratcher fended off two grand jury investigations, one into improper campaign contributions (he'd funneled union money to retired firefighters in a scam to skirt spending limits, and laundered developer kickbacks through his lawyer), the other for orchestrating a pattern of HUD fraud, relating to abuse of the Officer Next Door Program.

Cops and firemen and teachers could purchase HUD foreclosures for 50 percent of the outstanding loan if they agreed to live in the house three years. It was a way of getting respectable community members into marginal neighborhoods. But HUD lacked the manpower to enforce the terms; scammers had a field day. Buyers got in low, rented or turned the properties around in just a few months with minor, cosmetic changes, and walked off with a killing. Bratcher, after a decade of hassles with the agency over his drug dealing problems, saw this as sweet revenge. He had his hand in locating properties for willing takers, finessing the back end sales and rentals, keeping tabs on HUD investigations, and again letting his attorney's client trust account serve as a slush fund for unreportable cash.

He'd paid a fine on the campaign charges. The results of the second investigation were strangely vague. There were rumors Bratcher and his lawyer were cooperating, which of course made sense. Amazing, the crap you can manage with federal juice.

Then last fall, Bratcher resumed contact with Ferry. He had a different problem, he said, a bigger one. He didn't need to drive out just a few problem bangers. He needed more.

It was tricky, given the rumors that he stooled for the feds. But Ferry knew this about Bratcher: he was too cutthroat to betray someone still useful to him, too hard-nosed to let the law badger him into it. And Bratcher could hardly bring down Ferry on his drug dealer drop plays and killings—juries never let the paymaster snitch off his muscle, it went against the American grain. Besides, Bratcher was earnest, he wanted this thing done, and from just a glance you could see the money at stake. It made sense. That kind of making sense, it protected you, unless you got sloppy.

Manny's killing the old spade, that was sloppy. Demented and sloppy. Which was why Ferry could feel his heartbeat kick a little as finally, pulling onto the gravel at the end of Green Island Road, Bratcher's Escalade appeared—big and white with gold hardware and gaudy horsepower—kicking up dust as it left the asphalt.

Bratcher parked beside the van, got out, removed two fly rods from the back of the Escalade, and charged forward.

"You weren't supposed to take me serious, Clint, when I said I wanted to fish."

"You showing up like that, it's no good, understand?" Bratcher's face was red; he gripped the two fly rods tight in his huge hands. "End of the day, the risks you thought were no big thing, they're the ones do you in."

Ferry didn't like the feel of this. "Clint, we've met there before, alone, first time, remember?"

"That was then. I brought you into this thing because you've got the kind of head can handle it. Pull a stunt like that, I gotta think—"

"I poked my nose in the damn door. Get real. Anybody recalls my face he's lying. I page you, beep you, call your cell, there's a record. I did the right thing."

Bratcher grunted and held out one of the rods. "Grab that. Walk with me."

Ferry obeyed. Secretly he preferred not meeting in the Escalade, which could be bugged. That was paranoia for you, it never slept. The rod Bratcher gave Ferry came fitted with a Penn Sixty reel, a decent

rig for the stripers he said were here. Not that Ferry'd seen any. All
he'd spotted so far was a few schools of threadfin shad darkening the
water, surging upriver from the bay.

"I'm not seeing any bait here, Clint."

"Shut up for once, will ya? I'm gonna practice casting, used to do
it here all the time. You can do what the hell you want."

Bratcher pulled up at a divide in the cattails edging the water, then
let out his line, stretching it to remove the memory. Ferry didn't bother
to do the same. He was thinking. It was a good sign, he decided,
Bratcher's foul mood. The crankiness seemed genuine. That and his
plan to come out here, where they might get seen but not noticed.

When Bratcher started to restrip his line, Ferry said, "It's gonna
happen tonight."

The look, you'd have thought he'd tried to feed the guy a clump of
mud.

"You're not serious."

"It's okay, we're ready."

"That's not the point."

On the far levy, a woman in a sweat suit walked down to the dock
beneath her house, accompanied by a toddler and a dog. The woman
threw a tennis ball into the water, the dog sailed in after it, and the toddler applauded with mittened hands.

"Some old dusk got killed last night up on the St. Martin's side of
the panhandle. Turns out my guy was crashing at the house next door.
Cops found that out."

Bratcher stopped what he was doing. "Gonna tell me how?"

"Guy they've got as their chief suspect, he's a banger, works for
people my guy hung with."

Bratcher grimaced and shook his head. "Nice class of people you
bring into this."

"Yeah, well, I thought about an ad in *Boys' Life*, but the last couple issues, I dunno, just didn't ring my bell."

"You think this is funny?"

"Cops're looking for my guy now, got him pegged as a possible material witness." Ferry had thought it through. This seemed like the
most readily defensible lie at his disposal. Besides, it was at least half-
true, which was pretty good as lies went.

Bratcher twitched, shook his head. "So keep him under wraps, like you shoulda done in the first place."

Oh, sure, Ferry thought. Blame me. "Too risky, Clint."

"He goes in, says he didn't see anything." Bratcher turned, glared. "Did he?"

"Not the problem. He's got baggage, he's suspected in some heavy fires up north. He goes in for questioning, he stays in."

Without warning, Bratcher snapped his rod back to two o'clock, listened for his line to hit ground, then snapped the rod forward. One smooth movement. No de-barbed lure or yarn ball for this guy. Hook catch your eye? Shoulda ducked. The lure hit water with a *thunk*.

"This thing's gotten so fucked up," Bratcher said.

What else has gone wrong, Ferry wondered, knowing better than to push his luck and ask. He'd already heard Bratcher's rag about the last project that had fallen through. His buddies Glenn and Craugh had bought up a dozen warehouses near the river, operating under long-term leases from the city at negotiated low rents due to promises to rebuild. But then the project got tied up by the city when it tried to squeeze out extra CAM charges and pass-throughs. None of Bratcher's muscle had gotten the city to budge. Craugh was overleveraged and couldn't get more financing. Now squatters had taken over some of the buildings.

Worse, the city, feeling its oats after backing down Bratcher, had dug in its heels. It wanted any businesses lined up as tenants to pay triple rents, working it through a Municipal Services District that didn't exist when the leases were formed. The city had also invoked Mello-Roos and tried to form a new district for extra taxes to bounce up school funding. As if all that weren't enough, insurance was going through the roof due to the World Trade Center attack and the threat of reparations lawsuits.

It was that last part that really galled Bratcher. In their first meeting, when Bratcher explained the vision he had for Baymont—gated community, all wired for satellite or cable, high-speed Internet, multiple phone lines, exterior surveillance and home theater surround sound, the wiring package alone worth five grand, plus peninsula kitchens, built-in gas fireplaces, master baths with jetted tubs and custom glass—he described his plan for ridding the hill of its current structures and tenants by saying, "Think of it as reverse reparations." He got the biggest kick out of that.

"There is," Ferry said, "a bright side to what happened last night. Rains got the sewers backed up, which means the gas will move slow through the system. Fumes will build up and ride high. You got smoke crews working the top of the hill, where everybody can see. Nobody's gonna second-guess the problems up there with the storm drains. And every other Sunday night, mom-and-pop gas station up top, it gets its delivery. That's tonight. It's the key to the whole thing."

"Gonna be true as long as there's an every other Saturday night. Besides, the rain cuts both ways, it's too wet."

"There's a good wind today. Dry enough."

"That's crap." Bratcher scanned the westward horizon. "You got storms coming in. What's the point, the thing doesn't spread?"

"It'll spread. We've got eight houses that'll go up quick, the fire source is inside, not out. And they're gonna burn hot. Radiant heat'll dry things out as things move."

Bratcher's eyes darkened. "Who's talking about eight houses?"

"You'll have the sewers full of gas fumes. They'll back up through the drains. All they have to do is hit a pilot light."

"Just because you got fumes and a flame source in the same room doesn't mean—"

"Fumes back up into a sewer, they find a flame source every time. Ask anybody who's worked on a flipped tanker."

Bratcher screwed up his mouth, shook his head. "Don't like it. Too soon. No. Feels all wrong."

Ferry bit his lip to control his impatience. "You get eight houses, fast full engagement, plus others on top of the—"

"I understand the plan. I'm the one came up with it. I'm just saying—"

"You came up with what and where. How and why and when are my department. I've got the kind of head that can handle this sort of thing—your words, remember? I'm serious, it's gotta be tonight."

Bratcher rolled all but about thirty feet of his line back onto the reel. Slow. Thinking. "If this chickenshit backwater worked the way it ought to work, none of this would be necessary." He grimaced, like an ugly premonition had just snuck up on him. "The hoops you gotta jump through anymore," he muttered, "just to build something, make life better for a place like this." He turned toward Ferry and shot him a baleful look. "Give most people half a chance, they'll waste their lives sitting in their own stink. The only thing new and better they'll ever make is the next excuse for why nothing's ever their fault."

Ferry'd heard this before, or something much like it. In this rendition, though, he detected a hint of regret in Bratcher's tone. More likely, it was fear. "Not much point worrying over things like that."

"Yeah. Sure. True enough." Bratcher turned back to the water, shook off his mood. "Back to the point—this was supposed to happen in April, you know? After we get Polhemus in, have a majority in place."

"Can't wait that long, Clint."

"Fire doesn't solve squat without the council on board. Haven't got the votes for the package we want—the right consultants, the bond brokers, the lawyers we need to write up the DDA."

"With the way that hill's gonna look tomorrow morning, the council will come on board in a heartbeat."

"What do you know about it?" Bratcher shot Ferry a rum look. "Know what I think? I think there's something you're not telling me."

Ferry shook his head, looked off. "There's a lot I'm not telling you. That's the way you want it, believe me."

"Yeah? Why's that?"

"Get too hands-on, you'll wear it on your face. I'm doing you a favor."

"Don't worry about what I do or how I handle it."

This is getting too strange, Ferry thought. He laid his rod on the ground, turned to leave, then heard a cry from the far side of the river. Something was wrong with the dog; it was struggling in the current. The woman was calling to it, her voice becoming shrill. She crawled down onto the pier and into the water as the little girl began to shriek, sobbing hysterically. Ferry and Bratcher stood there, helpless, watching. Serves her right, Ferry thought, cold as that water must be. Poor dog.

"One other thing," he said finally. "This goes tonight, I'm gonna need my money tomorrow."

Bratcher laughed. "You nuts?"

"Route it the same as last time."

"No way I can move it that quick. No way I should. That's insane."

"Don't do this, Clint. Take you thirty minutes, tops, you move it over the Internet. Just like last time. I'm not telling you anything you don't know."

Bratcher readied to cast again. "Maybe that's not the point."

"Think of it this way: First installment bought performance. Second buys loyalty."

Bratcher stopped his cast and shot Ferry a thin, hateful smile. "You trying to shake me down?"

"I'm letting you know what you're paying for."

Bratcher grabbed his arm. "No. I'll tell you what I'm paying for. And it ain't eight houses. It ain't *eighteen* houses."

16

No sooner had Murchison arrived back at the station than word came from the front desk that a lawyer wanted to see him. Tina Navigato, he thought, and it put a little kick in his step as he headed toward the lobby. Through the lettered glass of the final door, however, he saw that the lawyer there to greet him was a man. Murchison knew him. His name was Grantree Hamilton and he specialized in civil rights law—suing cops for use of force—in addition to handling the headline drug case now and then, the occasional murder. Murchison had suffered through a few of the man's cross-examinations and had a grudging respect for him, despite the shaved head.

Murchison wondered if Sarina Thigpen had hired Hamilton to protest Arlie's treatment in custody. Or maybe Carvela Grimes had retained him on behalf of Francis Templeton; she'd said she'd talk to her lawyer at church and Hamilton looked dressed for Sunday services: cream-colored suit with a double-breasted jacket, sky-blue shirt, navy-blue tie. The shoes were two-tone Stacy Adams, a little touch of old school, still the homeboy. As Murchison finally stepped through the door, the lawyer charged forward, plowing the air with his outstretched hand.

"Detective, good to see you."

He smiled that shameless smile; it could give you sunburn. In contrast, the handshake was limp, indifferent.

"Mr. Hamilton."

"I understand you're lead detective on the Carlisle matter."

"You represent?"

"Veronique Edwards."

Murchison couldn't help himself, he smiled. "No fooling."

"She's Mr. Carlisle's next of kin."

"Not the way I hear it."

"Yes, well." Hamilton gestured for time, opened his briefcase, sorted through some papers, and withdrew a manila envelope. "I believe this may interest you."

Murchison took the envelope, opened it, and removed two photocopied documents. The first was a birth certificate: Tobias Marchand, no middle name. The father was listed as George Prescott Marchand. Felicia Marchand's signature appeared under the heading "Parent or Other Informant." The second document was a petition for child support—Felicia Marchand, Complainant; George "Sonny" Marchand, Respondent. One page was marked, where "Children of the Marriage" were listed. There were two girls. And Toby. More to the point, Hamilton had them on a Sunday morning. He and his client had been ready.

"The petition for support, that's penalty of perjury," Hamilton said. "So if there's been any talk, from Ms. Marchand in particular, that this Toby individual is the decedent's son—"

Murchison held up his hand. "Let me stop you, okay? This is the police department. Not the probate division."

"You still find perjury under the Penal Code."

"It's a civil matter."

"My point is, Detective, this Marchand woman and her son have tried to bleed my client's brother his whole life. Woman showed up first thing when her marriage fell apart, begging for money. Tried to piggyback her son's music career onto Mr. Carlisle's. Since he got sick late last year, they've had their eyes on that house up there. It's not for me, Detective, point the blame—"

"No. It's not." Murchison slipped the documents back inside their envelope. "Even if what you're saying's true, it's not you I need to hear it from. I need to talk to your client."

"Of course. Now is impossible, she's bereft. Her brother—"

"Everybody's bereft. They always are. I know, I talk to them. Now, I doubt this next bit comes as a surprise—we got a tip and searched the Victorians to either side of Mr. Carlisle's property. Owners gave us your client's name as the person to talk to. One was empty, but inside the other we found signs of a guy who was hanging out there, had an obsession with the victim's son's girlfriend."

"Detective, listen to me. The victim had no son."

"Doesn't change where I'm going. I need your client to come down, fill me in on the property, her brother." He raised the manila envelope to his ear and shook. "And anything else she thinks I need to know."

"Perhaps in a few days."

"Try a few hours." Murchison turned, reaching for the doorknob. "She drags it out, just makes us think. You don't want that. Right?"

Stluka, back from four hours off, sat at his desk, wrestling with paperwork. He looked miserable but rested.

Murchison pulled up beside his desk. "You heard?"

Stluka glanced up like he smelled abuse on the way. "Yeah, one of the Victorians. Swear to God, Murch. I checked. The place was tight."

"I know." Murchison gestured for him to relax. "The door he used, it was padlocked. We needed bolt cutters to get in."

Stluka sat back, looking vaguely relieved. "I like that." He scratched his ear with his pen. "Find anything? In the Vic, I mean."

"No weapon. He's a firebug. And I say he's got a thing for this Lazarenko girl."

Stluka thought about that. "Or didn't like the company she kept." He stretched, a yawn that expanded into a groan. "You look like crap, incidentally. Knock off. I'll drive the bus."

Murchison told him the rest of what the last few hours had produced. When he'd finished, Stluka said, "What I'm hearing, we haven't given up on this Mooney character."

"Too many things lead back to him. The house, I figure, he likes property. That's motive. We just gotta figure out if he did it on his own or one of these other characters did his bidding." He shook his head, get the cobwebs out. "The vic's sister has ties to the guy, and whatever anybody says—she's got a lawyer already, ain't that interesting—she's in this somehow."

"Lawyer?"

"Grantree Hamilton."

Stluka smiled. "You're shitting me."

"She's bereft."

"Oh, I'm sure. So hire Hamilton. Guy missed his calling, shoulda been a funeral director. That smells like Mooney, too."

"Everything does. Arlie Thigpen has ties to him. Kid who hung out at the Victorian was balling with some of Mooney's crew, they're the ones who steered him to the squat. The only ones we haven't tied to Mooney so far are the son—this Toby kid—and his abscond pal Francis. Which reminds me."

Murchison left Stluka at his desk and hunted the squad room for Holmes. No sign. He checked Dispatch, learned Holmes had gone off-duty. Voice mail, he thought. If he'd come up with anything, he'd have left word.

Murchison went back to his desk, checked his messages. Sure enough, Holmes had come through. His source in Mooney's circle knew nothing about a Toby Marchand. But Francis Templeton? He was nothing more than an occasional customer, and then all he wanted was pot—*dank*, Holmes said this guy called it, a new one for Murchison—but the crew knew who he was, and he knew them.

Murchison came around to Stluka's desk again. "Got news," he said, not happily.

In contrast, Stluka was beaming. "Me, too, oh yeah," he said, putting down his phone. "You first."

"Francis Templeton, Toby's alibi. He bought his weed from the Mooney crew."

Stluka's smile widened. "Oh, that's sweet."

Murchison couldn't share the joy. He wasn't sure, precisely, why.

"My turn." Stluka sat back, clasped his hands behind his head. "That dyke who showed up for Mr. Toby, the probate lawyer?"

Murchison winced. "Why dyke?"

Stluka shot him a puzzled look. "Don't tell me she rocked your world."

"Jerry, I'm just . . ." He dragged the word out, not sure what came next.

Stluka studied him. "I mean, hey, could be wrong. Maybe she's just confused. Lot of that going around these days."

"Can we get back to—?"

"She comes from a real interesting family. Father was a low-level Mob mutt, tied to gambling in North Beach like decades ago. Disappeared. Nobody knows where. Some folks think he's dead. And her brother." He glanced down at notes he'd written. "I'm not even gonna try to pronounce his name, but he was some kind of big-time dope smuggler, did ten years in federal stir, Safford."

Murchison glanced down at the notepad, read the name upside down. Dan Abatangelo. "They've got different last names. Him and his sister." He didn't remember a wedding ring. "She's divorced?"

"Nope. Not even. Changed her name." Stluka grinned, loving it. "Felt ashamed of the men in her family. Disappearing dad. Doper bro. She had an innocent heart and a bar card to protect. Took her mother's maiden name."

"How'd you learn all this?"

Stluka nodded toward the phone. "Lawyer buddy here in town. A dyke herself, if I may say. No cracks—I'm more broad-minded than people think. Anyway, local bar, it's very, how shall we say . . ." He snapped his fingers once, twice.

"Cliquish?"

Stluka fluttered his eyelashes. The coquette. "*Incestuous* was the word I was after, actually."

Toby rode in front, Nadya in back, as Tina's brother, Dan, drove them up the hill to Baymont to stay with Francis's great-aunt. Darkness tinged the edges of the afternoon sky. The huge trees lining the narrow streets swayed with a strong westerly wind, which carried with it a prickly scent of salty mud from the marshes. It felt strangely warm for February, almost balmy, like spring.

Toby had wanted to drive up alone, but Tina wouldn't have it. "Think about what they've found out. This character next door, hiding. He may think Nadya, or you, saw him come and go. Maybe saw the shooting. I'd feel better if Dan was with you. He's been through some trouble in his time. He can handle things."

Toby wondered what "trouble" meant, but he had to admit, there was an almost hypnotic gravity to her brother. Not just because of his imposing height, his build. He had wise eyes. Like he'd figured out and put behind him every single thing you were still too scared to face.

As they reached the top of Baymont, turning onto Miss Carvela's street in Home in the Sky, Toby glanced around at the drama. Tatted-up muscle—gripping bottles, blowing smoke—slouched on porch stoops. Hood rats perched on cars. Illogic's "Hate in a Puddle" thundered from a tape deck as a throng playing roundball hustled around a portable hoop planted in a tire. They stopped playing as the car approached, parting lazily as it passed, a few of them leaning down to get a good look, flash some hooride cheese through the glass.

"We're making an impression," Toby said, reading in their eyes the same message he'd heard most of his life: Only fools, cowards, and children bother to befriend white people. Sonny, his stepfather, breathed fire on the subject. Toby'd recoiled from the rant. Not that he didn't see the truth to it—he wasn't stupid—but it was a small, mean truth.

Besides, he wasn't immune. He played his own games. Jazz crowds were overwhelmingly white; you didn't play long and not figure out how to angle that. Most white people wanted so badly to be liked you could get them to agree to almost anything, while the others either kept their distance or wanted to be congratulated for hating you. And, of course, there was Nadya. He felt ashamed sometimes, how easy it was. I'm not just different, he thought. I'm exotic. If I can't figure out what to say, I'm not just sitting there stupid—I'm mysterious. Even a nitwit stammer comes across somehow quaint. He wondered sometimes who he hated more, her or himself, for getting away with all that. Just as he wondered what had possessed his father to bare the uglier family secrets to his white woman lawyer.

Stop doing this to yourself, he thought as he pointed out Miss Carvela's house. Dan pulled the car to the curb in front. As he did, one of the ballplayers cakewalked behind, to laughter from his friends. He was shirtless, lean but muscular, boxers hiked up, painter pants tugged down, his hair in a fade. As the car stopped, he stopped. Leaning down, he feigned stupefaction at what he saw. Snapping back straight, he called out over his shoulder, "Yo, money, check this shit out. Coulda sworn Zip Coon come on up, pay his props, blackface and all. Him and his Babylonians."

As some of the others laughed again, one called back, "Stop choppin', fool. Come on, Spoonie. Play ball!"

"No, no, serious now. This nigger's black as Clarence Thomas. Come look."

Inside the car, Toby said, "I'll go up alone first. Miss Carvela, she's older. I want to make sure she's ready for us to come in."

Dan, eyeing the young man just outside the car, said, "You're sure—"

"You think I'm scared?"

Dan's face went blank. "I didn't—"

Toby opened the passenger door. "I'm fine."

As he got out, the one named Spoonie circled behind the car to meet him. Toby eased up to him, not shunning eye contact and even offering a sly little smile, the jokester, his usual defense. His voice, though, was cold and low. "You looking for Swanson," he said, "you need a new nigger. We straight?" The young man's face snarled up in puzzlement as Toby slipped on past. He was halfway to the top of the steps before, from behind, Spoonie recovered.

"Hey, Clarence! Left your flossy little boo behind! What's up with that?"

Nadya watched Toby climb the cracked cement steps that led uphill from the street to the old saltbox house. Dan, watching as well, said, "I could have handled that better."

"We're both a little on edge. Don't take it personally."

He turned around in his seat, cast a glance at the young men outside in the street, then said, "Actually, I'm glad we've got a minute alone. I wanted to speak with you." He fixed her with his eyes, a stare somehow intimidating but not frightening. "My sister, Christina, filled me in on what happened, what you did. It's difficult to describe for people what it's like. See someone die like that. Not like TV."

Nadya's heartbeat quickened. At the sound of a shout from the street, she turned around, watching as the young men resumed their game. Here and there, one or another of them stole a glance toward the car. As her eyes met theirs, she could feel them daring her to be just who they knew she was.

Dan continued, "If you need to talk to someone, Shel or I might be good. We've been through some things, too. Not the same as you, but not much different, actually. The after part, it's hard. And people who haven't been through it, they mean well, but . . . Can't blame them. Not their fault."

She turned back around to face him. "Talking doesn't seem to help much, actually."

He smiled. "Give it time. Don't brood. Dive inside your own head, you just get lost."

Nadya lowered her head, nodded. "It's crazy-making."

Her worst fear was that Toby would feel for her, but only to a point. Only for a time. His patience would wear thin, and it would be gone long before she was even halfway close to getting a handle on what was happening to her. He'll keep on saying he understands, she thought, but it gets old, if you're not the one going through it. She could forget about sleep. She wasn't going to make it through the night for a long, long while. The nightmares, she knew, would be fierce, and she already suspected that the deeper she slept, the more vivid they'd become.

She turned, glanced up at the old house into which Toby'd disappeared. Her longing for him, it grew by the minute. The neediness made her feel repulsive.

"Some advice?" He followed her glance. "The best thing you can do—guaranteed, one hundred percent best. You can try, ask for kindness, comfort—but maybe it's a male thing, I always found that hard to do."

"It's not just a male thing," she assured him. "But what else is there?"

"Reach out." He nodded up the hill, Toby's direction. "Take care of him. Same way it's obvious he means to look after you."

He meant well, and it was kind advice. "I wish," she said, brushing the hair out of her face, "that didn't just seem like a pretty picture."

"I'm not talking denial. It can cure a lot of ills, taking care of someone. And you're in this together."

You have no idea how much I hope that's true, she thought, glancing once again over her shoulder at the fierce and jubilant young men in the street.

"The worst part is feeling helpless." He smiled, a brotherly glint in his eye. "Reminds me of a story. There was this priest, chaplain at the prison I was in, perfectly decent guy. Hokey, but nice. 'Good listener.'"

She looked at him quizzically.

"It's what we used to say about ugly girls in high school."

"Oh."

"Anyway, this chaplain, he had a sign over his desk: THE ROAD TO DESPAIR BEGINS IN HELPLESS."

She chuckled. "The geography of gloom." Her hands felt cold; she buried them in her armpits. "Your wife, she's not well."

The brotherly light dimmed. "No."

Nadya had noticed the glassiness in Shel's eyes, the dark patches beneath them, the slack smile. The cane she used to walk. Cancer, she'd guessed, afraid to ask. "I was really moved by how you treated each other, the way you talked and touched each other. Can I tell you a secret?"

"Sure."

"I felt jealous."

That seemed to please him, but from the look on his face, the pleasure was a kind of heartbreak. "No need. I see much the same thing between you and Toby."

Is that a compliment, she wondered, or a curse? "Can I tell you another secret?"

He studied her. "Of course."

"I'm afraid." She shook her head. "I'll say this badly. I'm afraid, yes. Afraid . . . I might die. Before I can make it up to him. Toby." She winced. "It sounds so stupid—"

He reached out for her hand. Please don't tell me I'm not going to die, she thought. Don't patronize me.

"You can't make it up to him. I mean, I should probably tell you there's nothing to make up, but I know how guilt can work on your head. Trust me on this, okay? You did all you could. Knowing what you know now, you'd do better, but you don't get those kinds of second chances."

She looked at her hand in his. "I'm afraid of what his mother, the rest of his family, think. I hear them, in my head I mean, I hear them saying something like, 'This is the white girl who didn't see a thing.' "

Toby appeared on the porch, waving them inside. Dan squeezed her hand one last time. "Try to focus on the things you can control, not the things you can't."

He got out, opened her door, and walked at her elbow up the steps. It seemed the whole neighborhood came to a halt. Nadya could feel their eyes on her back.

Inside, the heater had warmed the old house with the dense, slightly ticklish smell so similar to that in Toby's father's home. Needlework sat everywhere—Nadya recognized Gobelin and *tramé* patterns on a pair of sofa cushions. A candy dish filled with butter creams rested on a maple veneer end table, and a sweating tumbler of ice water sat beside the candy dish.

Francis's aunt wore a belted black knee-length dress with white lace trim at the neck. Elegant and small, the old woman came forward, silver hair combed flat to her head and held fast with pins. She wore eyeglasses mended with tape and took both Nadya's hands in her own.

"Well, look at us," she said, her fingers dry and cold. "Two tiny women."

Murchison didn't go straight home. He detoured toward downtown, then stopped at Tina Navigato's office. Bad move, he knew, even as he got out, strode from the car through the gate and up the walk beneath the trees. He rang the bell like he'd knock the door down if it didn't open, and shortly a petite, dimpled Filipina stood there, eyes the size of quarters behind gold-rimmed glasses.

"Miss Navigato, she here?"

"Yes." The voice fit the face. Murchison wasn't fooled. He knew enough Filipino families to know how tough the women could be, how hard they worked to hide that from outsiders.

"Tell her Detective Murchison is here." As an afterthought: "Please."

He stepped inside before the woman could close the door on him. He waited in the entry, surveying the decor. Luxuriant but subtle, he thought, white plaster and wood with strangely mannish furniture—

Morris chairs with leather cushions, a matching settee, and library tables. A lawyer thing, he supposed, or a dyke thing. The floors were pegged white oak, and watercolors provided color along the walls. Joan, who had an eye for such things, would kill to have a place like this.

Tina appeared, and again he felt caught like a boy in her stark blue eyes. The Filipina trailed behind with a pinched face, not so angelic now. Something charged the air between them, a concern that went beyond business. Stluka had it right after all, Murchison thought. Jesus, what a sap you can be.

"Your client lied. Or his mother did. But you know that already."

Tina studied him, thinking. Behind her, the Filipina twisted her head brusquely toward Tina, toward Murchison, back and forth.

"You mean the birth certificate."

"Don't forget the divorce papers."

She gestured for him to calm down. "A birth certificate does not establish paternity. It's not under oath."

Murchison laughed. Lawyers, he thought. "But the petition for child support is."

"Detective—"

"So you knew about it?"

"I'll say it again, the issue of paternity is irrelevant to the issue of who murdered—"

"That's touching. Your concern for the murder victim. Must be a family trait. I hear the men in your family are known for their soft hearts."

The Filipina leaned forward, whispered something urgent in Tagalog. Tina cut her off.

"The men in my family?"

"I heard—"

"I haven't seen my father since I was six. I was estranged from my brother for almost twenty years, but that's over now. It was hard, but we worked at it. I'm glad he's in my life again. Beyond that, my family has nothing to do—"

"Know how I found out? My partner, he's the one, actually, got the tip. From a lawyer in town. Gay woman. That surprise you? My partner, for all his faults, he has very good instincts about some things."

Murchison himself detected the vulgar pitch creeping into his voice. The Filipina stared at him like he'd just zipped down his fly.

"Detective," Tina said, "I really think it would be best if you left now."

"Where's your client?"

"He's in town, with friends. If you need to speak with him you can do so through me."

Murchison wondered if it would be too much to ask if he could sit down. His head swam. Muscles aching with weariness. "I need to speak with him."

"No. Not now. I meant what I said, Detective. Please leave."

Murchison lived in one of the newer developments on a hill overlooking the old salt evaporation ponds. The homes had been built by Bob Craugh's company, known for its below-market pricing and bottom money down, financing its own mortgages, like Jameson Carswell had done in the Black community decades before. Carswell had built to last. These houses were crap—a decade old and falling apart. Worse, the city had to raid the general fund to service the construction bond, because tax assessments had stagnated. It meant no raises for cops or firemen in the foreseeable future.

He removed his service piece, tucked it in the vault he kept in the garage, and locked it up. Joan had become increasingly paranoiac since reading about how an Indiana state trooper's boy had blown off the top of his head with his father's side arm. Murchison saw the point, though he'd resented the tone she'd used when she pressed it.

Sun streamed through the kitchen window, reflecting thousands of dust motes suspended in the downward slant of light. A musty stench of old clothes and sitting garbage hung in the air, too. Joan prized her job, she could dress to the nines when called upon, and she had the knack for motherhood, too. But her disdain for homemaking was absolute. She could be at times the most inspired slob one could imagine. The girls adored her for it.

She stood at the sink with her back to the door, washing dishes. She did them by hand. The dishwasher leaked. She wore just her bra and a wool skirt, stockings but no shoes, caught in transition between dressed up for mass and dressed down for her weekly trip with the girls to Granite Bay to see her parents.

Despite his recent urge for Tina Navigato, made all the more half-assed by his pushiness at her office, he felt instantly aroused by the sight of the smooth whiteness of his wife's back, the elasticized cotton of her bra pinching her skin. The three moles above her waist he knew well. And the scar acquired at the age of eight, when she'd slipped on a diving board at Girl Scout camp and bled into the pool. One of those stories women tell you.

Beyond a slight stir, nothing moved below his belt line. Sometimes hard-ons do have a conscience, he guessed. He already knew they possessed a memory. Once before when he'd come upon her like this, put his arms around her, and tried to kiss her neck, she'd cut him short with, "What is it about a woman with her back turned, hands stuck in grimy water, that invariably gets guys horny?"

Sensing him behind her, she glanced over her shoulder. "You look tired."

It was not a statement of sympathy, just an observation. "Yeah," he admitted. Trying for humor, he added, "I'm two steps from a snooze."

Upstairs, the girls thundered up and down the hallway, giggling. The sound, it seemed a universe away.

Turning back to the sink, Joan said, "Your mother called. I think you better go over."

She might as well have handed him a sack of stones. "Sound that bad?"

"You really have to ask that?"

"She say why—"

"She didn't say anything, Dennis. She never does. Not to me."

She rinsed a plate and racked it, probing the washtub for the next one. What is it, he wanted to ask. Tell me. But he knew he'd never say such things. He'd gone inward, like his old man.

"You'll probably be at church by the time I get back. Girls need money for the basket?"

"I've got it," Joan said, still not facing him.

•   •   •

His parents lived down the hill in one of the bungalow-style homes built during the war for the influx of shipyard workers. Sixty years old, these houses were small, plain, sometimes dreary, but seldom junk like Murchison's.

He let himself in and found his mother sitting in her bathrobe, smoking a cigarette in the living room, her hair uncombed. On the mantle above her, a triptych told the family story: his parents on their wedding day; Willy in his Special Forces uniform, frozen for all time at age twenty, his portrait bearing a small black ribbon; Dennis as he appeared in the program for Homecoming senior year, number 29, San Diego State Aztecs.

Seeing him enter, his mother neither waved nor smiled. "He's killing me, you know that? I'm worn out. I can't cope." She stubbed out her butt in the ashtray. "And when I'm dead, when he's driven me to my goddamn grave, then what? Ask him that for me, will you, please?" She immediately reached for her cigarette pack, prepared to light another. "Not like I care, though, right? I'll be dead. God willing."

"He's where?"

She flicked her hands toward the back of the house. "The yard. Out where the whole damn world can see."

He went through the kitchen and out the back, found his father sitting naked at the white metal patio table, watching a portable TV connected by a long extension cord to an outlet beneath the deck. His knees were scrabbled with mulch and dirt from crawling under there and back. He was smoking, coughing with each inhalation.

A face looked down from a neighbor's window. Murchison drew up a chair beside his father, who took no notice of his arrival. His hands, age-spotted and knobby from arthritis, were still thick and callused. Wisps of white hair floated atop his freckled scalp.

"Pop. You need some duds."

His father grimaced and snarled as though to continue an argument he'd been conducting inside his head for days. Then, just as suddenly, the expression faded, his eyelids fluttered, and he took another drag from his cigarette, after which he once again convulsed into a coughing jag.

Regaining his breath, he nodded toward the TV screen. "That coulda been you, ya know." It was one of those NFL Films programs put on for football junkies suffering the first throes of postseason withdrawal, full of slow-motion clips, thundering music.

"I'm gonna go back inside, get you something to wear."

"Don't bother." His voice was oddly detached. As though it wasn't really him speaking, wasn't really his son there to hear it, the subject wasn't his nudity. Some other bother, buried in the past, not to be troubled with.

He said, "It was Halburton's turn to go down."

"Sit tight. I'll be right back."

Inside the house again, Murchison said to his mother, "It would have been nice, going out the first time, knowing he needed clothes."

His mother said nothing.

He made his way up the stairs to their room. A strong smell of disinfectant filled the air. He went to their closet and withdrew a pair of dungarees and a sweatshirt. The closet was in chaos. His mother had been a patron saint of tidiness once. Now, his father's succession of small strokes, the overwhelming burden of new chores, and his escalating incontinence—not to mention the dementia, his meanness—it had swallowed up any impulse to care. It was all she could do to keep the bathroom sanitary. The rest could go to hell.

Rummaging through the bureau for some socks, Murchison reflected on his father's bringing up the name Halburton. It was one more symptom of the way his brain was turning to sand. Thirty-eight years he'd worked as a welder on the ships. Never a word about anything wrong, any accidents. Then, after the strokes began, little things started popping out. The name Halburton, for one. Murchison had prodded his dad for a little more information, but it all came out in cryptic asides: "Underwater job. . . . The hull breaks, the thing caves in, it's the suction, see? . . . We took turns. Everybody did." When Murchison had enough of these disconnected bits to put the question to his mother, she just stared at him. "Honestly, you think he ever told me anything?"

Outside, it took almost ten minutes to get his father into his pants, and Murchison gave up on the sweatshirt. The profanities were vicious and oddball. He finally just tossed the pair of socks into the old man's lap and said, "Enjoy your program."

Back inside, Murchison took a moment in the kitchen to gather his thoughts. For some reason, Toby Marchand came to mind. In particular, the way he'd cared for his father after surgery, only to see him start up drinking again. Still no hard suspect in that shooting, Murchison reminded himself. And if there was anything he could understand at that moment, it was wanting to kill your old man.

He walked out to the living room, sat down across from his mother, who now nursed a tumbler full of orange juice that looked suspiciously thin. Vodka, he guessed.

"I thought you guys had nursing care coverage."

His mother laughed acidly. "He won't go. Says I'll have to kill him first." Eyeing the service piece in its holster at her son's waist, she added, "Leave that behind, I'll put it to good use."

"You get the doctor involved?"

She grimaced with disgust. "Which doctor? The one this last visit or the one before that? Or the one before him? It's like a merry-go-round. 'Let's do an MRI. Let's get a CAT scan. Tests? What tests? Better do them all over again.' Then they just end up saying the same damn thing. 'Alzheimer's-like symptoms.' What the hell does that mean? What do I do? Nobody has a clue." She lifted her glass to drink. "Why should they care? It's not like they have to cure him to get paid."

Murchison felt an impulse to suggest something, anything, regardless how bankrupt, at the same time knowing it wasn't a solution she was after.

"And I'll tell you what else. This fat-ass nurse down there? I'm desperate, I'm crying, I'm on my knees. You know what she has the gall to tell me? 'There's no cure for growing old, dear.' Like I'm an idiot. Like I'm a child." She lifted the glass again, shrugged. "But what am I telling you for?"

Nodding toward her glass, he said, "You given any thought to antidepressants?"

Her expression collapsed, the eyes turned cold. Raising her hand, she pointed at him with a bent, arthritic finger: "How dare you say a thing like that to me."

17

As Ferry drove up to the storage locker, he discovered Manny sitting on the pavement out front, his back propped against the wall, knees swaying dreamily to and fro. His bruised eye still swollen shut, he blew a smoke ring into the air, studying its ascent as though it conveyed a secret message. Ferry inferred from all this that the kid had already cooked up and fixed and withstood his afternoon retch and nod. And who saw him at it, Ferry wondered, slamming the van door shut.

"I told you to stay out of sight."

"You're paranoid." Manny tapped tobacco ash onto the pavement. "I've seen, like, three people around here since you left."

Ferry took the cigarette out of his fingers, crushed it with his heel. "Yeah? Well, I took a drive around St. Martin's Hill, past your little home away from home. Your so-called friends handed you up. Took 'em no time at all."

Manny trembled a little, but his face glowed with smiling tranquillity. It's not just the smack, Ferry thought. The work, the smell of diesel fuel, it must have calmed him down.

"Like I said, you should get me out of here."

"Give me four more hours' honest labor." Ferry rolled up the locker door. "I'll get you as far away as you want."

He checked the detergent tubs, now filled with the silvery gray mix of ammonium perchlorate and diesel fuel and cut-up strips of aluminum. A flare impaled each tub.

"I figured we'd add the top-off of diesel fuel later." Manny nodded toward the last remaining nonempty jerrican. "You know, so they don't all slosh and spill in the van."

"Slow us down, messing around with the can each stop. Here." Ferry picked up the tin snips. "Make a hole in the tub lids, for the flare to stick out. I'll pour in the diesel now. What spills won't matter, too little to bother with. We'll take the lids off as we fire the little fuckers up. Hot as these burn, won't be a problem."

Manny went to work on the plastic tub lids, his high slowing him down just a notch, but that made him meticulous. Ferry doled out the diesel fuel, no more than a half inch in each tub. When they'd both finished they snapped home the lids and had a dozen self-contained bombs. Rocket fuel, basically. Things would go up so hot and fast they'd take with them anything in a ten-yard radius almost instantly.

"Let's pack 'em up."

They loaded the empty jerricans first, so they'd sit farthest from the rear doors. Then one by one they arranged the tubs—easy to reach, just open the doors and grab. From behind the passenger compartment Ferry dug out a pair of coveralls, a white cloth cap, and a huge pair of rubber boots, handing them all to Manny. "You're a plumber. Delivering supplies for repair jobs this week. Look the part."

Manny stepped into the coveralls as carefully as a kid putting on his pajamas. When he got to the boots, he said, "How come so big?"

"Same reason as mine." Ferry pulled his own boots on. "Keep them from matching our shoe prints from what they find at the scene. Stuff some paper in the toe, you want."

Ferry packed the rest of the debris from the locker into plastic bags. Nothing left but dust.

"We'll find a Dumpster for the garbage on the way. Get in."

Manny climbed into the passenger seat. "Where's the first stop?"

"Set a decoy." Ferry turned the ignition key, slid the tranny into drive. "There's an empty warehouse down around Dumpers in south-town."

"Could be squatters there." Manny bit into a fingernail as the van started to move. "I mean, you know, all those warehouses, same deal."

"I've got it figured out," Ferry said.

• • •

Miss Carvela sat in her recliner, Toby and Nadya on the sofa. The room was warm and softly lit. They'd been discussing Toby's father, reminiscing. At one point, Miss Carvela read aloud the Thirty-ninth Psalm. Dan, sitting by himself near the living room window where he had a view of the street, said, "Were you expecting someone?"

Toby rose, crossed the room, looked out. "Good God."

"Who is it?" Miss Carvela put her Bible aside and turned in her chair to stand, slipping her feet into her shoes. "I wasn't expecting anyone."

"Aunt Veronique."

Toby's aunt scaled the concrete steps in the twilight, reedy like his father but shorter, pinch-faced beneath a honey-colored wig, wearing high heels and a calfskin car coat. The woman who'd come up to him in the police station lobby, Arlie Thigpen's mother, followed behind, holding her purse like a bucket.

Dan looked at Toby. "Should I let them in?"

"Sure, I guess. Miss Carvela?"

The tiny old woman shrugged helplessly, stepping forward. "Is there a reason not to?"

"Possibly." Dan pointed. "The guys down there."

Down at the pavement, three men looked up, waiting beside a silver BMW parked behind Veronique's Mark IV. The tallest one had a short-cut natural and wore a putty-colored sport coat over a plaid shirt and jeans. The second was shorter but massive, with a thick head crowned with jeri curls lathered in gel; he wore a black turtleneck beneath a powder-blue suit, a pair of white loafers on his feet. The third wore charcoal slacks and a black blazer, a snow-white V-neck sweater, no shirt beneath, with gold rope chains looped around his neck. A few of the young men still out on the street ventured up, paid their respects.

"Which one's Long Walk Mooney?" Dan asked as the two women reached the porch. "If you know."

"I don't," Toby said.

The doorbell rang. Everybody looked at everybody else. Dan got up from his chair, but Miss Carvela held him back with a raised finger. "This is my home." A voice like a plucked string. "I will decide."

She brushed the creases from her dress, patted the lace at her collar, then stepped to the door. She could have chained the lock, spoken through the tiny space, but chose instead to swing the door wide. "Good evening, ladies. I do not believe I've yet had the pleasure."

Before they could answer, Dan, standing now, said, "Showtime."

He moved to the door as Toby looked out, saw the three men taking the steps two at a time. He spun toward Nadya, who remained on the sofa, looking lost. She was the reason they'd come. The only witness. He sped to the hallway, found a cordless phone. It had a speed dial function for 911. Back in the living room, he delivered the handset to Nadya.

"Just hit this button if things get out of hand. The police will know just from the call where to come."

She took the phone from him, nodded her understanding. As their eyes met, he wanted to tell her he was sorry. Instead, he turned and hurried to the door.

Dan placed a gentle hand on Miss Carvela's shoulder, towering over her. "I'm hoping we won't have a problem here."

The three men arranged themselves on the porch with a poorly feigned casual air. "Miss Carvela," the one in the white V-neck said, like Dan wasn't there, easing between the two women, who'd yet to say one word. His voice was strangely clenched and high. "Miss Carvela, you know me. Union Elementary, one through six. James Mooney. Kids called me Long Walk."

"You were called a great many things," Miss Carvela replied. A withering tone, echoes of detention. "Not just by the children."

"Yes, ma'am. Yes, ma'am." His deference was genuine. He spread his hand at his chest, an apology, an oath. "I mean no disrespect to you. I'm not here to disrespect your home, neither. Let me introduce folks here." The two women, Veronique and Sarina, stood stiff and eerily dull-eyed as he said their names. The two men—the chunky one in the suit was named Mack Silas; the taller one in the jeans and plaid shirt, Chat Miller—traded stares with Dan. "We have business to discuss with Mr. Carlisle's son."

"I have difficulty," Miss Carvela said, "embracing any concept of business that would include your activities."

"Miss Grimes, we wish to come in." It was Veronique. Toby'd never heard her voice so meek, so false.

"Any reason we can't talk like this, right here?" he asked.

"Cold out here." It was Mack Silas. His voice came from deep inside his barrel-shaped body, like he meant to be heard throughout the house. "Almost dark."

"The lady did ask nice," the tall one added, much gentler, stammering just a little.

Up close they both looked rough-edged but in distinctly different ways. The tall one, Chat Miller, was older than the other two, maybe as old as his mid-forties, with huge, bony hands so scarred and thick with calluses Toby guessed he was a handyman or a carpenter. His face had a high-cheeked, sharp-nosed angularity, with steady eyes and a deep, ugly, hook-shaped scar running from one edge of his mouth to beneath his chin. The thick one, Mack Silas, had his share of scars as well, but they didn't look the kind that came from work. He had swollen, pebbly knuckles and a gold tooth, plus a flat, shovel-shaped nose and a heavy, low-slung jaw. There was a scent to him, too—junior-high locker rooms, cheap cologne, sweat.

Mooney, in contrast, with his choirboy voice—and despite the chains and shirtless V-neck—seemed almost gentrified. Except for the eyes. They were deep-set, a mesmerizing amber color.

"Miss Carvela. I promise, word of honor, we come to talk. Nothing but."

Miss Carvela turned around. Toby met her gaze. Seeing concession, he reached out, touched Dan's arm. "Let me." He stared at his aunt, who looked off, then addressed them all at once. "My girlfriend's inside, holding a phone. One false move, she connects with the police. That good? If not, leave now."

Mooney smiled in a way that made Toby uneasy, agreeing too soon. His two sidekicks just stared; the women looked numb. Dan eased back and Mooney didn't wait. He slipped past everyone with graceful speed, spotted Nadya on the couch, and went straight for her, reaching inside his coat. Nadya stared at him like he was death itself. As though sensing the wrongness of it himself, Mooney stopped halfway in, removed not a weapon but a picture from his pocket, and held it high for all to see.

"I'd like her to check this out. Okay?" Turning this way, that.

Toby took it from him. "Who's this?"

"Just show it to her, if you would." He made a "scoot" gesture with his hands. "Go on."

Toby crossed the room, handed the picture to Nadya.

Mooney said to her, "Tell me who that is."

Nadya studied the picture, clutching the phone. "I don't know."

"You never seen him," Mooney said.

"No."

"Not once. Never."

"She answered you," Toby said. "What's your point?"

"My point?" He gestured across the room at Sarina Thigpen. "Young man's mama right there. Boy's name's Arlie. He's a good boy, ain't nobody's idea of trouble."

Sarina made two steps forward, her eyes red. She seemed uneasy on her feet, not from fatigue so much as misery.

Nadya greeted her with a self-conscious nod. "I heard the detectives mention your son's name, ma'am. They asked if I knew who he was, I said no. They asked if I saw him shoot Mr. Carlisle. I didn't—"

"Thank you," Mooney said in a loud whisper.

"I didn't see anybody shoot Mr. Carlisle."

"Then why won't the police release my son?" Sarina's eyes ballooned with outrage and fear.

"I don't know."

Mooney folded his hands, put them to his lips. "Arlie ain't but nineteen."

Dan stepped in. "That the extent of your business? If so—"

Mooney stopped him with a look. "Just a minute. Hold on now." He stuck out a hand. "Name's James. You are?"

It took a second, but Dan reached out for Mooney's hand, shook. "Dan."

"Pleasure. But no, the extent of my business, as you put it—more to it than that."

Toby's aunt finally made way into the room and dropped into a chair as though afraid she might collapse. She sat, eyes closed, breathing like she'd run. Mooney glanced at her briefly, his brow creased.

"People I know," he said, turning back to the room, "they been telling the rollers all day they know who shot Mr. Carlisle. They *know*. This deadbeat named Manny. Been hanging around the house next door to Mr. Carlisle's."

"I saw him last night," Nadya said.

Everybody froze. Mooney said, "One more time?"

"I saw him—"

"You just said you *didn't*—"

"Not at the house. I saw him at the club. Where Toby was playing. At least I think it was him. There was a fight, he tried to control Mr. Carlisle. Mr. Carlisle didn't like that."

"A *fight*?"

"Yes."

Arlie's mother stared at Nadya like she'd just confessed to the killing herself. Mooney edged closer to her. "And you told this to the heat."

"Who?"

"Po-lice."

"Yes."

"What you just said."

"Yes. Yes."

For the first time, a genuine ugliness rose up in Mooney's face. "Mother*fuckers*."

"James Mooney, you are in my home, you will control your tongue."

He snapped to with an instant deference, stonily sincere. "Miss Carvela, I *am* sorry."

Arlie's mother said, "They know this, you told them, they know who shot Mr. Carlisle. Why won't they let Arlie go?"

"Trumped-up drug charge," Mack Silas said, voice again booming, too loud for the room.

Mooney added more quietly, "Ain't sellin' drugs for me, Miss Carvela. All long ago. My past life."

Nadya swallowed. "I don't know, ma'am. Why they're holding your son, ma'am."

"It's not up to her what the police do," Toby said. "Believe me, we'd love to have some effect on what the police do."

"Sounds to me," Mack Silas said, "you got plenty goddamn effect."

Miss Carvela rose from her chair. "I have had just enough vulgarity, gentlemen."

Dan stepped toward Mooney. "I think that's your cue. We're done."

Mack Silas slid up, grabbed his arm. "You gonna take a seat now." The first thing he said quietly. Dan shook him off, but the big man regained his hold, two-handed now. "Don't mess. Hear?" They struggled for a second in the middle of the room. Then, with a swiftness Toby hadn't seen since his days watching playground fights, Dan snapped his arm free, spun around, and landed three fast punches—the nose, the throat, the stomach, right, left, right. Mack Silas bent double, staggered back, and dropped hard to one knee, the breath coming out of his mouth in a soupy whistle.

"Stop it!" Miss Carvela pointed to Mooney. "Stop this."

Mooney just stared. A smile formed. "Seems to me pretty much stopped already." He made a gesture of peace to Dan, then told his man, "Plant yourself in a chair someplace." He looked from face to face, Miss Carvela, Dan, Toby, to be sure they were all appeased. Then he turned, eased toward Nadya, gesturing to the picture in her hand.

"Can I have that back, miss?"

Nadya held out the picture and Mooney took it from her, but instead of returning it to his pocket he studied it himself for a moment, thinking. Slowly, he sat down beside her, placing the picture on the coffee table and positioning it so they both could study it together.

Finally, he glanced up, trained those honey-colored eyes on her. "It's hard sometimes, for people like yourself, to understand what it's like. Be accused of something you didn't do. Go to prison for it." His face was blank, not threatening, not kind. His voice was soft, hypnotic. "For folks like us, it's everyday. That don't mean, though, we gonna sit still for it." He glanced at the picture, tapped it several times with the tip of his middle finger. "Now, unless I'm mistaken, the po-lice didn't quite get what you had to tell them. Might be their fault. God knows that happens. Then again, maybe you didn't understand how important it was. So maybe we ought to work on that."

He glanced around the room, face to face, as though to be sure everyone agreed. He'd made no threats; he'd crossed no lines. This was too important to get wrong. Turning back to Nadya, he continued, "I'd like to know if you're gonna tell them again what you saw, okay? 'Cause to me, sounds like you saw this Manny, same one tangled with Mr. Carlisle, outside that house. I believe that. I do. Maybe it's buried inside, maybe you're scared, but you know—you *know*—the truth. You know what he looks like, you saw him there, front yard, pull out the gun, rain comin' down. Boom." He mocked up a gun with his hand, lowered his thumb. "*Boom*. Am I right? Say it. Like I'm the po-lice. Tell me what you saw."

The warehouse was U-shaped and stood on a three acre lot, surrounded by an aging hurricane fence. The grounds showed long neglect, waist-high grass thick with weeds and haphazard piles of toxic debris—old paint, dirty motor oil, rusty cans of acetone and other solvents—fruits of illegal dumping. Spotlights once lit the perimeter, gone now, victim to kids who'd used rocks. Same with the windows.

"I know the crowd, one that squats here," Manny said. "This won't work. They're smart."

Ferry steered around the southerly side of the building, down a strip of buckling asphalt outside the fence line. "Guess that means we gotta be smarter."

He'd cased the building. The squatters numbered half a dozen at most, and they clustered in the northeast corner. You could tell by the black plastic hung where the windows used to be. Given the need to hijack water and power, there was no advantage to spreading out. They'd be at the opposite corner of the project. The place was big enough, they might as well be in a different neighborhood.

"There's a toolbox, behind the seat," Ferry said as he killed the motor. "Got a bolt cutter inside. Get it out and follow me."

He went around back, opened the doors, and took out the first tub. Manny brought the bolt cutter, holding it like a dowsing rod. "What about light? How we gonna see?"

"Stay close." Ferry closed the door and headed for the fence.

Someone—kids again, or vandals, or the same toxic dumpers,

Ferry supposed—had cut a passage through the fence along the rear perimeter, the clipped edges of the chain link weathered with rust. A truck yard and loading dock waited beyond. Thistle and blackberry sprouted through cracks in the asphalt. The rusted clamp on the tether on a fifty-foot flagpole chimed metal-to-metal in the wind.

"First door on the dock, this side, that's where we're headed."

They crossed fifty yards of busted asphalt, weaving past scattered junk and thorny coils of blackberry bush. Manny stumbled twice, Ferry reaching back each time without a glance to drag him along. Their steps echoed in the silence as they neared the warehouse wall and climbed up the iron stairway to the loading dock.

"Give me the bolt cutter."

Ferry took the tool from Manny and cut the weatherworn padlock on the roll-up door. He eased the door up, one hand on the corrugated metal to keep it from rattling. It snagged a foot from the floor, the rollers thick with rust. He had to work it free with a gentle up and down, needing to clear no more than the distance required to slip in the tub with the flare sticking up. "Don't just stand there. Help me, work the other side. Gentle. No noise." Manny joined in. They rocked it up and back, inch by grating inch, till they had the clearance. Pushing the tub in first, they crawled in after.

"I can't see. It's like pitch-black in here."

Ferry knelt. "What's to see?" Pushing the tub against the wall, he eased the lid off, then ripped off the cap of the flare. "Make a wish." He struck the tip of the flare twice and it caught. A willowy spume of white smoke rose as the flame burned hot and bright. Not pitch-black now. He saw the exposed framing of the wall above the flare. Old dry wood.

Manny stared at the flame. "Can we stick around, out in the van, I mean. At least watch the first few minutes?"

"You can't be that stupid. Come on, move."

They slid back beneath the door, jogged across the asphalt. Ferry nudged Manny along, the kid wanting to turn back every few steps. He lost his hat going through the fence, fumbled around in the grass for it. Ferry'd had enough. He grabbed the kid by the ears, hissed into his face, "You fuck around like this the whole damn night, I swear to God, you'll pay."

The space beneath the open roll-up door grew brighter with a rubbery light. The flare had hit the floater layer of diesel fuel.

"We've got five minutes. Run."

"You ain't even trying," Mooney said.

"I've been trying ever since it happened," Nadya replied.

"Not hard enough."

"You have no idea how hard I've tried."

Mooney rose from the couch, tapping the photo of Arlie against his knuckles with growing impatience. Nadya, her face ashen, remained seated.

"She didn't see what happened," Toby said, stepping in to protect her. "There's no other way to say it."

"Oh, well now." Mooney uttered a caustic little laugh. "That's deep."

Toby sighed and shook his head. "Think what you want."

"What I *want*?" Mooney's eyes flared. He looked at Toby like he wanted to shake him. "What I *want* is to set the record straight. I didn't shoot your daddy. Arlie didn't, neither. I know. He was with me. But I ain't puttin' my head on a chopping block to prove that point."

"Course not," Toby said. "Better to use her head."

Mooney stared at him, eyes dull. "Like cops gonna fuck with a white girl says she saw who really killed your daddy."

"But something did happen downtown. Between you and Pops. That's not just made up."

Mooney recoiled a little, clenched his fist to his lips, then wagged a finger.

"Your daddy." He turned toward Veronique. "I mean no offense now, a'ight?" Back to Toby. "But your daddy, he had a mouth on him. Arlie was just minding his own, outside Fielding's Liquor's, no bother to nobody. Up walks trouble. Your daddy, tacked to beat Jesus. To' up from flo' up. But he ain't done for the night. Heads on in, buys himself a pint, then swerves on out and lights right into Arlie. No cause."

"You were there."

"That point, yeah."

"So Arlie wasn't just minding his business. He was minding yours."

Mooney pressed his hands against his chest. "I am a *promoter*. I stage *events*. I provide *a venue*. Arlie and other folks I employ, they bring the people in."

Sarina Thigpen sat listening, a sad, faraway look in her eye, like this was the one last thing she needed to believe. Mooney's two men sat there, too, Mack Silas still rubbing his midriff, Chat Miller tapping his callused fingers together between his knees, otherwise the two of them inert as stones.

"He's handin' out handbills—"

"Handbills?"

"*Handbills*. I go down, check it out. That's my *job*. Your daddy, half in the bag, starts callin' Arlie and his whoadies a bunch of punks. 'Dumb as ducks,' he says, I remember that. Arlie asked him nice, 'Mind your own, old man,' but your daddy'd have none of that. I step in, try to broker the peace. Your daddy just escalates. Off on me, now. Me, his sister here, calling us names I won't repeat outta respect for the dead. Took out a matchbook, all theatrical and shit. 'Tell you what, Mooney,' he says. 'You want my house, you put down on this matchbook what you think it's worth. Then stick it up your ass and strike.' "

Toby had little trouble picturing the scene. Meanwhile, sensing another scolding on the way, Mooney spun around. "I'm just repeating what he said, Miss Carvela. His words, not mine." He did a little conciliatory nod, then spun right back around to Toby. "Some point, enough is enough. Arlie stepped in, gave your daddy a nudge." He demonstrated, hand on Toby's shoulder, like waking a sleeping bum. "Told your daddy to go on home, before he embarrassed himself."

"A nudge," Toby said.

"Just."

"Then?"

Mooney shrugged. "Staggered his wackity ass on up the hill and that's the last time I saw him. Me and Arlie both."

Miss Carvela rose from her chair. Tufts of silver hair had sprung loose from their pins; she looked eccentric, fragile. "James Mooney, you will leave now." She pivoted, made eye contact with Veronique and Arlie's mother, Mooney's two men. "All of you."

"I told you I meant no disrespect, Miss Carvela. But this business is crucial."

"I said get out."

Mooney just stood there, like he hadn't quite heard right or didn't want to. A meanness crept over his face. His eyes flared and he marched to the window, pointing out into the night.

"Where's the money come from, people up here need cash? Millie and Big John Summers need to patch their roof. Serella Jones got to get a new furnace, Mazy Roberts a water heater. Other folks—you want the names, I'll give you the names—fix the dry rot in the bathroom or the plumbing, build an add-on for the grandfolks they gotta take in. Who, I'm asking. I'll tell you who. They can go to one of those check cashing joints, like Payday America, get ripped off that way. Or they can sign up with the thieves down at Frontline Financial. Bleed the needy. Christ, you even got real estate brokers coming up here, pushing hard money seconds on people, just so they can foreclose."

He scoured every face with those cold amber eyes, making sure everyone was paying attention

"People can put up with that. Or they can come to me. I'll pay off Payday America or whoever, so you can get out from under the nine hundred percent yearly vig. You pay me a straight ten percent, no compound interest, no bullshit fees on top of fees."

The vehemence built as he talked. He'd schooled himself. He was proud.

"You need to refinance, I'll take a deed of trust, ten percent again, straight as a rod—sure, it's above market, but you tell me where people up here gonna find a deal like that. You got a dozen houses on this hill sitting empty, people run out of their homes. That ain't me. Know why? I believe in the neighborhood. Call me names, go on. But hear me out—I am the one source of money on this hill who's jake for real with folks up here, knows what they go through, how they gotta struggle, gives a good goddamn about it."

Miss Carvela locked eyes with him. "To hear such talk. Make yourself out like Jameson Carswell himself."

"I can live with that. Man I admire."

"He built these homes up here. *Built* them. What can you honestly say you've—"

"Miss Carvela, don't push now. There are things you just don't know."

"I shudder to think what happens when people foolish enough to trust you can't pay."

Mooney's eyes went wild. "How many people up here lost their homes 'cause of me? None. Not one." He was shouting. Veins bulged in his neck. "Those homes Frontline foreclosed? I sent her"—he pointed at Veronique—"to the bank auctions, tried to outbid the loan folks and the vultures show up at those things, buy back the property so folks could stay put. Had cash in hand, just like they wanted. But every time, property got yanked off the bidding block. Every goddamn time. Not because folks paid up, got a grace period. Unh-uh, nothing like that. Because the properties got sold on the sly. That's illegal." He looked to Veronique for confirmation. "Something's goin' on, Miss Carvela, I don't know what, but every one of those houses is just sittin' on that hill, no fix-up, no turnaround, no nothing. If it was me there'd be people living there. You ought to give me props, thank me, 'stead of trying to shame me way you do." He pointed again at Veronique. "Ask her, you don't believe me. Go on. Ask."

Veronique winced at the focus, avoiding the glances that turned her way.

"I've got a question." It was Toby. He stared across the room at his aunt. "What's all this have to do with the forged deed you recorded?"

Veronique shot up straight, eyes livid. "That's a lie. I forged no deed."

"Okay, Exeter did." Toby nodded toward Mooney. "Or he did. Why else would Pops lump you together the way he did, home in on you two wanting the house?"

Mooney cut in, "Look, look. I'm not saying I wouldn't like that house. Already own the two Vics either side. Give me three in a row, like Monopoly. Don't mean I wanted to chalk the place. Beyond that, your daddy, his house, you, the whole family, not my concern. That woman there"—Mooney again pointed to Veronique—"helps me with my paperwork. And that's all."

"Then why bring her here?"

Mooney cupped his hands. "Seemed right, bring you all together. Got a lot to work out. Or you can piss the whole thing away paying lawyers."

Veronique took this as a cue. "My brother, and my mother before him, wanted that house kept in the family."

That sealed it, Toby thought. In it together. That old sorry house. Bad as grave robbers. Now they're scared they'll get dragged into a killing. If that wasn't the case already.

"I'm family," he said.

Veronique scoffed, "Hardly."

"Check out the will."

"There's a will?" Mooney was stunned.

"No." Veronique's eyes narrowed. "Not one's that signed."

How does she know about the unsigned will, Toby wondered. "Maybe there's one you don't know about."

For the first time, she smiled. "I know all I need to know."

"That's right. I forgot. You've got a key."

"A will that cannot be found is presumed revoked."

Mooney chuckled. "That's the law. Woman knows her law."

"Yeah," Toby said. "Probably even knows what a holographic will is."

That shut them both up. Toby smiled. "Never much cared for his music, did you? Thought that big old horn was slimy. Vile."

"Jesus goddamn man alive."

It was Chat Miller, gazing out the window as a muffled, faraway roar made the glass tremble. Everybody jumped, got up, joined him, looking out. He pointed. To the south, on the far side of town along the river, a fireball plumed the darkness. It burned high and white, a huge tapered shock of flame, brightening the night sky. A gas jet, maybe. A broken feed line.

"Where is that?"

"Fuck where is it. *What* is it?"

"Looks like Dumpers. Near there. Some warehouse."

They edged in, clustering at the window to peer out side by side, the last hour forgotten for a moment. Not a word among them as they watched the ragged stitchwork of flames, embers sailing high into the air like rockets. Faraway sirens wailed as patrol cars responded and the engine companies headed out. The eerie keening sound and swirling lights seemed so distant, unreal.

18

anny cranked down the passenger's side window and leaned out into the wind, craning for a good look back at the flames. Frustrated, he stuck his whole torso through the window, like a sheepdog, perched sideways on the seat. Ferry marveled at the sheer girth of the kid's butt as he snagged the back of his massive overalls, pulled hard, and dragged him back in.

"There some kinda blue ribbon for dumbfuck I don't know about?" The van veered as Ferry got control of the wheel again. Then he reached out, slapped at Manny's head. "Come on. Answer."

"What the—stop it. What's *wrong* with you." Manny scuttled back against his door, arms up to protect his head.

"Face front. Shut up."

"All right, okay, all right. Jesus." Manny sank into his seat. He lowered his arms from his head, but just a little. "You know, calling you an asshole is an affront to assholes everywhere."

Ferry laughed. "That's good. I like that." He thrummed his fingers against the steering wheel, thinking, Nothing hones the instincts like abuse.

He turned into the stonework gate at the bottom of the hill to Baymont. As the street formed a T at the panhandle, he turned again—not left, but right. Toward St. Martin's Hill.

"Hey," Manny said. "This is the wrong way."

"We gotta clean up your mess."

He climbed the hill beneath the Monterey pines and eucalyptus trees, following the narrow, tightly curving streets. Already dark, still windy, people kept inside, this part of town especially. No witnesses walking about.

He passed the Carlisle house and the Victorian where Manny'd holed up. With a major fire on the south of town, they'd called away the patrolman stationed outside. Ferry turned at the end of the block, then turned again, heading back up the alley behind the properties. Tall fences and ramshackle garages flanked the alleyway, making the van all but invisible, but dogs barked here and there. He pulled up behind the Victorian and killed the motor, then reached behind the seat for the bolt cutter again and took a wrench from the tool chest.

"I don't like being here," Manny said. "This feels bad."

"Get out."

Around back, Ferry opened the doors and took out a five-gallon tub, handed it to Manny. "You take the Vic." He passed on the bolt cutter next, pocketing the wrench for himself, plus a roll of duct tape. "If they didn't just ram the door, they changed the lock. Cut it off. It's important to get inside. Place your tub downstairs. You got a low ceiling, lots of exposed wood framing there. Near the furnace or the water heater—you know where they are—so the welding melts on the gas jets."

Manny scrunched up his face. "Won't that kinda be like throwing a Bic into a bonfire? I mean, a gas plume in the middle of something like this, what's the point?"

Ferry took out a second tub for himself, closed the van's doors. "Stop wasting time."

"Meanwhile, you do what?"

"Smack you again, you don't do what I tell you."

"Wait. Wait. This just—" Manny pounded the side of the van softly with his fist. "This wasn't part of the plan."

"Not before you offed the old spade, no."

"They're gonna know it's me."

"They already know it's you. I told you. You're not gonna be safe because that's a secret. You're gonna be safe because you disappear. Get a new life. That's where I help. Now go. Do it."

Ferry turned toward the back gate of the Carlisle property. From behind, with juvenile gall, trying for tough, Manny said, "You're gonna just leave me here, aren't you?"

Turning around, Ferry felt stunned by the kid's face. Moon eyes, almost teary, but a clenched frown, too, the kind that told the world you knew you were gonna take some punishment, but you weren't scared.

"If not leave me here, somewhere."

"I need you," Ferry told him. "I'm not gonna just leave. Not now. Not later."

"You'll wait."

"Five minutes, yeah, I'll wait. Don't fuck around. Now go. Get it done."

Ferry tore away the crime scene tape at the back gate to the Carlisle yard, threw the latch, and headed in. The rain had all but washed away whatever gravel had once covered the path to the back door. Just a muddy aisle through a muddier backyard. He aimed for the grassy patches, hoping for better traction, but even so almost slid the last few yards. He taped one of the windowpanes on the back door, tapped with the wrench till the glass gave way, then picked away what larger pieces he could, reached in, and threw the lock.

He felt his way through the dark. Eyes adjusting, he found himself in a vast open room with egg crate foam on three walls. A banner he couldn't quite read hung from the back wall. Rolled-up carpet smelled of mold. He didn't see a furnace.

Continuing on, he found himself in a small cluttered vestibule between the addition and the main house. Shelves lined the walls, full of piecemeal hardware and tools. Cans of paint and varnish and thinner were stacked on metal shelving near the same corner where the water heater stood. Here, he decided. This is the spot.

He pried off the tub lid carefully, broke the seal on the fuse, struck twice, and lit the flare. He made sure it was going strong, then backed away, hustled into the addition, where his eye again caught the massive banner draped along the back wall. This time he could make out the words:

STRONG CARLISLE & THE MIGHTY FIREFLY
MF R&B

Manny should see this, he thought, smiling. Snag himself a handle, steal it from the man he killed. The Mighty Firefly. Multiple Fires Raging & Burning.

He hurried out the back, negotiating the mud the same way he had on the way in. Manny wasn't at the van. Ferry slid behind the wheel and eased the door closed.

Dogs in the nearer yards began to bark again. Above the fences and through the trees, lights came on in windows. He leaned back in the seat, trying to hide. Sweat beading on his face, tricking down his back, he listened for footsteps and checked his watch until Manny yanked open the door and scrambled in.

Stluka and Murchison sped south from the station, passing through Dumpers where, on the brickwork wall of an abandoned foundry, a tagger had laid out the roll call for a gang called the Southtown Punk Stoners. The names of the dead wore large black *X*s, relic of the turf war with Baymont, but two of the *X*s were new.

When they turned onto the river road, the fire came into view. Flames cut high above the roofline along the whole south flank of the warehouse. Smoke boiled out of windows, churning from the wind and heat—black in places, gray or white in others, depending on what was burning—sparked with embers as it billowed up into the night sky.

The watch commander had sent them down to interview a handful of squatters detained by patrol units already on scene. The squatters claimed they had nothing to do with the fire. "Get them away from each other," the watch commander said. "See what shakes out."

The fire crews had cut their way in and thrown the gate wide open. Pumper engines and boom trucks and rescue wagons thronged the warehouse grounds. The blaze was a worker, three alarms, with every firehouse in town except one on scene, the last held back for other emergencies. Assistance was en route from Vallejo and American Canyon, Napa and Benicia, even the nearer refineries across the strait.

Firemen garbed in turn-out gear, bunker pants, and lug-sole boots hustled everywhere, manning hoses, hefting ropes and axes and chain saws and halligan tools into the building, raking through charred debris blown out through the roof and stamping out glow coals, shouting down from inside the building and shouting back from the ground amid the deafening thrum and hiss of their machinery and trucks and the roar of the fire itself. They'd already cut holes in the roof to let the smoke escape, and clouds of it roiled up into the night.

Murchison felt the heat prick the skin on the back of his neck as he turned around to eye the road and the tree line on its far side. The fire freaks had already arrived, picking up the dispatcher calls on their scanners. They stood atop cars and in pickup beds, peering in like dads at peewee football. Like my dad, he thought, years ago—that was me, Daddy's little house afire, ha ha. None of the sightseers matched Manny's description.

"Murch," Stluka said, gesturing toward the gate. "Snap to. Let's get this done."

The boom trucks had hoisted ladders to the second floor in front, a way in through the broken windows. Murchison saw the beams of hand torches roaming around inside through churning waves of smoke. The dull flickering lights reminded him of something he couldn't bring to bear at first, but then it came to him: fireflies.

He and Stluka checked in with the officer manning the gate, logging entry and exit, and got pointed north, where, about seventy yards away, a line of squatters stood inside the perimeter, against the fence, detained by patrolmen. They thanked the officer at the gate and headed that way.

There were five of them, and in accordance with some unspoken rule of youth, they bore themselves not with fear, or awe at the raging fire, but an instinctive surly contempt for the police. A study in slouches and extreme hair. What was it about being young these days, Murchison wondered, that made every kid you met so full of shit, and hostile about it to boot?

Reaching the northeast corner of the warehouse, he glanced up and spotted the sheets of black plastic where the windows on the second floor used to be. The fire hadn't reached here, not yet, but the wind came freighted with heat and his pores opened as he looked up.

The patrolman in charge was named Maples. He wasn't getting very far.

"Let us back in, *now*, we gotta get our *stuff*."

Maples said, "Nobody gets back in—"

"You can't *do* this."

"—till the fire commander—"

"Nazi motherfucking USA."

"—gives the all clear."

"You can't frame us for this."

"This is harassment."

"Nobody wants to frame—"

"Blackshirt motherfuckers. This is against the goddamn *law*."

The mouthiest of the bunch seemed to be the girl—sixteen tops, burrheaded, small and wiry. She wore a T-shirt reading SQUAT THE LOT!, plus khaki pants and rag socks, no shoes—probably abandoned inside once she smelled smoke. Rings and studs bristled everywhere, ten to an ear, plus the eyebrows, cheeks, nose, lip. She hopped around like a bantamweight.

"Cocksuckers! Give it or guard it!"

Other than Maples, the patrolmen just stood there in a semicircle, containing the group, thumbs in their gun belts. Maples saw Murchison and gladly stepped back.

"They want to go back in," he said needlessly.

"Not possible. Safety, one. Crime scene, two."

"*Sieg heil!*"

"I tried to tell them."

"Looky looky here, will ya?" Stluka headed straight for the burrheaded girl. "You look like you fell face first into a tackle box, know that?"

"Up your ass crack."

Stluka cackled. "Spunkita!" He turned back to Maples and dropped the act. "Take her in, call Social Services. Send her back to her weaselly, boo-jwah parents." To the other patrolmen he said, "Divvy these scuts up. Find out who's been poking L'il Miss Squat the Lot."

Every guy sank a half foot shorter, the same guilt lighting face to face. But it was the girl who darted. Eyes ballooning, she sprang for the road, dodged the one cop close enough to grab her, spun out of his grip, and kept running. Stluka and the cop who'd missed ran after. They caught her at the fence, boxed her into the corner. Before they could lay hands on, though, something in the northerly distance caught their eye. Whatever it was, it showed in their faces to where even the girl turned to look.

"Keep them here," Murchison told Maples, gesturing to the four young men. He jogged up behind Stluka, followed his sight line, and saw at the top of St. Martin's Hill a vast wash of tapered flame shooting up like a jet tail. Embers sailed high, drifting with the wind into nearby pines, which shortly glowed with flame. A moment later, a second ignition, same as the other, close by. The noise of the warehouse firefight drowned out the explosion. Given the distance, it seemed strangely innocent, the silence.

The Carlisle house, Murchison thought. The Victorian next door. Manny.

From behind, an eerie monstrous crack split through the firefight din, giving way to a rolling howl that ended in something like thunder. Everybody spun toward the sound as the earth beneath their feet shuddered and a vast new surge of smoke boiled out of the warehouse. The roof had crashed in.

Stluka was the first to move. He turned back to the cornered girl and three times, fast, punched her in the face. Her eyes rolled back as her knees buckled and he snagged her arm, gripping it tight. "You are going to tell me every single thing you know about this fire. About the fires up there on that hill. About Manny."

She winced, face bloody. "Fuck you, let *go*. I don't—"

Murchison came up behind Stluka, grabbed his jacket. "Jerry—"

Stluka fought him off. "Some men just got trapped in there. Men with families, I'll bet. They're likely to die. That's murder, understand?" He shook her. "You talk. Or we'll go in for your *stuff*. And so help me God, I'll shoot that shiny crap off your face before I let you come out again."

Manny leaned back in his seat, hoping to hide his face in shadow. He was breathing through his mouth. "We can't just sit here like this. We'll get spotted."

"Be quiet."

"There's gonna be people."

"Keep it together."

Manny unfolded the list of addresses for the Frontline foreclosure properties they were due to hit in Baymont. "Why we stopped here, anyway?"

"Quiet, I said."

Manny sank down a little, not to hide but to get the best angle on the fires uphill. Like a kid at Christmas, Ferry thought. Good. Keep him entertained.

They were parked beside the stand of old, towering Monterey pines just inside the stonework gate at the bottom of the hill. A funeral home, still sandbagged against the flooding from a recent water main break, sat dark across the way. The pie shop next door was empty, too, same as the other stores in the slummy strip mall on the other side of the street.

The nearest houses were around the corner on either side, seventy-five yards away at least. Manny was right—soon, people would start bubbling out of their homes, heading up toward St. Martin's Hill, drawn by the sirens and word of the fire. Likely they'd head through the panhandle, though. It'd be safe here.

Ferry checked his watch. The tanker was late. Maybe the station had canceled its order. Maybe the driver had spotted the flames, stopped to CB in and tell the refinery he was circling back. Soon there'd be pumpers and ladder trucks heading in. Should've timed the fuses different, Ferry thought. Given us more time. Too late now. One more miscalculation.

Air brakes hissed and squealed beyond the trees, announcing the tanker's arrival. The driver downshifted for the turn through the stonework gate. He didn't see the fire after all, Ferry thought. Too busy worrying about his schedule, his load, making it up the hill. The truck was a brand-new Peterbilt ten-speed, 400 horsepower Cat, Muncie Fuller tranny, pulling a shiny aluminum DOT 406, nine thousand gallons. From the groan of the tranny Ferry figured he had the standard load, at best 10 percent outage in the tank trailer. The truck throttled low toward the next turn, then braked and downshifted again, at the panhandle, where the long, slow seesaw uphill began. A sign posted on the back of the tank trailer read: SAFETY IS NO ACCIDENT.

"Okay," Ferry said. "Follow me."

He got out, walked to the back, and opened the door as sirens approached down Magnolia Street. Manny came around, too, walking clumsily in the oversize boots. Ferry grabbed the next tub as a pumper truck, sent from the only local firehouse crew not called to the warehouse fire, pulled through the stonework gate. He stopped, Manny standing beside him, both of them watching as first the pumper, then a ladder truck moments later, and finally a rescue unit made the turn at the base of the panhandle and headed up St. Martin's Hill toward the fires.

"That was luck." Manny stared at the rescue unit's taillights as they vanished uphill. "The timing, I mean."

"Close the doors," Ferry said. "Be quiet about it."

Manny eased both doors shut, then followed Ferry beneath the canopy of the trees. The ground was thick with pine duff, still spongy and wet from the rain and the recent main break and flooding. Up top, though, the trees would be dry. Credit the wind, Ferry thought. He set the tub down at the base of the centermost pine, placing it deep in shadow and away from the sight line from the street. As he pried off the flare cap, Manny gazed up into the dense branchwork.

"Monterey pine. Trash heap of trees."

"Upright log pile," Ferry said. "All it means to me."

The flare caught fire. Ferry pointed back toward the street. "Go slow. Easy."

They walked single file across the pine duff to the van. Manny stared out the window as they pulled away. "That's gonna light up like crazy."

"No joke."

Manny spun his head around. He finally got it. "How are we gonna get back out?"

"Like I told you before. Stay close."

It took them twenty-five minutes to plant the rest, one after the other up the hill, the whole time hearing the howl of sirens in the night while ahead of them, unseen but always audible, the Peterbilt tramped and clutched up the incline, back and forth through the neighborhoods, to avoid anything steeper than a 7 percent grade. It shuddered up the narrow winding streets, taking corners in the lowest gear possible to avoid scraping parked cars or peeling alligators off the tires by hitting a curb. No doubt the driver heard the sirens, too, Ferry thought, even saw the fires now, but he was trapped in the maze. No way back down till he reached the top.

At each stop, Ferry kept the van running as Manny hurried to the back of the van, collected the tub, hustled businesslike, but not too fast, to the already jimmied door, stole inside the abandoned house, planted the bomb in a cellar if it had one, near a gas line in any event, and lit the flare, then scurried back to the van. He'd begun to enjoy himself finally.

At the last house, Ferry reached into the glove compartment once Manny was gone. He withdrew the kid's .357 and tucked it into his belt beneath his overalls, right beside his own gun, a Smithy 645. Make sure everybody's stepped away from the tanker, he thought. One stray bullet and the whole thing fails. To put it mildly.

By the time Manny climbed back into the van, the first bomb went hot downhill in its stand of pines. The only crews to arrive so far were fighting the St. Martin's fire—the next ones in would be turn-out crews from out of town; their hoses wouldn't fit the hydrants. They'd be forced to fight the tree fires with just the water in their pumper reservoirs, five minutes max. Once the crowds started down, you'd have chaos. Everything else up here would rage hot for a good long while.

At the crest of the hill, they both looked back. From this vantage, the warehouse, the Carlisle house, and the Victorian next door, the Monterey pines downhill, they burned hot and high, still uncontained, the blazing corners of a citywide triangle. As they watched, the first of the downhill houses exploded, the roof melting away where the jet from the bomb burned through like a massive blowtorch.

Manny stared at the fires with a kind of reverence. "Thank you, Richard."

Ferry let off the brake and steered toward Home in the Sky. "Thank me for what?"

"You know for what." No more whiny objections. The boy had settled into what seemed like an almost ethereal contentment. "This is awesome. Just awesome."

As they pulled into the gas station, the owner and the tanker driver argued nose to nose, yelling, gesturing to the fires. The driver was beside himself, his thumper pole in one hand, the other sailing wildly around his head. He was white and string bean tall, with long sandy-colored hair, pinpoint eyes, and a hatchet-shaped nose. The owner was black, short but muscular. Despite the cold he wore shorts and a T-shirt from which his arms bulged like hams.

Ferry eased the van near where they stood, rolled the window down to listen.

"Safest place for the damn gas is in your tanks, now unlock the latches."

"Safe? How 'bout where it's sittin' right now, inside your truck. Now turn the damn thing around and head on off my lot."

"I'll burn up my brake lines I try to go back down that hill with a full load."

Ferry parked the van just beyond the Peterbilt and gestured for Manny to get out with him. "Act scared, like you don't know what the hell's going on." Ferry eased out onto the pavement and edged toward the two men. Manny did likewise, except he had an edgy grin on his face.

Ferry called out, "You guys see what the hell's going on down there?"

The owner and driver ignored him.

"Nothing more dangerous than an empty truck. Jesus, listen to me, will ya? It's the fumes'll blow you sky-high." The driver pointed to a blister on the side of one of the trailer tires. "Got that taking a damn turn up here. I could lose that tire, understand? I stop at a guillotine, they'd nail me for sure. My container's empty? They wouldn't let me budge. Like a bomb on wheels. I'm sure as hell not driving down into no fires. Jesus."

"And you sure as hell ain't unloading, and you ain't staying here."

"Your tanks are safer loaded than they are now. You deaf? I unload, park out on the street, down the hill, I don't care. Wait till the fires burn out. What's the problem? You're being seriously fucked about this."

Ferry edged to position himself between the tanker and the two men, figuring ten feet was good. He feigned bafflement, like he couldn't figure out why all the yelling, then turned toward the truck briefly, subterfuge while he opened his overalls and removed the .357. Turning back and raising the gun in one movement, he aimed, sighting the driver and firing twice at his back, high left side, the heart. The tall man jerked from the impact and the blood spray showered the owner. The driver didn't fall, though, just stood there wavering, but Ferry'd planned for that, moving quick to his right and taking aim now at the owner, who stood rooted to his spot, stunned, eyes perplexed as his hands went instinctively to his face. A big man, he'd require closer range, even with the Magnum, so Ferry closed another five feet, aimed again for the heart, and landed three fast shots. Like shooting a bear. He didn't fall, either, just tottered, still blinking the other man's blood from his eyes.

Ferry realized he'd missed by the gaping wound on the big man's arm. It had shielded his chest from at least one of the shots. Ferry stepped closer, avoiding the driver, who'd fallen to his knees now, one hand to the ground to keep himself upright as he coughed up blood. The owner could do no more than clench his jaw in rage and swing loosely with his ruined arm as Ferry stepped in and fired the last round in the cylinder point-blank. Even with that, the man wouldn't fall. He twisted away, eyes blind, staggering toward the door of his station. Fine, Ferry thought, go on, go. He turned back to the driver, kicked the man's arm away so he fell to the pavement.

Searching for Manny, Ferry called out, "Get over here!"

Manny had taken refuge near the pumps, crouching once the gunfire started. He rose to his feet, mouth agape.

"I said move, damn it. Here. C'mon."

Manny edged toward him, eyes trained on the owner, who stumbled, fell to his knees, dragged himself to his feet, but then just stood there, weaving, five yards from his office door. Blood bubbled from his chest.

"Jesus, you didn't say—"

"Search this guy's pockets for his keys."

Manny grabbed his stomach, like he was ready to hurl. "Maybe they're still in the cab."

"Search his pockets!" Ferry reached out and grabbed Manny's shoulder, driving him to his knees. "Don't argue."

Manny stared at the .357. "You used my gun. You were going to get rid of it."

"I am getting rid of it. Here." He wiped the .357 clean, then laid it on the pavement, right beside the boy's knee.

Manny stared at it. "No. Wait. No, this is—"

"I don't have time to explain. Search his pockets."

Ferry waited as Manny, still on his knees, finally obeyed, inching closer to the driver. The man lay sprawled in his own blood, still alive, his eyes open as he worked his mouth, trying to breathe. Manny couldn't get the nerve to touch him at first, but as he finally reached into the dying man's pockets, Ferry drew the Smithy 645 from inside his overalls, crouched down low, and shoved the barrel up into Manny's neck. The shot blew open the boy's carotid artery and took half his jaw away. He windmilled onto his haunch, his neck spewing blood. Ferry caught backspray, too, this time. He used his arm to wipe it away so he could see.

Edging over, he took out a handkerchief, wiped his prints off the 645, and forced it into the driver's hand, molding his finger onto the trigger. The man, still alive, fought, but weakly. Ferry managed to get the right fit, pressed his own finger over the driver's, and fired the gun one shot after the other, aiming once for Manny, hitting him in the shoulder, then just wildly, emptying the clip. The shoulder shot knocked Manny back onto his elbows. He was whimpering, "No no no no no," his hand clasping around an invisible something.

Ferry ran to the Peterbilt, climbed into the cab, and threw the internal plug valve switch—no need for the pumps, gravity would do the work—then hurried to release the other two valve switches at the front and back of the trailer unit. Before opening the outside discharge valves at the hose couplings, he went back to Manny.

The boy's mouth still opened and closed of its own volition, no sound. If Ferry had never killed a man before, he might have wondered if the boy was praying, but he knew it was just the brain shutting down from blood loss. He crouched before Manny and grabbed the collar of the boy's overalls in one hand, rolled his bloody body onto its front, with his free hand grabbed the overalls again, this time in the small of the back, and half dragged, half trundled the all-but-dead boy over to the tanker. It was hard, the kid big and heavy to begin with, doubly so like this. The blood trail left behind would never convince a cop with any smarts, but the trail wouldn't be there long.

Panting, he dropped Manny's body beside the discharge piping, eyeing how things stood and measuring it against the scenario he hoped to concoct. The boy had tried to hijack the truck, things went queer, he opened fire and got return fire. Everybody hit, bad. As a last gasp act, he'd dragged himself to the tanker, decided if he couldn't blow up the truck where he'd wanted—the local branch of Frontline Financial, death to the predatory lenders—he'd just let the gas loose up here, let it flow into the sewers. He'd die watching the fires, foreshadow paradise.

A schematic of the bank branch sat folded up inside Manny's backpack in the van. Ferry had given it to him earlier as they'd run through the plan, the one Manny had thought he was part of. Assuming flames didn't take this whole area, there'd be that left behind. You couldn't get everything perfect.

The tank had four compartments; Ferry opened the discharge valves one by one. The gasoline, nine thousand gallons, surged out onto the pavement like spillover from a dam, drenching Manny and knocking him onto his side, burying him and washing away his blood trail as it flooded the pump island, eddying here and there but most of it flowing on, downhill toward the sewer grates.

Ferry covered his mouth and nose with his arm as he ran from the fumes, heading for the bluff behind the gas station, scrambling up the tiered rock, the sandstone crumbling beneath his hands and feet as he dug for purchase. He slipped, fell, regained his feet, then finally reached the top. Below him, four of the empty houses now blazed hot, spreading to their neighbors, the string of fires creeping uphill as the nine thousand gallons of gas spilled down. People were already scrambling for cars, trying to escape those first fires near the bottom. That'd just continue as the new fires lit and the old ones spread. Every man, woman, and child on the hill, if they had any sense and two legs to carry them, would be heading for the safety of the bottoms. Either that or risk burning alive where they sat. They'd swarm the entrance for hours, keep the fire crews tied down.

He turned and scrambled down into the star thistle and lupine on the bluff's far side, skating down the steep decline beneath the power lines and high-tension towers, tripping in coyote holes and ground squirrel burrows. His ankles buckled, knees, too, but nothing so bad he feared a break. Numb from adrenaline, he kept moving, tumbling twice headlong through the rocky weeds, cutting a gash in his face once but jumping right back up again to regain his feet and vanish farther into the dark ravines.

19

---

oby realized at last how much his father's home was his own as he
stood on the street with the rest of the crowd, watching it burn.
Another morbid instance of déjà vu—like last night, and earlier
that day, the police were there, but now it was firefighters inside the
fence line. The police edged onlookers back as matters got worse.
The fires had burned so hot and fast the houses were fully engaged by
the time the fire crews arrived, and spreading to the next houses
down.

The back addition of his father's house—built not just for The
Mighty Firefly but Toby, too—had gone fast. Only a skeleton of
charred studs and headers and roof beams remained visible through
the smoke. The front walls stood eerily whole, but the cinder blocks
had acted like chimneys, ramping the heat inside till the roof caught
and caved in. The fire spread to the whole interior then, the furniture,
the old piano, his father's clothes, the family pictures.

He felt a queasy kind of relief at having had the sense to remove
his father's horn from the place earlier in the day. But he'd left behind
sheet music, reams and reams of it, including charts for tunes his father had written years ago for The Mighty Firefly: "Pump Action,"
"Red Planet," "Snakebit," "Bone Deep," dozens of others. He'd always
wanted to rechart those numbers, add a little texture to the straight-
ahead blues lines. A lost chance. One more thing to mourn.

Long Walk Mooney, his two men, and both Veronique and Sarina
Thigpen had fled Miss Carvela's when the first tower of flame had shot
skyward in the night on this side of the panhandle. They knew. Just by

direction, they knew. Toby followed, telling Nadya to stay behind, Dan to stay with her and Miss Carvela. "I'll be back quick," he'd said, meaning it at the time. Now he couldn't tear himself away.

Once here, Mooney and his men had soon fled, knowing better than to stick around a crime scene, this one in particular. Sarina Thigpen had wandered off, she had no place here. Only Veronique remained, and Toby could hear her as she wept, no one but strangers to console her. Precious few of them. She stood up front, transfixed, shuddering as she watched the flames reduce her childhood home to ruin. Hardly half an hour before, she and Toby had squared off, blame and recrimination, no pity, just to claim it. A pointless feud, like all feuds.

Her voice as she mewled out her grief, it haunted him, a cry not just for what she'd lost, he supposed, but for things barely guessed at. He wanted to go over, lay his hand upon her shoulder, but he knew better. She wanted none of his pity. And a part of him knew that some of her tears were not for the memories but her pride. What stakes—how much money and what vindictive dreams—had she invested in that sad old house? He supposed he'd never know.

Word came about other fires, downhill, over in Baymont. Panic rippled through the crowd, an instinct of something horribly wrong.

Toby ran back the way he'd come, across the panhandle, into Baymont, then two blocks uphill to Home in the Sky. He could smell it then, not just the rising smoke from below but the heavy stench of gasoline, so thick it seemed to seep up from the ground. When he got to Miss Carvela's, he realized there was no escape indoors. The smell hung everywhere.

"We have to get out," Dan told him. "I don't know what's going on, but we have to get out."

"Nadya's where?"

"Up helping Miss Carvela. Look, I'm serious. The cellar reeks of gasoline. We're not safe here."

Toby headed for the stairs. "I'll bring them down."

He found Nadya with Miss Carvela in her bedroom. Nadya greeted him with a breathless look of relief, then nodded helplessly at the tiny old woman. "She won't go."

Miss Carvela clutched a decorative tin box to her chest, eyes locked on some invisible thing. Toby had some idea what the box contained—letters and photographs from decades ago, her fiancé, never forgotten—and as he came closer, she looked up suddenly, a steely defiance in her eye, daring him to take it from her.

"It's dangerous here, Miss Carvela, we have to go."

Her resistance softened. "You do, yes. Of course. But I can't. This is my home."

"You're not safe here."

"You should go, yes." She waved her hand. "Both of you. Please."

"Not without you."

She dropped her gaze again. Dreamily she said, "I have lived in this house a great long while. . . ."

Toby knelt down in front of her, reaching for her hands to press his point, but she fought him off, clinging still to the small tin box.

"Miss Carvela, no. You know this isn't right. You know."

"I'm so tired," she whispered. "I can't tell you."

A tremor shook the house, rattling the windows and joined by a dull hammering sound, like thunder.

"We'll help you."

"No."

"You're just frightened."

"No, I am not." The steeliness returned. "I assure you, absolutely, I do not fear—"

"All right them." Toby moved to the bed, sat beside her. "We'll wait with you."

She looked at him with a helpless puzzlement, almost anguish. "You can't—"

Dan bounded up the stairs, his footsteps echoing against the bare walls. Entering the doorway, he said, "The basement, it's caught fire. We leave. Now." He took one look around the room, strode forward, dipped his shoulder into the small woman's midriff, and hefted her up like a large flour sack. "I'm sorry, ma'am. If I didn't have to do this, I wouldn't. You two, down the stairs. Now."

Out on the porch, Dan put Miss Carvela down. She turned right around toward the house. He tried to grab her but she struggled free.

"Let me," Toby said, following her back in.

She didn't run to the stairs, merely claimed a picture from the entry wall. Holding it in one hand, the tin box clutched in the other, she studied the photograph while all around her black smoke poured from the heater grates.

"We'll bring it along," Toby said as he gathered her toward him, turned her around, and half pushed, half guided her out the front door onto the porch.

"Good Lord," she whispered, looking out at the chaos of the neighborhood, smoke billowing from basement windows, cars edging downhill through crowds on foot.

"We need to get off the hill," Toby told her, easing her down the steps. "It's not—"

An explosion blew out a window in the house across the street. Flames shot up the outside walls through the shattered glass. Then a second blast followed the first, this one from somewhere deeper inside. The crowd in the street came to a halt, watching in stupefied horror as the figure of a boy appeared, maybe seven years old, trapped, outlined at the picture window and backlit by flames.

The boy's father—backing a station wagon out of the garage—jammed the car into park at the sound of the first explosion. He barely got out from behind the wheel before the second blast knocked him to the ground. His wife came out of the garage screaming, holding an infant in her arms, following her husband into the yard, shouting, "The stove, good God, JuDon—" Then the two of them together glanced up, saw their boy, his clothes on fire, pounding against the windowpane. The mother let loose a chilling scream.

The father shouted at the boy, "I said wait for me, JuDon!" his voice filling the street. "In your room. Stay *in your room!*"

People in the crowd stood paralyzed, unable to believe what they saw. Dan snapped to, turned to Nadya. "You have to take care of her," he said, gesturing to Miss Carvela, then taking off at a run down the stairs to the street. Toby followed.

Others responded. Men in the crowd scrambled down the sides of the house, pounding at windows, trying to smash the glass and climb in. Women came forward to restrain the mother, talk her down. The father tried getting in the front door, but the smoke held him back. He staggered off the porch, eyes dazed. Trying to return through the garage, he again met a wall of smoke, billowing out from the kitchen. The mother kept screaming, "JuDon, JuDon," the infant in her arms now bawling, too. The father regained his bearings, ran around to the back of the house. Toby could see through the window, though, that smoke blocked that direction, too.

Dan searched a flower bed and found a rock the size of a melon. Running forward, he hurled it full force against the picture window. The glass broke, but a hole no bigger than a hand appeared. As Dan searched out another stone, Toby spotted a baseball bat on the porch. He went for it, scrambling on his knees as heat and smoke poured out the screen door. Back at the window, he couldn't look at the boy—the sounds were horrible enough, the child still slamming himself, arms and body and head, against the glass. Toby lowered his head and began hammering with the bat against the glass where the rock had torn its hole. A crack formed. He hit it again, the crack split, the hole widening as he slammed the bat over and over at the glass, a mindless fury, till someone shouted, "Now!"

An army of bodies surged forward, engulfing him as they went for the glass, tearing away loose jagged shards and reaching in through the scalding heat for the boy. But the boy didn't wait. He threw his body into the opening, clothes on fire as he tumbled past the out-stretched arms and hit the ground. Dan lunged after him, covered him with his body to put out the flames, but the boy fought, kicked, screaming nonstop. He tore loose, jumped up, clothes still smoldering as he fled the yard, leaving bloody footprints on the pavement down-hill till at last he collapsed in the middle of the street, rolling onto his back, the whole time crying out. Only then did Toby recognize the sickening, sweet smell, like charred meat, the boy left in his wake.

A woman with long beaded braids came running with a blanket. Dan, smeared with sooty blood, gestured for Toby to follow him as he stumbled down the street.

"We gonna carry him now," the woman with the braids said. "Hold on to the edge, we'll get him in the car."

She laid the blanket out on the asphalt. The boy, skin blistered with burns, shook fiercely, going into shock. His father ran up: "JuDon, JuDon! It's me! It's Daddy! It's me—"

"Help us get him on the blanket," the woman said.

The father, eyes raw with panic, took one shoulder, the woman the other. Toby and Dan each placed one hand beneath a hip, the other hand lifting a leg beneath the knee. They eased the boy onto the blanket, their hands coming away with blood and scorched fabric and burned skin.

Another man appeared, nudging the father aside. "Go help your wife and get the car started," he said. "I'll do this."

Toby recognized the voice. He glanced up. "Francis."

Francis made no acknowledgment, just grabbed his corner of the blanket, nodded for the others to do likewise. "On three, we lift. One. Two."

They hoisted the boy up and headed back uphill toward the parents' car. The mother fought through the restraining arms of neighbors to greet the makeshift stretcher halfway, one hand still clutching the infant to her body, the other hand reaching for her son's face, telling him in a choking voice, "You're gonna be fine, JuDon. Listen. Listen. You listen to me, this is Mama, you listen, you're gonna be fine fine fine now."

At the car, someone in the crowd opened the tailgate so they could lay the boy out in the back. The mother crawled in after, the wailing infant gripped tight to her chest as she tucked into the small space and folded the blanket around her son's body. The father climbed in behind the wheel and cranked the engine.

They backed out into the street and were gone, horn blasts sounding as they reached the fringe of the crowd and the other cars edging downhill. Dan and Toby and Francis, all the others who'd stayed behind, looked around helpless, suddenly returned to their own plight. Behind them, up the hill, smoke poured out of every cellar window in Miss Carvela's house, flames darting out and licking up the walls.

Francis grabbed Toby's coat and shook him. "You get Auntie C down, you get her safe, you understand me?"

"Francis—"

The punch came from nowhere, a roundhouse to the head that knocked Toby sideways and off his feet. Dan rushed in, spun Francis around, but Toby cried out, "No. Don't. It's all right."

Toby straightened his glasses and climbed to his feet, hearing

Francis call out, "You heard what I said," as he glanced up one last time at his great-aunt's house, checked to be sure she was safe with Nadya, then started to jog downhill.

Dan tugged Toby's sleeve. "The car. Get everybody in the car."

Miss Carvela stared up at her burning home, emitting a soft, throaty wail. As Toby approached, she spun toward him with faithless eyes. "Francis. He was here, he—" She searched the street, trying to find him.

"Miss Carvela, we have to get in the car."

"But Francis—"

"He told me to get you away. We'll find him down the hill. He's gone. He's fine. Please."

At the top of the block, smoke spilled out of another house now and flames rippled in the dark beyond its windows. Other fires raged downhill. They'd have to drive past the fires to get out. Airborne cinders sailed into the pine trees, the dry needles smoldering till whole branches popped into flame with a sudden glancing wind.

Toby opened the car door, helped Miss Carvela inside, and Nadya climbed in with her. Toby and Dan got in the front and they were moving, pulling into a makeshift caravan that budged downhill in fits and starts amid a sea of bodies on foot, away from one nest of fire, down toward others.

Along the edges of the street, boys on bicycles sped as fast as they could, dodging the people on foot. Fright-eyed mothers pushed toddlers in strollers and clung with free hands to other children running alongside. One man rolled a wheelbarrow, his three girls inside, legs dangling over the lip as they reached out their hands for their mother, who struggled to keep pace.

Dogs ran free, searching out pathways through the yards, knocking people down as they darted in and out of blind pathways. Cats fled, too, sprinting through the crowds and along fence tops, across roofs. Squirrels traveled the power lines, a knotwork of scuttering shapes, while birds soared low overhead, in and out of the dense smoke clouds.

Two-thirds of the way down, they met a wall of motionless

taillights. People were gesturing for them to back up. A dozen cars ahead, they could see the burned boy and his family, fleeing their grid-locked car and continuing on foot, the father clutching his blanket-wrapped son as he ran, the mother with her baby trailing behind in the crowd. In the far distance, the garish swirl of a fire engine's roof lights spun red and white in the drifting haze of smoke and airborne cinders, its horn bleating helplessly for people to make way.

"There another way out?" Dan asked Toby, putting the car in reverse.

"You can try up or down, but everything bottles up at the bottom."

Dan backed up crooked to the curb, jammed the transmission into park. "From here on out we walk."

Miss Carvela could barely stand, drained and fearful, confused. Toby hunched down. "Climb on, Miss Carvela." Nadya took the tin box and picture from her as the old woman wrapped her arms around his neck. He hoisted her up, tucked his arms beneath her knees, and jostled her into place. "We're set."

A hundred people flooded past the congested cars that tried to nudge back so the fire crews could pass. The cars couldn't move for the foot traffic. Finally, police officers shouldered their way through, waving people to the curbs, pushing them sometimes, swinging their batons, waving the cars back. The whole time Toby just kept moving forward, glancing to his side only to be sure Nadya was there. He lost track of Dan, but every now and again he caught sight of him in the corner of his eye, swimming through the crowd.

Time lost all measure—it could have been an hour, half that, or half that again—but finally they got directed through a dirt track alleyway toward the stonework fence along Magnolia. Farther down, a fire among the pines near the gate still burned. Officers in reflective vests, swinging their flashlights in the haze, gestured them west toward the river. Following others, their backs now the one constant thing in his field of vision, Toby clambered over the stonework with Miss Carvela clinging to him piggyback. Nadya followed after, assisted by Dan, who brought up the rear.

Lungs aching, Toby eased Miss Carvela to the ground. Dozens of others, dazed and restless and panting, thronged Magnolia. Sawhorse barriers blocked traffic. A rescue wagon sat parked in the street, its red light spinning as people clustered at its rear doors. EMTs handed out wet cloths to wipe away the soot, cups of water to slake thirst and rinse away the gagging taste of smoke. People drank and spat, coughing miserably.

Sooner or later, everyone stared up at the hillside—in the firelit night, it seemed hardly more than a patchwork of angular shapes engulfed in scattered fires, shrouded in smoke. Here and there in the crowd you heard a wail or muffled sobbing, while in the dark beyond the bodies Toby spotted a loose-knit pack of dogs, clambering over the stonework fence, scurrying across Magnolia for the riverbank beyond.

The chief set up his control and command in a storefront just inside the Baymont gate, appearing in person to steer the ship. News crews stood ready to film, and no doubt he thought he'd been ready, decked out in his blues and brass. But the youngest man on camera—not to mention new to the force, an outsider—he came across like a spin flack, sweating and vacant-eyed beneath the lights. Murchison almost felt sorry for him. The guy was photogenic, smart, but his inclination toward the grand, mixed with a free-form wordiness, did him in. Shooting from the lip, the older hands on the force called it.

Baffled by some of his commands, detectives and uniforms conferred in private or devised their own protocols on the fly as they headed up the hill to pound on doors, aid the evacuation, check every house to make sure no stragglers remained behind to burn up and die.

Murchison and Stluka, pulled off the warehouse fire, joined the others, fighting against the spilling crowd as they pushed uphill on foot. There'd only been time to collect walkie-talkies to communicate with the watch command, none to don vests or windbreakers identifying them as police. They'd have to chance it in just their sport jackets and slacks.

Stluka, still fuming from his encounter with the burrheaded squatter at the warehouse fire, sank deeper and deeper into a helpless fury as they went house to house. Sometimes you couldn't tell whether a family had already fled or hid inside in the locked-up dark, waiting for luck they had no reason to hope for. Murchison and Stulka came across both in the first block alone, wasting fifteen minutes each place.

"Let the damn fools burn," Stluka muttered as they headed up the next walkway.

Smoke from fires less than a block away drifted like fog along the rooftops. Stluka covered his mouth, hammered his fist against the front door, calling out, "Police! Open up!" Murchison cupped his hands around his eyes, checked the windows, looking for signs of someone inside. Through the dark interior he spotted a sliver of light eking out beneath a hallway door.

"I think we got a holdout here, Jerry. Let me try around back."

Stluka, coughing, pounded harder, kicked at the door. "Come on! Police! Show your goddamn face! Now!"

Murchison slid in mud along the side yard. A smell of gas, but no idea from where. Light bled through curtains at a window, and he heard battling voices within as he passed beneath the sill. Uneasy, he drew his piece as Stluka's shouts and fistfalls continued in front.

A chain-link fence surrounded the backyard. Fearing a dog—they lurked sometimes beneath the porch, silent till the very last second— Murchison kept the gun ready as he draped one leg over, lifted the second behind, dropping onto the mud and grass beyond the fence. Beef bones and waterlogged mounds of shit littered the yard, confirming his instincts.

Through trailing smoke he made out a handcrafted staircase of wood slat steps leading up to a plywood landing and a dark back door. Edging closer, gun held out at the ready, he listened hard and heard at last the low simpering growl from deep in the subporch shadows.

"Jerry, heads up. Got ourselves at least one dog back here!"

He waited for acknowledgment but heard instead the sudden fast slam of an opening door, then a shotgun blast. The ratchet of a pump, a second blast.

"Jerry!" He kept his gun trained on the shadows beneath the plank steps. "Call out, give me your status! Jerry!"

From the front of the house he heard only the scramble of footsteps as one, maybe two people fled. He fired twice into the darkness beneath the porch, heard the hidden animal yelp in pain and flee—a

Doberman, sleek and huge—dragging its hindquarters. It circled into the far corner of the yard, pitching its head back to emit an open-throat howl.

Murchison ran up the steps, kicked at the door till the wood gave way. The entrance led through a short dark hallway to a kitchen that reeked of mold and rubbish. "Anybody here, come out. Identify yourself, hands where I can see them." All he could make out was the glowing blue gas flames of the stove's pilot lights.

"Jerry! Call out! Status!"

The kitchen led to another hallway, this one longer and leading to the front. He saw again the same closed door with the light bleeding out along the floor. He pounded, stood back, called out, "Police!"

"I am, I don't—" A woman's voice, ancient, weak.

"Answer me—are you alone?"

"Yes. No."

"Who else is in the house?"

"Who are you?"

"Who else is in the house?"

"My grandson. Roderick? I heard noise. Shots, oh my Lord, my grandson—"

Murchison ran to the front. The door was ajar, slammed open so hard it had bounced back and almost closed again. Pulling it toward him, he found Stluka struggling to lift himself off the porch, his whole chest bloody, his face and neck pocked with small wounds. One in the neck bled bad, an artery. Licking his lips, trying for air, he swatted at his holster, still hoping to draw his piece. The shotgun lay on the porch, discarded. At the bottom of the hill Murchison glimpsed a figure darting through the smoke around the street corner.

Murchison drew the walkie-talkie from his pocket, thumbing the transmit button and coughing as he shouted into the mouthpiece, "Code Nine Nine Nine, officer down. Respond!"

He checked the wall for the house number and, when the watch commander confirmed response, gave the location, identified himself, told him Stluka was hit. "It's bad, he's losing blood fast."

"Sit tight, Murch. I can't promise you. Sorry. It's a mess down here. I'll get someone to you. Hang on."

He signed off, pressed his hands against Stluka's neck, trying to stem the blood, but it kept seeping through his fingers. From behind, the same ancient female voice as before, suddenly close, said, "Away with your noisy songs! Offer me holocausts. . . ."

The woman stood just beyond the doorway, well over six feet tall, thin as a rail, toothless, with dried spittle caking her lips. Her matted gray hair tufted and peaked atop her head. She stank of sweat and unwashed skin, barefoot with yellow nails, dressed in a ratty green robe.

A crack house, Murchison figured. The old woman, delusional, feeble, probably owned the place. Her grandson and his crowd had taken it over. Hands still pressed to Stluka's throbbing neck wound, he shouted, "Stand back from the door!"

"Roderick, he knows I'm here to do—listen, he . . ."

"Stand back from the *door.*"

The woman didn't move. Her eyes were blank and red, her face an etchwork of deep creases and folds around the eyes, the mouth. "Don't let nobody in. Nobody." Her voice was strangely clear and calm and steady. "Two men in a van come around, set the whole hill on fire."

Murchison felt a tug on his shirt cuff. Turning back to Stluka, he saw his partner's eyes swell, hazing in their sockets. He tried to speak. Nothing but a spurt of breath came.

"Jerry, don't—"

Stluka's hand flailed, he caught Murchison's jacket, grasped it tight, and pulled. Murchison leaned down, put his ear to Stluka's lips. He whispered something, too soft. It sounded like, "Macon Bay." Blood and spittle coated his tongue. He clenched Murchison's jacket harder, shook. "You—"

"Jerry, lie still, I've got—"

Stluka swatted at his holster again; the hand caught, he pulled his service piece out. Jerkily he pushed the weapon into Murchison's free hand. "May . . . gun . . ."

The old woman stepped out from the doorway. Murchison shouted, "Ma'am, stay in the house," but she heard nothing. Like a sleepwalker, she stepped out to the edge of the porch, reached out her hand beyond the overhang, palm up. Smiling with a childlike innocence, she closed her eyes and lifted her face to the smoke-filled sky, by which time Murchison felt it, too, smelled it, heard the pinging sound on the roof gutters, the soft thump on the roof and the dirt of the yard.

Rain.

Part III

Goin' Down Slow

20

erry had hidden the car, a Chevy Caprice, in the same storage facility where Manny had mixed the tubs—different locker, two
aisles away. It took him an hour to walk there from the hill, his
ankle sprained, his face cut from thistle lashings, but with a little Dex
for clarity, plain aspirin for the pain, he felt ready for the all-night
drive.

At a water spigot near the locker, he washed the stickiness of
Manny's blood from his face and hands. He balled up the overalls,
stuffed them into a plastic sack, and tossed them in a random Dumpster while en route to the vacant office where he'd bivouacked the
past two months. After shoving his gear into a duffel and gathering his
collection of mobile phones and his laptop, he hit the freeway and
headed south.

He crossed the border from San Ysidro into Tijuana well before
dawn. At the border no one bothered with southbound traffic, but
Ferry still checked his mirrors as he passed through the international
gateway. Before continuing south on the coastal toll road, he headed
into town, toward the Zona Norte, where the brothels were.

It wasn't a girl he was after—at least, not one he'd pay for. He
headed for the edge of the district, near the *colonias* where the poor-
est working families lived. At the end of a dusty thoroughfare, lined
with bus stops for transport of the female workers to the *maquilas* on
the Otay Mesa, he parked outside a cantina called *El Gallo*. The
Rooster.

Monday morning, five o'clock, it was already open for breakfast.

Some of the girls ventured in to grab a quick taco or *pan dulce* before their buses arrived to carry them to their shifts. Ferry liked the factory girls. Even the shy ones flirted.

He ordered *horchata*—a sweet rice drink spiced with cinnamon—to soothe the acid in his stomach from the Dexedrine. He drank it slow at the counter, every now and then sneaking a glance at the girls, relishing the sight of so many plump butts packed tight into faded jeans.

Finishing his *horchata*, he stepped outside and scanned the dark trashy street. In days past dozens and dozens of women would have been out here, too, waiting at the bus stops, ready for work. A number of factories had closed in the past year, the companies moving their assembly work to Malaysia, where the labor glut was even more desperate.

He collected his laptop from the trunk of the car, then headed into the Zona Norte. After walking several blocks, he turned into an alley of hard-packed dirt and stepped inside an unmarked cinder block storefront. A bald, gap-toothed *cholo*, wearing a loose white *guayabera* to disguise his fat, sat in a torn leather swivel chair behind the counter, leaning into a cone of lamplight to read his comic book.

There were shelves behind him, scattered with cloned cell phones. Ferry was already equipped in that department; for him, the item of interest was simply a door. He withdrew a twenty from his pocket. The *cholo* collected the bill in a large, soft hand and gestured with a tug of his head that Ferry could pass through to the back.

Beyond the door sat four men wearing *cremas de seda*, their backs to one another as they hunched over laptops linked to phone jacks along the walls. A single bulb in a ceiling socket dimly lit the room, which stank of sweat and cat piss. Ferry chose an open jack, plugged in his laptop, fired up the PGP encryption program, and logged on.

First, he checked E-mail. Marisela had written. It hadn't been easy, Ovidio had been obliged to call in some very old favors and offer in return a few of his own, but yes, a boat would be waiting—Bahía de San Quintín, four hours farther south. He was to meet a man named Rafael at the Old Mill launch ramp. He'd wait till two. His fishing boat was named *La Chica de Buenas*. Lucky Girl.

Next, he checked his account with Pennington International

Trust, Ltd., a dodge shelter located in the Cook Islands. He got his cash through ATM transactions drawn off the account, which was held in the name of an offshore asset protection trust. The trust had a flight provision, requiring the bank as trustee to move his assets to another offshore jurisdiction if any threat to the trust or its corpus should materialize, and no such threat could arise without ample notice through a local court action. He closed out accounts after every job, so any inquiry into past acts was doomed to come up empty. Another benefit of working narcotics for so many years—you learned a lot about hiding money.

No new deposits appeared. Bratcher hadn't come through.

Ferry logged off, left the storefront, and walked back to his car. Heading south on the toll road, he passed the new liquid natural gas plants serving the American Southwest, built here to avoid EPA guidelines. Farther south, industry gave way to the beaches at Rosarito, the golf courses at Bajamar. This part of the peninsula resembled what Orange and San Diego counties had looked like twenty years ago, gated housing tracts cropping up everywhere to accommodate the latest wave of bourgeois flight.

Eight miles south of Bajamar, he pulled off the tollway onto a dirt road leading west to Playa Saldamando. The road descended steeply to the beach, which tall bluffs protected from wind. Kayakers camped on the sand, the predawn sea glassy and calm.

He rummaged through his duffel, pulled out one of the Rohde & Schwartz digital phones he had, the encrypted ones designed for European executives paranoid about American surveillance. He dialed Bratcher, routing the call through a reorigination service that would complicate even further any attempt to triangulate his location. Bratcher picked up on the third ring, a good sign.

"This who I think it is?" Drowsy, he slurred his words, his voice almost a growl.

"North Bay Services, sir. Sorry to catch you so early, but you told me to call this line if I had any urgent concerns. I'm looking at a rush invoice here, remains outstanding. I was hoping we could close this."

Without a specific number or identification code to target, it was highly unlikely law enforcement would have a way to focus in on his cell, and the encryption would make it difficult to snag and decode the signal for all but the most sophisticated eavesdroppers. Not much chance of that, this soon after the fires. The order-and-invoice jargon was more to put Bratcher to the test.

"I'm not showing full delivery on that order." Bratcher had picked up the cue, albeit with a little menace in his voice. The fact he played along, didn't just jump in discussing the fire, it was a good sign. "And I didn't order the rush."

"Code's been entered here, it's off our inventory. I think there might be some confusion concerning the back-end service portion of the contract. That what you mean?"

First half buys performance, Ferry thought. Second buys loyalty. Remember?

"Just because it's off your shelf doesn't mean we're satisfied with the product."

Ferry had caught news reports on the car radio during the trip south. You couldn't trust the media, of course, but from what he'd heard the fires had done enough damage to qualify as a job well done.

"Could you clarify what you mean?"

"Supposed to be weatherproof, for one thing."

The rain, Ferry thought. He'd heard about that, too. "What portion of the shipment we talking about?"

"Third at least. Maybe half. I made it clear, nothing but full delivery and complete satisfaction."

"I think we should turn our attention to the service part of the contract. No support services will be forthcoming until payment is made in full. I think if you review the contract—"

"Contract specified full performance. I'm sick of saying that. Besides—"

"I'm gonna have to be firm here. I expect to see the balance paid by noon. And I think your definition and mine concerning full performance? Let's just say we'll have to agree to disagree."

"No. No, you listen." The menace switched to anger. "You pushed this, not me. Truth is, your guy, one of your employees, he fucked up. That problem you mentioned—he wasn't just hanging around, he was involved. You needed to act fast to cover your own ass. You think I don't know this? You've been paid all you're gonna get paid. You're damn lucky to have that."

Somehow, Bratcher had already tapped into the full story on Manny's involvement in the Carlisle killing. They wouldn't be broadcasting that through the media yet. That meant juice, no more doubt about it. Feds most likely.

Get off the phone, he told himself.

"I'm gonna give you a chance to reconsider. It won't get cheaper, in the long run, doing it this way."

Bratcher laughed and broke the connection. Ferry stared at the cell phone for a moment, puzzled, then enraged. He considered slamming it against the dash but thought better of it. Instead, leaving it on, so they could continue tracking the ping if Bratcher tipped them off to the call, he dropped it outside the car into the sand. Maybe one of the kayakers will pick it up, he thought, take it out into the Pacific with him. That'd make for an interesting hunt.

He cranked the ignition, put the Caprice in gear, and headed back out toward the toll road.

Toby and Nadya spent the night on the floor with Miss Carvela in the basement of Mission Baptist. They'd slept there, shoeless but in their clothes, lying on thin foam mats, polyester blankets for warmth, like dozens of others from Baymont and St. Martin's Hill.

Dan had left them in the hands of the Red Cross, then walked off to his sister's office to let her know everyone had survived. There was no point in trying to phone; if one worked it had twenty people queued up to use it.

He offered to come back with another car to take them to Tina's home, where they could wash, sleep in a bed or at least on a couch, have something decent to eat. Miss Carvela declined, and Toby refused to leave her alone. She needed to be here, she said, where her neighbors and friends, their children and grandchildren, would be. She needed to know who was safe, who needed her prayers. And Francis, he might show up at the shelter, there was that chance.

During the night, dozing off from exhaustion, she'd finally loosened her hold on the tin box and picture she'd insisted on saving from the fire. Toby, who'd slept not at all, reached over at one point and ventured a peek. As he'd thought, the box held letters—penned by someone named Reginald, his words filled with a clumsy boyish tenderness. Toby read no more than a few lines, felt ashamed, then refolded the old brittle paper and returned it to its box.

The picture was a sepia-tinted black-and-white photograph of a young Carvela Grimes. Slender and small, but with that same proud sadness in her eyes even then, she stood at an auditorium lectern beside a double-chinned matron, both women wearing orchids and sashes and floor-length gowns. Beneath the photograph, a yellowed scrap of newsprint read: *"Mrs. Augusta Jones presents Carvela Grimes with the Worthy Miss Sash for Fidelus Chapter No. 9, Order of Eastern Star-Prince Hall Rite of Adoption, Firma Lodge Hall."*

And those were her most perfected memories, he guessed. The love of a young sailor long dead and the recognition that once, years ago, in the aftermath of that sacrifice, she'd been deemed worthy.

Nadya slept fitfully, her fists tucked under her chin. Toby pulled the blanket up above her shoulder, tucked it tighter around her legs. He'd spent the past two months caring for his father. He'd lacked any idea how important the role had become to him, but he felt it now, grateful to have these two women, one old, one young, Black, white, to look after. He anticipated with dread the day they'd no longer need him that way. There'd be his own business to sit with then.

He felt changed. Like he'd turned a corner, but his shadow had continued on in the same old direction. He had no idea what that meant, what he'd do about it. It frightened him, that not knowing. In particular, he cringed at the thought of actually being there when Nadya woke up, opened her eyes. Feared being the first thing she saw. Feared being seen for who he really was.

The detective conducting the shooting review—a Kentucky transplant named Jimmy Johndroe, not a bad guy—wore jeans and a hooded sweatshirt. Like Murchison, he'd already been up on the hill aiding evacuation and only sat here because Stluka was dead.

Johndroe worked IA for the Rio Mirada force. They wouldn't bring in an outsider, not for something as clean as this. He'd started by offering his condolences, then thanking Murchison for sitting down so soon, while the memory was fresh. Murchison ran down what had happened and Johndroe taped it.

The issue of charging uphill without vests came up. Murchison blamed lack of foresight, lack of time. A crisis dictates action, detectives don't wear vests, there you had it. Secretly, Murchison thought, I hate this, every single bit of it. Hate myself.

After a few follow-up questions, Johndroe recited their names, badge numbers, and the time and date, then turned the machine off. As though it was just the next item on his checklist, he said, "There's counseling available, Murch. If you want, I can—"

"Maybe in a couple days," Murchison lied. Counselors were thought of as spies for the brass. And he didn't need reminding of his limitations as a talker. "We're undermanned on the hill. Still a lot to get done."

Johndroe nodded. "No lie to that." He shivered a little. "Be honest with you? Nothing perks up my pucker factor like fire."

"Yeah."

Inwardly, Murchison thought: Fire's the easy part. He no longer had to guess at what the Lazarenko girl had gone through. Like her, he'd been bloody when the EMTs reached him. And like her, he'd been unable to make it matter. Stluka died right there as Murchison blew worthless air into his lungs. It had taken forty minutes for help to arrive. They'd had to fight through the crowd and smoke and chaos, find their way through all that to the house. The whole time, the gaunt, feebleminded old woman just stood there, like he and Stluka were invisible, toeing the edge of the porch as she tried to catch rain on her tongue.

"Reminds me of that booby-trapped tank truck full of jet fuel they found headed for Bagram Air Base in Afghanistan," Johndroe said, shaking his head. "Gives you the willies seeing that kinda thing so close to home."

Not close, Murchison thought. Home.

"Been catching the radio broadcasts? Worst fire since the Oakland Hills firestorm, they say, and a lot of the same problems. But Stluka's the only man we lost. I mean, not like that's some small—"

"It's okay, Johndroe." Murchison worked up a smile. "Don't. Really."

Johndroe squirmed a few more apologies into his chair, then went on. "Fire companies lost four so far, got maybe five more in critical. Bunch of minor stuff, them and us both."

"How many people from the hill?"

"Still counting. Sixteen dead we know about. About two, three dozen in ER for burns, a lot of them critical. One seven-year-old boy, he's touch and go. Father carried him in a blanket all the way down into the command center, screamed out, 'Somebody, please, help my son!' Chief looked at him like he'd pulled a knife. But they got the kid to ER quick enough to save his life, for now any rate. Won't know the whole story, on him or the hill, for days."

The rain had slowed but not stopped the fires. Given the mismatch in hydrant couplings, the nearby fire companies had been forced to stand down, providing manpower for support while their trucks stood helplessly idle, their pumper engines all but useless beyond five minutes. Helicopters had been called in, filling their monsoon buckets in the river, then flying over the smoldering houses. HAZMAT crews had made it to the top of the hill and were laying foam into the sewers to sit on the gas fumes. Meanwhile, clear through dawn, officers trudged door to door—some from in town, the whole force on mandatory overtime, others called in by the Office of Emergency Services from as far away as Santa Rosa and Oakland—trying to root out the hideaways, the stay-behinds, the ill and crippled not yet accounted for.

"The Roderick guy you mentioned, one who shot your partner, now there's a real piece of work."

Murchison stared blankly.

"You wouldn't believe what they found inside that house."

"Sure I would."

While still at the scene, Murchison learned from an EMT that the old woman wasn't just undernourished, dehydrated, and mentally ill. A brief inspection suggested she'd also been subjected to repeated sexual assaults. The EMT said his wife worked for the ombudsman, you saw that kind of thing more and more—old women with dementia pimped off by family members for drug money.

"And the botched tanker heist up top of the hill? Your perp in the Carlisle killing got found there. Or at least they think it's him, pending dentals and prints, if they can get any off him. Did you know that?"

"I heard. Yeah."

The gas from the tanker had flooded the sewers but left only a film at the station itself, so when a spark source hit it only a surface fire caught, and that got handled by the rain. Luckily, none of the vapor inside the empty tank compartments went up. Too rich a mixture. It meant they had a relatively intact crime scene, complete with three dead men—singed by the fire but not burned to char and bone, they'd be identified—plus a long-bed van. They'd found, too, a .357 and a Smith and Wesson 645, both now being matched against the Carlisle ballistics through IBIS, and a knapsack containing the personal property of one Manuel Turpin, aged twenty-one, with an Oregon conviction for felony arson.

"FBI's arrived, because of this Turpin mutt. They're keen on him in a weird way."

"How so?"

"You'll find out. They want you in on the big sit-down once they're through with their preliminaries. ATF's in town now, too, because of the way the houses went up. Some kind of bomb they've seen before, but only in Mob jobs."

"Fed's sharing anything real?"

Johndroe laughed. "Get serious."

Murchison got up from his chair. "Holmes paged me from the hill. He's got something he wants me to see."

Johndroe didn't stand up. "Holmes, he'll probably get that detective shield now. Got the vacancy, with Stluka gone. Chief's got no reason not to put Holmes in his place. God knows they've both been eager. Might even make him your partner. How's that sit with you?"

The question, folksy in tone, had insidious intent, but Murchison couldn't be sure he wasn't just imagining. Still, he knew pretty soon the nicknames would start. Ebony and Ivory. Ugly and Uglier. And it would be odd, going from partner to the most unapologetic racist on the force to partner of its first Black detective. There was a mood swing for you. But he knew it wouldn't make him look versatile. It'd make him look like he wasn't even there.

He shrugged. "Holmesy's a good cop. Why?"

Johndroe gestured for Murchison to sit back down. "Just a few last questions."

He didn't bother to flip the recorder back on. Murchison sat.

"Did Stluka slug one of the kids taken into custody for trespass at the warehouse fire near Dumpers?"

Murchison sagged in his chair. "Kinda late in the game to be asking that. Can't sue a dead man."

"Department's still on the hook."

"Then I'll wait for a lawyer. No offense."

"None taken. Got anything you want to tell me about Officer Gilroy's handling of the Thigpen arrest?"

How did he know these things, Murchison wondered. "I wasn't present during the arrest."

"Anything at all? The hospital? The fact you tore up his booking sheet?"

Murchison felt his mouth get dry. "Like I said—"

"Did you tell this Thigpen kid's mother you had an eyewitness?"

It was a prickling sensation along his neck Murchison felt now. Sarina Thigpen, she'd already complained. Maybe hired a lawyer. Everybody'd be hiring lawyers.

"That's permissible deception, Johndroe."

"The kid's mother? How about this—you continue to question her son after he made a clear and unequivocal request for counsel?"

"He wasn't a suspect in the shooting at that point."

Johndroe rolled his eyes. "Ah, Jesus, Murch—"

"A material witness, I don't—"

"Murch, stop. You had his clothes. The door was locked. You know better." Johndroe edged closer. Same as Murchison had with Arlie. "Not like we hide the SOP binder." Standard Operating Procedure—a three-ring binder filled with the latest great idea on how to avoid the last big blunder. Fifty Years of Fuckups, it got called. "You nuts? You want to lose your house?"

"Over the piddly beefs you just brought up?"

"You want to answer any of my questions?"

Murchison wondered where all this was headed. Whatever he did in the room with Arlie Thigpen seemed wildly irrelevant at this point. What charge was the kid facing, resisting arrest? That would depend on Gilroy, and it seemed pretty obvious he'd decided to hedge his bets and get down first with Johndroe. The Carlisle killing would stay unsolved or get pinned on Manny, depending on the call from IBIS with the ballistics match, unless somebody came forward with something different. Even if Murchison's questioning of Arlie got admitted in whatever prosecution came up—and that was doubtful—no evidence resulted. Reversible error, if that. Even a civil suit would get settled fast for next to nothing.

Then Johndroe laid out his cards. "Like I said. It's not just us now. The feds are falling all over themselves. This fire on the hill, it's a very big deal. Rumors are flying everywhere, the whole town's scared or pissed or both. Gonna be a feeding frenzy."

"Yeah. But, Johndroe, this thing here, between you and me—it's a shooting review."

Johndroe finally stood up, his eyes strangely sad and cold at the same time. "I know. That's why the recorder's off. But if any of that other stuff comes up, it won't be me running the show, okay? They'll bring somebody in from outside. Just a heads up."

That was Johndroe. Not a bad guy.

21

Murchison lowered his window and showed his badge to pass through the various checkpoints outside Baymont. Some were manned by MPs from the National Guard brigade out of San Francisco, called in by the sheriff. The uniforms evoked an eerie sense of déjà vu that stayed with him as he drove on. It accentuated the awkward unreality of driving itself. Stluka had been the wheelman so long it seemed not just backward but, in a certain sense, wrong to be steering the car himself.

The Red Cross had set up shelters in local schools and church basements, but a lot of the crowd still waited out on Magnolia, restless, combative. Stirred by rumors of looting, they argued with the officers manning the perimeter, wanting permission to go back to their homes, get clothes and valuables left behind. Some, sick of the runaround, slipped over the stonework fence and tried to steal uphill unnoticed—thus becoming themselves suspected looters. Murchison saw a few of them sitting on curbs as he drove up the hill, women as well as men, all ages, dressed as they'd been when fleeing their homes, their hands now secured behind their backs with come-alongs.

On top of the hill, firemen still battled a line of house and underbrush fires, but elsewhere the destruction was done. Here a line of homes reduced to blackened timber and brick and smoldering char, then one untouched, grimed from smoke but still standing, eerily whole. This neighborhood gutted, that one spared. Hundreds of trees had burned down to scorched shafts, horror movie stuff, while others looked as green as yesterday. It felt a little like mockery, that randomness. Meanwhile, the heavy stench of smoke hung everywhere, stinging the mouth and throat and lungs, while grayish swirls of ash fluttered through the air, like fine dry snow.

Along the streets, sanitation crews pried open manholes to ventilate the sewers. Smoke ejectors chugged noisily, pumping out fumes, while utility crews bled gas lines, creating eerie plumes of blue flame amid the ruin. If you watched long enough, out of the corner of your eye you'd spot a crouched shape, edging from one shadow to the next, as a pet ventured back into its former neighborhood, nose piqued, ears and tail slack as it hunted for food or just something, someone, familiar.

A few of the stay-behinds showed up in their soot-black doorways to watch, blinking like sleepers suddenly wakened. Neckerchiefs obscured their faces, to help against the smoke and windblown ash.

Patrol and fire units were parked in front of the house where Holmes was waiting, if *house* was still the word for it. The front window was shattered; the roof and walls had burned away in places. It seemed a miracle of sorts the thing still stood there. Other houses up and down the block had suffered, too, but not like this. He showed his badge to the officer manning entry/exit and ducked inside.

Unfolding a handkerchief, he covered his mouth and nose. Like shoving your face in a damp ash pit, the smell. The fire had reduced the living room to cinders, the furniture nothing but blackened debris from the flashover. Everything, ceiling to floor, dripped black water, sodden from the pumper hoses and bucket drops. Toward the back, where the fire damage was less, window glass bellied in toward the room in syrupy shapes, and the aluminum frames had melted, too, like wax, oozing down the walls to form hardened shapes on the floor. Above, you could see sky where the fire had eaten through the ceiling. The floor underneath was a mulchy bog of char and ash.

The overhaul crew plodded about in their turn-out gear, prodding the ash beds with hooks and halligan tools as they hunted for melted copper or brass that might reignite. An arson investigator, holding a tool intended to check tire tread, plunged it into the wall, trying to measure char depth. How in God's name do you control your crime scene, Murchison thought, when you throw in fire, the men who fight it, and the way they have to do their job?

Seeing Murchison, the arson man gestured toward the back. "Through there."

Holmes, dressed in street clothes, conferred with a uniformed officer outside a bathroom just inside a black gutted doorway leading out to the garage. Seeing Murchison, he broke off the conversation and came forward.

"This one's mean." Holmes nodded back over his shoulder toward the bathroom door. "Seen two houses up here already look like the folks who lived there set fire to the place before taking off. Or somebody else did."

It was a common problem in major fires and riots. Storekeepers torched their shops, figuring blame would fall on looters. Renters who hated their landlords got revenge.

"We'll see some insurance fraud," Murchison guessed.

"Or covering up crime scenes."

"We got that here?"

Holmes gestured him back. "What we got here defies description."

The bathroom had been sandwiched between the two advancing fires. Part of the wall had burned away, revealing melted copper piping, oxidized black and coiled into oddball shapes. The floor tiles had peeled up, the edges curled like plastic flower petals. The floor beneath was spalled and tarred with ghost marks.

The glass in the mirror above the sink, melted slightly from the heat, reflected back funhouse images of Holmes and Murchison in the doorway. The faucet handles and water spout were weirdly malformed as well. A body sheet lay across the blackened tub. The aluminum shower rod and plastic curtain were history, melted. No windows. Up top, the ceiling, made of Sheetrock, had survived reasonably well. And trapped the smoke, Murchison guessed.

"Owner here worked on a landscaping crew and did handyman jobs around the hill. Garage was filled with mowers and blowers. All junk now. Plenty of gas and oil, too, I figure. Some solvents, maybe. One side of the fire started there and all that stuff just blew. Other fire started in front and moved in from the opposite direction."

"The owner," Murchison said, "the landscaper, we know where he is?"

"Yeah," Holmes said. He stepped to the tub and pulled the drape away. "Owner, plus his wife and child, maybe five years old."

All three lay facedown in the tub, charred black from soot and smoke, their bodies twisted into inhuman shapes, muscle shriveled up on bone from the fierce heat. Here and there, reddish pink skin blistered through the grime. Nothing like faces remained, but their tongues protruded, revealing smutty teeth. Worse, the tub was gory with blood spatters, a lot of them. They'd clawed each other raw, fighting for the last gasp of air trickling up through the drain.

Holmes gingerly covered them up again. "Never seen anything like that."

"I have."

Murchison suffered another disquieting surge of déja vu, like he had with the MPs at the checkpoints, this time recalling that first killing, almost thirty years ago, the naked young woman cut to shreds in the shower stall by the drunken Spec. 4 from Fort Ord. It seemed a bad omen, that echo.

"People run to the bathroom because the surfaces are cool. There's water, and the tub, it seems protective. They think it's safe."

Holmes couldn't stop staring at the draped bodies. He chewed his lower lip hard.

"People stay strangely rational in a fire," Murchison told him, "unless they have to compete for an exit. Or air. That's when panic sets in."

The arson investigator called out from the front, "You guys ready to talk?"

Back in the living room, the guy introduced himself. "Name's Gladden. I'm with the CDF." Rio Mirada had no arson investigators with either the fire or police department, a sore spot during the recent spate of SUV and carport fires. Thus the need for the California Department of

Forestry to step in. "You've got a broken window in front, next to no glass shards outside, almost all in. And the point of origin is in a direct line from that window. So first guess? Somebody walked up, shattered the window with a hammer or ax, then tossed in not one but three Molotov cocktails." He pointed to the center of the room. "There's shards of bottle glass all over."

"How come that didn't melt, like the windows?" Murchison asked.

"It's on the floor. Coolest place in a fire like this. Even right next to the point of origin. Know what else is interesting?" He pointed in turn to three intact bottle necks, all clotted with singed rags. "This was clever. You want a Molotov to work, the bottle needs to shatter. Lot of guys forget that, throw the thing into a house, it hits the carpet? Oops. These guys planned for that. The rags, they weren't fuses, they were stoppers." He pointed to a curled-up sliver of fabric, a hint of silver under the char. "They put firecrackers of some kind, M-80s be my guess, slapped them to the sides of the bottles. Used duct tape."

"They've done this before," Murchison said.

"Or know someone who has. You're gonna want to preserve all that glass, check for prints."

"Fire didn't destroy them?" Holmes asked.

"That's a myth. Your evidence techs should know all about that, if they don't they can connect with ours. By the way, we're gonna need a protocol for who bags and tags—you guys or us?"

"Us," Murchison said, jealous for control by instinct, not even sure yet if this was his scene. "But it'd be great to have you walk us through, point out what you want saved."

"What about the garage?" Holmes pointed toward the back. "The fire there, I mean."

"Same deal. You looked?"

"A little."

"Back door, the window's broken, from outside again. My guess is it went second. Created a fireball when all the gas and other accelerants went. Whoever did this, he started in front. I figure the family was in the kitchen. There's a phone there, they were calling somebody, let them know they were heading out to someplace safe. Maybe they tried to fight the fire, then gave up. Can't get out the front through here, so they head toward the garage. By that time your perp, or an accomplice, had hit there, too. They're trapped. Father probably put the mother and kid in the bathroom, figuring that was the safest spot at that time. He left them, tried to find a way out. Smoke got to him, he crawled back. Looks like they tried to lie still, stay calm, but they ran out of time. Fire burns like this, sucks out all the oxygen. They were breathing smoke, carbon monoxide, hydrogen cyanide."

Murchison turned away. "Leave you guys alone for a minute?"

He walked out of the house and onto the scorched lawn. He thought of just getting into the car and driving, till nothing and no one looked familiar. But he knew it wouldn't help. The horror show came from inside as well as out. Stulka, dying. The remembered smell of his blood, tinged with the stench of smoke. Doubled now, by what he'd just seen. And strangely, Willy had been on his mind, too. As though scraps of memory from every pointless death he'd ever had to face were floating up from the brain's graveyard, each one whispering, *Feel this.* Or worse: *Do something.*

He heard footsteps behind. Holmes rested a hand on Murchison's shoulder. "You okay?"

Murchison shrugged off the hand. Too harshly. He didn't know why. "You look none too okay yourself."

Holmes flinched at his attitude but let it go unremarked. He nodded back at the burned-out house. "I knew these people. Not well, but we'd met on a call." He looked out across the neighborhood, the ruin, his eyes red from the smoke. "Father worked two jobs, the landscaping and handyman gig plus he drove a truck for a mover, too. Mother worked in the cafeteria at the high school. The little girl, she was a preemie, weighed three pounds at birth, been sick her whole life."

"Why them?" Murchison felt sick to his stomach. The smells were getting to him. The new ones, the remembered ones. "There a story?"

Holmes pointed up the block. "See that fence?" The chain link was twisted and coiled by the heat, blackened by smoke. "People lived there kept fighting dogs. Mean-ass pits, you would not believe. Let the monsters out sometimes, just to fool with people, scare them. Man here, he called the tip line twice."

Murchison's jaw dropped. "All this—over a dog call?"

"Guy inside, he took it into his own hands. Dumped strychnine mixed with birdseed over the fence one night."

"Ah, Jesus." He felt disgusted with the thing now. "That works? Birdseed?"

"Killed one of the dogs, two others got real sick. Couldn't prove who did it, but the fool who owned the pits said he'd get even."

"We know where to find this guy?"

"Now? Hell no. I know his name, though. Spoonie McNown. I'll find him."

A helicopter thundered low overhead, its monsoon bucket leaking pumpkin-sized spillage as it headed for an uphill hot spot. At the same time, Murchison's pager throbbed on his hip. Checking the display, he recognized the number for his in-laws. Joan was trying to get in touch.

"Need to get that?"

"I'll do it later," Murchison said, knowing he wouldn't. What would he say? What had he ever said? "So what exactly do you need from me here?"

Holmes looked chastened. "Word is—I mean, nothing's official yet, but word is, you and me, we'll be partnered up."

"This is my scene?"

Holmes didn't look chastened now. He looked pissed. "Our scene."

Murchison suffered a clash of emotions he doubted he'd make sense of for a long while, if ever. And even if he did, what then? He'd spent much of his life keeping a lid on his insides, why change that now? What was different, really? Just more dead.

He was spared further reflection on the matter as a cruiser pulled up, chirping its siren. The cop driving rolled down his window and poked his head out. "Yo, Murch." It was Hennessey. "Chief's got the conniptions, trying to track you down. You, too, Holmesy. You're wanted."

Murchison just stared, like he'd been called out. Holmes said, "Reason being? We're trying to process a crime scene here."

"The big sit with the *federales*, I think. Figure out who brags, who begs."

● ● ●

In the basement of Mission Baptist, the Red Cross served soup with sliced white bread for breakfast, and there was coffee to be had. Volunteers handed out portions with apologies and promises of better fare come noontime. The smells mingled with those of sleepy, unwashed bodies still tinged with smoke.

Toby collected soup and coffee for him and Nadya and Miss Carvela and returned with it on a tray, only to find a stranger sitting with them now. The man was dressed in a three-piece suit, sitting cross-legged on the floor.

"It doesn't seem fair," Miss Carvela was saying as Toby walked up.

"You have to see it from their side, Miss Grimes." The man spoke in a fluid, chesty baritone. "Now I've been your insurance agent what, five years? Seven years?"

"Since Walter Toomis retired, sold the agency."

"And I've done right by you. But what happened last night, those are arson fires, and arson can't but slow down a casualty claim. Here you got dozens, hell, hundreds of claims—between you and me, Miss Grimes, way too many of those gonna show up inflated—and that means the insurance company's sure to dig through every single one."

Toby cleared his throat to let them know he was standing there with food. Miss Carvela looked up. "This is Ralston Polhemus, Toby. My insurance agent."

The man popped up, shooting out his hand with a smile—broad shoulders, ramrod posture, thinning hair cut just so. Even his fingernails were pared to perfection and glossy. Toby gestured with the tray that the handshake would have to wait. At the same time he looked at Nadya, who in two movements of her eyes conveyed that Ralston Polhemus vastly overrated his welcome.

"I'll set this down," Toby said, dropping to his knees and handing out bowls of soup to Miss Carvela and Nadya.

"Absolutely. Food for the body, food for the soul, am I right?"

No one responded. Toby dipped a corner of bread in the soup. The broth tasted like weak powdered chicken stock laced with dish liquid. Celery and onion, boiled to transparency, bobbed with carrots amid dubious bubbles of fat.

Polhemus now directed himself toward Toby. The man. "I was just explaining to Miss Grimes that the claims process in the wake of those fires will go slow. She's going to need a place to live, and—"

"Her coverage doesn't provide for an interim rental?"

It caught Polhemus off guard. The charm faltered. "It's a bare-bones policy. She owns the property outright, no lender to indemnify, she's on a fixed income."

"You've got a copy at your office?"

"The carrier does. I'm sure—"

"Miss Carvela, don't make any decisions till my lawyer gets a chance to look your policy over, okay?"

The agent tried to rework his smile, but his lips only crept back halfway, the eyes not even that. He was finished with Toby.

"I'm going to tell you what will happen, Miss Grimes. The carrier's going to make a good faith offer of seventy percent of face value, give or take, right up front. I mean, I don't know, but that's my educated guess. So you can take your money now, move on, find yourself a new place—"

"New?" The old woman looked heartsick. "But I've lived—"

"Rebuilding alone will take years most likely. That hill is destroyed. And with all these claims, and arson in the picture, carriers will have a right to investigate for fraud. They'll foot drag—I'll tell it like it is—because they can't afford the losses. World Trade Center disaster hit the industry hard. And there'll be eminent domain hearings, an appraiser will be called in to determine fair market value—"

Toby cut in now. "Eminent domain?"

Polhemus shot a baldly spiteful glance toward Toby, all the while trying to keep a grip on that smile. "That hill was a disaster waiting to happen. That was one reason I chose to run for council. Every time the subject came up, all people wanted to do was bicker. Who's the blight consultant gonna be? The bond brokers? The lawyers who draw up the Disposition and Development Agreement? Bicker and bitch and get nothing done. Time to straighten out all the problems up there. It's what eminent domain is for."

"I understand what eminent domain is. My question—"

"City's got to act. It's a question of *morality*." He said the word like it had been flying around inside his brain for weeks, searching for a way out. "Sewer lines all fouled up, water mains crumbling, streets too narrow, only one way in or out, fire hydrants fifty years old. And those houses up there, half of them firetraps to begin with and burned down to the slab now. City's going to buy up the property for a fair price and put out the bid so somebody does it right."

"And the people who live there now?"

"Nobody lives there now." The contempt poisoned his voice now, too. Toby thought he heard as well an undertone of panic, like the man felt trapped. "That's the tragedy of it. Place will be condemned. Not safe for anybody."

"That can't be right." Toby looked at Miss Carvela. "I want you to talk to my lawyer—"

"Seventy percent of face value, cash in hand. Now, not later, Miss Grimes. Get yourself a little town house, a nice place, new. That old thing up top the hill, it needed work bad, and that'll come into account when they figure your payout. Too big for a woman your age anyway. And those walls, thin as cardboard. How much you spend in heating bills?"

"That's bad faith," Toby said.

He might as well have thrown the bowl of soup at the man. "You want to argue that, you got to go to court. That's foolish, just goddamn *foolish.*" His own intensity caught him off guard. He shifted back to Miss Carvela, softened. "That's three to five years before you see a penny, if you see that. Again, Miss Carvela, I gotta point out that the World Trade Center changed everything. You heard what happened with the Victims Compensation Fund. People had to agree to a fixed sum up front or see the whole thing grind to a standstill. And there's so much confusion surrounding this—I will tell it like it is—insurers got a million excuses built in. No jury will ever bring back a damage verdict worth the bother, you go to court. You figure the cost of the lawyers and experts, there's no benefit." He tented his fingers, a plea. "Sometimes, Miss Carvela, we have to put aside what we think is just and do what's wise."

"I would like to be left alone now," Miss Carvela said wearily. She fingered a slice of bread. Following Toby's example, she dipped it into her soup. Her nose curled. "I will call you."

"Absolutely. Fine. We'll see what the carrier does. Just think about what I said, all right?"

"I shall. Thank you."

Polhemus ambled off toward the next familiar face, extending his hands and offering condolence. Once he was out of earshot, Miss Carvela said, "Why do I feel as though I've just been bathed in muck?"

"Something not right about all that." Toby ventured some coffee, forgoing more soup. "I'm serious, Miss Carvela. Let my lawyer—"

"Your lawyer, yeah, that's a *damn* good idea."

Everyone turned at the sound.

"Francis!" Miss Carvela almost sang his name, her hand held out for his. He looked wired, uneasy on his feet and wild-eyed. He scanned the room, face obscured by the hood of his sweatshirt, as though he feared being seen. His clothes smelled damp. He'd slept outside somewhere.

"Just what I wanted to talk to you about. Your lawyer, yeah. Got a thing or two to talk through."

He finally took his great-aunt's hand. But his eyes stayed fixed on Toby.

"I saw a thing or two last night. And talk I'm hearing, about how those fires started? What I saw and that talk, two different things. Two goddamn *different* things." He rubbed his eyes, then shook his head hard, willing himself awake. "But I talk to your lawyer first. I get a deal. Then I tell what I saw."

22

———————

"There are three main groups connected nationwide to this kind of economic sabotage. Earth First, the Earth Liberation Front, and the Animal Liberation Front."

Peterson, the FBI agent in charge of the presentation, handed out a flowchart with supporting memoranda, plus a diagram of the scene at the gas station, the tank truck, the van, the three bodies. They've already been up there, Murchison thought, but I haven't. He felt brushed aside. It stung.

He'd worked with the Bureau dozens of times, mostly on gang jobs, the occasional car theft or bank robbery ring. The guys called in for this, though, were strangers. The materials they'd brought got passed hand to hand around the conference table. Just the kind of thing the feds loved: compelling visuals, a grim narrative, eye-popping numbers. Murchison recognized a few of the names—Greenpeace, Rainforest Action Network, People for the Ethical Treatment of Animals. Others were new to him—the Rukus Society, Carnival Against Capitalism, the Evan Meecham Eco-Terrorist Conspiracy.

Peterson himself was classic: a wool suit, off-the-rack but pressed, princely jaw, sportscaster hair, eyes of a pitiless banker. His partner, named Chadwick, had more the look of a lifetime cop—rumpled gabardine sport coat, coffee-stained tie, beginnings of a bald spot and paunch. But those same eyes.

"The suspect found dead at the scene, Manuel Turpin—he had ties to the ELF."

ELF, Murchison thought, smiling at the acronym. The handouts were littered with them: ALF, RAN, ATF, CDF, BLM, PETA. Cops, like the military—compress the idea of a thing into its initials, you somehow got smarter.

"By 'ties' I don't mean anything like gang affiliations or even the kind of cell organization we see in foreign terror outfits, except maybe the IRA. It might even be a misnomer to call the ELF a group at all. These people seldom meet each other. They share a program—basically, class warfare disguised as radical environmentalism—and a so-called set of principles which they routinely betray, then just disavow something when it goes wrong. They communicate through a variety of handles over the Internet using routers that disguise the message's origins."

Then how do you know anybody in particular has "ties," to the "group," Murchison wondered. He saw the wisdom in not saying it out loud.

"All told, since 1996 these outfits account for six hundred incidents around the country, forty-three million dollars in damage."

"Twelve million in that ski resort arson in Vail alone." It was Chadwick, chiming in.

"There were sixty-seven incidents last year, with an uptick in the numbers here in California."

"They're listed on the chart." Chadwick picked up his copy to read from it. "A BLM hay barn near Susanville. Lab equipment and records at Sierra Biomedical in La Jolla. Big one, seven hundred grand in damage, a cotton gin fire in Visalia."

"They encouraged targeting FBI headquarters after that one," Peterson said.

"And they've been active back east lately. Etching acid on SUVs."

"Understand you had some SUV targets here." Peterson directed the remark to the room.

"Fires." It was the chief. He said it a little too earnestly, as though afraid no one was listening. He still wore his blues and brass, looking tired in them. "We've had SUVs set on fire."

The man was desperate to get back into the Bureau's good graces. He'd been frozen out since demanding to be present when agents questioned local Filipino Muslims in the aftermath of the World Trade Center attacks. Elections often turned, in Rio Mirada, on the Filipino vote. The chief knew who he worked for.

"Carport fires, too. Detective?"

The punt sailed across the table and into Murchison's lap. He forced a shrug. "We were unable to identify a suspect in those. But there are hints from witnesses brought in on the Carlisle killing that this Manny kid, Turpin, he bragged about setting those fires."

"No suspects?" It was the chief again.

"Typical problem with arson," Murchison said. "Sir."

He'd realized early on in the meeting that the role of goat was his. He could see it not just in the chief's eyes but the eyes of every other man in the room. Stluka got himself killed, that's bad luck enough. But the partner of a killed cop, he was the king of jinxes.

"No hard suspects except, like I said, this Turpin kid. And we didn't have time to confirm."

"A little more about him," Peterson interjected. "He only has that one conviction we discussed earlier, out of Oregon, but he's suspected in as many as five incendiary events in the northern end of the state, including the BLM hay barn fire near Susanville."

"His target here for the tank truck," Chadwick said, reading from jottings in a spiral notepad, "from what we can tell, given the stuff found on him and in his knapsack, was the Frontline Financial branch down at . . . Riverview Plaza." He shot a glance around the table. "You guys know where that is, I assume."

"There's a lot of Internet chatter about lenders like Frontline." It was Peterson again. "Banks like that, the hard money lenders, they're a relatively new target. They get tagged as predatory lenders, then comes the vandalism, sabotage."

"He'd never have made it." Murchison decided what the hell, he didn't have any status to lose here. "He would have burned up his brake lines coming down that hill with a full load. Presuming he knew how to drive the rig."

"We understand," Chadwick said, "he took some big rig courses in Lassen County and hijacked a lumber truck up around Quincy. Admittedly, he didn't drive it far, he just wanted to set it on fire."

"We're not saying the plan was perfect," Peterson added, "or that he was smart enough to pull it off. We're saying what the materials found on him and in his belongings tell us. Plus, the houses that got targeted for the incendiary devices, they were all foreclosure properties, I'm right about that?"

"Frontline foreclosures, yes." The chief spotted a chance to nudge in another good word. "That's been confirmed."

"Except for two," Murchison said. "The Carlisle house and the Victorian next to it."

"Those seem personal, not part of the plot per se," Chadwick said. "Cover up any evidence of his having been in the Victorian—"

"We'd already bagged the evidence."

"—then set fire to where he saw that white girl coming and going each day."

"It matches his profile," Peterson said. "The 'power assurance' type. Dissociated anger. Sexual obsession. Ineffectual sense of his own masculinity."

After the Unabomber and Yosemite tourist killings and Virginia sniper fiascoes, Murchison would've thought they'd soft-pedal the profile concept. But cops never apologize—even if they get something wrong, it's always for the right reason. Beyond which, who in this room could say with a straight face his masculinity was *effectual?*

"The old woman at the house where my partner got shot, she said something about two men, not just one, starting the fires. Anybody but me seem to think that might be relevant?"

"Remind me, Detective." The chief shot a put-upon smile across the table. "That woman was, I believe, delusional?"

"There's been corroboration, that there were two men in the white van, from others who I've spoken to," Holmes said. "People who live up there."

"Rumors get a little nuts in a thing like this," Peterson offered.

"I didn't say rumor." Holmes sounded testy. "I said corroboration. Witnesses who saw a van—"

"Okay. Good." Peterson drummed his pen on the tabletop. "There were two guys. Maybe. I can live with that. Your point?"

"I made it," Holmes said, backing down.

"Well, I didn't make mine," Murchison said, "so here it is. I think all these"—he pitched his handouts into the center of the table—"are just an elaborate fairy tale till we find out who this second man was."

"If he exists." Chadwick now, defending himself, his partner.

"Well, that's what we do, right? We find out."

Peterson leaned forward. "Yes, absolutely. It's what we do. And what we've done." He nodded toward the handouts Murchison had discarded. "We're not ruling out a second man or a third man or an entire cell of individuals lending support. You've had a squatter influx here, ever since the dot-com boom drove up rents in San Francisco. They haven't moved back, even now that the dot-commers are gone and rents have settled back down. Those people are a breeding ground for what happened here last night."

"Look, granted, they can be a pain in the ass." Murchison remembered the five at the warehouse fire. "But we've never—"

"There hadn't been loss of life before—and, Detective, no need to remind you, I'm sure, one of those killed was your partner."

Murchison fought an impulse to jump across the table. "My partner," he said quietly, "wasn't killed by Manny Turpin."

"Might as well have been," Chadwick said, his eyes cold, like he'd be ready if Murchison lost it. "Or doesn't that matter?"

"There a point in all this?"

The chief squeezed in. "Gentlemen—"

"*My* point," Peterson said, "is that it was only a matter of time before somebody got killed. Country's drifting right, these groups have gotten more and more desperate for airtime."

"They're not a bunch of tree-hugging hippies." Chadwick was still staring. "They're criminals. They're well funded, smart, and sneaky as cats."

"My point," Murchison said, still struggling to contain his temper, "is that you're shaping facts to your theory, instead of the other way around. On the basis of—"

"Detective, if I may. It's important at this point we not confuse signal with noise."

Murchison couldn't help himself. That was worth a laugh. "That like 'forest from the trees,' just snotty?"

The chief went red. "Detective—"

"Okay." Murchison got up too fast. His vision blurred, his head spun. It wasn't just Chadwick staring at him now. "I get it. Sorry to be so contrary. Well, let's get to it, fellas." He clapped his hands like a softball coach. "What're we waiting for?"

He was halfway down the hall before Holmes caught up. "Burning some serious-ass bridges in there."

"Interesting choice of words, given circumstances."

"What is it with you?"

That stopped him. "Come on, Holmes. They waltz in from out of town, don't have more than six hours to get the lay of the land, haven't so much as listened to one word we've had to say, let alone ask. But they've already got it figured out?"

"Murch—"

"You grew up here, Holmes. Like me. We're not ignorant."

"Look, granted, nobody likes the Feeb."

"Chief's scared shitless they're gonna make him look bad. It's wrong. It stinks."

"Not like there isn't evidence, Murch, get real. This Manny kid—"

"No. No. Something's wrong, Holmes."

"With you, Murch."

Murchison froze. That was too much. "No, Holmes. Not with me."

"Granted, a lot's gone on—"

"Now I get your pity?" He squared off. "Stluka's dead, you don't miss him much, I can understand that. Gotta climb over bodies sometimes to get where you wanna go."

Holmes took a step back. "I'm gonna do us both a favor and pretend—"

"This kid who shot Jerry, Roderick Whatever, the crackhead pimping his grandma for scratch—he wouldn't be your source inside the Mooney crew by any chance, would he? Guy you've been so eager to protect?"

He could have hardly done worse taking a swing. "You are *way* the fuck outta line."

"Stop being so damn scared you're gonna screw up your big chance, Sherlock."

Holmes stood there, close. But from the eyes alone Murchison could tell inside he was miles and miles away now. "That the way it is?"

Murchison turned to go. "I've got work."

He headed off down the hall. Holmes contained himself for a bit, then called out from behind, his voice straining for control, "Need to go home, Murch. Been too much to handle last few hours. Go home, get straight. Come back fresh."

● ● ●

In the dispatch room, two female operators were handling 911 calls, supervised by a sergeant named Gump. On a slip of notepad paper Murchison scrawled out the number where Joan had taken the girls, her parents' place.

"Gump, hey. Do me a favor? Call my wife, here's the number. Tell her I'm alive."

Gump's hand dwarfed the notepad slip. "Why not you?" He frowned. "Alive? That's it?"

"Alive. Okay. In one piece. She wants to know more, make something up."

Back upstairs in the detective bureau, he spotted Sheila Stluka. She sat at her husband's desk, going through it with a uniformed officer, claiming the personal items.

She wore a slicker over a housedress, rain boots. Her hair hung limp; all the color had drained from her skin. Even her eyes and lips looked drab. Wrung out and left to hang, that was how Stluka once put it when he saw a woman who looked like that. He'd never said it of his wife, not in front of Murchison. They'd seldom discussed much private between them or socialized; their wives disliked each other, Sheila finding Joan stuck-up, Joan considering Sheila vulgar. Hardly surprising. He and Jerry, they'd been partners, not friends.

In the few things Stluka had said, Murchison got the sense Sheila had proved an equal match when it came to emotional firepower, and that alone had engendered what appeared from the outside to be a genuine respect, if not exactly romance. She'd been fronting a lounge act for conventioneers in Long Beach when they'd met. "Woman likes swagger, or thinks she does." Murchison remembered him saying that.

He came up, said to the uniform, "Could you leave us alone for a minute?"

"No." Sheila grabbed the officer's sleeve. "Don't."

The officer looked trapped. Sheila ignored him, her focus solely on Murchison now. All that anger, he thought, all that hate. It's mine now. Not the killer's. Mine.

"You know, Dennis, Jerry always told me he'd have to hope you'd be there for him if things went bad. Because he didn't know."

It was Murchison's turn to feel trapped. Worse, it seemed right. "Sheila—"

"You understand? He had to hope. Because he didn't know. Well, now we know. Don't we?"

Ferry refilled his tank just north of Ensenada and bought three cups of coffee at a *panadería*. He added heavy cream to each cup, in deference again to his stomach, then mindlessly drank two fast. He carried the third with him back to the car.

Route I veered inland at the southern rim of the peninsula, meaning Punta Banda would be his last chance till Colonio Guerrero to see the ocean. This time of year, dolphins and gray whales schooled through the kelp beds, seeking out lagoons for breeding. There'd be boats moored off the *malecón*, too—American yachts, new ones, beauties—anchored there or out in the Bahía de Todos Santos for six months to escape taxes. It was why some people called it Tax Cheat Harbor. Meanwhile, like a monument to pipe dreams, the listing hull of the SS *Catalina* lay at the harbor mouth, empty and forsaken.

With Carnaval coming, traffic through town moved slow, and then the rocky point was fogged in, a mass of gray haze so thick he could barely make out the road in front of him. Pulling to the roadside near a locked-up *churro* stand, he parked, waiting for the burn-off. As he sat, he tried to picture the drive south. Vineyards covered the hillsides for a while, not unlike Napa. In fact, the development here was starting to match that up north, making the California–Mexico distinction all but academic. People here knew what the future held.

La Escalera Náutica, they called it. The Mexican government intended to build or improve marinas around the entire Baja coastline, from the Coronado Islands to the mouth of the Colorado River. Tourism—the great brown hope—followed by luxury homes in enclaves built like fortresses. The rest of the coast south to San Quintín would be next to go, along with Cabo and the tourist towns on the Gulf of California. And if the Mexican government shit backwards on the idea, like they always did, American developers would fill the vacuum—like they always did.

Ferry figured he'd be hiring himself out to some of those developers next time around. Plan against kidnappers, play the bag man for the local *politicos* and *narcos*—sometimes they were the same guys— track down work site thieves, scare off union organizers. Too risky to reenter the States for a while. Maybe a good long while. He'd have to reinvent himself, come up with a brand-new past, the usual chore, but that had become shamelessly easy with the Internet. He'd spend a few months working on his Spanish in El Salvador. About time, he supposed. Marisela's English would have to suffer.

This is the place Bratcher and his cronies should be thinking about, he thought. Better margin on your money, less red tape, unless you thought of bribes that way. That's what I'll say if we ever come face-to-face again, Ferry thought, smiling. Plenty of opportunity down here, Clint. Just your style. Because you're gonna be on the run, son. That I promise.

23

Murchison left the station house with no clear idea of where he should head. He had to get out, though, and not just to escape Holmes, the chief, the FBI, or the wrath of Sheila Stluka. The looks from the other cops were taking their toll.

You have to think you're invincible, on the street especially. It's how the job gets done. Stluka's death, any cop's death, put the lie to all that. Murchison—drifting hollow-eyed down the halls, exhausted—served as a kind of stand-in for his partner's ghost. The other guys, they didn't mean to be cold, but they had to think of themselves, too. Their glances said, *I feel for you, I'm serious. Now get out of my sight.*

As tired as he was, he couldn't sleep. Home held no invitation; he'd come unglued sitting there alone. Double that, his parents' place, where he'd be twice as alone. There was a crime scene to process in Baymont—dozens actually, the whole hill was a crime scene—but he needed time to get his head right about Holmes. His new partner. How to forgive him for that. Forgive him not for his guilt but yours.

He started the car. So where?

Feeling the tug of unfinished business, he drove to the edge of downtown. The thrum of helicopters continued in the distance. The stench of smoke lingered. Otherwise, this part of town seemed strangely, unjustly safe. He crossed the yard beneath the oaks and chinaberry trees, climbed the porch, rang the bell, waited. Tina Navigato answered.

"Detective."

The surprise in her voice, it came out almost pleasant.

"I came to apologize. For the way—"

"Don't, please. Apologize, I mean." She stepped back. "Come in."

Murchison felt too stunned not to oblige. Once inside, he saw Toby Marchand, Nadya Lazarenko, and Miss Carvela Grimes all gathered together over food in the conference room to the right of the entry. Another African American male sat with them, about Toby's age, maybe a few years older. He looked at Murchison edgily, then averted his eyes.

Murchison smelled toast and oatmeal and cinnamon. Bowls of walnuts and raisins sat with a coffeepot and a milk pitcher atop the cherry wood table. The scent of potatoes on boil and a chicken roasting with onion and rosemary came wafting from the back of the house. The sight of them all eating together, the aromas, it unraveled a knot in his chest. A painful longing welled up in its place. Not hunger. The thing that hunger disguises.

"You got my message on your voice mail."

Murchison snapped to. "I beg your pardon?"

Tina gestured him down the hallway—my God, he thought, she wants to be alone with me—stopping at the first doorway. "I left a message for you, asking you to come over. I have some information I think you might find important."

Information. Well, yes. That. He could feel the warmth in his face, blushing. "I didn't check. I'm sorry, no."

The office was small, packed tight with a desk, file cabinets, and bookshelves. A thick text titled *California Decedent Estate Practice* sat on the desktop, a candy wrapper lodged among its pages as a bookmark. Leaving the desk for Tina, Murchison sat in the only remaining chair. She closed the door, and instantly he caught the soapy apple scent of her shampoo. She was barefoot, wearing a lumpy sweater and loose drawstring pants. Not quite the wardrobe for a Queen of Naps, but close enough. He averted his eyes when she turned back toward him.

"The young man you saw in the conference room with my client, he's—"

"Francis Templeton."

Tina blanched. It was attractive, he thought. He considered telling her that Joan, his wife, had left with their children. For reasons he barely understood, he doubted they would ever return.

He said, "I could take Mr. Templeton into custody." Actually, Murchison felt far too tired for that.

"I'm going to ask you not to. For a reason. I think a good reason."

"He knows something."

"He saw something."

"About Mr. Carlisle's murder."

"No. About the fires last night."

The way she looked at him, less than hopeful, almost untrusting, it made his heart sink.

"I'm listening."

"Is there a lawyer in the district attorney's office you have confidence in? I said that badly. I mean, my court cases up here have largely been in probate division, I don't—"

"Mr. Templeton wants immunity."

She made a resigned smile. "You're always a step ahead of me."

"Not really."

"You told Miss Grimes you would be willing to speak on his behalf if he came in early."

"He didn't."

"He's going one better, Detective. He's coming in with crucial information."

Murchison chuckled. "*Crucial.* You'd be amazed how often that word comes up."

"It's my understanding that at this point, the police believe that the fires were caused by a truck hijacking that went wrong."

Murchison brushed some lint from his knee. "Something like that."

"That's not what happened. There was no hijacking."

She said it with such conviction, and yet an undertone of apology crept in, too. As though she understood that what she was about to say would make Murchison's life impossible.

"Explain that. If you don't mind."

"There was a man who wasn't apprehended. He arrived in the same white van as the younger man who was killed and left there. This man, the one who fled, he was older, late thirties or early forties. White."

Her voice again, it threw him off. Her conviction had faltered, but the apology remained. She seemed to be worrying her way through her thoughts.

Murchison said, "We've heard there might've been a second man. But excuse me, I'm a little slow. Francis. The gas station? He was—"

"There's a house right behind it. The owner lived there. He was hiding Francis, knowing you were looking for him. They were friends."

Were, Murchison thought. He remembered the FBI's diagram of the scene. The owner was one of the three men found dead.

"Francis was staying in a spare room, on the second floor. When the tank truck arrived, an argument broke out, between the driver and Francis's friend. Francis stood at the window, watching, wondering if he'd need to come down. Help. A white van pulled up. Two men got out, both dressed in overalls. The one who got away, the older man, he drew a gun and, out of nowhere, shot the truck driver and the gas station owner. Then he lured the third man over, the one he'd come with, and shot him up close. In the face."

She was clearly horrified by what she'd just described. Horrified and disgusted. Murchison envied that.

"Rig job."

"I beg your pardon?"

"What you're describing—"

She shook her head, confused. "It's what happened."

"It's what Francis Templeton says he saw."

There, finally he'd pissed her off.

"He watched his friend get killed, Detective."

I watched my partner die, Murchison thought. "He never called nine-one-one."

"You know his position."

"That's no excuse. He could have saved his friend."

"He tried. He ran down, but his friend had already bled to death. There was gasoline everywhere."

"Should've started down sooner."

She winced, as though he'd mocked her. "Is being scared and confused a crime now?"

Certain circumstances, yeah, Murchison thought. Or it ought to be. He sat back in the chair, tried to test the story mentally. Before he could come up with anything, she continued, "I want to say something. Every single person in that conference room out there has been through hell."

"They're not alone."

"Of course not. But they're the ones who are my responsibility."

Whose responsibility am I, Murchison wondered. It seemed a perverse kind of luxury, having someone say that about you, an adult. Perverse and, again, enviable.

"Can I be frank?"

"Please."

"For that story to be worth a grant of immunity, somebody's got to be interested in it. And right now, there seems to be a general consensus that what needs to be known is already known. They want to nail it down fast, blame the obvious players. That's it."

"That's corrupt."

One gets used to it, he thought. "I don't like it much, either, but I seem to be in the minority."

She looked disconsolate, expecting more from him, he supposed. It would have been flattering, that expectation, had he not let her down. Lowering her glance, she picked up a paper clip and tortured it out of shape.

"Something else. This morning, while she was at the Red Cross shelter, Miss Grimes was approached by a man named Ralston Polhemus. Insurance agent, he placed her home owner's coverage. Do you know him?"

Murchison shrugged. "Gas bag, like everybody else who runs for council. Special election's next month."

"Yes, well, he said some odd things. He seemed extremely eager for Miss Grimes to accept a seventy percent cash payout on her policy amount for the fire damage. This before any contact with the insurer, let alone a claim submission. I mean, just pulled the number out of the air."

"Excuse me. Again, I'm not too clearheaded—"

"It's as though he was saying everybody up there's so desperate they should prepare themselves to take cash in hand and walk away."

"You think the insurance companies—"

"Maybe. They may have put him up to it. I mean, it's possible. But he brought up eminent domain, too, said the city would condemn the hill, buy up the properties, and put out the rebuilding for bid. I mean, basically, lowball the people who lived there, drive them off, then let the developers in. This the morning after everybody's lost their homes. It was odd. Beyond odd."

Murchison puzzled it over. "Not what you expect from a guy running for office."

"No."

"Dumb. Unless . . ."

The word hung in the air.

"Unless what?"

"Unless it's his job. Not on the insurance end, the political end."

She shook her head. "Now I'm not following."

"Whoever's behind him, they want him to soften the blow. Be the human face bringing one more shot of bad news. Before there's even a chance for people to get their hopes up."

She picked up the paper clip again, but it was beyond further damage. "And a man running for office, he'd do this why?"

Murchison pressed his palms together, tapping his fingers against his chin as he thought. "I don't know. Maybe the fix is already in."

Before he left, Murchison went into the conference room. They'd finished eating, but the aromas lingered. The Filipina—Tina's roommate, sidekick, squeeze, whatever—cleared plates and everyone else looked as contented as they could hope to, given recent events. He nodded hello to Toby, Nadya, Miss Carvela, then said to Francis, "What Ms. Navigato just told me, I need to hear it from you."

Miss Carvela began to protest, but Francis laid his hand on her shoulder, said, "It's fine now, don't worry," and followed Murchison back into the same small office.

He had Francis tell him the story backward, a common trick. Even reversed, the account came out reasonably identical to the one Tina had provided, and when Murchison probed details he considered a little loose on deck Francis looked straight at him and offered what he could, admitted it when he couldn't. He liked to play it tough at times, stare you down, but he didn't seem a bad sort. Had a chip on his shoulder, but that could mean any one of a dozen things, few of them equating with criminal. Prisons were filling with guys just like him. Murchison had put some there himself. As for Francis's story, it held together, more or less, which was one step toward the truth. It made Murchison restless. This sort of truth, it never ended the way it should.

When he was finished, Tina walked him out to the porch. She made small talk he could barely hear for the buzzing an incipient migraine was causing. He caught her last words, though: "So what do you think you'll do?"

He attempted a smile, jerking down the steps so awkwardly he nearly fell. "It's never too soon to get desperate," he said, wondering where on earth the thought had come from.

Tina drew Francis away to confer with him alone. Joyanne led Miss Carvela up to a bedroom where she could rest. Suddenly Nadya and Toby were by themselves for the first time since collecting their things at his father's house.

Toby, feeling awkward, unsure why, pulled a walnut from the bowl, placed it between the heels of his hands, and pressed until the shell cracked open. The effort made him smile, like he'd performed a trick. He felt so tired.

"There's something I've wanted to tell you all morning," Nadya said.

Her dark eyes seemed unusually large, as though her face was opening to him. It created a kind of vertigo, like he might fall in. He lowered his glance, looked at his hands, plucked bits of shell from the meat of the walnut.

"I could tell."

"I had a dream last night." She reached for his hand, brushed the crumbling walnut from it, pressing her own hand in his palm, so he would have to look at her. "I was scared to fall asleep, afraid I'd have nightmares. And I did, but I had this dream, too. So vivid, you know? And because of that, it felt more like, I don't know. This will sound so stupid."

"I can handle stupid."

"It felt like a communication."

Toby read her expression. "My father."

She began kneading his fingers. "The silly part, it took place in a shop, where they sell coffee and tea. All that glass and wood and the smells. Your father was working there, behind the counter, he had an apron on, and—"

Toby chuckled. "Tea?"

"Yes, I know, that part's so obvious. Like I said, it's silly. But the other part—there was light streaming through the window. He was bathed in it."

Toby felt a sudden resentment but managed a smile. "You'll see the stars a-fallin'. You'll see forked lightnin'."

She cocked her head, puzzled. "That's—?"

"A spiritual. 'In That Great Getting Up Morning.' It refers to Judgment Day."

She seemed bothered by his flip tone. "He seemed so happy, Toby. Please, hear me out. At the house, before we went to the club, we sat at the piano, he listened to me torture 'Well You Needn't,' then told me to play what I know. And he said he knew why I was always saying I was sorry. I feel guilty for being alive. After my grandmother, then Jeremy. Now your father—"

"You talked about all of that? With my *father*?"

"Let me tell you the rest of the dream, Toby. He came out from behind the counter, took my hands, so glad to see me. It was just all so—"

"Perfect." He was unable to suppress the sarcasm.

"It was real, Toby. It didn't feel like a dream."

Her voice cracked. With his thumb he wiped her cheek, expecting a tear, but her skin was dry. She was frightened.

"Maybe he forgives you."

Trembling, she pressed her face against his ribs. Stroking her hair, kissing it, he said, "I'm glad."

"Thank you," she whispered.

"Can I tell you a secret?"

"Please."

"I'm jealous."

She gripped his hand. "Come upstairs. There's a place we can lie down."

"Nadya—"

She got up, tugged at his arm. "Please. It's too hard, too lonely. Lie down with me. Hold me. Tell me you won't go away, even if it's not true. Please."

Her eyes shamed him. He pulled her back to avoid them. "Stop. Stop." He held her tight, stroking her back, then made her sit. She looked stricken, hands in her lap, ready for a scolding. Or a betrayal.

He reached for her hand, laced his fingers in hers. "Remember your dream. You're forgiven. Right?"

They both heard it, the thing not said.

Murchison arrived in the courtroom in the middle of cattle call. Shackled defendants in orange jumpsuits, groggy, yawning—eager to save themselves as long as it didn't get in the way of their boredom—filed one by one from a side door to confer briefly with their attorneys, public defenders mostly. Calling them forward, the judge heard their pleas, set bail, assigned a department to hear the case, and set the date for the preliminary hearing. After that, the lawyer sat down and the defendant vanished once again behind the telltale door.

Once cattle call had run its course, the judge ordered everyone out. He wanted to prepare the courtroom for his own morning calendar. As the lawyers filed toward the doors, Murchison rose from his seat in the back and snagged the sleeve of the assistant district attorney he'd been waiting for.

"Billy, got a minute? Something's come up on the Baymont fires."

Bill Reeves was a former cop out of San Francisco, night school law degree type. He was smarter than most of that breed, talked to you like a human being while deciding whether to go forward with a case or not, always bought a round for the rank and file. Murchison had worked at least a dozen major crimes with him.

In the hallway, Murchison ran down what Francis Templeton and Tina Navigato had told him about the fires and about Ralston Polhemus. It came out ragged, he had to backtrack once or twice to claim a neglected detail. Reeves cut him short.

"Murch, Murch. Let me stop you, okay? First, what you're telling me here? I gotta be honest, it's a little, I don't know, untidy."

Murchison nodded. "Been a long night."

"I don't doubt that."

"Jerry's dead."

Reeves sagged. "Ah, Jesus. I didn't hear—"

"I was there."

Reeves stared at him like he was nuts. "What are you doing on-duty? Murch, go home. You look like hell."

"If I had a nickel for every time—"

"I'm serious. Go home."

"Billy, I'm okay. Fine. This guy, his story. He wants immunity on his parole beef."

"No doubt. But if he's the only guy who can tell this story, he's out of luck. He needs a corroborating witness. A credible one. He's a convicted felon."

"What about the bit with Polhemus?"

"He's a wank, what can I tell you? He's on a Bratcher slate, which means he's tied in with Wally Glenn and Bob Craugh and just about every other redevelopment whore around here. They've been wanting to sink their teeth into that hill for ages. So? Now they've got their chance, they're a little greedy about it. The commission on the bond float alone on a redevelopment deal that big'll have brokers and lawyers on their knees for a piece. Polhemus, what he did, it's tasteless, he's got bad timing. Not a crime." He reached out for Murchison's shoulder, squeezed. "You need some sleep."

Murchison averted his eyes. "Easier said than done."

"Try." Reeves, a big man, broad and hard, spoke with a strangely gentle concern. "One more thing? Way I'm hearing it, nobody in our office is gonna move on those fires till every agency involved gets its ducks in a row. The last thing, absolute last thing, we want is a bunch of cases heading into jury rooms with different fact patterns. That'd be a disaster. For everybody. So nobody's going to grant your guy immunity unless every other prosecutor involved signs off on it. That means federal *and* state. Okay?" He patted Murchison's shoulder. "Now go home."

24

---

erry crossed the Rio San Miguel before noon and entered the Valle de San Quintín. Extinct volcanoes encircled the flatlands under a bright coastal sun, with the Sierra San Miguel to the east, Isla San Martin offshore. Hundreds of tottering shacks lined the road—fashioned of scrap wood and tin, with lashings of chicken wire. Indians from Oaxaca and Chiapas flocked here to work the vegetable farms that thrived among the irrigation canals fanning across the plain.

Soon he passed between the lines of stucco and clapboard stores along Mexico 1 that comprised San Quintín itself. One of the town's curiosities was its Internet café—not as colorful as the *cholo's* storefront he'd visited in Tijuana, just strange for its location here, on the final edge of civilization before the Baja wilderness.

He pulled in and parked, ignoring the two khaki-clad infantrymen from the Sixty-seventh Battalion loitering with *minutas* at an ice wagon. Ferry felt no threat, despite the carbines slung from their shoulders. American law enforcement didn't trust the Mexican military enough to ally them in a manhunt, not on such short notice. He withdrew his laptop from the trunk of the dust-caked Caprice and headed up the café's wood plank stairs.

Inside, an overhead fan spun lazily over a scuffed wood floor. The proprietor, a light-skinned Mexicana of matronly girth, breathed deep from a cactus blossom, eyeing Ferry as he took a seat, plugged in his laptop, and logged on.

Even an arrogant pirate like Bratcher deserves a second

chance, he thought, checking his trust account. As expected, though, it still showed no activity. All right then, Ferry thought. Have it your way. He E-mailed the Pennington executive with whom he did business, provided his confirmation code, and ordered all funds be transferred into a new account in conformance with the trust documents on file with the bank. In keeping with past practice, he then sent a second message, repeating the request, using a second confidential code.

Last, he checked news reports of the fire. Unlike the radio accounts, here the names of some of those killed and injured were provided. A fleeting discomfort trickled up from somewhere, then he reminded himself it wasn't his fault. I don't dream these things up, he thought. I just do what I'm paid to do. There's hardly fault in doing it well.

How many years had the city put off repairs of the sewers and storm drains, upgrades to the hydrants? How many years had they scotched the street work that would have made simple an effective evacuation and firefight? And there were reports of collateral "opportunity" fires, people torching their own places once they saw the hill go up. You can hardly blame me for that, he thought. Part of the rage people would be lathering themselves in would be solely to disguise their own guilt. The virtuous always scream loudest. They're the most dishonest.

Glancing down the list of the dead, he came upon the name of Detective Gerald Stluka. It stopped him. He wondered if he read right. Checking again, he saw it was true, and logged off. He was still musing on how unforseen that was, how useful it might prove, as he settled up with the ample Mexicana, trying not to stare at her cleavage.

He drove south toward Lázaro Cárdenas, then turned west on a gravel road just beyond the Benito Juárez military camp. About seven miles in, just past Monte de Kenton, he followed a still smaller road, this one of rutted dirt, forking left toward the fishing village of Pedregal. Soon he was parked at the tidal flats at the north end of the Bahía Falsa, not far from the airstrip that brought the fishermen here from up north.

He reached into his duffel, pulled out a satellite phone, figuring he was too far from any transmission towers to make a cell phone usable. He dialed the Rio Mirada police department, and once the operator connected he asked for the voice mail of Detective Dennis Murchison. Soon he was listening to Murchison's outgoing message, then came the beep.

Ferry found himself curiously unable to speak for a second. Collecting himself, he began: "This message will serve as my full confession."

By midday, the war of words had commenced.

The chief, squaring himself before a battery of microphones and television cameras—flanked by Peterson on one side, Gladden, the CDF's arson man, on the other, an ATF agent standing in the wings— read from a brief prepared statement.

" 'The investigation to this point indicates that all but a handful of the fires last night in Rio Mirada were the direct result of a sabotage plot against a local subprime lender named Frontline Financial. The fires were caused by a number of sophisticated incendiary devices planted in empty foreclosure properties and gasoline released from a tanker trunk that the perpetrators had hoped to hijack, then explode outside a local Frontline branch office. The principal saboteur, Manuel Turpin, was found dead at the scene of the failed hijacking. He was a convicted felony arsonist with suspected involvement in a number of incendiary fires in Northern California. He also had known ties to radical environmental groups, and the investigation is continuing, particularly concerning the possible involvement of one or more accomplices with similar ties.' "

In the question and answer period that followed, one of the reporters asked if the incendiary devices used were similar to others employed by radical greens. Gladden, showing a little initiative, stepped up to the microphone before either the chief or Peterson could stop him.

"No," he admitted. "And they don't match the kind of devices described in the bomb-making manual the ELF posted on its Web site, either. We've seen these before mainly in arson fires believed to have been related to organized crime."

Peterson stepped forward. "You shouldn't read too much into that." He reclaimed the microphone, nudging Gladden aside. "The use of increasingly sophisticated methods is no more surprising than the increased level of violence and harm. Terrorism escalates. It's what it's meant to do."

The denials came almost instantly. An organic grocer in Boulder, Colorado, who disavowed membership in the ELF or any of the targeted organizations but who admitted serving as an ad hoc spokesman, rendered a statement on their behalf, which he claimed he'd received anonymously over the Internet.

" 'The Baymont fires,' " he read, " 'did not and could not have been the result of any effort by environmental direct action advocates or their allies. The parties responsible for the fires made no attempt to educate the public concerning the damage being caused by the targeted bank, and no effort was made to protect human life. These are two core requirements of all direct action.

" 'Furthermore, as was seen in the attempt to frame Earth First activists Judi Bari and Darryl Cherney in 1990, and as revealed in the resulting civil trial this past year—a trial which resulted in a multimillion-dollar judgment against the FBI and Oakland police— these law enforcement agencies, along with private security forces working on behalf of corporations and others, are willing to fabricate evidence, lie under oath in support of illegal search warrant affidavits, and even stage violent acts themselves in their attempt to discredit the entire environmental movement. Such tactics are increasing—in one year alone, over one hundred intentional acts of violence or harassment were perpetrated not by, but against, environmentalists.' "

At his desk, the recriminations and disavowals Murchison suffered were more personal in nature. Trying to make headway through paperwork, he kept seeing Stluka, eyes howling with pain, shoving his bloody side arm into Murchison's hand. Worse than the image was the wretched sick feeling, the pit of his stomach dropping out and his throat clamping shut in a gag reflex. Like he was still kneeling there. Like time meant nothing. Right now was back then, forever.

His mother tried to contact him, but he refused to have the call patched through. He did not much see the point of speaking with her. When Willy had died, he'd attempted, just once, to feel her out, see if solace might be offered. She'd stared at him with a cold bewilderment. "It's not all about you," she'd said.

He was unable to duck Joan's call. She phoned from her parents' home in Granite Bay and told Gump it was an emergency. Gump sent up one of the operators to stand at Murchison's desk till he agreed to pick up.

"It would have been nice, Dennis, if you'd called yourself, instead of having someone else do it for you."

He heard his mother's voice, buried inside his wife's. The one brittle in its despair, the other stiffly confident, two sides of the same obstinacy, he supposed. But both disappointed *in him*. No real surprise to that—wasn't it the eternal curse? We marry our most pathetic secrets.

"I'm not much up for blame right now, if you don't mind."

"Blame?" She sounded genuinely hurt. Misunderstood. She did that. Then her voice softened, as though finding the direction she'd meant to take all along. "I heard about Jerry. I'm sorry."

With unforeseen intensity, he hated her. "Are you, now."

She caught it, the shift in his voice. "Dennis—"

Now he hated himself. A lot of that today. "I'm sorry. That was—"

"It's all right, Dennis. Really."

Murchison felt ashamed and yet unable to apologize. Something unsaid too long lurked just out of reach. He feared what that might be. He'd barely begun puzzling it through when Joan said, "Why don't you drive up, Dennis? There's no need for you to stay down there. Take a leave, you're owed that. My God. The girls have seen the news. They're scared. You've needed a break for ages. If you can't take one now, I don't know . . ."

Her voice was oddly, mechanically resilient, even cheerful. Murchison let the receiver slip in his hand, away from his ear. He could still hear her voice, though her words became unintelligible, just a rhythmic hiss of sounds that echoed strangely with another conversation, one from a year before. Joan again, but she hadn't been speaking to Murchison.

She'd been at the bedside of a childhood friend, a woman named Chessy, dying of cervical cancer. The woman, only forty-five years old, lay in her sour bed, gaunt from chemotherapy-induced nausea, her head shaved. They'd gone to the hospital to visit. Joan brought flowers, held the woman's hand, looked into her ravaged face, and spoke in tones much like she was using now, on the phone. Her sister, Ellen, was there at the time and in the middle of Joan's monologue got up abruptly and left. Chessy seemed hurt, Joan looked puzzled. Murchison excused himself, following Ellen into the hallway to see if anything was wrong.

He found her in the waiting room, by herself, arms folded so tightly around herself it looked like she was afraid she might literally come apart. She was two years younger than Joan, middle child, the family misfit—a childless divorcée with dirty blonde hair cut close, quick temper, wild laugh, six years sober. She was dressed in jeans and a sweater, no makeup. Murchison sat down next to her.

"Everything all right?"

She looked at him like he was insane. "How do you live with her?"

Murchison flinched, feeling accused by the remark and yet spared, too. "I don't know what—"

"You don't see it, do you?" She shook her head, wiped at her eyes, which were raw and red. "The way she acts, the way she talks. Like she's performing for the class." She reached into her pocket, dug out a handkerchief, and blew her nose. "Chessy was our closest friend in the neighborhood growing up. She spent more time at our house than her own. It's not some stranger in there."

"Ellen, I think Joan knows—"

"No. No, you don't get it. Listen, Dennis—it's not just the way she talks, the way she acts. Chessy's been here three weeks. A bunch of us, we've traded off, taking turns to stay with her at night, spell her husband so he can take care of the kids. It's hard, okay? For all of us. Chessy can't sleep. Doesn't matter how much morphine they give her, she's in pain. So we walk. We get up and walk the halls. All night, sometimes. And she's not all there anymore. The medication, it's got her loopy, she hallucinates, she's paranoid. She vomits and pisses the bed and hears stuff that isn't there. It's just—it's the hardest thing imaginable, okay? Joan hasn't offered to spend the night once. Not once. Today, this visit? It's only the second. In three weeks, our best friend growing up, like family. Two visits in three weeks. She's going to die, Dennis."

"It's my fault," Murchison said, not hesitating to take the blame. "My hours, they're unpredictable. Joan can't be sure I won't get called in the middle of the night—"

Ellen shook her head. "Dennis, stop it. I offered to stay with the kids if that became a problem. That's not it." She sniffled, shoving the handkerchief back into her pocket. "Joan's just incapable of dealing with anything that can't be solved by pretending it isn't important. You know that, right? A positive attitude and busy-busy-busy solves everything." She laughed caustically, thought for a moment. "She ever talk to you about your job? I'm serious. She ever ask you to tell her the really awful stuff, the stuff you can't tell anybody else?"

Murchison couldn't respond. Not because he didn't know the answer.

"It's not that she's scared. Christ, we're all scared. It's that she's such a phony about it. I mean, I wonder sometimes, I really do, if Joan came across a drowning man, whether she'd even think of diving in the water. Or if she'd just go and buy the guy a tasteful card."

Sitting at his desk, Murchison felt it hard not to think of the memory as a premonition. He bobbed the receiver in his hand, tilting his head a little closer to listen.

". . . time away plus rest, Dennis. It's what you need. It's what you've needed for a very long time. Everyone knows that. I spoke to my mother about—"

He pictured a future filled with that voice, sincere in its own false way, and couldn't bear the thought of pretending it would be okay anymore. He lifted the receiver. "I have to go." His heart pounded, he felt sick to his stomach. "I'm being called into a meeting. Something's come up. I'll call back later."

"Dennis—"

He pressed the plunger, cutting off the connection. A second later, lifting his hand, he listened to the hum of the dial tone, feeling unpleasantly numb. He sat there like that for what seemed a very long while. Finally, he noticed the receiver clenched in his hand like a weapon. He set it down in its cradle. The hum of the dial tone went away, but not the numbness. It occurred to him, then, what it was Stluka had tried to say as he died.

Not "Macon Bay."

"Make them pay."

He tried to bury himself in the Carlisle murder book. It seemed a drudge task now, writing up reports on his dead-end interrogations of Toby Marchand, Arlie Thigpen. A lifetime ago, he thought, kneeling in that man's front yard, walking through his house. Jerry's lifetime.

I should be up on the hill, he thought, not here. With Holmes. Except he doesn't want you.

The station house was thronged now, everyone on duty, everyone buzzing about, ignoring him. He reached for the phone, dialed his voice mail, hoping for a callback from Joan—wanting to hear her relentless cheerfulness again, convince himself he was wrong about it. Instead he heard an unfamiliar male voice. The voice said the following message would serve as a full confession to the Baymont fires.

Murchison pressed the receiver close, listened to the entire recitation, ran it back, played it again, cupping a hand to his other ear to shut out the background noise. He rummaged a microcassette recorder from his desk drawer, stuck the suction cup microphone to the earpiece of the phone, and played the message back a third time, recording it now, wanting to make sure he had at least one copy in his own hands. He played the tape back to make sure it was audible and complete. He then recited his own name, the date and time and place, at the end, and rewound the tape. After writing down this same information on the cassette label, he placed the tape in an envelope and sealed it shut, then stuffed it into his pant pocket.

He ran down to dispatch. Gump, seeing him, seemed about to complain about being dragged in as a marital go-between, but Murchison cut him off.

"I've got a voice mail message. It's evidence. Log it in, Gumper, do it right."

• • •

"No way we can authorize a warrant." The chief sat at the conference table with Murchison, Peterson, and Chadwick. Gladden, the CDF man, was out in the field, as were the ATF agents and the other Rio Mirada detectives. "We need a reliable informant, with a proven track record of solid leads. This—I mean, good God—for all intents and purposes, this is an a anonymous tip."

They'd all just listened to the recording twice. The chief looked sick. He'd completed his press conference less than an hour before, going on record across the country as to who was responsible for the fires and why. Now this.

"It's bogus," Peterson said. The press in his suit had begun to sag. His eyes hollowed out his face. "And no surprise, given how these people operate."

"Yeah. Kinda convenient." It was Chadwick, looking not much better than his partner. "All he has to do is bare his sad little soul, from God knows where. Such a deal."

"And developers." Peterson again. "Gee, who'd want to pin this on a bunch of developers?"

"The eco-trash?"

"You think?"

"He's reliable," Murchison countered, "because his information tracks the fires down to the smallest details. Things not made public." Like the incendiary ingredients used, he thought, the exact location of each placed bomb, the time progression of how they went off, entry and exit points, precise descriptions—of the truck, the tanker valve releases, the driver, the gas station owner, the guns used and the placement of wounds, down to which side of Manny Turpin's face had been blown away. "And the court in *Camarella*—"

Peterson cut him off. "*Camarella* granted a *Leon* exception on the basis of good faith reliance on a warrant that lacked probable cause. You can't fudge up a warrant based on tips you know going in are loose on deck and expect a *Leon* ruling."

"Okay, then what about *Gates*? *Gates* gives us a totality of circumstances criteria with an anonymous tip, and this information tracks exactly with the facts surrounding the fire. That should give the court its comfort zone. And this isn't an anonymous tip, the guy gave his name."

"*A* name," Peterson corrected. "Not necessarily *his* name."

"Which reminds me." Chadwick rose from the table and left the room. Murchison watched him go with a sense the whole thing was pointless.

Peterson added, "And in *Gates*, what made the information credible was the tipster didn't just provide facts about past acts. He predicted events that hadn't yet occurred."

Murchison's head pounded, his migraine was worse. Every few minutes it got hard to breathe.

The chief went back at him. "Look, everybody agreed all along there could be a second guy involved. And yeah, that guy's going to know everything about the fires. He should. He helped set them. But you want to drag in third parties who've got—I mean, Clint Bratcher, for fuck's sake. Ralston Polhemus, Wally Glenn, Bob Craugh. Christ, we're talking—I mean, why not the goddamn mayor?"

"What if I said I had a corroborating witness?"

"To Bratcher's involvement?"

"To how the thing at the gas station went down."

"Reliable?" Peterson was shaking his head. "That's the whole issue here."

"He wants immunity."

"Well, knock me down."

"He's an abscond. A parole beef. That's all, but he—"

"Wants it to go away. Shopping stories. Detective, really, tell me you're not this stupid."

Murchison checked his anger. Slowly, he said, "I spoke with him earlier, before I got this recording. Understand? *Before.* He says it wasn't a botched hijack. It was meant to go down that way. Baymont was the target all along."

"Not given everything else—"

"I've got another witness, too. He'll confirm Ralston Polhemus, the candidate this Ferry guy mentions on the tape, is already pushing eminent domain and negotiating lowball payouts to home owners on the hill, trying to pave way for redevelopment."

"None of that is going to justify a search warrant of Bratcher's accounts."

"I won't authorize it," the chief said flatly. "I'll put a call in to the presiding judge, every other judge and commissioner in the county while I'm at it. Probable cause, Detective. Good Lord."

Murchison turned to Peterson. "What about phone records? Find out who Bratcher's been talking to and who's been talking to him. You guys don't need a warrant for that, not anymore. If you really think this is domestic terror, use the Patriot Act—"

"Let's slow down for a minute, shall we?" Peterson leaned forward, forcing a smile. "This tape. There's no small problem, Detective, with the scenario this character lays out. I mean, just for argument. Let's say this Ferry character planned to do the job with the Turpin kid the way it looks at first blush."

"The bank as target," the chief said.

"But the thing goes haywire. Truck driver has a gun."

"My witness saw the whole thing. It didn't happen that way."

"Eyewitnesses get things wrong, you ever find that to be true? Especially ones trying to buy their way out of trouble. Look, just bear—"

"It couldn't have happened—"

"Shut the fuck up, Detective, and listen to me." It came out eerily quiet. Peterson wasn't smiling now. "This Ferry character, he can't drive the truck, he's up there alone with Manny Turpin dead, and Manny was the one supposed to move the rig downhill."

"I said it before: they'd never have made it."

"Not the goddamn point, Detective. Once the Turpin kid dies, the plan is meaningless. Regardless how harebrained it was to begin with, it's over now. This Ferry character, he's going to run, no matter what. So the only question is: Why wouldn't he just do that, disappear, instead of empty the tanker?"

"Exactly."

Peterson leaned forward, as though tutoring a child. "Because we're not talking about people who are idealistic. I don't care what load of crap they use to defend what they do. They just . . . like . . . setting . . . fires."

Chadwick reentered the room. "Okay," he said, sitting back down, "a little show-and-tell." He had several pages of fax paper curling up in his hand. He spread them out on the tabletop, smoothing them flat with his palm. "Bratcher's name has come up in a few investigations out of the Sacramento office. I called up there, asked if they had any-thing we might find interesting."

He turned the top page around so the others could see it. There was a photograph from an Illinois driver's license, paired with one from a Chicago PD personnel file. The latter seemed more recent. The man had black hair and a drooping mustache, raw features, and an un-pleasant intensity in his eyes, not so much menacing as cold, unavail-ing, empty. Stubble darkened his cheeks and neck and chin. He wore a black leather jacket over a crew neck sweater, his hair longish, brushing the tops of his ears.

"You can see under 'Suspect's Name' this guy is named William Malvasio. There's a couple AKAs, none of them Richard Ferry, the one he used in the phone call, but that could be because it's new."

"If it's him," Murchison said. He had to admit, this face, the voice, they went together. "How do we—"

"It's him. Stick with me here," Chadwick said. "He worked under-cover narcotics on Chicago's South Side for several years, part of a tac squad that got brought down hard by IA. Nothing too original—jack-ing some dealers, running protection for others, that story. Malvasio here shot dead another cop he suspected of laying numbers on him and his pals."

"A cop killer," the chief said, fingering the page for a better look.

"Cop-killing cop." Peterson made a point to look straight at Murchison as he said it.

Chadwick continued, "He'd worked with some Salvadoran police units in an exchange of sorts before disappearing from Chicago, but there've never been any solid leads down there. Either he's hidden somewhere else or he's got connected friends in country, watching his back."

"What's his connection to Bratcher?" The chief was still reading.

"Turns out Mr. Bratcher is a cooperating individual with the Sacra-mento office. He's proved to be a reliable asset in several investi-gations concerning HUD fraud, abuse of the Officer Next Door Program."

Murchison couldn't believe it. "He rats out cops?"

"You'd rather he killed them?" Peterson's impatience was mount-ing. "Would that make him more reliable in your book?"

Chadwick gestured for everybody to calm down. "Agent handling this guy Bratcher assured me he's a tough nut, but he'd never have anything to do with a job like this guy Malvasio, or Ferry, or whatever the hell he calls himself—"

"But the connection," Murchison said, knowing it would mean little. Bratcher had juice. You'd have to have hard evidence, not just probable cause, to get anyone to move on him now. "What's Bratcher's connection to this Ferry guy, Malvasio?"

"He advertises himself as a security consultant. Had a Web site—Bureau tried to sting him twice with that, set up phony clients, but he's been too smart to fall for it. Web site's closed down now."

"But Bratcher fell for it," the chief guessed.

"Once. Yeah. Bratcher owns property in Sacramento. He had a drug problem with tenants, a bad one. He'd tried everything else, figured he'd give this solo hotshot a chance. Malvasio ended up killing two kids, gangbangers living in one of Bratcher's buildings, then tried to extort Bratcher, claiming he ordered the hits."

"He didn't?" Murchison glanced around the table, wondering if anyone else had doubts. "Order the hits, I mean."

"He says no. And like I said—"

"He's a valuable asset." Peterson again, tag-teaming.

"He's provided critical information in several successful investigations, one of which is ongoing."

"Which means you risk being in contempt of the grand jury you try to push this joke of a confession too far."

Chadwick shuffled his fax pages together. "Yeah. I'd have to weigh in here and say we need a lot more than the word of this sociopath before we moved on a guy who's proved to be reliable and has cooperated with us. Arrests and convictions, all good." His glance circled the table. "Anybody else?"

"He didn't even level with us about who he is." The chief's voice was stronger now. He'd made up his mind. "His being a bent cop, the IA business, the killing, nothing."

Murchison wasn't letting go. "How did a guy like this end up with a bottom-feeder like Manny Turpin? This Ferry guy, Malvasio, whatever, he does what he does for money. You telling me he'd work for a high five and 'attaboy' from a bunch of green freaks?"

"There are people connected with the movement," Peterson said, again like he was schooling an idiot, "who are supportive of the more extremist elements but who prefer to retain an image of moderation. They channel money—"

Murchison was stunned. Talk about hypotheticals. "You saying the Sierra Club hired this guy?"

Chadwick said, "There are a lot of weasels in Hollywood, actually—"

Murchison howled, "Oh, come on. What, Susan Sarandon was behind this?"

Peterson, leaning forward again, responded, "You're not privy to the kinds of intelligence we are, Detective. It stops being funny real quick."

Chadwick chased him down in the hallway this time, like Holmes had before. "Look," he said, stepping in front. "Sorry if that got rougher than it should have. We're all on the same side in this."

"Oh yeah." Murchison tried to pull away, but Chadwick stopped him.

"Try to see it from our perspective, okay? You track this stuff as long as we have, I mean, it's like trying to bottle up smoke. You can't infiltrate these people. Even if everything falls out right, you nail some dweeb, turns out he knows nothing or just clams up. Meanwhile, the shit just keeps mounting. Seven years now, it's just gotten worse. We've solved damn few of these things and it gets to you."

"So blame them for a fire they didn't set."

"You know for a fact they didn't set it? You've got a tape recording from a killer on the run, trying to blame somebody else for what he did. You can hardly blame us for not taking it as God's truth, okay? Now listen to me—we're not wedded to this Bratcher guy, understand? He's not our snitch. We could give a rat's ass about him. And yeah, we'll see whether this story that he's involved has merit. We'll work it, I promise you that. But we're not going to just ignore everything we know, everything we've learned over years of tracking this kind of deal, everything we see here, on the basis of what you've got so far. Especially when this kind of disavowal is almost predictable given how bad this thing turned out. That'd be nuts, and you can call us a lot of things—"

"I'm not going down with you like those guys in Oakland, okay?" Murchison glanced up and down the hallway. There were men coming and going, so he kept his voice low. "They fell for your line and jumped on those two Earth Firsters just like you told them to. Look what happened. If I'm gonna get a multimillion-dollar judgment against me, I want it to be because I followed my own instincts, not yours."

"You can't compare this to the Oakland deal."

"Sure I can."

"And neither Peterson nor I worked that case."

"Lucky for you."

"Look, I said it before. These aren't idealists. They're criminals. I'm not making that up, Detective." He took a second to collect himself, playing something in his head as he looked past Murchison down the hall. "Can I run a hypothetical by you?"

Murchison laughed. "If you guys are so convinced you've got this figured out, what's with all the hypotheticals?"

Chadwick ignored that. "There's a similarity between these radical groups here and what we see abroad. Just a total hatred of the West and what it stands for. There's another element to that, actually, that I'd like to run by you."

It came out surprisingly guileless. Murchison shrugged, thinking, Truthfully, what else is there to do? "Sure. Shoot."

"It's the drug angle. This kid Turpin, he was hanging not just with rads but a pretty heavy drug crowd, too. Especially here in town, that right?"

Murchison wondered who'd briefed him on that. Not like the mutt hunt of yesterday morning was any great secret, he realized, the whole Sunday squad had been on it. "Yeah. From what we know."

"You raised a good point in there. If this Malvasio guy, Ferry, if he was in this, and his information's too specific not to think he was, then somebody was bankrolling him, because he's not the kind to be in it otherwise."

"You're thinking—"

"We understand there's a guy named James Mooney, goes by the name Long Tall—"

"Long Walk."

"Him. He's a major player in the local drug scene, right? He's also got his hand in a lot of property on that hill."

"Where did you hear—"

"Your partner talked about it yesterday, with some of the other detectives. It's true, then."

"Yeah, what I can tell. We haven't followed up, there hasn't been—"

"I think that might prove a viable area, Detective. There may be a motive for setting those fires we don't see yet. Insurance fraud, maybe, on Mooney's part. Building inspectors were beginning to find out he'd financed renovations that didn't meet code. Pretty soon the home owners were gonna get grilled about where the money came from. This Mooney character, he was going to be exposed. He may have thought a bunch of fires would solve his problems. Wouldn't be the first guy to think like that."

Murchison thought it through. Chadwick could be right, he realized. Regardless, it only made sense to take a look. "We should bring Holmes in on this. He has a source inside Mooney's crew."

"We don't think it would be wise to bring Sergeant Holmes in just yet." Chadwick hunted Murchison's face, looking for a flinch, a tic, a giveaway.

"Explain that," Murchison said.

"He has a source. Exactly, you said it. We want to make sure the information flow doesn't become two-way."

"You think Holmes would—"

"This early, we don't want to risk anything we don't have to."

"You can't keep him out of the loop."

"We think we can. And we'll need your help."

Murchison saw it then. The voice didn't match the eyes.

"I think you need to find somebody else."

"He trusts you."

"I wouldn't be so sure about that. Besides, if it were true, why would I want to betray that trust?"

"For the greater good."

Murchison gave in to his disgust and pulled away. "You gotta try harder than that."

"This is an extremely touchy deal, Detective. I'm asking."

"And I answered. No."

"You don't know how dangerous these people are. We do. Mix that with drug money—"

Murchison stopped. "I just saw an entire hillside in my hometown burned down, seen my partner killed and a family burned to death in a bathtub while they clawed each other to pieces. I don't understand that the people responsible are dangerous?"

When he got to his desk, he found Hennessey waiting. No smiling Irish eyes this time, he'd drawn a short straw, been sent on a bad news errand. Concerning me, Murchison guessed.

"Hey, Murch." The words came out barely loud enough to be heard above the noise. "How ya doing?" His big body sat perched on the corner of the desk, so Murchison couldn't get past him to sit.

"There a problem?"

"No no no. No problem. I just..." His voice trailed away and bumped into a sigh on the back end. "Just got something I need... There's a..." His mouth tightened, he shook his head. "Chief wants—"

"For God's sake, Hennessey. If it was really that bad you'd have shot me by now."

Hennessey couldn't make eye contact. "Chief wanted me to tell you that he appreciates your staying on-duty this morning, us being short-staffed and all. But, you know, with the shooting, the usual procedure—"

"He's putting me on admin leave."

"It's paid."

"I know it's paid. That's not the point." Murchison gestured for Hennessey to stand so he could get to his desk. "Okay, I'm on leave. Now let me get back to work."

Hennessey seemed in agony. He didn't move. "Murch, please."

Murchison realized finally he held no cards. It unnerved him. "Please what? Come on, Hennessey, say it."

Hennessey uttered a breathy, almost inaudible groan. "I'm just the messenger, Murch, okay?" He stood up finally, placing his hand on Murchison's shoulder. "I'm supposed to walk you out. Gotta make sure you leave the building."

25

It was Nadya's turn to lie awake while Toby slept. He'd come up-stairs with her, as she'd wished, into a small guest room where ex-haustion had finally won out. He lay on his stomach upon the narrow bed, again in his clothes, like this morning in the church base-ment—not even his shoes removed now, only his glasses. He'd pulled a thick wool blanket across his body. His arms lay flat to either side, his head turned, mouth slightly open as he breathed in, breathed out.

Nadya watched each breath, envying his tranquillity. Inside her, the relentlessly vile memories continued like a howl of curses, no matter how still she sat, no matter how intent her focus on him, not her. If anything, calming down just made it worse. And, yes, focusing on Toby made it worse.

Finally, she surrendered, got up, taking care not to wake him, and padded out of the room, carrying her shoes. She ventured into the conference room, sat down at the massive table where Toby's father's horn still lay exposed in its red velvet case. As though it were lying in state. She reached out and touched the cool, shimmering brass, the soft leather pads for the keys, ran her finger along the rim of the bell. If you forgive me, she thought, why do I still feel all these terrible things?

She ventured downstairs, sauntering through the kitchen and the hallway toward the front. From the conference room she heard voices. The detective, Murchison, was here again. He was talking with Francis and Tina. Francis was yelling.

"That can't be. It's wrong!"

"There's not much I can do," the detective said.

"But the tape. One you played just now. It's clear as can be."

"They don't see it that way."

"Because you didn't try to make them see."

"Francis—" It was Tina.

"Perhaps." The detective, his voice, it seemed so defeated. So disheartened. "Perhaps you're right."

"And this fixer, this Bratcher guy, he walks."

"He's smart, he's connected, he plays rough. Everybody knows that. But to pin something like these fires on him, what I've got now—"

"Well, ain't that the goddamn evening news."

"There may still be a way to obtain immunity," Tina said. "I'm not going to stop believing—"

"All a fucking joke. Truth? Don't bother. Worse than that."

"I still believe there's a way—"

"I don't," Murchison said. "Not the way things stand. I wish I did."

Nadya drew away, ducking into one of the offices along the hall. She closed the door, needing to shut out their voices. Heart pounding, she found a notepad and pen on the desktop. Sitting down, she began furiously to write.

Dear Toby,

It seems that only one of us at a time can find a way to sleep. I hope you dreamed, and hope your dreams were a comfort.

To be honest, what kept me awake was remembering your silence when I asked you to tell me you'd never leave, even if it wasn't true. I should thank you for being unwilling to lie, but honestly, given all that's happened and how I feel, I find myself hating you for that.

I feel a lot of hatred, actually. It's as though a scream is building inside me and when it finally breaks through to my voice I will die from it. What frightens me is that I have begun to look forward to that.

I can't expect you to deal with any of this. I've given up any hope that what we feel for each other would survive what we've been forced to deal with. It would make a pretty story, if

that happened, but I've lost my capacity for investing hope in
pretty stories. I'll be lucky if I just get through this, and that's
no way to be with someone.

I spoke of hate. I've felt your hatred for me, too. You've tried
hard to hide it, and I appreciate that, but it's in your touch,
your eyes, your distance. If I were you, I'd feel the same. It's
the guilt, the helplessness. It's too much, the horror out there,
plus all these maddening, disgusting images and sensations
and feelings on the inside, too. I assume it's true for you, as
well. I don't know, you haven't spoken of it. It would take a
saint to endure that and not rage with hatred. We're not saints.
Maybe someday we can sit together, find a bond in that—here
we are, two people who wanted so much to be loving and brave
but who failed to be saints.

Nadya

She found an envelope, sealed her letter inside it, and returned upstairs on tiptoe to deposit it on the floor beside Toby's glasses. She
wanted to kiss him good-bye but feared waking him.

Downstairs again, she came upon the detective alone in the hallway. He was pacing, a lost look on his face, waiting for Tina, who was
arguing plaintively with Francis behind the closed door to one of the
offices.

"Hello," she said.

Murchison tottered, as though about to fall over from fatigue. Still,
he managed a smile. "How are you? I mean, how are you doing?"

"I need to ask a small favor."

He cocked his head. "If I can."

"A ride to the bus station is all. I need to go home."

He studied her, no doubt wondering why Toby wasn't being called
upon for the task. A hint of sympathy softened his gaze. "How soon?"

She shrugged. "When you can."

He looked morosely at the closed office door, then all around him,
as though trying to find out where he was. Or why he was there. "I'll
take you now."

•   •   •

Murchison noted she'd brought nothing with her, not even a purse. "You have money?"

"Yes." She reached into her pocket, pulled out a wad of mangled bills—the way you found them in a junkie's pocket, except they didn't look quite so grimy. This was quite possibly the most eccentric young woman he'd ever met. And he'd met some oddballs. He wondered how many times her beauty had spared her being thought of as just a little crazy.

"I want to apologize for how rough my partner and I were on you yesterday at the hospital."

She stuffed her money back into her pocket. "It doesn't matter now."

"It doesn't?" Stluka's dead, I may as well be dead—is that what she meant? "Why not?"

"I understand what you had to do."

"And what was that?" For some reason, he felt testy.

She looked up at him with helpless eyes. "Your job."

"That's an excuse? My job?"

"I don't know." Her voice withered. She surrendered. "I was trying to be kind."

Inwardly he chastised himself. Apologize for being rough, then rough her up some more. "I'm sorry. Thank you."

"You're welcome."

At the waterfront he turned south, toward the Greyhound terminal. The Bay Area buses all picked up there. The streets were eerily empty.

"I wanted to tell you," he said, "that I understand a little bit better now, what you went through. With Mr. Carlisle. Finding him like that, trying—" He couldn't get the rest out.

She regarded him with a vaguely troubled sympathy. "I wish you didn't have to understand that. I wish no one did. I heard about your partner. I'm sorry."

"Thanks." He felt his heart pounding. His eyes burned. His migraine throbbed. "We don't get to choose what we have to deal with."

"No. We don't." She gazed out the window at the vacant streetscape. "I used to believe we at least had a choice as to *how* we dealt with it, but I no longer even believe that very much."

"I understand that, too."

She puffed her cheeks, spat out little bursts of air, then said, "Life upon the wicked stage ain't everything a girl supposes."

He dropped her off at a covered shelter outside the terminal. The weather was dry for now, but rain clouds loomed to the west. The wind gusted; leaves and scrap paper whirled in the gutters. Two other riders waited for their buses—a middle-aged black woman in a red watch cap and wool coat clutching a bag of groceries, and a scrawny white teen with limp, long hair chain-smoking as he bobbed on his feet in the cold.

"You sure you'll be all right?" Murchison knew the question was too hopeless, too vague, to elicit anything but a false answer.

"I just need to go home," she said, and got out of the car.

The house was empty, and though Murchison had expected that, had no reason not to, it stung in a way he'd not anticipated. Standing in the kitchen, he drank three glasses of cold tap water. The rubbish stank. The counter was smeared with something sticky, jam or honey. He left his glass in the sink and bothered with none of it.

He couldn't get himself into the bedroom. In a while he'd pack some clothes, let Joan know she could come back with the girls, stay here while they worked things out. Or didn't. But he knew he'd never sleep with her in that bed again.

He sat down on the living room sofa and leafed through a Bible Joan had left out. It was her practice, before taking the girls to church, to have them bone up on the week's Sunday school lesson. He thumbed through the pages—the paper felt brittle, almost powdery to the touch—looking for something that might make sense of what he'd been through the past forty-eight hours. One came from the Thirty-eighth Psalm: "My friends and my companions stand back. . . . For I am very near to falling and my grief is with me always." The other, from Ecclesiastes: "Better the day of death than the day of birth."

Shortly, without knowing how or why or when he came to that position, he was lying flat and, finally, dozing. But it was a twitchy, restless sleep. At first, he didn't so much dream as suffer the same nightmarish thoughts and words and images that had haunted him all day. Jerry, dying. The family of three found gruesomely dead in their tub. The stench of the burning hillside, the crazy old woman tonguing the rain, Raymond Carlisle shot in the back and rolled over by the girl who couldn't save him—all of it, tinged with other things, worse things he'd seen over the years, thought he'd dealt with, clearly hadn't—the images lined up, a freak show. Then he heard a dog barking. He saw its eyes, staring out from the dark. He raised his side arm, but the gunshot he heard wasn't his own. It was loud, far away, like a rocket blast. He ran through a maze, it stank like the garbage in his own kitchen, pitch-black, he stumbled, a door opened, and there he was, lying there. Dying.

Willy.

He nearly toppled off the sofa onto the floor. Heart pounding. Stomach ready to heave. He sat up straight, shook the haze from his head, and tried to focus. What the hell was that, he wondered.

It's wrong, he thought, any comparison of Willy's death with Jerry's. Jerry was my partner, sure, and that's nothing to belittle. But I never pledged my life to the guy, didn't even like him all that much. Hated him, sometimes. But respected him, as a cop. Granted. And, sometimes, despite all my groaning about how isolated it felt, being partnered with him, secretly I think I wanted it that way. I like being alone. It feels right. It feels just. And, someday, death will perfect that solitude, won't it?

You feel guilty, he told himself, for being there, being unable to save him. Yes. Absolutely. Like he died for me, in my place. Not just Jerry. Willy, too. There, that was it. And not just them. Every stranger whose death had never come out right, since that first young woman in the Monterey hotel room cut to shreds up to this morning, the people burned alive up on Baymont.

In my place.

The phone rang. Joan? You'll have to find something to say, he thought, staggering to the kitchen. He grabbed the receiver from its cradle, put it to his ear.

"Detective. This is Richard Ferry."

Images from his nightmare quickened at the sound of that voice. Hypnotized, he tried to shake off the feeling, couldn't. At the same time, he realized he'd left the taped confession at Tina Navigato's office.

"How did you get this number?"

"It's my business, knowing things." The line hissed and popped with static. "Besides, home phone. Child's play. Rookie who knows how to talk his way past a door can manage it."

Ferry sat beneath a palm-fronded *palapa* atop the pier at the Old Mill Resort, one hand wrapped around a smeary glass of *aguardiente*, the local white lightning. His other hand held the satellite phone to his ear.

"I was curious how it went. A confession in hand."

"Where are you?"

The grass-bottomed shallows stretched south beneath a bright sun. Siesta hour, no one walked about. The rustic pier, the old resort, the ramshackle fishing shop, the restaurant, all stood locked up and empty. Ferry risked no one overhearing. A thin veil of sweat covered his skin. The heat, finally, had begun to melt away his tension.

"That's a pointless question. I said I confessed. I didn't say I was turning myself in."

"Talk about pointless."

"Hardly. You know plenty. Mr. Bratcher—you brought him in for a sit, I hope."

"They say it's bogus."

"They as in who?"

"Everybody. FBI, in particular. They're convinced the fire was set by the people you meant to hang it on. The rads."

Talent doesn't pay, Ferry thought. Sometimes you're your own worst enemy. "I got it right, and it turned out all wrong."

"Sounds like a song title."

"Yeah. But back to Bratcher."

"They won't bite. You worked for him before, three years ago. Your name's Malvasio, you hire yourself out as a security consultant—lot of that these days—then shake down your employers. Lot of that, too. You killed two bangers in Sacramento, then tried to extort Bratcher."

"Who told you that?"

"Let's talk in person."

"Not possible. Who told you that?"

"Bratcher's a snitch. Federal. His handlers sent down the info. Agents working the fire got it from them. They vouch for him. Large. No one seems to vouch for you."

"That extortion story? It's horseshit."

"Sent pictures, too. You could use a shave."

"I gave you an account number, I said get a warrant, check his accounts, his partnerships and LLCs, closely held corporations. He's got dozens. You'll find the money trail. Probably more than that."

"They'll just say it was a payoff on your extortion."

"Three months ago?"

"I can't get a warrant. Got closed down. You're a bad man."

"Bratcher's more bad. Way bad. Most bad."

"You and I seem to be in the minority on that. Could have something to do with your killing a cop."

"Oh, that."

"Yeah. That."

Ferry marveled at the thoroughness. Bratcher had planned this out long ago. It meant he'd probably been more careful about the money than Ferry had realized. A search warrant, even if they got it, would most likely come up empty. No paper trail. And the feds were going to bat for their boy. Devotedly—not so much for Bratcher's sake as their own reputations. They hated a mess; no surprise, given the recent history of fending off shit storms. The world's best stonewallers.

"They tell you the story, about the shooting?"

"Said you were bent, took out one of the cops who'd rolled."

"That's a lie."

"Had a feeling you'd say that."

"Want to hear the truth?"

There was a long pause.

"Go ahead and record this if you want."

"Had a feeling you'd say that."

"Want me to wait?"

"Where are you?"

"Nice try."

"My phone here says you're calling from a local line."

"It's a trick. One you won't figure out in time. You ready?"

There was another silence. Then: "Sure."

Ferry took a sip from his glass. He hadn't thought about this in a while, except for bits and pieces every single day.

"I shot a cop. They're right. His name was Hank Winters, he worked vice. He was leaning on one of his snitches, this pimp on the South Side—utter waste of a human being, king roach of the crack-heads, walked around with his fly open, red-eyed, nasty. His girls were filth.

"Among other problems, this pimp was staring at a felony bad check beef. Winters was using that, squeezing him, trying to get him to serve up who he paid his protection money up in the street. Pimp wanted no part of that, knew he'd get dealt with if he named names. So Winters made sure the bad check thing sailed through. There was a bench warrant out on the pimp, failure to appear. Winters handed it off to a couple of uniforms to serve.

"One of those cops was a friend of mine. Great guy, played center field in college, Notre Dame. Partner material, kind of cop I should've been. Maybe. Any event, Winters says nothing about this strong-arm effort to my friend or the other cop, doesn't tell them the pimp's scared—been told he goes to jail, he's dead—doesn't tell them he's threatened to wax anybody who comes to get him and lately is jacked so high on crack he can't tell a whore from a hayride. Oh no, why tell this to the cops serving your warrant. They might say, 'No, thanks. You do it.' Besides, pimps are such pussified little skels anyway, what's to fear, unless you're one of his women.

"My buddy and his backup, they show up at this loser's crib, figuring it's a routine warrant—be polite, 'Yes, sir, come along, thank you.' Get him in the car, no problem. Cancel that. Mr. Pimp—he's been up three days, chasing shadows around the room—he goes postal. My friend takes one in the head. Other guy has to chase this fuckstick up the fire escape to the roof, call for backup, while my buddy bleeds to death in the pimp's doorway.

"I hear all this, I went a little nuts, yeah. There's an IA review, sure. Pro forma, you know what I'm saying. Winters, he's got wheels. Skates in, skates out. Nothing.

"I started in on the piece of shit. Wasn't hard, he was big news on the grapevine. Found out he had a slice on the side—call girl he'd busted once, that a picture or what?—found out when he went to see her. Found out where, this condo rehab up off Milwaukee. So I waited. This alley, where he parked the car. He saw me, went for his piece." Ferry stopped for a second, noticed he was breathing hard. "Funny the way some things just stay in your head. His own damn fault. Haven't been back to Chicago since. Way I hear it, though? Lot of guys thank me."

He finished his *aguardiente*, wanted another, but no one had awakened from the midday nap as yet. He might raid the bar himself if no one showed up soon.

"You're kind quiet," he said finally. "You heard that story before?"

"I know one that's kind of similar."

"Your partner."

"Kind of. How'd you—"

"Like I said, I know things. Your partner. Sent in without everything he needed."

"There was no time."

"Goes in and doesn't come back out again."

"Yeah, it rings a bell. You're right."

Murchison's voice sounded thready and lost. He was getting dragged inside, Ferry figured. Into the house of no hope. Meanwhile, at the mouth of the harbor, Ferry spotted an approaching dinghy, its aluminum hull glinting in the sun. A lone man sat astern, guiding the outboard. Ovidio's friend, coming in from his fishing boat, anchored out beyond the shallows.

"So what are you going to do, Dennis?"

"Excuse me?"

"I've told you all I can. All I'm going to. You know my side of things. What I told you, my last voice mail. It's true, every word. I think you know that. So what are you going to do?"

"It's not . . . I'm not the one who gets to decide."

"Let me put it another way. It's your hometown. You grew up there. What would your brother want you to do?"

The silence was much longer, almost agonizing. Long enough for the dinghy to drift in to the pier, its outboard cut. The boatman—Rafael,

Ferry remembered—he was thirty-something, slender and dark, wearing a Packers jersey and cutoffs, Keds with no socks. He made the boat fast, tying its painter to a bollard.

Finally, Murchison said, "How do you know about my brother?"

"We've been through this, Dennis. I know things. It's my reason for being."

As Murchison drove, his migraine worsened, hammering behind his eyes, like something inside his head couldn't escape. I'm losing it, he thought, not with fear but a kind of wonderment. It took two hours, along winding two-lane roads, before Murchison reached the place— Ferry had told him how to get there, just before hanging up—located in the wetlands northwest of Lake Berryessa. There was little to announce its being there, just an ironwork fence topped with press-metal silhouettes of ducks. LA CASA DE CAZA, a sign read at the gate. The House of Hunting.

In fact, it was a rice farm. Not the best region for rice—you found that fifty miles farther northeast up the Sacramento Valley—but Murchison remembered reading a story in the paper about how Bratcher had managed to finagle his way into the farm subsidy program while building himself one of the more enviable duck clubs in the area. He got money for production and a second payment to reimburse any differential between loans and cost. He was guaranteed a profit by the government, for a ruse.

That's the sign he ought to have out front, Murchison thought. RICE PAYS TWICE.

The plan—if it deserved such a word—was to ask some tough questions point-blank, judge for himself by Bratcher's carriage, his eyes, his tone, whether he was a liar or not. He wasn't sure what this would prove or to whom it would prove it beyond himself, but it had seemed enough when he'd gotten in the car. Even if he couldn't prove anything, at least he'd know. And if Bratcher stonewalled, resisted? Murchison hadn't quite thought that part through. Improvise, he guessed.

A security guard manned the gate—retired sheriff's deputy from the looks of him, bald with a mustache, wearing black slacks and a blue windbreaker. Daylight was fading, the sun had gone down. A cold drizzle whirled in the headlights as Murchison showed his badge. The guard held his umbrella with one hand while the other flipped open his cell phone.

Murchison reached out, stopped him. "Just let me go up. Unannounced."

The guard looked at him like he'd asked for money. "My job we're talking about."

"You won't lose your job. I promise." Murchison let go of the man's sleeve. "You heard about the fires down my way last night."

The guard shrugged. "Sure."

"Some guy claims your boss had something to do with it. I've got to prove this loon wrong. But to do that, I have to come on like I'm serious. Can't just go through the motions."

"I don't see why that means I shouldn't call up, tell him you're here."

Murchison smiled. "Look, you're a cop, right?"

The guy looked vaguely defensive at first, then nodded, sensing comradery. "Yeah."

"Napa County sheriff?"

"Lake County."

"Lake County? You're a ways from home."

"Not so bad. Just over the hill. Middletown."

"Well, look. Here's the thing. I gotta look like I'm doing my job, okay? Put a little element of surprise into it. Besides, if I thought I'd have to do anything serious, I'd have come with a squad, not like this."

Sent in without everything he needed.

The guard glanced around the interior of Murchison's car. "Yeah. I was thinking that."

"This is just a formality. But if I show that up front, let Mr. Bratcher call all the shots, it won't pass the smell test. Look like I came up, kissed his butt, and turned back around. Which won't solve anything. I'm doing him a favor."

The guard winced. "Not likely he'll see it that way."

"He will once we're done. I promise."

The guard looked off into the growing twilight, agonizing. Rain droplets fattened along the lip of his umbrella. "I could tell him my cell battery died. Wouldn't be the first time." He chuckled disconsolately, as though recalling a browbeating. "Let's say you told me you were just here to pass along some info, okay? Cleared it with him beforehand."

"That's good. Put it on me."

"Said you knew about the meeting, figured they'd want to know."

"Meeting?"

"Him and his lawyer and a couple other guys, Craugh the developer, that Glenn guy—"

Sure, Murchison thought. Time for champagne. Roll out the plans for a brand-new Baymont. "They still here?"

"Naw, they came out, shot some skeet, left once the rain started. Just Mr. Bratcher and his lawyer, guy named Peter Gramm. Know him?"

"His lawyer's there. Perfect. That'll square things on both ends."

"I sure as hell hope so." The guard finally turned around and opened the wrought-iron gate. "Pay some mind once you're up around the house. He's got the damn dogs out."

The driveway wound for a half mile through thick groves of oak and walnut trees. Rice fields stretched low and green to the east, with duck blinds tucked along the levees. More trees, dense and dark, stood to the west, all the way to Putah Creek.

Cracking a window, he could smell the bay leaves from the trees clustered around the stock ponds and wellheads, where the geese and ducks collected on their journeys north and south along the Pacific flyway. Duck season was over, had been for several weeks. The guard had said they were shooting skeet, but that could be a ruse. Who from Fish & Game would actually come out here and write the citation? He spotted snow geese, some Canadas, plus ruddies and stiff tails, gadwalls and mallards. Willy would have loved this place, he thought, which brought the whole thing full circle.

Just this isn't nothing, he reminded himself. One sacrifice can't redeem another. Unless, finally, it somehow does.

For the rest of the drive, he couldn't help imagining everything out here burned to the ground. Beyond the last turn, the house sat atop a low rise, ranch style, modest in its lines but huge. Lights glowed in the windows, but no one appeared to be inside. Murchison, feeling his pulse throb in his neck, put the transmission in park and checked his side arm. The clip was full; he had an extra round in the chamber, ten shots. He flipped off the safety and holstered the piece as the dogs appeared.

There were six of them, an odd pack, a mix of pets and protection: two birders, a wolfhound, two rotts, and a sleek, needle-faced Doberman leading the charge. They barked with an ugly vehemence, outdoing one another, baring fangs and flaring their hackles—he remembered the guard at the gate, shame as well as fear in his warning—but it wasn't that so much as simply their presence, the Doberman especially, that started it. He felt his mouth dry up, his skin grow cold. His heart raced as he tried to draw breath. From around the corner he saw two men, but more to the point, he saw the barrels of their pump loaders as they came to investigate the unannounced car. It all seemed of one piece then—menacing dogs, shotguns, a house that might be empty, might not be. Rain. We don't live in a world of things, Murchison thought. We live in a world of shadows.

He got out of the car, drew his piece, and shot the first dog, the Doberman. So much for the plan. There'd been another plan at work all along, he realized. The 9mm's report stopped the charging men. The other dogs whirled backward, yelping in fear, whimpering for a moment as they gained safe ground. Then the barking began all over again, even more savage than before. They nosed forward. Murchison took aim at one of the rotts as a voice called out, "Hey! Hey! What the hell are you doing?"

Better the day of death.

Make them pay.

"Restrain your dogs, sir." Like he was there to read the gas meter. He steadied his aim.

"Who the hell are you? How did you— What are you doing on—"

Murchison fired again, took out the rott with a slug to the head. It collapsed like a switch got thrown. The end of things. Again the remaining dogs spun backward, regrouped. The men lugged forward.

Murchison recognized Bratcher from city council meetings. Murchison, contemptuous of politics in all forms, had never paid him or the stories about him much mind. Now the man who'd inspired so many rumors strode toward him—big, hulking, an aging onetime fireman, which was the sickness at the heart of the whole damn thing—a shotgun in his hands, waist level, trained in Murchison's direction.

"Put the fucking pistol down. Now."

"Police!" Murchison reached in his jacket, withdrew his badge. "Restrain your dogs or lose them all."

"Put the damn gun down."

"Dogs first."

"Wait. Wait. Wait." It was the lawyer, Gramm. He was wearing a Redman cap—looking foolish in it with his gold-rimmed aviators and jowly, stubbled face—plus a down vest and camouflage pants. "There's no need for this. What do you want here? This is private property."

It came out like a plea to a madman. Bratcher kept edging forward. He wore waders and a lumber jacket. Murchison removed his aim from the nearest dog and switched to Bratcher.

"You. The shotgun. On the ground. Now."

Bratcher ignored him. He knelt beside the Doberman's carcass, felt for its heart. "You killed my best damn dog."

"What is this *about*?" The lawyer's voice peeled high. He stayed back, beyond the dogs. "You can't just come here—"

"Both of you. The guns. On the ground."

"This is insane, you can't—"

"On the ground!"

He saw the barrel of Bratcher's gun float upward, a clean swift movement, sign of long practice. It seemed a kind of deliverance. You killed my best dog. *This is insane.* By the time Murchison had his own trigger squeezed, firing off three rounds, he'd registered the shotgun's report and muzzle flash, caught its blast in his chest. Not trap shot. Nine shot, he guessed, feeling eerily calm, buoyed on a flood of adrenaline, despite the horse kick of the shotgun's load slamming his flesh, the pain. In an eerie slowdown of time, like he'd felt once during a car accident, he tumbled backward, hitting the ground hard, the whole time watching Bratcher spin off his haunches into the dirt with a startled cry. The lawyer stood there gaping, like an innocent.

The dogs charged while Murchison scrambled through a daze

onto his knees. He shot one at close range and was aiming at the second when the lawyer fired. The blast caught Murchison high, the chest again, the face. He was blinded but raised his gun anyway, aiming toward the remembered sound through pain and blood and firing till he heard the man scream and fall.

Murchison lifted himself onto one elbow, dragging himself back toward his car. He couldn't breathe, gagging on the blood. He heard the lawyer sobbing, the sound punctuated by gasping cries for help. The dogs continued barking but kept their distance, confused, scared, not sure who or what they had to defend now. In the background he heard Bratcher coughing up blood, too, his only sound. Justice in that, Murchison told himself, pulling himself into a sitting position. Through his smeary field of vision he found Bratcher's body, then readied himself to use the gun in case the dogs regrouped. Pity they were here, he thought. The dogs, they really set me off.

Things swam and he felt himself closing down, growing cold, his vision hazing darker. So hard to breathe—he convulsed, trying to inhale, gargling blood. As the adrenaline drained away, he felt the pain more clearly and couldn't help himself. His eyes filled with tears, he soiled himself, descending into a formless place of terror and want. I know this place, he thought. Known it all my life.

You're gonna miss me when I'm gone.

He caught the sound of a vehicle roaring forward, slamming to a stop and then the door opened. Steps churned across the damp gravel. The security guard from the gate, Murchison thought, unable to see. He heard the man wailing, "Good God, no, fucking hell, no, no . . ." A voice like a strangled trumpet. Then shouts into the cell phone, calls for an ambulance, but the nearest hospital was so far away.

Murchison eased himself onto his side, laid his head down. Time to let go. Embracing the terror and want, in time he felt them give way, till a vast cold stillness encircled him. *Too hard to breathe,* a voice said, *and what for?* His own voice, and yet—

Above him, a presence, the security guard: "Go ahead and bleed. Lying bastard. Go ahead." Well said, Murchison thought, as the guard kicked the gun away from his hand. You tell the tale now. Look at the bodies, figure it out, save yourself.

26

The funerals began. Every church in Rio Mirada, it seemed, served double duty, a shelter for the homeless, a chapel for the bereft. Services ran nonstop, packed with mourners who offered ritual prayers and tried to steady their voices as they joined together in hymns.

Murchison and Stluka were honored together—matching flag-draped caskets carried in identical white hearses, proceeding at dirge speed behind row after row of motorcycles and squad cars, cruiser strobes flickering blue and red. Over one thousand officers came, as though to say, *You can't kill us all.* They traveled from across the state and as far away as Denver, Phoenix, Portland, Seattle, each cop wearing a funereal armband or a black-banded badge.

News crews stationed themselves at the base of the charred hillside, pointing their cameras toward the devastation, framing it as backdrop, while the mile-long motorcade edged solemnly past, heading toward the high school stadium for the memorial service as the public, held back behind barriers, looked on.

The stands were full—men and women in uniform, a mosaic of blues, plus mayors from across the state, the families of the fallen men and selected local officials. The public, again, was excluded, in keeping with custom. This ceremony was for the brotherhood. Twenty motorcycles in slow procession led the two white hearses around the cinder track, then a bagpipe played "Amazing Grace" as Holmes and the others in the honor guard, wearing their white gloves and dress blues, carried the flag-draped caskets to the stage and placed them on stands marked by wreaths bearing each man's badge number.

The speeches came next, some sweetly personal and teary, others droning, pompous things that made Holmes cringe. If I hear one more politician say, "We're all family here," or "They paid the ultimate sacrifice," he thought, I'll draw my piece and fire. Officers from the outside departments, growing bored, chatted or cracked jokes among themselves in the stands. Later they'd hit the bars or show off the latest bells and whistles in their cruisers.

No one mentioned how Murchison died, nor the deaths of the men found with him. It seemed eerie and odd and almost poisonous, that silence. The circumstances remained a riddle, made no more clear by the brief, implausible, self-serving tale proposed by the security guard on the premises at the time, who promptly hired a lawyer and said no more.

The chief had refused even to honor Murchison without first consulting the mayor's office and legal counsel regarding its propriety. They'd been able to keep his being on administrative leave under wraps for now, but it would come out eventually. Sarina Thigpen had hired Grantree Hamilton to pursue a misconduct claim, which was more nuisance than threat but still cast a shadow. As for the families and business associates of Clint Bratcher and his lawyer, Gramm, they stayed quiet, retained counsel with an expertise in wrongful death, and waited.

Word leaked concerning the chief's misgivings, prompting a cry of outrage not just from some on the force but the community, too. Rumors flew, each more insidious than the last and only intensified by the details of the Ferry confession, now well known. Tina Navigato had passed along Murchison's tape to the press, and not all reports bothered with restraint. A typical headline, this one in the normally modest *Rio Mirada Index*, read:

TRAUMATIZED COP KILLS TAINTED POWER BROKER
LINKED TO BAYMONT FIRES

The community rose up. Ralston Polhemus, one of their own, had been in league with arsonists—worse, killers—knowingly or not, that was for him and God to work out. People vowed that they would burn the rest of the city down before they saw Bob Craugh or Wally Glenn or any of their henchmen so much as turn a shovelful of dirt on

Baymont or St. Martin's Hill or let the council approve such a thing. And Murchison, he'd shown true courage, "our homegrown hero," sacrificing himself as he had.

So easy to praise the dead, Holmes thought, when he heard such things. So hard to forgive the living. Stluka, it was true, he did not much miss, except for the sake of pity. Murchison, that was different. Despite the ugly side he'd shown that last day of his life, he'd been fair overall, more or less honest, smart, decent. Hard to know what had gone so wrong inside him. Holmes wondered, though, remembering the sight of Murchison twisted up inside, the lost look in his eyes, the scattershot rage, whether the heroic self-sacrifice everyone felt so compelled to honor wasn't actually a sort of death wish. Whether noble sacrifice wasn't just suicide dressed up for company.

As irony would have it, the chief spoke last. Holmes prepared himself for a final insult of numbing pomposities, but the man surprised him.

"Cops think they're invulnerable," he began, sounding for once not quite as young as he looked. "We're convinced we'll die from a heart attack two weeks after retirement, not in the line of duty. And so when one of us goes down, that illusion gets exposed for what it is."

A restlessness rippled through the crowd as he spoke of how the awareness of our own waiting death only intensified when two men, partners, were killed. And how it was easy, but wrong, to blame the dead for reminding us so starkly of that one inescapable part of the future.

"It happens," he said, "that blaming. It already has."

Holmes felt oddly moved, first from the surprise of hearing this man so roundly despised by the rank and file speak so honestly on a touchy point, then finally by the words themselves, the man's recognition that they were all gathered there not just in grief but also in fear. He'd be ridiculed by some for saying as much. Holmes found courage in it, and in that courage, solace.

As the chief stepped away from the microphone, six helicopters flew low above the stadium, performing a twofold missing man formation as first one then a second chopper peeled away, returning back the way they had come instead of continuing on with the others.

At the cemetery, while "Taps" played and Murchison and Stluka received their twenty-one-gun salutes, the honor guard rolled up the flags from each casket and presented them to the widows. Sheila Stluka—defiant and tearless one moment, then shaking with sobs the next—received her flag like she intended to hurl it down into the grave with the casket.

Holmes presented the second flag to Murchison's wife, Joan. She accepted it with a nod, her face stoic in its sorrow inside her veil. A bit too stoic, Holmes couldn't help thinking as he snapped to his salute.

Coast Guard planes patrolled the ocean as *La Chica de Buenas* kept to the ten-mile mark. Ferry and the boat crew, watching the sky, spotted a C-130 or Falcon Lear jet pass overhead at least once a day, usually twice, but no patrol boats or buoy tenders appeared to send out a boarding crew, scour around, looking for drugs or weapons under the guise of checking to be sure they had enough life vests and fire extinguishers aboard.

Ovidio's friend Rafael had made a point in San Quintín to demand Ferry relinquish any weapons. "They'll seize the boat on that alone, even if it's your own gun." Ferry had tossed a perfectly fine Walther P5 overboard under those pretenses, and then, as it turned out, not a boarding to bother over the whole trip down.

Now, anchored off La Libertad, they lowered the dinghy from its boom and Rafael and Ferry disembarked, heading in for the huge long pier stemming out from the old town of ruins. Late in the day, the fishing boats headed in, too, aiming for the crane that would pull them up from the surf to the pier itself with a blast from its smokestack whistle.

Rafael brought the dinghy in close to the pier. As the boat jostled in the late day surf, Ferry stowed his laptop inside his duffel, tossed the bag over his shoulder, and grabbed hold of the wood ladder and climbed to the top.

He entered a circus of activity. Makeshift stalls lined the pier, the deck slimy and fetid with salt water and fish entrails. Old women sat shelling *camarones* or cleaning *boca colorada*, selling their wares from ice-filled tubs and haggling with buyers. Boat crews wheeled their vessels down the pier on homemade dollies—some built from toy wagons or bicycles—shouting, *"¡Con permiso!"* as they pushed through the crowd, down the gauntlet of fishmongers' stalls, guiding their boats into their proper berths for the night.

Just beyond the pier, Ferry bought a cup of ceviche made with lime juice and bitter orange, chasing it with two pilsners as he sat with a group of *pescadores* at a stone table in the shadows of the old train station. Once majestic, the old station now sat empty, a ruin—and in its decrepitude, it served as a kind of cautionary backdrop for the weekenders from the capital who flocked here, as well as the expatriate surfers you still found lolling around the beach.

For dessert, he bought a fresh coconut, drinking the clear sweet milk first, then shaving pieces of the meat from the shell, eating the slivers one by one as he paced, waiting. In the shadows of the palm trees, black crabs emerged from the dark volcanic sand and skittered away from his footfalls. Down the beach toward Punta Roca, a pack of shirtless boys stoned a rat.

"*¡Hola!* ¡Guillermo!"

He turned at the sound of his given name, rendered in Spanish. Marisela waved from her car, unwilling to pay the old men who would watch it for her if she wanted to park. Ferry hoisted his duffel and hurried toward the street.

She beamed at him, waiting for a kiss behind the wheel. Ferry apologized for his cabin stench. She was wearing a flowered sundress and sandals. Seeing his eyes run up and down her body, she blushed.

"How I see me?"

She meant, "How do I look?"

"It's nice, the dress. Does you justice."

He realized the expression lay a little outside her grasp, but his tone seemed to register. She blushed again.

"I don't have nothing for put me on." She shook her head prettily, putting the car in gear.

The road to the interior wove through low green hills. Traffic was light, psychedelic buses and smoke-spewing trucks mostly. Remembering his in-country manners, he extended his arm out the window and waved to the driver ahead when he sensed Marisela wanted to pass.

She attempted further conversation as she drove, bungling her English as usual—"She look me see when I be here," or, "She more young as me," or, "I feel me bad, it shame me"—then launching help-lessly into streams of Spanish when the translating impulse failed. Ferry nodded, understanding little of what she meant by her English and next to none of the Spanish, knowing he'd need to try harder at that, and soon. He had half the money he'd expected, and the boat had cost him an extra ten thousand, the cost of short notice. To make things worse, expenses here were through the roof now that they'd switched to the dollar. He'd be hiring himself out again sooner than he wanted.

They merged with the Pan-American Highway just outside Santa Tecla, passing the Col Don Bosco as they headed east. Since the 2001 earthquakes, whole sections of the city lay in ruins. The cinder block homes had collapsed like sand in the tremors, leaving skeletal re-mains. These areas looked like war zones, facing the sheared moun-tain face that had given way.

Nobody knew how many bodies remained beneath the debris, though from time to time government workers returned to spread lye around. Packs of *vagabundos* sniffed the rubble each day, side by side with trash pickers scavenging for pots and spoons and table knives. Marisela's family's lumber business should have prospered, but who had money to rebuild?

It wasn't just buildings that had fallen apart. The economy had tanked. Men with guns roamed everywhere. Six had appeared on a flatbed truck a week after Ferry had left for this most recent trip. They'd pushed Marisela, her mother, everyone else into the office, stripped the jewelry off the women, watches and belt buckles off the men, grabbed the money from the register, the vault, everyone's pock-ets. Not even a brother-in-law in the PCN with ties to *La Mara Diecio-cho* could protect them. As for the lumber, it stayed put—what good was that?

Remembering the story, and seeing again the ruins throughout the town, Ferry wondered what variety of weepy, woe-is-me hand-wringing would still be going on about the Rio Mirada fires. People in the States, he thought, they're like children. They have no idea how the rest of the world lives, what suffering really looks like.

Marisela lived in a second house on her parents' property, which lay inside a gated middle-class community of no particular ostentation.

Even so, uniformed men armed with machine pistols manned the entrance, and they jotted down Marisela's license number on a clipboard as they waved her through.

A brief visit with the folks in the main house was required. Marisela's father was Indian, a square-headed, jug-eared, gap-toothed man with an iron-hard body, a cagey mind, and a booming laugh. He drove into Guatemala every two weeks to cut trees single-handed, truck them to mill, then haul back the lumber. Her mother was fair-skinned and green-eyed, from a family of dentists, and she ran the office for the lumberyard.

In the small house, Ferry showered as Marisela prepared a supper of *camarones a la criolla* and *pupusas con loroco*. They ate on the porch in sling chairs, and once drowsiness hit they napped together, naked on a crisp, clean bed that felt like an impossible luxury after days on a fishing boat. Marisela, soft but strong, attended to him with passion and forgave him when he fell short. As she lay in his arms afterward, he felt badgered with an old, guilty disgust.

Ovidio appeared about nine o'clock. He wore street clothes, not the white shirt and navy pants comprising his PCN uniform. His smile was lackluster, his manner too polite. He told his sister he needed to take her *hombre guapo* away for a while, talk a little business.

Once in the car, Ferry said, "There's something wrong."

"Not here." Ovidio cranked the ignition, gesturing with a nod of his head to the lamplit windows of the neighboring houses. "The people on this street, they're like the old *orejas*." The term referred to the secret underground of informants bribed by the military during the civil war.

They drove to a shabby café on the edge of the technical institute. The local coffee being notoriously bad, despite the crop being a major export, they both ordered *guanaquita*, a bittersweet hot chocolate served without milk. Ovidio made sure no nearby tables were occupied, then began.

"You know the Southern Command has installed an air base at Comalapa."

Ferry nodded. "We saw the planes as we sailed south. Sure."

"The FMLN says it's illegal, it violates the peace accords." He chuckled, like it was a childish joke.

"You didn't drive me here to discuss current events."

Ovidio turned his cup slowly in its saucer. "Well, not exactly. No. My point is to say your country's presence here is increasing, bit by bit, some secret, some not so secret." He smiled the universal smile of bad news. "It's the preoccupation with Colombia. This will be a southern staging area, along with Aruba and Curaçao in the Netherlands Antilles. They're improving intelligence, which means some of their old friends in the Treasury Police, the National Guard, the National Police, are being rerecruited." Ovidio glanced across the table with a look that said, *I can't protect you like before.*

"What's Colombia got to do with me?"

"It's not that. It's the fact everybody will want to buy his way into good graces. Everybody. The embassy flacks are handing out money like business cards." He took a sip of his chocolate. "And your name has come across the wires again. It's different this time. They aren't just going through the motions. They're making noise. They think you're here. They want you found."

Ferry reasoned it through. He'd learned of Bratcher's and Murchison's deaths while en route, listening to the shipboard radio and getting translations when necessary from Rafael. Not like they can blame me for that, he thought, but no surprise, either, that they'd try. He'd managed to hide here for half a decade, relying on American distrust of the locals and local contempt for Americans. Now the war drums were ratchetting up, and with it the heel clicking, the moneygrubbing, the secret little deals with the local breed of devil. Add to that the fact the FBI had egg on its face, a dirty informant not only exposed but killed, based on a tip from Ferry. Well, of course they were upset.

"I shouldn't stay with Marisela."

"Oh no. Definitely not. I'll make up something to tell her if you like."

"That'd be good. Thanks."

"But that just leaves us with the question of where you should go. It's not a minor difficulty. There's a very substantial price on your head."

Ferry looked into his friend's eyes and saw something unappealing. "That just means I have to outbid the bounty. How much are we talking about?"

Ovidio smiled, turning his cup slowly in its saucer again. "How much, yes, that is the question."

Toby marveled at the crowd amassed inside Mission Baptist for the service. His Uncle Lamont and Aunt Glovina had flown in from Bremerton, and for the sake of peace sat with Veronique and Exeter. Across the aisle—it might as well be across the universe—Toby's mother sat with Sonny Marchand and their daughters, Toby's stepsisters. Cousins and relations further removed, some of whom had traveled from as far away as Cleveland and Montgomery, took seats where they thought best, hoping not to tip the scale of sympathy too far in one direction or the other.

Musicians with local roots had come, too—Sly Stone, Lowell Fulson, Felton Pilate—and they sat with Johnny Otis, Strong Carlisle's onetime boss. John Lee Hooker's nephew and children—Archie Lee, Zakiya, and John Lee Jr.—came to pay respects on behalf of their late father, another old local, together with his longtime slide guitarist, Roy Rogers. Elsewhere in the packed church Toby spotted jazz and blues musicians from around the region, some of them friends, some players he knew only by name, all of them there to pay homage. Others, unable to attend, had sent flower arrangements, so many they crowded the aisles, and a thick and heady fragrance lingered heavily among the pews. Toby wondered at the irony of how a man who rattled around in that sad old house by himself while alive could pack a church like this once dead. It seemed sadly fitting, he supposed. Meanwhile, the only person missing, besides his father of course, was Nadya. And in that regard, the place felt empty.

He sat with Francis and the members of The Mighty Firefly, positioned across from the choir. The choir began the service with three spirituals: "There Is a Balm in Gilead," "I Believe I'll Go Back Home," and "Didn't It Rain."

Next, the pastor rendered his sermon. He was a massive, gray-haired man with a voice that could coo and thunder by turns. But today he did not offer solace—no verdant pastures or overflowing cup. He breathed fire. He'd been building all week, one homily after the other—for people he knew, children as well as adults, murdered for money if the rumors were true—and his rage had burned hotter with each climb to the pulpit. He no longer asked God for pity. He wanted justice. He exhorted the congregation to see in the senseless death suffered by this man, Raymond Carlisle—as it turned out, just some reckless hireling's lashing out—see in this death and all the others that followed a measure of the evil they faced.

"You hear it time and time again. Whenever someone dares to ask, 'What in God's name has gone wrong?' So-called welfare reform, packaged with tax cuts for the rich. Wages no family can live on, scraping by, mothers with two jobs, three jobs, while thieves and hustlers sneak millions upon millions into offshore accounts. Corporations evading billions in taxes, while our sons and daughters, from this community right here—*our* community—man the front lines and risk their lives when the military gets the call to fight. Someone dares to say, 'This is wrong. That isn't right.' What do they hear? 'Why, you're talking *the politics of envy*,' they say. *'Class warfare,'* they say. Well, good God almighty—if what has happened to this community isn't class warfare, I fail to see what is."

He concluded by reading from Psalm 17, David's "Prayer against Persecution." Its conclusion was the Firefly's cue. Toby had conferred with the band members on which tunes to play. His father had been right, they'd accepted his lead. It humbled him. He admired these men. You heard them and understood what it meant to pay your dues, heard in their solos what a savage business music was, full of stolen promises and night-after-night of having the gift but not the prize. And yet, for all that, there was the music, and the rule there was: Hold Back Nothing.

For the sake of solemnity and to suit the surroundings, they began with "Come Sunday," from Ellington's *Black, Brown & Beige*, with an alto from the choir singing the part made famous by Mahalia Jackson. Next came a more secular offering, "Goodbye Pork Pie Hat," Mingus's elegy for Lester Young, followed by the most personal of the set, Toby alone with just piano and bass, playing J. J. Johnson's "Lament," a haunting modal tune that Toby punctuated with a high, lilting solo on the second chorus, a whispered cry.

The band had insisted they finish with a roof raiser, something to truly conjure the image of the man they'd known as Strong. "God knows he'll haunt us if we don't," Toby'd agreed. The choice was automatic—"Moanin'," with Francis assigned the missing man's lead.

The intro hook resonated eerily with the pastor's sermon; you could feel the collective shiver up every spine in the place. They built the tune up till its echoes rocked the packed church. Every man took a solo, a final tribute to the man who'd brought them together, and members of the congregation rose from their pews, crying out in praise or grief, lifting their arms above their heads to handclap. The choir followed with "I'm Gonna Walk Right In and Make Myself at Home", then the choir and band joined together in one of the few spirituals Toby knew had gained his father's fondness, the old Sister Rosetta Tharpe and Lucky Millinder rendition of "Lonesome Road."

The reception afterward was held at the Masonic Temple, with a reprise performance by the church choir. Toby felt uneasy—Veronique held court, queen for a day, the grieving little sister. Rumors of her involvement in Long Walk Mooney's schemes, the forged deed, had yet to ripple very far outside the police and the family, and Toby was obliged to play along. In return, no more questions were raised regarding his status as his father's son. It seemed a backhanded victory, given all he'd been through. Even as he accepted the kindness and affection of other family members, struggling with their own grief, and the well-wishing of so many others who'd come so far to pay their respects, he couldn't shake his sense that there was a grating dissonance, a lie, at the heart of the occasion. It made him feel oddly alone, even with his own family, Francis and Miss Carvela, the players from the band. That, combined with a numbness, an inescapable, leaden sensation in his body and soul, made him realize where he needed to be.

As the reception wound down, he excused himself, then found his car, drove to Berkeley, and parked outside the music store where Nadya worked. *If she didn't come to the service, she wants nothing to do with you*, he thought. On reflection, that seemed cowardly. *Let her tell you herself what she wants or doesn't want. Go from there.*

The store was thickly carpeted and had that bright, clean, polished smell that since childhood had conjured an ineffable sense of welcome. Behind the counter hung a poster from Ernst Krenek's 1927 opera, *Jonny spielt auf*, with its jazz-oriented score about a Black musician and his white girlfriend. He and Nadya had always joked about its being a good omen, having that poster right there in the store where they'd met. Even portents can be mistaken, he supposed, or short-lived. He feigned browsing, saw she wasn't there, nodded hello to Mr. Kurtzmann, the owner, then went back outside, climbing the stair along the alley that led to her tiny two-room apartment.

Peeking through the window curtains, he saw her at her table eating a bowl of egg noodles with salt and butter, comfort food. He rapped gently on the windowpane, and when her eyes lifted at the sound he didn't know whether to smile or not. Looking pale, unhealthy, she wore a long-sleeved blouse to conceal the scars on her arm. Her expression seemed grave but uncertain, even a little lost. And yet she put down her fork, came to the door, and opened it.

"I missed you," he said. It hung there like a guilty secret, so he added, "At the service."

"I wanted to go," she said, unconvincingly. "Thank you for inviting me. I just felt—"

"Can I come in?"

The place was too small for more than the one chair at her table. The only spot for him to sit was the futon they'd shared when he stayed over. He ached for that, wanting it again more than he'd realized. To hold her, be held. His heart pounded as he looked about the room, his eyes registering the plants and the books and the shoes and the arty or cartoonish postcards taped to the walls. He felt returned to the one safe place he'd known lately. He feared it was gone for good now.

"You belonged there, at the service. As much as anyone. More than most."

She picked up her fork, poked at her food. "It's been difficult."

Dark patches rimmed her eye sockets. A slight twitch flickered along her cheek.

"I'd like to help."

She smiled sadly, tucking her shoulder up in a half shrug. "Like it's been easy for you. Easy for anyone up there."

"Doesn't mean we avoid each other."

She looked up finally. For the first time, he saw in her eyes what he'd dreaded he'd find there. Finality.

"It's just been very difficult," was all she said. Then: "I should get back to work."

She put down her fork and rose from her chair and straightened her skirt. Toby didn't move.

"Can I wait here for you?"

She seemed confused, like he'd posed a riddle. "I don't get off till six."

He reached out for her hand. "That doesn't matter."

She stepped toward him, placed her hand in his, trying to smile. When he gently pulled her toward him, she knelt down clumsily. Bending to him, she at last rested her face against his breastbone. He felt a shudder ripple up her back, and so he circled his arms around her.

"I can't forgive myself," she whispered.

"It's my fault." He stroked her hair. "I felt so guilty, so jealous. You caught that. I want to help now. Let me help."

She was shaking. Her hands gripped his jacket. "I think about what happened day and night. I'm afraid to sleep, I can't—"

"Let me help," he told her again, kissing her hair. You can't bring him back by killing yourself, he thought, though he understood the impulse. "Then—if you can, if you want—you help me."

They stayed like that a moment, then with a jerky suddenness she pulled herself free of his arms and rose. "I really do have to get back." Her face contorted in a wrenching smile and she tucked a strand of hair behind her ear. "If you decide to leave, please lock the door."

"I'm not leaving," he told her. "I'll stay. If that's all right."

The merest smile flickered across her lips, at the same time her eyes welled up. She nodded, then fled. He waited a long while, hoping she'd come back. Make some excuse, cut work. Once a half hour passed he knew it was futile, for now. I'll wait, he thought, like I promised, till six. He lay on his side, curled up his knees. Closing his eyes, he waited for sleep. He needed so badly to dream a convincing dream.